Also by Dylann Crush

HOLIDAY, TEXAS

All-American Cowboy

Cowboy Christmas Jubilee

COWBOY
Christmas
JUBILEE

DYLANN
CRUSH

sourcebooks
casablanca

Published by Sourcebooks Casablanca, an imprint of Sourcebooks, Inc.
P.O. Box 4410, Naperville, Illinois 60567-4410
(630) 961-3900
Fax: (630) 961-2168
sourcebooks.com

Printed and bound in the United States of America.
OPM 10 9 8 7 6 5 4 3 2 1

For Mr. Crush—my own happily-ever-after hero.
This one's for you. YAYFY

chapter
ONE

JINX JACOBS GLANCED AT THE CUSTOM-RIGGED CUCKOO clock behind the bar of the cheesy North Hollywood biker club she'd been working at for the past six months. At any moment, an engine would rev, and a Hulk Hogan action figure decked out in pleather would roll out on a miniature Harley, marking the half hour. Her boss thought the clock was classy. Jinx thought it looked like an overgrown child's failed mixed-media art project.

Yep, there it went. She had fifteen minutes before her boss/very-ex-boyfriend would strut in. Hooking up with Wade hadn't seemed like such a big deal when she'd taken the job. But over the past six months, his true colors had shone through. She couldn't afford to be around when he discovered she'd taken the back pay he owed her from the till.

"Whatcha doin', sweets?" Geri, the gussied-up, full-time waitress who should have turned in her red leather mini about thirty years ago, leaned her hip against the bar.

"I'm done. Can't take it anymore." Jinx carefully counted the cash, not wanting to take a dime more than her fair share. She'd never taken from the register before, but Wade had strung her along for too long.

Geri pulled a compact out of her short apron and lined her lips in her signature fuchsia. "Wade know you're heading out?"

Jinx grabbed her arm, causing the bright line to swerve across Geri's cheek. "No. Please don't tell him, okay?"

"He's not that stupid, hon." Geri wet her finger with her tongue and rubbed at the pink mark. "Thousand bucks or more gone from the till? Even Wade could figure that out. Don't take a genius to put two and two together. And we all know Wade ain't no freaking genius!"

"Think you can buy me some time?" Although Jinx hesitated to call her a friend, Geri had been her only ally in this hellhole.

"I'll see what I can do. He's gonna be pissed though. They got that Halloween costume contest coming up, and now he'll be short a bartender."

Jinx wrapped a rubber band around the cash and stuffed the wad of bills into her bag. "It's his own fault. You know he's dealing drugs out of here. I can't be involved in that—and you shouldn't be either."

Geri shrugged. "The pay's good. Wade's always been fair with me."

"You can't keep buying those gift cards for him. He's using them to pay off the guys running drugs. He thinks he's covering his trail, but someday, someone's going to catch on to him. I don't want you to get caught up in that."

"Where else am I gonna go?" The older woman crossed her arms under her chest, dragging her low-cut tank even lower.

For half a heartbeat, Jinx thought about suggesting they take off together. But there wasn't enough room for both of them on her bike, and there was no way she was leaving that behind. The 1953 Indian Chief Roadmaster was the only thing she had left from her dad.

Jinx slung an arm around Geri's neck, wrapping her in

a half hug. "Just take care, okay? You've got my new number if you need to call me."

Geri nodded, wiping a tear away from her electric-blue lined eyes. "Be careful, Jinx."

"Promise me you won't give him my number."

"Sure, kid."

Jinx slipped a few bills from the stack of cash and handed them over to Geri. "For the cats."

That small gesture opened up the waterworks, and Geri dissolved into a puddle of tears. The woman may have looked like she got stuck in the 1960s, but she had a heart as sweet as honey and ran an unlicensed cat rescue out of her two-bedroom mobile home in Kagel Canyon.

"Get outta here before he gets back." Geri nudged her with her shoulder. "Take care of yourself. Hendrix too."

"I will." Jinx bent down to scoop up her tiny traveling companion. Taking a Chihuahua on a cross-country motorcycle trip probably wouldn't end up being one of her wisest decisions, but she couldn't leave the little guy here. He'd been with her for three years now, by far the longest relationship she'd ever been able to—or wanted to—maintain.

She slung the strap of her bag over her shoulder and pushed through the door to the gravel parking lot. The door slammed closed behind her, causing the giant *Z* in the Beer & Geerz sign to come loose and swing down like a sickle, missing the top of her head by a mere few inches.

The sunshine-yellow paint job on her bike sparkled in the bright California sun. She wrapped Hendrix in a baby blanket and tucked him into the pricey dog carrier she'd attached to the rear of her bike. After securing the rest of her stuff in the saddlebag, she straddled the seat. Her fingers shook as she buckled the helmet under her chin and slid her shades in place.

She hadn't driven the vintage motorcycle more than a couple hundred miles in the past two years. With any luck, it would hold together until she made it to New Orleans, where her friend Jamie had promised her a high-paying bartending job. She could save up some cash and eventually see about turning her artwork into some sort of money-making opportunity.

But even if her bike crapped out on her along the way, she needed to head south. Wade had his hands in too many questionable activities along the West Coast. Wouldn't be safe to go home to Seattle. The way she figured, the only place he wouldn't be able to come after her would be Louisiana. Wade had told her once he had a warrant out for his arrest in his home state. She hoped that hadn't been another one of his lies.

With a last look at the desperate, run-down bar she'd considered a temporary home for the past several months, she revved the motor, let the tires spin on the dusty gravel, and accelerated onto the two-lane highway.

⟶

"But, Daddy, I want to be a unicorn."

Cash Walker ground his molars together and took a deep breath in through his nose. "Kenzie, honey, it's getting late. We've still got a few stops to make before we head home."

The seven-year-old drama queen clamped her fists to

her hips and narrowed her eyes. "I don't wanna be a cowgirl for Halloween again. All I do is dress up in my regular clothes."

"That's not true. Nana made you that suede vest with the fringe you wanted. She spent a lot of time on that costume. You don't want to hurt her feelings, do you?" Trying to reason with his daughter once she made up her mind about something was more difficult than trying to talk sense into some of the repeat offenders he dealt with on a regular basis as the deputy sheriff of Conroe County. He made a move to grab her hand. She was faster, wrapping her arms around the sparkly unicorn costume hanging on the rack in front of her.

"She didn't make it new, Daddy. It's the same one Ryder wore two years ago. It's a boy costume. I want to be a unicorn, not a cowgirl this year." Her lower lip stuck out in a pout.

Glancing toward the filtered sunlight streaming through the suburban mall's skylight, he counted to ten in his head. He should have known better than to bring Kenzie with him today. But when his mom found out he had to go into Austin, she'd asked him to stop by the mall and pick up a baby gift she'd put on hold for his sister's shower.

"Come on, Tadpole. Can't you pick something else? Aunt Darby has lots of other choices."

"They're all boy costumes, Daddy. A storm-trooper. A policeman. A fireman. I want a girl costume this year." She stroked the unicorn's long, rainbow-colored mane. "Why can't I dress up like a mommy like Aunt Charlie?"

Over his dead body would his seven-year-old stick a pillow up her shirt and dress up like a pint-size pregnant woman for Halloween. Kenzie's fascination with her aunt's bulging belly bordered on obsessive. Sure, he was just as excited as the rest of the family that Charlie and Beck had tied the knot and were expecting the newest member of the family. But it also rubbed like a burr in his boot, seeing his baby sister get her happily ever after while he struggled to find his own way after Kenzie's mom had passed. Being a single dad had never been on his bucket list, although he wouldn't trade his little tadpole for anything.

As his mother never tired of telling him, maybe it was time for him to try again. Kenzie deserved the best. He knew one thing for sure—if he ever decided to go looking for a potential partner, he wouldn't let himself get swept away like he had with his ex. He'd learned his lesson the hard way: love made a person blind. Any future relationship he went into would be with his eyes wide open.

He put both hands on his daughter's waist and hoisted her up over his head to sit on his shoulders. "We'll talk about it when we get home. Now where's that shop Nana wanted us to stop at?"

Kenzie let out an exaggerated sigh. He bounced her up and down a few times with no reaction. Even at seven, she could hold a grudge longer than most grown men. Finally, he pulled out all the stops and tickled the underside of her knee. She kicked her hot-pink cowgirl boots against his chest and erupted into a fit of giggles.

"You better hang on up there. Don't want to fall off," he warned.

She grabbed a handful of his hair in each fist. "Walk faster, Daddy!"

If he ended up with a receding hairline, he'd know who to blame. He stopped at the mall directory and figured out the store he needed was two floors up and on the opposite side of the mall. By the time they picked up the custom onesies his mom had ordered, his shoulders ached. He carried Kenzie out to the truck and waited as patiently as his type A personality would allow while she buckled herself into her booster. She'd always been bullheaded, but since she had started second grade this fall, she'd been especially independent.

After a few more stops, he turned the truck southwest and started the hour-plus drive back to Holiday, Texas. This had been a relatively quick trip, and Kenzie had only talked him into a few things not on the list—a big bag of cotton candy that would probably be stuck all over the leather seats, a sparkly collar for her grumpy old barn cat, and a new stuffed dog. The kid could already outfit an entire stuffed zoo, but as the most important female in his life, she pretty much had him wrapped around her pudgy little finger.

He might curse her mother with every four-letter word he'd ever heard, but the woman had given him one good thing—Kenzie.

"Turn it up, Daddy? Please?" Her favorite song had come on the radio—Johnny Cash's "I Walk the Line." Not that kiddie crap his older brother had to play when his wife and kids were in the truck. Hell no. He'd raised Kenzie on classic rock, country, and the country-western star who'd inspired his name— the Man in Black.

"Should we stop by the big house when we get back or go home and eat dinner first?" he asked.

She clapped her hands together in time to the music. "Stop at Nana and Papa's. I asked Nana if she'd make cookies today."

"All right. Nana and Papa's it is."

The truck ate up the miles of asphalt until they turned off the pavement and onto the private road that ran through the Walker family ranch. When he had first moved out on his own, he had found it stifling to have a house on the edge of the family compound. But now, with Kenzie, it was comforting to know he had family close by. They passed Waylon and Darby's place, then turned down the long driveway to the big house.

He brought the truck to a stop behind his sister's dually.

"Yay! Aunt Charlie's here! I can pretend to be an almost-mommy just like her!" Kenzie scrambled out of the back seat, her sticky, cotton candy–covered hands leaving traces of syrupy pink goop all over the seat.

Great, just great. That fifty-dollar sparkly unicorn costume suddenly seemed like a reasonably priced alternative to Kenzie wanting to dress up like his pregnant sister.

chapter
TWO

JINX CLIMBED OFF HER BIKE AND SET THE KICKSTAND. Thank goodness for modern rest areas, although she'd just about kill for a shower. The grit and dust from driving halfway across Texas had somehow managed to cover every inch of exposed skin. Even with her old motorcycle jacket and a pair of windproof pants protecting her from the elements, the dirt had worked its way into all kinds of places she couldn't clean with a quick wipe down over a sink.

"How ya doin', Hendrix?" She nuzzled him against her cheek. He yipped and rewarded her with a sloppy kiss, then took the bit of kibble she held out to him. Stopping every couple of hours for him to water the bushes and stretch his legs hadn't been as bad as she'd thought. Better than leaving the little guy behind.

"Spare some change?" A woman sat with her back resting against the building. She appeared to be in even worse shape than Jinx. A mottled purple bruise covered one side of her face, and she looked like she hadn't bathed in weeks.

"Where you headed?"

"Does it matter?" The woman didn't make eye contact, just focused on a spot on the ground in front of her.

Jinx crouched down, putting them on the same level. "What's your name?"

The woman let out a harsh laugh that sounded more like a moan. "Why? Are you gonna try to save me?"

Jinx recognized the familiar signs. The last time she'd seen her mom, her face had reflected the same defeated hopelessness along with some similar bruises. She reached into her pocket for a couple of bucks. This woman needed help. If someone had provided a leg up for her mom, would she have found the courage to lift herself out of her own desperate circumstances?

"The only one who can save you is yourself, you know." She handed the money to the woman, who slid it into her pocket.

In a voice so quiet Jinx had to lean closer to hear, the woman spoke. "Mona. My name is Mona."

Jinx reached out to squeeze her hand. As she did, Hendrix hopped down and scrambled onto the woman's lap. Before she could grab him, he put his front paws on Mona's chest and gave her a half dozen Chihuahua kisses.

"Hendrix!" Jinx grasped the dog. "I'm so sorry. He's usually much better behaved."

Mona smiled. "What a sweetie."

"Sometimes." Jinx grinned back. "He can also be a giant pain in the ass. Good luck, Mona."

A tear slid down Mona's cheek. "Thanks."

Jinx nodded, making sure she caught Mona's eye before she headed into the bathroom. If only she had more. A couple of dollars wouldn't make a difference for someone in that kind of situation, but at least she could get something warm to drink out of the vending machine, maybe ease her suffering a tiny bit.

Jinx cleaned up as best as she could using a sink that stopped running every time she took her hand off the faucet.

Digging through her bag for a fresh shirt, her hand hit something hard and heavy at the bottom. What the hell? She felt around the item, the size of a brick. How could she have missed that when she packed?

As she pulled the plastic-wrapped bundle out of her bag, her heart skipped a few beats, then picked up the pace.

Wade's gift cards.

Shit, shit, shit. How in the hell had those gotten in there? And what was she going to do about it? She locked herself in a stall and unwrapped the plastic with trembling hands. There must be thousands of dollars' worth of cards—enough to keep his thugs and runners paid for a couple of months, easy.

Think, Jinx, think. Geri had borrowed her backpack a couple of days ago. Maybe Wade had sent her on one of his special errands and she'd forgotten to put the cards in the safe. That was the only logical explanation. But what could she do with them now? There was no way she could keep them—she'd taken what he owed her, and that was it. She didn't want anything more from the bastard. But it seemed such a waste to just throw them away.

A vision of Mona sitting on the floor flitted through her mind. Wade might be a complete and utter ass, but at least something good could come out of the time she'd spent with him. She pulled a huge handful of cards out of the stack and tucked the rest away at the bottom of her bag. Hundreds of miles separated her from New Orleans. She may as well save the rest of the cards in case she had a chance to dole them out along the route. Once she got there, she could make an anonymous donation to a women's shelter or something with whatever she had left.

"Here." Jinx handed Mona the gift cards on her way out. "Get away from whoever did that to you."

Mona reached for them, but Jinx held fast.

"Promise?" She wanted to shake the woman, tell her that no man was worth letting her body be used for a punching bag.

A glimmer sparked in Mona's eyes. "Yes."

"Good." Jinx released the cards, silently sending a wish to whomever or whatever might be listening that Mona would find her way.

Satisfied she'd done what she could, Jinx consulted the map on the wall. She'd been on the road for days. If she pushed it, she ought to make San Antonio before dark. She could splurge on a cheap hotel with a shower and let Hendrix run around a bit.

She climbed back on the bike, but it wouldn't shift into gear. *Please, not now.* When she got to New Orleans, she'd find a garage to take a look at it. Until then, she just needed to get as far as she could. She wrestled the bike back into gear and opted for a side road. No sense in overdoing it on the highway.

Thirty miles later, she must have taken a wrong turn, since the setting sun ended up behind her. She needed to be going south, not due east. The bike gave one final surge, then died underneath her. *Dammit.* Jinx climbed off the bike and circled it, looking for obvious signs. She'd done some basic maintenance on it in the past, but a standard oil change fell far short of diagnosing a possible transmission problem.

If she'd sold the motorcycle back in LA, it could have

added a cool ten grand or more to her pathetic bank account. She could have spent the cash on a cheap compact car and avoided the inevitable breakdown in the middle of freaking nowhere, but she'd chosen to be sentimental instead of practical for once in her freaking life.

Now what was she going to do? The burner phone she'd picked up before leaving California offered no solution. Service out here in the sticks was limited. She rolled the bike off the road into a scrubby stand of bushes, hopefully hiding it from anyone who might pass by.

What to do with the gift cards though? She didn't want to have them in her bag in case something happened. How would she explain thousands of dollars in gift cards? Not that she paid much attention to Wade's side dealings, but even she'd heard him bitching about a recent bust in Arizona where the feds had recovered hundreds of gift cards along with a sizable stash of heroin.

But she didn't want to leave them on the bike either, on the off chance someone found them. Scanning the side of the road for a potential hiding place, her gaze caught a hollowed-out log about twenty feet away. She wrapped the plastic tight around the cards and pushed them deep into the decaying wood. That ought to work until she came back for her bike. She'd crossed a four-lane road a few miles back. If she could get to the highway, she could hitch into the nearest town and see about finding a garage. She tucked Hendrix into her backpack and pulled her coat around her, her heavy black boots crunching onto the gravel shoulder.

Just another minor setback. She'd been down before. It would take a hell of a lot more than a fickle engine to knock her out for good.

_HH_

Cash held Kenzie's tiny hoof in one hand and the pillow-case containing her massive haul of Halloween candy in the other. Trick-or-treating sure wasn't this easy when he was a kid. Back then, he and his brothers would ride their bikes from ranch to ranch almost all night long. They probably pedaled fifty miles by the time they hit up the few neighboring houses close enough to reach on two wheels. For all that effort, they were lucky if they got a fourth of what Kenzie had managed to shake down in less than forty-five minutes at the annual Tot Trick-Or-Treat at the Rambling Rose. Back when Sully owned the historic honky-tonk, he didn't cater to the half-pint crowd. But ever since Cash's sister and her new husband—Sully's grandson—had taken over, they held all kinds of events and activities for the kids.

"Go say good night to Aunt Charlie, Uncle Beck, and Nana, Tadpole." Cash prodded Kenzie toward his sister and mom. She sashayed away, her glittery unicorn tail swishing with each step. Leave it to his brilliant sister to suggest Kenzie stuff a pillow in her costume and dress up as a unicorn with a tummy full of candy for Halloween. Charlie thought she'd reached a compromise with Kenzie, but he'd overheard his daughter telling people she was a pregnant unicorn. Best of both worlds for her, but he'd pretty much lost on both counts on that one. At this rate, he'd be doomed by the time she reached puberty.

Kenzie doled out hugs and kisses, then scampered back

to his side. "Can I have some more of my candy, Daddy?"

"One more piece, okay? You've got to get to bed. There's school tomorrow."

She held out a king-size bag of Skittles. "This one?"

"I said one piece, not one giant bag. Who gave you that, anyway?" He peered across the crowded dance hall, trying to find the most likely source of the abundance of sugar. Had to be someone without kids.

"Uncle Presley." Kenzie dug through the pillow-case and withdrew another giant bag of candy, this one M&Ms. "He gave me this too."

Presley, of course. Probably better than him handing out single shots of his new favorite whiskey to all his nieces and nephews. Cash had spent years wishing and hoping for his younger brother to get tamed by some two-stepping Texas beauty. Presley wasn't just the black sheep of the family; he caused enough trouble for a whole damn flock.

"Why don't you pick something else tonight, and you can start in on those Skittles tomorrow?" He dropped the candy back into the pillowcase and pulled out a single Starburst. "Yellow, your favorite."

"I love yellow." Took her less than a second to unwrap the candy and pop it in her mouth.

He led her out of the building and crossed the parking lot to the truck. Once she got settled in her seat, he pulled out onto the road for the short drive home. As he navigated around a bend, he squinted at the dark shape standing on the side of the road up ahead.

"What the hell?"

"Bad word! Gotta put a quarter in the curse-word jar when we get home."

Stinker. He'd probably be able to pay for her first car with the amount he owed the curse-word jar. Her toothy grin filled the rearview mirror. But seriously, what the heck was that? The headlights bounced off what appeared to be a person. They got closer, and he could make out a black jacket, black pants, and a mass of bright hair. The figure turned to face the truck, thrusting a thumb out to solicit a ride. Cash wouldn't pick up a hitchhiker around Austin or San Antonio, but on the backroads surrounding Holiday, he didn't run across many strangers. Probably some kid on her way to a Halloween party in town. He slowed the truck to pull off the road.

The girl grabbed the backpack at her feet, slung the strap over her shoulder, and approached the passenger side. Cash lowered the window before leaning across the front of the cab.

"Hey, where you headed?" His gaze raked over her teal hair, shaved to the scalp on one side, exposing an ear full of metal piercings. At least she didn't have any of that crap on her lips or eyebrows. He couldn't understand the kids who poked holes all over their faces. Made booking them a pain in the ass too, since he couldn't rely on the sensitive metal detectors.

"Thanks for stopping. Is there a garage somewhere around here? My bike broke down."

"What, did you slip a chain? Tire go flat? We can throw it in the back, and I can run you home." Easy fix. His hand wrapped around the door handle, ready to exit the vehicle and give her a hand.

"Sorry, it's a motorcycle, not a bike."

Cash turned his head back toward the window. She moved into the light coming from the overhead dome. Hmm, she wasn't as young as he thought. Had to be early twenties.

"Where did you leave it? We can still toss it in back. I'll drop you off at Dwight's, and he can take a look."

"You got a ramp?" She patted the doorframe. "It's kind of heavy."

"Is she gonna ride with us?" Kenzie unbuckled and leaned into the front seat. At the sight of the stranger's bright-teal hair, her eyes widened. "Are you a mermaid?"

Great, now his daughter would be begging for a trip to the salon for her first dye job. "No, babe. She's probably just dressed up for a Halloween party. What are you supposed to be, anyway? A punk rocker? Some sort of survivor of the zombie apocalypse?"

A hint of pink tinged the woman's cheeks. "I'm not going to a party. Look, can you just give me a lift into town? I can come back later with a trailer to get my bike, okay?"

The color drained from Cash's face. "I'm so sorry. I just thought, with that getup, I mean…"

"It's fine, really. I'm used to it." Her gaze flitted around the cab. "About that ride?"

Nothing like opening his mouth and inserting both boots at once. He needed to shut up before he buried himself completely. "I'd be happy to give you a ride. Do you live close by?" Cash gestured to Kenzie to buckle up again as the gal climbed into the cab.

She pulled the door closed behind her. "Not exactly."

He didn't recognize her as anyone he'd seen around town. "Where you from?"

"Um, how far is the garage?" She sandwiched her backpack between heavy black motorcycle boots and pressed herself against the door.

"Not far. You just passing through then?" She didn't strike him as threatening, but something about the crazy-ass hair and vintage black leather jacket put him on edge. Or was it the way she looked like she wanted to crawl right out of her skin every time he asked a question?

"Something like that. Is there a hotel in town? Somewhere I can lay up for the night?"

"There's a bed-and-breakfast just off the main road. Otherwise, the typical chain places are a few miles away along the interstate. Plenty of options closer to Austin."

Kenzie's hand reached over the seat back to pat the woman's hair.

Cash shot a glance toward his daughter. "Kenzie, keep your hands to yourself, hon."

"But it's so pretty. Can I have my hair like that?"

"We'll talk about that when you're eighteen."

The woman let out a soft laugh. It seemed to surprise her, since she covered her mouth with her hand.

"What's your name? Do you like cats? What's your favorite color?" Kenzie must have taken that tiny break in the woman's outer armor as an invitation to pepper her with her own questions.

The woman turned to face the back seat. "My name's Jinx. I like your costume."

"Thanks. My aunt Charlie is going to have a baby."

"Oh. Um, congratulations. How old are you, Kenzie?"

"Seven. My birthday is in August. When's yours? Do you have any pets?"

"Just one." She reached into her backpack. Cash

instinctively stiffened in the seat next to her. She must have noticed. "Relax. I've got a dog in my bag."

Kenzie squealed as Jinx pulled a small ratlike creature out and held it up.

"His name is Hendrix."

"That's an interesting choice of name," Cash commented.

Jinx shrugged. "My dad was a huge fan of Jimi."

"He's so cute!" Kenzie's grabby hands reached for the animal.

"Kenz, you need to ask if you can hold it." He cast a quick look at the animal. "Does it bite?"

"No, he's super gentle. Here, you can hold him. He likes it when you scratch him behind the ears." She passed the scrawny thing to Kenzie, who nestled it against her chest.

"Daddy says I can't have a dog."

"Dogs are a lot of work." Cash felt an unfamiliar need to defend himself. "You've already got a cat."

"Yeah, but Chucky doesn't live inside. I want a dog like this." She ran her fingers over the dog's back.

Jinx gave him the side-eye. "You've got a cat named Chucky?"

"He's got some anger issues. It's a long story." Great, just great. With Christmas coming up, Kenzie would probably tell Santa she wanted a dog. He'd have to figure out a better excuse to head her off before she made the request. His schedule was barely sane keeping up with Kenzie. Adding a dog to the mix wouldn't be fair to the dog or his parents, who took in Kenzie when he had to work nights.

While Kenzie fired question after question, he

kept one eye on the road and the other on Jinx. Cash let Kenzie do the dirty work; his daughter would make a fabulous interrogator someday. Jinx didn't appear to be threatening, but she definitely had her guard up.

Who could blame her? With the crazy hair, pounds of metal piercing her body, and hardcore attire, she didn't exactly fit in with the small-town vibe Holiday was known for. But as his mama always said, what really matters is invisible to the eye. He'd always struggled a little bit with that one, especially in his line of work, where things often were exactly as they seemed.

Kenzie didn't let up. "Do you have any brothers and sisters?"

Jinx had shifted in her seat to face his daughter. "You ask a lot of questions."

"Daddy says I'm inquibative, right, Daddy?"

"Inquisitive," Cash corrected.

"He says it's a nice way of saying I'm nosy."

Jinx made brief eye contact with Cash. A tentative smile teased the corners of her mouth upward. "Your daddy sounds like a funny guy."

"Sometimes he's funny. He makes good jokes. Tell her the one about the skeleton."

"Aw, Tadpole, Jinx doesn't want to hear my jokes." His gaze darted to his right.

The light from the dash illuminated another smile from Jinx. "Sure I would."

Cash shook his head. "Just remember, you asked for it."

She raised her eyebrows, encouraging him to continue.

"All right. Why didn't the skeleton cross the road?"

Kenzie bounced up and down in her booster seat. "He didn't have any guts!" She erupted into a fit of giggles in the back seat, her sparkly, glittered sneakers battering the back of the center console.

Jinx's shoulders gave a little shake. "That's a good one. Do you know why the skeleton didn't want to go to school?"

Kenzie stopped laughing and furrowed her little brow, trying to come up with an answer. "No, why?"

"His heart wasn't in it." Jinx flashed his daughter a smile, turning toward him with the tail end of a grin still gracing her face.

"Can you come to our house, Jinx?" Kenzie reached out to pet the blue hair again.

The last thing Cash needed was for his daughter to form an instant attachment to an out-of-place punk chick. For all he knew, she might even be running from the law in some capacity.

Could be she was just passing through and her bike broke down. But then why was she so evasive about where she was from and where she was headed? He'd get her to Dwight's and let him help her with the bike. He had enough going on and couldn't afford to expend any energy worrying about the comings and goings of every single person who passed through Holiday on their way to somewhere else.

By the time they got to Dwight's garage, he'd learned more than he'd ever cared to know about hair dye and pierced ears. Kenzie passed the dog back to Jinx, who tucked it into her bag. Cash climbed out of the truck, leaving the motor running. He met up with Jinx as she hopped down, her boots thudding onto the pavement. Under the buzz of crappy overhead gas station lights, he got a better look at her. Ripped

black leggings, fingers full of rings, eyes lined in black—
she looked like a full-size version of one of those Monster
High dolls Kenzie got for Christmas last year.

"Dwight ought to be able to help you out from here."
He nodded toward the small convenience store where
Dwight stood staring out the window, then slid a business
card out of his wallet. "Let me know if you need anything
while you're in town."

She flipped it over in her fingers. "Deputy sheriff,
huh?" She bristled, then visibly made her shoulders relax.

"Yeah. I just tell bad jokes when I'm not busting bad
guys."

Her gaze met his as she slid the card into her pocket.
"Thanks for the ride."

"You bet. Good luck, Jinx."

He waited while she moved toward the door. Definitely
hiding something. He'd circle back with Dwight tomorrow and follow up to see if he could get any additional
info about the woman with the blue hair. Right now, he
had bigger issues—like how to get a sugar-loaded unicorn
to bed.

chapter

THREE

THE GUY IN THE DIRTY BASEBALL CAP STOOD BEHIND THE
counter. Staring at her. Mouth half-open. Whether it was
surprise, confusion, or just his natural state, Jinx hadn't
figured out quite yet. The rumble of Cash's truck pulled
her attention to the window. Taillights winked, then he
drove onto the road, leaving her with a guy who could
have starred in *Deliverance*. Even though she wasn't one
to typically put her trust in anyone, she somehow felt like
Cash wouldn't have left her here if she needed to worry
about Dwight.

"So, um, that guy who dropped me off here said you
can fix a motorcycle?" She thumbed toward the window.

"Do what?" Dwight's brow wrinkled under the brim
of his hat.

"You fix bikes here? I've got an Indian I had to leave a
few miles back. Engine died on me, and I need to know
what's wrong." She waited a beat, then two, for the guy to
say something.

The line bisecting his forehead deepened. "Bikes. Yeah,
I can fix just about anything. Where's it at?"

Finally. "About five miles down the main road, then off
on a side road in some bushes."

"Won't run?"

Didn't she just say the engine died? "No. You ever work

on Indian bikes? My dad rebuilt it about twenty years ago. Might need some work."

Now he looked like she'd just insulted his mother. A sneer stretched over his face. "I ain't met a motor I can't fix."

"Great. So can we go get it?" The sooner she figured out what was wrong, the sooner she'd be able to get out of here. Small towns gave her the creeps. She preferred to be surrounded by strangers, able to blend in to the anonymity of a big-city street.

"Yeah. Let's go." He snagged a ring of keys off a hook behind the counter and led the way through the store to the garage.

She wasn't crazy about the idea of jumping in a truck with another complete stranger, but what choice did she have? If he got out of hand, she could take him. She'd stood her ground against guys much bigger than him over the years.

An hour later, they'd unloaded her motorcycle into the three-bay repair shop. Dwight had taken a quick look but said he wouldn't be able to get started on it until the next afternoon. He had an ATV repair he'd promised to someone first. Based on what he'd seen so far, he thought it might require a total rebuild. At that news, a rock the size of that possum she'd seen on the side of the road dropped into her gut. She gathered as much of her stuff as she could carry.

"You got a phone number you want me to call when I know more?" Dwight pulled a pen from behind his ear and held it over his palm.

Like hell she wanted her phone number decorating any part of his anatomy. "I'll stop by tomorrow afternoon. Think you'll know something by, say, two?"

He shrugged. "Better make it three. You got a place to stay tonight?"

She hated small towns. If she said yes, he'd want to know where she was headed. If she said no, he'd make some suggestion, hopefully one that didn't involve his place, and he'd probably follow up to make sure she went there. She didn't want to spend the cash she'd brought with her at a pricey bed-and-breakfast. But there was no way in hell she'd want to entertain the idea of bunking at Dwight's for the night.

"I'll figure something out."

"There's a B&B a few blocks over that way." He pointed to a corner of the garage. "Probably ought to have space, seein' as how it's a weeknight and all."

"Thanks." She gathered her things and turned toward the door. "See you tomorrow."

The heavy weight of his stare pressed down on her as she walked in the direction he'd pointed. Once the door clicked closed, she looked back. No Dwight. She circled around, ready to make the five-mile trek to retrieve the gift cards from that log. Maybe she could find an out-of-the-way stand of trees to set up her tent for the night.

After days of having the bike between her thighs, her muscles twinged as she took long strides down the road. Things would work out. They always did. Hopefully, she'd get out of town before she had any more uncomfortable interactions with the law. Even if the local lawman had a sizzling gaze, a disarming smile, and a precocious little girl.

He was probably married anyway. Perfect nuclear family of three. Mom, Dad, well-loved, happy little girl. The kind of family a kid deserved.

Not like her fucked-up excuse for a home life.

She rarely allowed herself to dwell on the past, and no matter how much things sucked right now, she wouldn't let herself go there. That was her mom's MO. Instead, prepared to make the best of camping under the clear, starlit sky, she thought about the things she should be thankful for. She had half a sandwich leftover from lunch, a tent to shelter her from the chill in the air and whatever might be crawling around in the weeds, and Hendrix to keep her company. Yeah, life could be better. But it could also be a lot worse.

That she knew from experience.

<hr />

Cash removed his cowboy hat as he entered the elementary school. He slid his ID through the scanner and pressed the button.

The school secretary's grizzled voice floated through the speaker. "Welcome to Kennedy Elementary. The security system is broken this morning. Just come on in."

What good did it do to have the damn security system if it never worked right? The school board had pushed for it, and the whole town had worked together to raise enough funds for its installation last summer. He'd have to talk to the boss about that. But first, the meeting with Kenzie's teacher.

"Good morning." The secretary, Mrs. Aberdeen, hadn't changed a bit since he'd been a student at Kennedy nearly a quarter of a century ago. Still wore her hair in that frizzy bun. Still sported that hairy mole on her chin. Still sounded like she smoked three packs a day. Thanks to his day job, he'd learned Mrs. Aberdeen actually preferred a different kind of smoking—as in the illegal, recreational kind. Another drawback to working in the sheriff's department was he learned way too much about way too many people. "How are you doing today, Mr. Walker?"

He didn't bother to correct her. Most people called him Deputy Walker nowadays, or at least Cash. Seeing as how he managed to look the other way when he found her smoking a joint at the Chuckwagon Extravaganza last summer as a trade-off for all the times she hadn't reported him to the principal as a kid, he figured they might have achieved first-name status. Evidently not.

"I'm here to see Kenzie's teacher."

"They're in the staff lounge." She pointed to a doorway, then, without looking up, licked an envelope from the stack in front of her and pressed the flap closed.

"Thanks." He shuffled past her desk, still not comfortable being this close to the principal's office even after all these years.

"Cash, glad you could make it." The district psychologist whose name he could never remember offered her hand.

He set his hat down on the table and took her hand, looking to Kenzie's teacher, Ms. Pepper, for an explanation. His brother Statler had dated Grace Pepper all through high school and college. It was hard to take her seriously when he could still hear Strait and Presley singing that stupid song they'd made up...*Statler and Grace—sucking face*.

Grace shuffled some papers. "Lindsey, I mean Mrs. Blost, was able to join us today."

"Okay." Cash lowered himself into a chair that looked like it hadn't left the room since the school was built in the 1960s. "I thought you just wanted to touch base about Kenzie's progress so far this year."

"That's right," Mrs. Blost said, taking charge. "Kenzie is a special little girl." She twittered. "I know I don't have to tell you that."

Cash glanced to Grace. She didn't look up. "Now I know you didn't call me down here to talk about how special Kenzie is. What's going on?"

Mrs. Blost's hand fluttered against her collarbone. "She's doing just fine. Ms. Pepper noticed some issues with Kenzie's reading progress though, and I'd like to run a few tests."

"Wait a minute." Cash put his hands palm down on the laminate tabletop. "What kind of tests?"

Grace put her hand on his arm. He jerked it away. She'd always seemed like the touchy-feely type.

"Cash, it's standard stuff. Kenzie's not reading at grade level. She's barely reading at all," Grace explained. "I called in Mrs. Blost to check for dyslexia. Kenzie shows mild signs—"

"Whoa!" Cash put his hands out, palms facing the two women. Kenzie was perfect; what in the hell did they know about anything? "You're trying to tell me something's wrong with my little girl?"

"Nothing's wrong with her." Mrs. Blost clucked her tongue. "She's got some challenges, and we want to figure out how best to support her."

The pity in Grace's eyes looked just like it had when she'd called him in talk about how clingy Kenzie was the first few weeks of school. He'd had to remind her Kenzie didn't have a mama at home and guessed that was the reason behind her obsession with her new teacher.

"No matter what the test shows, it's obvious Kenzie is going to need some extra help with her reading. My schedule is booked, but I'd be happy to put her on the wait list for a tutor."

"What can I do to help?" Cash asked. Kenzie was his life. When her mom had walked out on both of them years ago, he had promised his little girl he'd never leave her, that he'd always be there for her. They'd made a good team so far. But being a single dad was hard. A hell of a lot harder than he'd ever imagined. And now, trying to navigate a learning disability on his own would only make it that much harder.

"Let's do the tests first. Once we have a clear diagnosis, we can take it from there. Sound good?" Mrs. Blost nodded like it was all settled.

"Cash?" Grace tilted her head. "You okay?"

He managed a nod.

"Kenzie's still the amazing, creative, darling little girl you know and love. This doesn't change anything. She just needs some extra help." Grace stood and pushed her chair in to the table. "I've got to get back to the classroom—the kids will be back from art soon. You have any questions or want to talk about this, give me a call, okay?"

Standing, he set his hat back on top of his head and thrust his fists into the pockets of his uniform jacket. "Yeah, okay."

He opened the door and let the women pass through first. His mom would know what to do about this. The matriarch of the Walker clan, she had a no-nonsense way of simmering things down to manageable pieces. She'd been there for him when he had decided to take on full custody, and since she'd kept him and his siblings alive to adulthood, she knew a lot more than he did about how to raise a kid.

"Thanks again for coming in." Mrs. Blost walked him to the front door, his daughter's future smashed in the manila folder against her chest.

Cash nodded and pushed through the doorway, thumping his hand against the piece-of-crap security system on his way out. As he passed through the main drag of town, he swerved into the parking lot of Dwight's place. Something about the night before still nagged at the back of his mind. He needed a distraction from the meeting at school, and checking up on the stranger with the bright-blue hair would do it.

"Hey, Deputy." Dwight strolled out of the open garage door, an oily rag in his pocket and a toothpick in the corner of his mouth.

Cash had known him since they were kids. Dwight usually called him "asshat" or something more along those lines. "Why the sudden respect? You do something illegal lately?"

"Who, me?" Dwight popped the toothpick out and held it between two fingers. "Want to see something special?"

"You haven't been putting together any more moonshine stills, have you?"

"One time. Damn, you gonna give me grief over that forever?"

Cash grinned. That was more like it. "I might. What do you want to show me?"

Dwight led the way into the garage where a gorgeous, sunshine-yellow, vintage motorcycle sat parked in the middle of the bay.

"Who did you steal that from?" Cash ran his hand over the sleek lines of the bike, then straddled the seat. "Hi there, gorgeous."

"Nobody. That chick you dropped off last night had it. It's a beaut, ain't it?"

Cash pulled his hand away as though the handlebars had burned him. The chick he'd dropped off last night? This bike belonged to Jinx? She looked like she couldn't even afford clothes without holes in them.

"You sure about that?" He cocked his head and looked to Dwight to see if he was messing with him.

"Yeah. She led me right to it. Said it was her dad's."

Cash sensed her before he heard her. The hair on the back of his neck stood on end as the energy in the garage shifted.

Jinx stood in the open garage door, in the same clothes as the night before.

"Speak of the devil…" Dwight muttered.

Cash shot him a shut-the-hell-up glare, and for once, Dwight took the hint. "Hey. Dwight was just showing me your bike."

She smirked. "Thanks for clarifying. I thought maybe you were about to ride off into the sunset on it."

Someone snorted. Damn, Dwight. Cash rubbed the back of his neck, feeling the beginning twinge of a headache. "So where'd you get a bike like this?"

"You think I stole it or something?" She walked in a wide circle around him.

He was a sheriff's deputy. It was his job to be curious. "No, that's not what I meant."

"Oh, so what you meant was I don't look like

the kind of girl who could afford a vintage, fully restored Indian motorcycle?"

"Hey, just trying to make conversation. I'll leave you and Dwight to it. Good luck with everything." He didn't need this crap. Especially not today. What he did need was to figure out where his mom was so she could tell him how to handle the bomb Kenzie's teacher had dropped. Stopping by Dwight's had been a bad idea. He climbed off the bike and tipped the brim of his hat toward Jinx. "See ya later, Dwight."

Dwight gave him a middle finger salute and a smile. Let him deal with the frosty biker chick. Cash climbed into the truck and pulled his mom's number up on his phone; she was the one person he might be able to manage a productive conversation with today.

chapter
FOUR

"YOU SURE ABOUT THAT?" JINX FOUGHT AGAINST THE fist squeezing her insides into a mishmashed mess. He had to be kidding. She didn't have five grand to rebuild the engine.

Dwight toed at the lid of a water bottle, scraping it along the concrete floor. "You're welcome to take it somewhere else. But I'm a hundred and ten percent positive it's gonna need a whole rebuild."

She didn't bother telling him one hundred and ten percent was mathematically impossible. He might not know math, but for some reason, she believed he did know engines. Maybe it was the permanent grease stains on his hands. Or the way the guy at the mini-mart talked about him this morning when she'd asked if he did a good job. Whatever caused it, her gut trusted him. And she'd gotten a lot further in life trusting her gut than she had putting her faith in anything else.

"When do you need the money?" That's what it came down to. She didn't have that much in her account, not after she'd had to move out of Wade's and into a hotel room when she'd found out he'd been cheating on her. She should have listened to her gut when it came to that asshole.

Dwight shrugged. "I can get started if you want. It'll take a few weeks to figure out what parts I need and how far I gotta go to get 'em. You wanna pay me a ten percent deposit and then I can let you know when I need to order stuff?"

"Um, can I get back to you about it?"

Dwight lifted his baseball cap and ran his fingers through his hair. "Look, if you don't want me to do the work—"

"No, it's not that." She was screwed. Not enough cash to get the bike fixed, probably not even enough cash to get settled in New Orleans if she gave this guy a five-hundred-dollar deposit. That's what she got for not splitting from LA as soon as she sensed things were heading south. "I need to get some cash together. Can you hold on to it for a day or two? Just let me figure a few things out?"

"Sure."

"You don't need any help around here, do you?" She cringed as the words left her mouth. Dwight didn't strike her as someone who was operating on all cylinders. Not that she wouldn't do what she needed to do to get by. Her need for survival had landed her in a crapload of undesirable jobs. Pumping gas and ringing up oil changes would be a vacation from the ass pinchings she'd endured at Wade's place.

"Nah. I pretty much handle stuff around here on my own."

She let out a tiny sigh of relief.

"But, hey. I know someone who might need some help." He snapped his fingers, then reached into his pocket and pulled out his phone. "You ever waited tables or pulled a draft beer before?"

Ha. What other kind of job could she expect to land? "Yeah, I know my way around the back of a bar."

"Hang on a sec. Lemme make a call." He stepped toward the store, holding the phone to his ear.

Jinx climbed onto the bike and let her head rest against the handlebars. The smart thing to do would be to sell the bike. Raise a little cash, get to New Orleans, and work her ass off. If things were as hot as her friend said they were, she'd finally be able to put some cash in the bank. Someday, she'd find another sunshine-yellow Roadmaster and could pick up again then.

Her heart squeezed, tapped out a drumroll, and squeezed again. It wouldn't be the same though. This bike was special because it had belonged to *him*. She remembered when her dad had finished restoring it. He'd set her in front of him on the smooth seat and driven her around the block. She'd squealed and giggled as the wind blew through her hair. If she closed her eyes as tight as she could, she could still feel the rumble of his chest as he laughed along with her, smell the scent of the unfiltered Camels he used to smoke.

"You're in luck."

Dwight's voice jerked her out of the past. She scrambled off the bike, tucking her memories back where they came from—somewhere deep and dark inside.

"Charlie needs help at the Rambling Rose. She's about big enough to pop and said she could use an extra body to pitch in behind the bar, maybe wait some tables and stuff. You up for it?"

"Yeah. Of course. Thanks. I really appreciate you making the call for me."

Dwight squinted and looked away. "You want a

ride? I may as well head on over there myself. They got a special on tamale pie today, and my belly's been bitchin' and moanin' like a bobcat in heat."

She cocked her head. Was that a thing around here? Bobcats in heat? She'd have to find out before she spent another night out in the wide open. "I'd love a ride. Thanks."

"I'll meet you out by the truck in two shakes, okay?"

Jinx nodded. Maybe it wouldn't be such a bad thing to get stuck in Holiday for a couple of weeks. The weather wasn't bad. She could find a nice patch of grass somewhere and pitch her tent. Working at a restaurant and bar would make sure she didn't starve, and she could make enough cash to get started on fixing the bike. Her backpack wiggled. Hendrix. He wouldn't be able to tag along if she was waiting tables. She'd figure something out.

Hopeful she was on the right track, at least for the time being, she let Hendrix out so he could stretch his legs and take care of business as she walked toward Dwight's truck. How bad could this Rambling Rose be?

~*~

Cash leaned over the fence of the pigpen to scratch Pork Chop behind the ears. The greedy sow knew he always brought a treat with him on the nights he worked security at the Rambling Rose.

"Hey there. Kenzie wouldn't let me out of the house without these." He tossed a few marshmallows Pork Chop's way. The pig grunted and snuffled, drooling as she searched out the sugary treats.

The screen door creaked open, then slammed closed. Cash squinted, looking toward the back of the Rose.

"Don't you go spoiling my pig." Charlie stood on the

wooden stoop. She looked like a balloon about to sail away. He hadn't gotten a really good look at her since last week. His niece or nephew sure had grown since then. "I was heading out to fill up her water bucket. You want to take care of that as long as you're standing over there?"

"Sure. Where's Beck?" His brother-in-law had taken on even more around the Rose since Charlie got pregnant. He was usually the one left dealing with the pig.

"He had to meet a contractor over at the house. I sure hope the baby's room is done before little Sully shows up." She rubbed a palm over her belly.

"I thought y'all weren't going to find out the gender?" Cash walked around the fence toward the hose. "You know for sure now you're having a boy?"

"Nah. I just have a sense. Did Lori Lynne know she was having a girl when she was pregnant with Kenzie?"

Cash's fingers paused on the faucet at the mention of Kenzie's mother. Hell, Lori Lynne hadn't had the backing of a loving husband or supportive family when she had found out she was expecting. She'd been strung tighter than a cat in a room full of rocking chairs by the time she told him she was pregnant.

He replaced Pork Chop's water bucket and walked over to where his baby sister still stood on the step.

Charlie held her hand out to him. "I'm sorry. I didn't mean to bring up bad memories."

"Not really anything *but* bad memories when it comes to Lori Lynne." He gave her a lopsided smile.

"Well, I should have known better. I just keep

hoping you can find somebody like I did. Someone to make good memories with, you know?"

He knew, all right. But pickings around Holiday were fairly slim, especially once he ruled out all the girls his brothers had dated. That was one rule the five Walker brothers never broke—they didn't go after each other's girls, no matter how long it had been. Presley alone had worked his way through more than half the eligible female population in Conroe County. Unless Cash was open to dating someone with an AARP card or a recent high-school grad, he was out of luck. Besides, he needed to focus all his energy and attention on the one female who needed him the most—his daughter.

"I'm glad you and Beck found each other. It's just not in the cards for me."

Charlie put an arm around him, propelling him toward the doorway. "Never say never. I didn't think I'd ever be able to open my heart again after Jackson died. But look at me now."

He slung an arm around his sister's shoulders. That was the truth. No one had thought she'd be open to love again after she lost her fiancé. Thank God Beck came along. Maybe she was right. He thought he'd found love with Lori Lynne. Looking back, he'd come to realize he'd been infatuated and just trying to do the right thing when she found out she was pregnant. But maybe there *was* someone out there who would be a good fit for him and Kenzie.

Charlie shrugged his arm off as she stepped through the doorway. "Now, how about something to eat before you start busting fights apart tonight?"

"You know I'd never turn down Angelo's ribs."

He followed his sister through the back hall and into the

kitchen. Angelo, the head chef, had his hands buried in some sort of dough. He nodded in acknowledgment at Cash. "Fix you a slab, bro?"

"You know I'd love it." Cash patted his stomach. *Finger-licking* didn't begin to describe the way Angelo cooked up a slab of ribs.

"I'll send an order out. Just give me a few." Angelo turned his attention to the floured surface in front of him.

"What's he working on?" Cash asked Charlie.

"New biscuit recipe. Why don't you grab a seat? The food will be out in a couple of minutes. We've got the twins from Abilene playing tonight. You know they always draw a rough-and-tumble kind of crowd."

"I can handle it." Might be good to have to break up a few fights tonight. He'd been pissed off all week and could use a way to blow off some steam. Since his folks kept Kenzie at the big house on the nights he helped out at the Rose or had to pull an evening shift, there'd be nobody to notice if he came home with a bloodied nose or a few scrapes and scuffs.

Charlie stopped him with a hand on his arm. "Oh, I need to introduce you to the new bartender."

"You finally found someone to pitch in?"

"Yeah. Crazy thing. Dwight brought her over. She's been working here the past couple of days."

The muscles in his shoulders bunched up, tense, waiting to round the corner and get his first look at the new bartender. Charlie couldn't be talking about Jinx. The last place that woman would fit in was the Rambling Rose, the oldest honky-tonk in Texas.

She'd be more at home at one of the raves he'd broken up at the abandoned grain mill in the next town over.

But there she was, commanding the space behind the bar. Teal hair spilled over her shoulders.

Bare shoulders.

A hot-pink Rambling Rose tank top clung to her frame like it had been spray-painted on. The scoop neck dipped low—too low—revealing an appealing glimpse of cleavage.

All the blood drained from his face to his crotch. Last time he'd seen her, she'd been covered in a black leather jacket that was at least two sizes too big. Now all he could see was skin. Skin covered in ink. Ink with swirls, drawing his gaze over her arms, her collarbone, her chest.

As he stood there staring, silently willing the blood to stop gravitating downward, she looked up. Her eyes locked with his. A flare of surprise flitted across her face, then she looked away.

"Wait. Do you two… Have you met her already?" Charlie squeezed his forearm, her attention bouncing back and forth between him and Jinx.

"Yeah. I ran into her earlier this week. Her bike broke down, and I gave her a lift to Dwight's." He faced his sister. "You hired her? What do you even know about her situation? She was evasive when I tried to talk to her. Didn't want to answer my questions. Could be trouble, Charlie."

She dismissed his concern with a scowl. "There you go again. Did you try to have a conversation with her, or did you grill her like a cop? You always think the worst about people." Charlie moved toward the bar. Toward Jinx. "She's on her way to New Orleans. Just needs to make some money to get her bike fixed up. It's too bad she's not planning on sticking around permanently though. She seems to know her way behind the bar, and with Beck spending more and more time on his craft brewery, I could use the help."

Cash reluctantly followed, moving closer and closer to Jinx with every step.

Jinx looked up, nudging her chin his way. "Hey."

Charlie twisted to face him, waiting for a response.

"Hi. Uh, looks like you're working here now." He tucked his thumbs through his belt loops, rocking back on the heels of his boots.

Jinx reached for a glass from the rack overhead, giving him a good look at the ink covering her triceps. Some sort of quote or something. "What gave it away? The fact that I'm standing behind the bar in a Rambling Rose tank top? Or did you think I sneaked back here to try to steal a beer?"

"Look, I'm in law enforcement. I'm suspicious of everyone."

"Cash…" Charlie drew his name out while she clamped her hands to her hips. "What did you do to Jinx?"

"Nothing." That was the truth. He hadn't done anything to her. Couldn't blame him for being a little leery of her though. Folks like Jinx didn't settle in tiny towns in Texas.

"Whatever he did, please forgive him. He takes after the bumpkin side of the family. He's just not sure what to make of a city girl like yourself." Charlie whirled around to face Cash. "And you"— she thrust a finger in his face—"you watch your step around here."

He rolled his eyes, snatched her finger, and flung

an arm around her. "Don't be making idle threats. Jinx and I are just fine. Right?"

Jinx swept a trio of empty mugs off the bar and stacked them in the bin below. "Sure. We'll be just fine as long as you stay out of my way, 'kay?"

"My pleasure." He took off his hat, bending into an exaggerated bow, then backed away toward a table to wait for his dinner. Charlie was such a bleeding heart, she'd give a complete stranger the clothes off her back if they looked like they needed them more. He'd have to keep an eye on Jinx. His gut told him she was hiding something, and he'd be damned if he'd let her take advantage of his sister's hospitality.

The ribs arrived, and he managed to get his fill before the band started. Jinx must have felt his gaze on her. She kept glancing his direction, that swoop of hair falling over her eyes. The guys sitting at the bar seemed to appreciate the new view. The regular bartender, Shep, was good at pulling a beer, but he didn't provide much in the way of eye candy.

Jinx, on the other hand, had all her assets on full display. The way the good ole boys nudged each other when she bent down to retrieve something behind the bar made his blood heat up a few degrees. Made him want to take off his shirt and throw it over her shoulders. Made him want to punch something.

Jinx looked like the kind of girl who could handle herself. As long as she didn't cause trouble and kept her hand out of the till, he'd let her bide her time here until she could get her bike fixed up and get out of town. Before he did something he'd regret, he headed out front to make sure the bouncer was actually carding people this week.

The night wore on. The band hardly left the stage. The beer flowed, and the crowd erupted into a few fistfights and borderline brawls, keeping him busy straight through to last call. By the time he made it to the bar for a water, there were only a few die-hard drinkers left.

"How'd your night go?" He leaned against a stool while he filled a plastic cup from the giant cooler of water Charlie kept on the edge of the bar.

Jinx looked up from wiping down the counter. "You talking to me?" She glanced around, obviously giving him a hard time, since no one else was within five feet of them.

"Look, I don't know what it is about me that's got your panties twisted into knots—"

"Chill out, cowboy. There's nothing about you that's got my panties or any other part of me in knots. You're not my type."

Cash laughed. He might have been rusty, but she sure as hell sounded like she was yanking his chain. Two could play at that game. "Why not? Because I don't have enough ink covering my torso to reprint the Constitution? Or because I've never let someone poke my body full of holes?"

She leaned across the bar, close enough that he could look down her shirt if he wanted. Too close. "You might just like some of my holes, cowboy."

chapter

FIVE

WHAT IN THE HELL WAS WRONG WITH HER? JINX BACKED away from the dark-eyed distraction at the bar. The last thing she needed to do was get on the wrong side of local law enforcement. Although, based on her limited interaction with Deputy Do-Good, she couldn't tell if he actually had a right side. He finished his plastic cup of water, smashed it in his fist, and tossed it into the trash can. Jinx finished wiping down the bar top and made her way to the back room to take Hendrix out for another potty break.

"Hey, buddy." She shrugged on her jacket, then unfastened the latch of his crate. He wasn't inside. It had been a long evening, and she hadn't been sleeping well, but surely she would have remembered if she hadn't shut the door. "Hendrix?"

A scratching sound came from a dark corner of the room.

"Hendrix..." Jinx half whispered. All she needed was for someone to find out she had a contraband Chihuahua in the storeroom. "Where are you?"

Nails click-clacked on the ancient hardwood floor. She turned around to find Hendrix covered from head to toe in something white.

"What did you get into?" She made a grab for him, but he dodged her and raced back to the corner. Jinx followed, peering under the floor-to-ceiling shelf to try to find him. "Hendrix. Get over here."

He snorted and continued working on whatever he'd gotten hold of in the corner. Jinx dropped to her knees and reached a hand under the shelf. Her fingers closed around the dog's thin torso, and she pulled him out. His nails scrabbled on the floor as he tried to wriggle away.

"What are you doing? Don't you know we need to keep a low profile?" She held him up in front of her to get a better look.

Something white and gooey covered his head, face, and paws. Smelled like…marshmallows? She swiped a finger across his nose and held it up to hers. Yes, definitely marshmallows. The little fiend was a sucker for sweets and could usually sniff them out if she tried to hide a piece of candy in a pocket. But this was the first time he'd gone after marshmallows.

"Let's get you rinsed off and back into the crate so I can finish cleaning up."

"Who are you talking to?" The storeroom door eased open. Dixie, the waitress who'd covered the restaurant tables tonight, stood in the doorway with a broom in her hand.

"Oh, no one. Just myself." Jinx held Hendrix behind her back and leaned against the wall, hoping the dim light from the bare overhead bulb would conceal the fact that she had a stowaway.

"I do that all the time too." Dixie moved past her to return the broom to its holder. "I'm heading out. Need a ride or anything?"

Hendrix nibbled on her fingers. "Nope, I'm good."

Dixie moved toward the door. "I'm glad you're here, Jinx. It's nice to have someone pitching in."

A high-pitched yelp came from behind her back.

"What was that?" Dixie turned back to face her.

"Um, me?" Jinx smiled.

"I don't think so." Dixie took a step toward her. "What are you hiding?"

"Nothing." Hendrix resumed licking his paws. For something so tiny, he sure did make a lot of noise when slurping marshmallow cream.

"Are you sure? Won't do you any good to lie about it."

"What do you mean by that? Why do you think I'm lying?" Jinx swallowed the rock that seemed to be lodged in her throat.

Dixie crossed her arms. "My gram always says little lies are what cause the biggest problems."

Jinx tried to divert Dixie's attention. "Great words to live by. Hey, did you happen to refill the napkin holders on the bar? I noticed we were getting low."

"Distraction won't work with me. But just know that you're doing yourself in." Dixie's shoulders rose and fell again in a shrug.

Jinx scoffed. "What are you talking about?"

"Karma." Dixie's curls shook as she nodded her head.

"Karma?"

"Sure. You tell a lie and put bad mojo out into the world, and that's what's going to come back to you."

"I'm not putting bad mojo out into the world." Jinx winced as Hendrix lapped at her shirt. Her backside was probably covered in marshmallow goop by now.

"Then what do you have behind your back? If you're

doing something funny in here, I'm going to have to tell Charlie."

"Would you please chill?" Jinx brought Hendrix out from behind her back. "It's a dog. Or should I say a traitor?"

"Oh my gosh, it's so tiny." Dixie reached a hand out, and Hendrix licked her fingers.

"He got into something behind the shelf. I think it's marshmallow fluff."

"Probably so." Dixie ran her hand between Hendrix's ears, the only place on him not covered in goop. "Charlie keeps it around as a treat for Pork Chop."

"The pig?"

"Yeah, she goes nuts for anything sugary."

"I suppose that's good to know. Hey, I need to take him out to go potty real quick, then I'll come back in and clean up. And, Dixie?" Jinx grimaced. "Can you please keep this a secret? Just for the next day or two until I find somewhere to keep him while I'm at work?"

"About that. " Dixie made her way to the sink to rinse off her hands. "Where *are* you staying?"

"I've been bunking down here and there for the past couple of days. I'm hoping to find someone who needs a roomie soon. Know anyone?"

"Actually, yeah, I do." Dixie dried her hands with a paper towel. "How would you like to take over my extra bedroom? I've been thinking of getting a roommate to help with expenses. It's not much, just an apartment over the antique store downtown, but it has plenty of room for two."

"What's your rent run? And how about him?" Jinx held Hendrix away from her chest. "Any pet restrictions?"

"Rent is eight hundred a month plus utilities, so about four fifty would cover it. And I think pets are okay as long as they're under twenty-five pounds."

Jinx ran through the pros and cons in her head. Having a place to stay that had actual walls would make her time in Holiday so much more bearable. But shelling out that much money in rent would mean it would take longer to get enough together to fix up her bike and be on her way. If she knew for sure the job in New Orleans would still be there when she got there, it would be easier to make a decision. "That sounds great. Let me check a couple of things on my end. Can I let you know in a day or two?"

"Sure. No rush. I'd need some time to clean out the second bedroom anyway. I've got a lot of craft stuff in there right now."

"What kind of crafts?" Jinx asked.

Dixie flicked her dangly earring. "Jewelry mostly, although I also dabble in photography. None of that pays the bills though, so if you want it, the space is yours."

"Thanks, Dixie."

"No problem. And just so you know"—she nodded toward Hendrix—"your secret's safe with me."

"No bad mojo?" Jinx wasn't sure she understood Dixie's stance on lies versus secrets.

"Nope. Keeping a secret is fine. Lying about it is what gets you into trouble."

"Glad we got that straight." She waited until Dixie left the storeroom, then tucked Hendrix under her arm. "Let's get you outside for a couple of minutes."

She took him out back and set him on the ground.

The light hanging from the tall pole outside the back door cast a circle of yellow around them. Hendrix sniffed around, venturing outside the glowing ring. While she waited for him to do his business, Jinx brainstormed places she could stay. When she'd worked janitorial in a high-rise building, she'd spent the night in one of the empty offices. But Holiday didn't look like it had a booming need for corporate cleaning services. She'd even slept in a shed at a gardening supply nursery for a few weeks before she had started working with Wade. It was easy to find places to hide out in LA. Not so much here in Holiday, where everyone seemed to keep track of everyone else's comings and goings.

"Hurry up, Hendrix." Where did he go? He usually didn't wander far, but she'd lost track of him. "Hendrix?"

Jinx crept around the grassy area, trying to catch a glimpse of him. She stopped when she came to the edge of the pigpen. Charlie had pointed out the Rose's mascot on her brief tour of the grounds. But Jinx hadn't seen the pig since. Soft snuffles and snorts came from a far corner.

"Hendrix? You'd better get over here, buddy, or your ass is grass." The flashlight on her phone didn't help much, but she held it out in front of her, trying to find where the noise was coming from.

There was Hendrix, on his back, the giant pig hovering over him.

"Get away from him! Hendrix, come here!" She clapped her hand against her thigh. Hendrix's head lolled back, and he yapped at her. She ran closer, waving her hands in the air above her, sure the pig was eating her traveling companion for a late-night snack. Finally, just a few feet from the pig, Jinx stopped. Pork Chop was giving Hendrix a bath with her tongue, licking off every dot of marshmallow fluff. And the little beast was loving it. His hind leg whapped the ground when Pork Chop started in on his head. He'd always loved to have his ears scratched.

"You little troublemaker. Get over here." She reached out and hooked his collar with her finger. He bounced to his feet and let her pick him up. The pig sat back on her butt. Jinx could have sworn she frowned at her. Then Pork Chop nudged into her, trying to finish what she'd started with Hendrix.

"Get away from me!" Jinx stumbled back, landing on her ass in a puddle of mud. Great, just great. Now she'd have to find a way to do laundry. Otherwise, she was down to a miniskirt and one pair of leggings.

She brushed herself off as best she could, then took Hendrix back into the storeroom and rinsed him off. "You stay put. I'll be back in just a few minutes."

With a thin layer of mud coating her backside, she poked her head into the office, where Charlie was counting up the till.

"You need me to do anything else?" She tried to block her mud-coated lower half with the door.

"Nope, I just need to finish up in here. Hey, do you have a sec?" Charlie looked up from the stacks of cash spread out on the desk in front of her.

"Sure." Jinx ventured into the office, careful not to turn, so Charlie couldn't see she'd taken an impromptu mud bath in the pigpen.

Charlie tucked her pencil behind her ear. "How are you liking it around here?"

"Oh, it's great. Thanks so much for the opportunity." Piles of dollar bills covered half the desktop. Wade would die, actually keel over and shit himself if he saw the kind of cash the Rambling Rose pulled in on a single Friday night.

Leaning forward to rest her elbows on the desk, Charlie sighed. "Can I be honest with you for a sec?"

"Sure." She was a little taken aback by the question. Jinx didn't usually inspire relative strangers to share deep thoughts with her, especially sober relative strangers.

"I need help." Charlie gestured to her humongous belly. "The baby's going to be here soon, and I need to start pulling back on my responsibilities at the Rose. I've already got Shep and Angelo taking on more than their fair share. With Beck devoting more and more time to developing his craft brew, I need someone I can count on to pick up the slack. Are you interested?"

"Like what?" If it meant extra pay or extra hours, she was in. The sooner she made enough to repair her bike, the sooner she'd be back on the road.

"Helping me with the accounting piece. Maybe take over the scheduling. I'm transitioning a lot of the special event planning to Dixie, but I know she could use some help with that too."

Sounded easy enough. And it wasn't anything she hadn't done in one of her many previous jobs. "Sure. I can use the extra hours."

"Great. You want to start by recounting the

deposit for tomorrow? I've got to run to the bathroom. This kid is sitting right on my bladder." Charlie struggled to rise from the chair. "I swear I must pee at least five thousand times a day."

"Um, okay." Jinx waited until Charlie waddled out of the room before turning to the desk full of cash in front of her. Had to be more than enough to fix her bike and get her to New Orleans with plenty to spare. Wade never would have let anyone near this kind of dough. Was Charlie that naive, just that trusting, or did being pregnant suck all the important brain cells out of her head and decimate her judgment?

Jinx wasn't there to figure out Charlie's mental health status. And she wasn't a thief. So she grabbed a towel to protect the seat, picked up the nearest stack, and began to count.

A half hour later, Jinx made it to the storeroom to get Hendrix. "Sorry, little guy. We'll figure something out soon, I promise." She should have found him a new home back in LA. Geri would have taken him if she hadn't had a trailer full of cats already. She was the kind of woman who couldn't say no to anyone, especially a male. Jinx let herself smile for a second as she thought about her ex-coworker. She wondered how long Geri had been able to hold off telling Wade that Jinx had taken off for good this time.

She stuffed the leftover wrap she'd had for dinner into her bag. Tips had been good, but she didn't want to spend all her income on food. The wrap would be enough for breakfast, and Charlie had asked her to come in for the

Saturday morning crowd, so she'd be able to grab something then. This living meal to meal would get old soon. Not that she'd ever managed to save more than a month or two extra in the bank. But living paycheck to paycheck sure beat not knowing where her next meal would come from.

At least working at the bar would ensure she didn't totally starve. And if it worked out to stay with Dixie for a month or two, she'd have a roof over her head. For now, she'd settle for a quick sponge bath over the utility sink. When was the last time she'd actually washed her hair? Tonight might be her lucky night.

She grabbed one of the clean washcloths and a hand towel. In less than five minutes, she managed to scrub down her whole body and wash her hair in the oversize utility tub. It would be nice to crawl into her sleeping bag without a boozy film on her skin. She threw on her last pair of clean leggings and a shirt, then tossed the linens in the washing machine.

Maybe this stint in Holiday, Texas, wouldn't be so bad. Maybe with the extra responsibilities Charlie was going to give her, she'd actually manage to save a little for a change. Maybe she'd turn her history of bad luck around.

Maybe.

Cash poured himself two fingers of whiskey from the bottle Charlie kept hidden in her bottom desk drawer, then settled into the chair across from her. She counted up the cash, slipping a rubber band around each stack when she got to a certain amount.

"Looks like a good night tonight?" He kicked his boots onto the edge of the desk.

She glared at him, holding out a finger, her lips moving as she counted.

"Sorry, Sis." The amber liquid slid down his throat, the burn a welcome distraction from what had been bothering him all night.

Jinx.

She'd laid that line on him, then barreled out from behind the bar, and he hadn't seen her since.

Charlie snapped a rubber band on the last stack. "There. Now, what were you asking that was so important you made me have to count that pile twice?"

"Nothing. Just saying it looked like the Rose did well tonight." He lifted his feet off the desk and leaned forward, resting his forearms on his knees. "Did your new bartender leave already?"

Charlie scooted back in her chair, crossing her arms under her chest. "What do you care?"

"What? I care if y'all do a good business here. Job security and all that."

His sister's head shook from side to side. "Not what I meant."

"What, then?"

"What is it with Jinx? I know you don't like her look—the hair, the tattoos, the metal. But what's your problem with her?" Charlie's eyes narrowed.

"Nothing." He scoffed, held his arms out to the sides, shrugged. Anything to make him look unaffected at the mention of the blue-haired bartender's name. "I just wondered how she was getting home. Where's she staying, anyhow?"

"Oh. I guess I didn't ask." A wrinkle appeared between Charlie's eyebrows. "I didn't even think about that."

"Yeah. I recognized all the vehicles left in the lot. Either she's catching a ride with someone, or she's walking wherever she's going tonight." For some reason, the thought of Jinx heading home with one of the frat boys down from San Marcos made his chest constrict. What the hell was that all about? She'd made it pretty damn clear he wasn't her type. Hell, he didn't even want to be her type. He wasn't looking for a hookup or anything else. Wouldn't mean a thing to him if she found a bed to warm. As long as she kept her word to Charlie—that's all he needed to be worried about. He set the glass tumbler on the edge of the desk, no longer in the mood for a drink.

"She seems like a big girl. I'm sure if she's biking cross country, she can look out for herself." Charlie lifted the tumbler to her nose and inhaled. "I miss Sully. We used to toast over big nights like tonight while we counted up the till."

Cash knew Charlie had a special place in her heart for the old owner of the Rambling Rose. "But if he hadn't passed, you wouldn't have met Beck, and you wouldn't be about to make me an uncle again."

"True." She set the glass down on the desk. "Speaking of my hubby, he's going to be here any minute to drive me home. I told him I'm pregnant, not completely incapable. He's been up since the crack of dawn, working on the house. I can get myself home."

"He cares about you. Let him spoil you for a

change." He offered a hand when she struggled to get up from the chair. "When are you going to start letting him work the late shifts around here? You ought to be taking it easy."

"Right. I told Beck, and I'll tell you—this place is in my blood. I'll probably go into labor during the New Year's Eve party or something. You'll have to haul me out of here kicking and screaming."

"That's what I'm afraid of." Cash could picture it now, Charlie scaring that baby into staying put until she was damn well ready for it to arrive. He didn't want to be the one to tell her that all her well-laid plans would get blown to bits as soon as that baby started screaming. He wasn't that far away from the sleepless nights and dirty diapers that he couldn't remember how it felt to be at the beck and call of a ten-pound tyrant.

Charlie gathered the cash and dropped it into a bank bag, then tucked it under her arm. "I did ask Jinx if she could pitch in on some of the office stuff. You proud of me for stepping back a bit?"

"What kind of office stuff?"

"Just counting up the deposits, maybe helping with staff schedules for the part-timers. She seems capable."

Cash clenched his jaw. "What do you know about her? Did you do a background check?"

Charlie put a hand on her hip. "Of course I did a background check. All clear. Obviously, she's experienced behind the bar. Plus, I had her recount the deposit tonight, and she actually told me the number I came up with was short a couple of twenties. Those brand-new bills stick together sometimes, you know?" Charlie shrugged. "She could have pocketed the difference, and I never would have known. What do you have against that poor girl?"

"Nothing." How could he explain the sixth sense a law enforcement officer had to deal with, even when off duty, to someone who trusted with her whole heart and soul? "Just be careful, okay?"

She shook her head, dismissing his concern. "Can you lock up for me?"

"No problem." He walked her to the back door just as Beck pulled up in his truck. "Have a good night, Sis."

"You too." She half hugged him before waddling down the steps to her waiting husband.

Cash turned back to the honky-tonk. Everyone else had cleared out, and an eerie quiet settled over the usually bustling building. He did a quick walk-through to make sure everything was locked up. As he passed the utility room, he thought he heard a dripping sound. He flicked on the light and noticed the faucet hadn't been turned off completely. Well, damn. He tightened the knob, then wiped his hand on his jeans. Something about the sink looked off. He leaned down to get a better look. Blue. Like someone had spilled some blue food coloring down the damn drain.

Or maybe blue hair dye.

Why the hell would Jinx be washing her hair in the storage room? No matter what Charlie thought, her new employee had to be hiding something. And he wanted to find out what it was. Not because she put him on edge, made him feel like he was standing at the rim of some deep ravine. No, he wanted to make sure she wasn't trying to pull a fast one on the people he loved.

Resolved to check her out more thoroughly in the morning, he locked the back door and pulled it closed behind him. Tonight, he'd do what he did every Friday night after a long shift at the bar—head home, pour himself a stiff one, and try to pass out before he started feeling sorry for himself for what a shitstorm his life had become.

Buried in thoughts of the past, he almost drove right by the black-jacket-wearing pedestrian. He slowed and pulled up beside her.

"Where you headed?"

"None of your business." Jinx didn't glance over.

"Let me give you a ride." At least she hadn't disappeared with someone else. For some reason, that realization shed a hint of lightness over his dark heart. "Come on, Jinx."

When he mentioned her name, she finally looked over. "Are you following me?"

"What? No, I'm not following you. I'm heading home. Why don't you get in the truck?" His tone didn't leave room for negotiation. But damn if she didn't keep putting one foot in front of the other.

"No thanks. I like to walk."

"Get in the damn truck," he growled.

She kicked at the gravel on the side of the road. "I said I like to walk."

He slammed on the brakes, threw the truck in park, and got out. He was used to people doing what he said. His job depended on it. He caught up to her and fell into step beside her. "You don't mind if I walk with you then, do you?"

She rolled her eyes. "I don't need an escort, Deputy."

"No. You need to get in the truck. But if you insist on walking, you don't leave me much choice but to make sure you get where you're going safe and sound."

"And you're really going to leave your truck here and walk with me wherever I want to go?"

"Well, I'd rather drive you, but my mama would whup me good if she found out I let a woman walk home alone at three o'clock in the fucking morning."

Jinx finally stopped moving. Turning to face him, she squeezed his cheeks together with one hand. "Would she wash your mouth out with soap for saying those four-letter words?"

Warmth radiated out from where her hand cupped his chin. The full moon bathed her in a shimmery glow, glinting off the dozen earrings and piercings she had through her ears. She smelled fresh, like she'd just doused herself in wildflowers, not spent the past eight hours sweating it out behind the bar. Come to think of it, her hair looked like it might even be damp.

"Did you shower?" As the words left his mouth, he wanted to chomp down on his tongue.

Her eyes sparked, then a vacant emptiness took over. She let her hand fall away. The cool night air seemed especially chilly after the warmth of her touch.

"Yeah. I reeked of beer, so I rinsed off real quick. Charlie said it was okay." She moved past him and continued to walk.

"Where are you staying? Let me run you over there so we can both go home and get to bed."

"Why does it matter so much? I appreciate your concern, but I can take care of myself."

Charlie was right. Jinx was a big girl. He'd be

better off putting the new bartender with the swirly ink and giant attitude out of his mind for good. "Fine. But if you get into a bind, give me a call. You still have my card, right?"

"Sure." She lifted a hand to wave over her shoulder. "See ya, Deputy."

He stood for a moment, watching her move beyond the reach of his headlights. Jaw clenched, he climbed back into the truck and inched past her on the pavement. With a final look in the rearview mirror, he pressed on the gas and left her behind. Stubborn woman. If she didn't want his help, he'd stop offering.

chapter
SIX

A BREEZE BATTED THE FRONT OF THE TENT, MAKING JINX want to burrow farther down into her lightweight sleeping bag and fall back asleep. Already November, and she could still sleep outside. Thank goodness for the moderate Texas climate. If she'd been home in Seattle right now, she probably wouldn't be able to stay in her tent. It didn't get that cold, but it was a different kind of cold—wet, bone chilling, damp.

Hendrix wiggled out from the sleeping bag and scratched at the front of the tent.

"Now? Seriously, you need to go out now?" She snuggled farther into the sleeping bag. "Just hold it."

He didn't come back, just sat near the front of the tent, pawing at the nylon.

"Cut it out. You're going to scratch a hole in it." She tossed a sock at him, hoping he'd give up and come back to the sleeping bag. He might have only been five pounds, but he generated enough body heat to keep her warm, and right now, she missed the little heater.

Hendrix barked, short, loud yips that pierced through the stone-cold silence of the night.

"Shh. You're supposed to be quiet so no one knows we're here." Jinx unzipped the side of her bag and shrugged into a sweatshirt. She clipped the leash on

Hendrix, then let him out into the eerie gray of early morning. Based on his behavior the night before, she didn't trust him not to wander.

She waited, trying to keep herself propped upright, wanting nothing more than to crawl back into her sleeping bag and catch a few more hours of shut-eye. But a quick glance at her watch showed she only had an hour until she had to be at the Rambling Rose to set up for the breakfast crowd. Charlie had given her a heads-up that it was a family-friendly shift and to be prepared for a slew of kids.

She liked kids. Other people's kids. She'd never let herself imagine having her own someday. Kids needed a mom and a dad. A home without wheels, a stable place to call their own. Not like the fun house she'd grown up in. At least until she'd turned fifteen and left home for good. Her mind wandered for a moment, back to roaming the streets of Rainier Beach with her friends late at night. Anything to get out of her mom's place. That was then. This was now.

And now meant she had about ten minutes to throw herself together if she wanted to make the trek to the Rambling Rose in time for her shift. She climbed out of the tent.

The walk back and forth to the honky-tonk was getting to her. She'd been keeping her eyes open for a spot to camp closer. So far, nothing beat this tract where she'd first parked the bike. The scrubby trees provided a break from the wind, and there was a freshwater stream just a few minutes' walk through the brush. But she did need to start thinking about a more semipermanent solution. She'd text Jamie today to find out how long she could hold the job in New Orleans. If things looked good on that front, she could bunk with Dixie for a while and still make it to Louisiana before New Year's.

Her backpack stuffed with dirty clothes and with a grumpy Chihuahua in his soft-side crate, she set off on the walk back to the Rambling Rose. She arrived in enough time to brush her teeth and put on a touch of makeup in the bathroom.

For the next couple of hours, she mixed mimosas and hauled trays of Texas french toast and huevos rancheros to the waiting crowd. The kids wanted to touch her hair, and more than once, she caught a skeptical glance from a surly local or concerned parent.

She was about to sneak off to the backroom to take Hendrix out when someone shrieked her name from the doorway.

"Jinx!"

Kenzie barreled across the room, legs and arms flapping like she'd just seen her favorite cartoon character. Jinx caught her right before Kenzie plowed into her. Scrawny arms wrapped around her waist, and a mass of light-brown hair pressed into her gut. Jinx instinctively hugged the kid back.

Kenzie took two steps backward, grabbed Jinx's hand, and began tugging her toward the doorway. "Daddy told me you work for Aunt Charlie now. Are you gonna have breakfast with us? I like the french toast sticks. Angelo always makes them look like a face and gives me extra whipped cream. Do you like whipped cream?"

"I...uh—"

"You gotta like whipped cream. Papa sometimes squirts it into my mouth from the can." Kenzie's voice quieted as she glanced at the older man standing next to her dad. "Oh, I wasn't supposed to tell Daddy that."

"You must be Jinx." A woman about Jinx's height enveloped her in a hug.

Awkward. Who in the hell were these people? So far, Texans sure seemed to like to dole out the hugs. All of them. Well, all of them except the tall, dark, and cranky deputy. Jinx stood still, waiting for the moment to pass.

Cash cleared his throat. "Sorry, my family's made up of huggers. Mom, enough already."

The words sounded funny coming from the man who couldn't seem to stand her. He definitely didn't strike her as a hugger. Or much of a smiler either. The chip on his shoulder seemed to be as big as the double-wide where she'd last seen her own mother.

Cash's mom backed away. "I'm sorry. It's just that Kenzie and Charlie have told us so much about you. It's nice to finally meet you."

Jinx side-eyed the beaming girl. They'd only met once. What could Kenzie have told them?

Cash gestured to his mother. "Mom, meet Jinx. Jinx, this is my mom, Ann, and my dad, Tom." He shifted from foot to foot, clearly uncomfortable performing the introductions.

Tom offered a hand, so Jinx shook it. Warm, rough, the way she imagined a rancher's hands would feel. Charlie had told her she grew up around here with a ranch full of brothers. Lucky for her she had so much family around.

"Can you eat with us? Nana, can she?" Kenzie grabbed Jinx's hand in one of hers and Ann's in the other.

"We'd love to have you join us. Kenzie, why don't you go find a table?" Ann pointed to the far side of the room, at the tables closest to the windows.

Couldn't they tell she was on the clock? Surely the logo T-shirt or apron ought to provide a built-in excuse. "Oh, I'm actually working right now. I can't—"

"Place is about cleared out, wouldn't you say?" Tom gestured around the mostly empty room.

The brunch crowd had come and gone. A few regulars sat on barstools watching a college football game. Dixie walked by at that exact ill-timed moment.

"You go ahead, Jinx. I'll cash out the table you've got left. Enjoy the break." She winked, and Jinx vowed to royally screw up her next cocktail order.

"It's all settled then. Looks like Kenzie found us a table." Tom guided his wife toward an empty table where Kenzie sat, swinging her legs in a too-big-for-her chair.

Jinx looked up at Cash, waiting for him to make up some excuse. She didn't want to budge her way into their little family lunch.

Instead, he pulled his mouth into a resigned line. "Shall we?" He gestured toward the table across the room.

Toward his mom and dad.

Toward his kid.

Toward uncharted territory.

HH

Jinx tensed as she stepped in front of him, moving toward the other side of the room. He didn't blame her. With a deer-in-the-headlights look frozen on her face, she let him direct her across the room to where his family waited. He should have known she'd be here this morning. With Charlie trying to step back a little, she was probably having Jinx work as many hours as she could handle.

They reached the table, and he held out a chair for her. Jinx cast a longing look toward the kitchen, then slid onto the seat. If she hadn't looked so miserable, he might have laughed out loud.

Kenzie pointed to the chair next to Jinx. "You sit there, Daddy." She leaned against the back of the chair on Jinx's other side.

Flanked by him and his daughter, Jinx seemed to grow more uncomfortable by the second.

His mom reached across the table and patted Jinx's hand. "Charlie told us you're from Seattle?"

Jinx nodded.

"How long are you in town?"

"Oh, I'm not sure. I need to get my bike fixed." Jinx slid her hand out from under his mom's.

Cash smirked. Hell, he could sit back and let the info flow. Between Kenzie and his nosy mother, he'd get all the recon he needed.

"Charlie said you'll probably be here for at least a month or two. You'll love the Jingle Bell Jamboree. So much fun. Here in Holiday, we don't need much excuse for a celebration. There's always a parade, a festival, or some sort of party going on."

Jinx's eyes widened. Her fingers gripped the edge of the table. The deer in the headlights appeared to be morphing into a wild animal caught in a snap trap.

"Chill, Mom. She's just passing through—"

"Oh!" Ann slapped a palm on the table. "You'll be here for Thanksgiving. You'll come to the house. The Rose is closed that afternoon, and we always have Charlie and the gang over for Thanksgiving dinner." She nodded to herself, satisfied firm plans had been made, and picked up a menu.

"Slow down. What if Jinx has other plans?" His dad smiled and nodded toward Jinx. "Do you have other plans, hon?"

Jinx took in a visible inhale. Her shoulders lifted, and her chest rose. The pink rose on the Rambling Rose logo perched in a precarious position. Every time she took in a breath, the rose on her chest moved. Cash became mesmerized with the rise and fall of her breath.

"Of course she doesn't have plans yet. She doesn't know anyone else in town." Ann slid her reading glasses to rest on top of her head. "Besides, Cash makes the best sausage stuffing in Texas."

"You can sit by me, Jinx. Nana lets us have pie *and* cookies on Thanksgiving, don't you?"

"That's right, baby doll."

Kenzie beamed under her nana's wink.

Cash finally managed to redirect his attention from Jinx's chest to her face. "How can you say no to cookies *and* pie?"

"Gosh, that sounds great. If I'm still here, I'd love to join you." The words spilled from her mouth, then she chomped down on her lower lip.

Liar, liar, pants on fire. She had absolutely no intention of joining his family for Thanksgiving. He could tell by the look on her face and the way she chewed on her bottom lip like she wanted to gnaw it off. Too bad for her. Once his mom got something in her head, didn't matter how crazy it was, she always saw it through. He'd been the victim of many of her harebrained ideas, and it appeared she had her sights set on Jinx next.

Kenzie poked Jinx in the arm and pointed to her menu. "What's that say?"

"Why don't you sound it out, Tadpole?" He'd confided in his mom about the teacher's preliminary diagnosis. Maybe now she'd see for herself what they were talking about.

"Eggs den…" Kenzie began.

"Benedict, honey," his dad chimed in. His mom poked his dad in the gut, and he gave her a confused look.

Cash watched his mom whisper in his dad's ear. They argued back and forth for a few moments, probably debating whether or not poor Kenzie needed as much help as the teachers thought.

As his parents muttered to each other, Jinx leaned over Kenzie's menu and pointed to some of the letters.

"See how the *d* faces that way and the *b* goes the other?" Jinx's finger trailed over the tiny print on the giant menu. "Sometimes they play tricks on me, and I have to think about it before I read the words."

"Me too!" Kenzie pointed to a capital *B*. "The bigger ones are easier. Do the words ever look like a worm and wiggle on the paper when you try to read?"

Jinx nodded, and the two of them put their heads together, giggling like they were sharing some sort of inside joke.

Cash stared at them, uncomfortable with the way Kenzie latched on to a woman she'd only met once but also grateful that someone seemed to understand what his daughter was going through. Why the hell did that someone have to be Jinx?

Dixie stopped by to take their order, and they managed to work their way through brunch. Jinx took Kenzie's recommendation and went with the Texas french toast. She practically inhaled it. Ann continued to pepper Jinx with questions. Some she answered. Some she deflected. Some she responded to with questions of her own.

By the time they finished eating, the room had emptied.

"Does Charlie have you working tonight?" his mom asked.

Jinx nodded. "I have a couple of hours before I need to clock in again."

"Can I see Hendrix?" Kenzie clasped Jinx's arm.

"Oh, um—" Jinx looked back and forth from Kenzie to Cash.

"Please? I want Nana to meet him." Kenzie whipped her head around to face her grandmother. "He's soooooo cute. I want one for Christmas, okay?"

His mom's brows knit together. "What's a Hendrix?"

"He's a Chihuahua." Jinx turned in her seat to smile at Kenzie. "If your dad says it's all right, you can hold him for a minute, okay?"

How could he say no to Kenzie when her face lit up like the angel at the top of the Christmas tree? "Okay, but make sure you wash your hands after. Where is he anyway? Did you bring him to work with you?"

Jinx frowned. "I couldn't leave him by himself. It's okay though. He's in a crate in back."

"Charlie know you're keeping a dog in her storeroom?" Cash asked.

"I…uh"—her eyes darted to the hall where the offices were—"haven't quite had a chance to talk to her about it yet."

Cash took his napkin from his lap and set it on the table. "Best make sure you do. She can't afford to have the health department close her down."

"I will. I'll ask her today." She stood and turned to Kenzie. "Want to come with me to get him, and then we can take him out back?"

Kenzie glanced his way. Cash nodded. She grabbed Jinx's hand and followed her to the back room. He couldn't tear his eyes away from the two of them, hand in hand.

"Kenzie seems to have found a new friend." His mom nodded toward the two of them. "What do you think?"

"What do I think about what?"

"Jinx. I'll admit she doesn't look like your type, but—"

"Whoa!" He stood and stepped back from the table. "Don't start trying to play matchmaker with me, Mom."

"Simmer down now. I'm not trying to play anything." His mother put her hand on his arm—her left hand. Her wedding ring sparkled. Like hell that wasn't intentional. "I'm just wondering if it isn't about time you try to find someone special. Kenzie needs a positive female role model in her life."

"She's got you…and Charlie. That's enough."

"I'm not saying you have to ask Jinx out. But promise me you'll keep an open mind about dating? You don't need to find *the one* tomorrow or even next week—"

"Enough, Mom, okay?" He covered her hand with his own and gave it a squeeze.

"I just want you to be happy. Kenzie too. Y'all deserve it."

He didn't hold it against his mom for wanting her kids

to have the best life had to offer. But he'd learned one thing—he didn't deserve shit. If he wanted something in this life, he had to work for it and take it and then fight like hell to hang on to it. He'd fought hard for Lori Lynne, and it hadn't made a bit of difference. He'd never forgive himself for letting her walk out of his and Kenzie's lives, for Kenzie's sake, if nothing else.

His daughter did deserve everything life had to offer. Maybe his mom was right about needing to find a positive role model for Kenzie. He'd never be able to tell his mother that. She'd hold it over him for the rest of his life.

"I'm gonna head out back and make sure Kenzie's not getting eaten alive by a rabid rat-dog. Y'all want to come?"

"We need to get back to the ranch. Tell Jinx we enjoyed meeting her though." His dad clasped his hand and patted him on the arm with the other.

"Will do, Dad."

His mom waited her turn, then grabbed him in a hug. "Tell Kenzie I'm looking forward to making cookies with her tomorrow. And remind Jinx about coming for Thanksgiving."

"Fine. I'll make sure she knows she's invited." He waited until his parents made it to the door before turning toward the back. Almost forty years of wedded bliss, and they were still going strong. Relationships like that just didn't exist anymore. He shook his head and passed into the outdoor beer garden.

Kenzie nuzzled the little critter against her cheek. "Isn't he so cute, Daddy?"

"Adorable." He pulled the brim of his hat over his eyes.

"Want to hold him?" She held it out. The dog scrambled to cling to her palm.

Cash reached for it at the same time as Jinx. Their hands bumped, both trying to grab on to Hendrix.

"It's okay. I've got him." Jinx smiled up at him, the sun glinting across her pale skin. Her eyes looked more blue than gray out in the sunshine.

"Yeah, go ahead." He untangled his hand from hers. "Kenzie, let's head out. I'm sure Jinx has stuff to do today before she has to be back at work." He studied her profile while she settled Hendrix against her chest. God, would he ever look at the Rambling Rose's logo the same?

"Can we take care of Hendrix while she works tonight? Please, oh please, Daddy?" Kenzie danced around in front of him, tugged on his hands, and shot him her best puppy dog eyes.

"I'm sure Jinx has a place for him."

Kenzie stuck out her lower lip. "No. He'll have to go back in his crate. But I could watch him. I'll hold him real careful, I promise. I'll even do all my homework."

"Reading too?" he asked. Ever since the meeting with her teacher, he couldn't help but notice how much she hated doing her reading homework.

She let out a huge sigh. "Do I have to do all of it?"

"Hey, I have an idea." Jinx paused, glancing over at Cash. "If your dad says it's okay, maybe you can read to Hendrix?"

Kenzie lit up like a sparkler on the Fourth of July. "Oh, please, Daddy? I promise I'll do all my reading if I can read to Hendrix."

They didn't have plans that night. He only pitched in

one weekend night at the bar so he'd have time to spend with Kenzie. Sure, why not? She could play with the dog, and he'd have a chance to catch up on some paperwork.

"If it's okay with Jinx…"

Tiny arms wrapped around his legs like a vise. "Thank you, Daddy."

"Sure. I think he'd like that. Why don't we put him in his crate so you can get him home?" Jinx offered. "And maybe I can show you a couple of tricks that might help with your reading."

Kenzie beamed up at him. "Jinx mixes up her *b*'s and *d*'s just like me, Daddy. She says she had diplexia."

"Dyslexia." Jinx laughed. "It just means I sometimes get my letters mixed up a little. I had a great teacher when I was about your age, and she taught me some ways to make it easier to see the difference."

Cash cringed at the mention of the d-word. Kenzie's teacher had put them on the list for a tutor, but the daily fights over getting the reading homework done were taking their toll. Maybe Jinx could offer a few suggestions. He hoped he wouldn't regret giving in this time. "So, how long until you need to be back?"

"Couple of hours. I was just going to walk over to Dwight's to see how things are going with the bike."

"We'd be happy to give you a ride."

"Oh, that's okay. It's nice out. I can walk."

"It'll take you an hour just to get there and back. This way, you can fill me in on how not to kill the critter while we Hendrix-sit for you tonight. What do you say?"

She didn't exactly smile, but the tiny upward tilt of her lips told him he'd won this round. "Let me just tell Dixie I'll be back."

"Yay! Jinx is going to ride with us!" Kenzie grabbed Jinx's backpack from where she'd set it on the ground.

Jinx reached for it as Kenzie tried to hoist it into the truck. "Oh, I'll get that."

Before she had a chance to grab it, the bag tumbled onto the ground. Clothes, toiletries, and a couple of credit cards spilled onto the gravel between them.

Jinx crouched down, trying to scoop everything back into the bag.

"I'm sorry." Kenzie's lower lip trembled.

"It's okay, sweetie. It was an accident." Cash squatted next to Jinx to help. His fingers closed around one of the shiny credit cards. Turned out it wasn't a credit card after all but some sort of cash card.

"Here you go." He handed it back.

She shoved it to the bottom of her bag without looking up. "Thanks. What a mess. I need to better organize my stuff, I guess."

"Here's another one." Kenzie held out a silver and red card that sparkled in the sun. "How much is five-zero-zero?"

Cash looked from his daughter to Jinx. "That's five hundred dollars."

Jinx's cheeks pinkened. "I didn't want to have a bunch of cash on me while I was on the road."

Cash nodded. "Okay."

"This way, I can store the numbers in my phone and don't have to keep track of it all."

"Makes sense." Sure, it might make sense—if he wasn't already getting a weird vibe from her.

"You ready to head to town?" Jinx stood and slung the strap of her backpack over her shoulder.

"Yep. Kenzie, let's go hop in the truck." He made sure Kenzie got settled, then climbed in the cab next to Jinx. What was she hiding? As he pulled onto the road to take them to town, he vowed he'd figure it out—hopefully before someone he loved, like Charlie or Kenzie, got too attached.

chapter
SEVEN

JINX PULLED HER JACKET TIGHTER AROUND HER. THE BAR
hadn't been as busy tonight. Storms had raged across the
county off and on for hours. Hopefully, she'd make it back
to the tent before the next shower started. At least Hendrix
was safe and warm at Cash's place. Maybe Kenzie would
be willing to watch him for a while until she could find a
better place to stay.

A fat raindrop plopped onto her head. Crap. This
was the one drawback to her freewheeling plan. Sleeping
outdoors in a non-waterproof tent meant she had a miserable night ahead of her.

Headlights appeared in the distance. She only had
another quarter mile or so to go. The drainage ditch sat
low on this stretch of road. She didn't want to scramble
down the embankment and get stuck trekking the rest of
the way through the tall weeds. Who knew what kind of
creatures might be slithering through the grass? Instead,
she pulled her jacket up and over her head, shielding her
face from the oncoming lights.

The vehicle passed her, and she let out the breath she'd
been holding. Just another truck. Did people around
here even own two-door and four-door cars? Seemed like
everyone had at least some sort of four-wheel drive vehicle.
The raindrops fell faster. She picked up her pace. Forced

her tired feet to move. Headlights shone behind her. Dammit, the truck that passed her had turned around. It pulled up beside her.

"God, you're stubborn." His voice floated through the window.

She lowered her jacket and turned to meet Cash's eyes. The blue glow from the dashboard made him look eerie. And mad. He was definitely mad. One hand rested on the steering wheel, the other draped across the back of the passenger seat, his fingers drumming on the headrest.

"Get in the truck, Jinx."

"I don't need a ride. I'm fine." She shivered as the rain found its way inside her jacket and rolled down her back.

"We can do this the easy way or the hard way. Your choice. Either way, you're about to get dumped on."

"Why can't you leave me alone?" That was the problem with towns so small they didn't appear on a stupid map—she couldn't blend in, lose herself, disappear among the tourist attractions. In Holiday, Texas, she *was* the attraction.

A crack of thunder rumbled across the sky. She hesitated. Part of her wanted to jump in the truck. At least she'd be dry. Part of her wanted to tell the deputy to go to hell. She didn't need him meddling in her business. Part of her wished she'd never left LA.

"Come on. I've got your tent and stuff in the back."

"What? Where did you get my tent?"

"From the edge of my property. Now are you gonna get in here with me, or do you want to ride in the back with your crap?"

"Wait a minute. Are you threatening me?"

"No. Just trying to keep us both nice and dry." He threw the truck into park and cracked open his door.

"Fine." She opened the passenger door and climbed inside, her wet clothes dripping all over his tan leather seats. Hopefully, they got waterlogged and ruined or something.

"Was that so hard?" He slammed his door shut and gestured to the seat belt. "Buckle up. Safety first." His mouth slashed across his face in a thin line.

She buckled her seat belt and crossed her arms across her chest. "Happy now?"

He pulled the truck onto the road. "I could charge you with trespassing."

"But?"

"But what?" He glanced her way.

She hated cops. When she was a kid, she thought they were the good guys, the ones she was supposed to look to for help. That was until her mom decided to make a career out of finding her next Mr. Right at the local precinct. Jinx learned the hard way that sometimes the people who were supposed to protect her could be the most dangerous.

"Seems like there was a *but* there." So what if he pressed charges? She hadn't damaged any of his precious property.

"But I won't."

Her breath left her body in a long, drawn-out exhale. "Why not?"

"Honestly?" His eyes cut to her.

She could just make out the wrinkle between his eyebrows. Nodding, she waited to see if he'd continue.

"I don't know." He shrugged his shoulders, shook his head. "My gut tells me you're hiding something. But hell if I know what it is. I don't suppose you want to tell me, do you?"

The skies opened, and rain pummeled the windshield. He flipped the wipers to full speed. She stared out the window, letting her finger trace the path of the cold raindrops as they split and rolled across the passenger window. Thing was, she did want to tell someone. She was tired of holding everything in, turning the other cheek, looking the other way, and keeping other people's secrets.

She tucked her hair behind her ear and studied Cash's profile. He could have been an actor with that jawline. Girls would have lined up for hours to pose for a selfie with him or get a glimpse at one of his rare smiles. Once upon a time, she might have been one of them. But she'd left giggling and gossiping about boys in the past, back when she had someone to giggle and gossip with.

"I'll take that as a no. Moving on to plan B." The inside of the windshield began to fog. He reached forward to adjust the defrost; she jerked her knee away. "Chill. I'm not going to touch you."

"What's plan B?"

"Head back to my place."

The hair on the back of her neck stood up. "If you think I'm going back to your place with you, you've—"

"What? You're out of options. Storm's not going to let up for a few hours, and I'm not going to worry about you getting washed away by a flash flood overnight. You'll be comfortable on the couch, and we'll find a better place for you to stay in the morning."

"And if I say no?"

He tossed her a smug, tight-lipped grin. "Do you have a better offer?"

"Dixie said I can stay with her for a while." She had another offer; she just hadn't officially taken Dixie up on it yet.

Cash let his head fall back against the headrest. "You want me to run you over there now?"

Jinx checked her watch. Dixie was probably sound asleep by now. "I don't want to wake her up."

"I can always drop you off at the sheriff's office if you don't want to stay at my place tonight, although I guarantee my couch is more comfortable than the cardboard they call a mattress."

Jinx crossed her arms around her stomach. "I'd prefer the couch." Half pissed off at the way he assumed he could boss her around, half looking forward to a night of dry, comfortable sleep, she caught herself before she let the relief she felt inside show on her face.

A few minutes later, he pulled off the main road and onto a long gravel drive. She couldn't see much of anything through the rain-splattered windows. They stopped in front of a two-story ranch house. The outdoor lights cut through the storm, a beacon guaranteeing warmth and a roof over her head, at least for the night.

"We're going to have to make a run for it. You ready?"

"Hey, Cash?" Jinx wrapped her hand around the door handle, ready to spring from the truck toward the house.

"Yeah?" His gaze met hers in the dim light of the truck cab.

Her breath hitched as she reached out to touch his shoulder. "I just wanted to say thanks." There, that wasn't so bad. She'd always had a hard time accepting help, especially from strangers.

He didn't say anything right away, just stared at her

in the semidarkness as the rain pummeled the roof of the truck. Then his shoulder rolled, making his muscle ripple under her touch. Could he tell how hard this was for her?

She let her hand drop. He caught it in his and gave it a squeeze before letting go. "You're welcome. Now, you ready to get out of this storm?"

Jinx nodded.

"Go!" Cash hopped out of the cab and waited for her to round the front bumper before leading her toward the porch.

The rain soaked through to her skin within seconds. She wiped at her eyes, trying to see where she was headed. Cash put an arm around her shoulders and tucked her against his chest, moving toward the door. By the time they reached the porch, her hair hung in wet chunks around her face. He fumbled with the knob before flinging the solid wooden door open and pulling her through.

The door closed behind them, shutting out the light. She stood in the calm, quiet darkness, the storm outside muted by thick wooden walls. The only sound was the *drip, drip, drip* of the rainwater trickling down her body and dropping onto the floor.

"You okay?" His voice came from her left. She turned toward it. He'd let go of her after they made it inside. He had to be close. She couldn't see a thing, but she could sense him. A zipper unzipped, and something hit the floor. His jacket.

"Yeah." The adrenaline surge left her chilled. Her teeth chattered, knocking against each other, the sound amplified, bouncing off the walls in the otherwise silent space.

"Come here." His hand grazed her shoulder. "Can I warm you up a bit?"

She nodded.

He held on, pulled her close.

Goose bumps raced across her skin as he slid her jacket off her shoulders and let it fall to the floor.

"You're freezing." His voice came out in a whisper, and she felt his breath float across her skin.

"Where's Kenzie?" She didn't want to wake her.

"I took her and your dog up to the big house before I came looking for you."

Alone with the deputy. He radiated heat. She gravitated toward him, craving the warmth. The layer of darkness provided a sense of safety and security. He couldn't see her, how vulnerable she felt. Not only had her hiding place been exposed, but she felt like he'd also peeled away a layer of her protective armor.

His hands rubbed up and down her arms. She rested her forehead against his chest. His breath caught, and his muscles tensed underneath her. Eyes closed, she burrowed into him. He relaxed, securing his arms around her, his head bending closer, his nose tickling the shell of her ear.

She wanted to bury herself in his arms. The solid weight of him felt like a shield she could hide behind. Safe and secure, far away from the troubles she'd fled in California.

His hand came up, and his fingers traced the line of her jaw, stopped at her chin, tilted her face up toward his. His mouth stopped half a breath from hers. "Tell me I shouldn't kiss you."

She swallowed the lump lodged in her throat and

rasped out a response. "I really don't think you should kiss me."

He nodded into her hair.

Her pulse revved like her bike just before she shifted into a higher gear. The moment stretched. He began to pull away, taking the heat with him. The contact had sparked something deep inside—a temporary connection. She'd been on her own for so long. It would be nice to give in to the kind of shelter Cash offered. If only for a night.

"But I want you to." Her hands slid under his shirt, fingers dancing across the smooth ridges of his abs.

He inhaled. Sharp.

Her nails raked across his back, not enough to leave a mark but deep enough to let him know she didn't want him to go anywhere.

That was all the encouragement he needed. His palms cupped her face. His nose bumped her cheek. His lips found hers. Sucking. Scorching. Searing.

He was everywhere at once. Need bubbled up inside her. The need to feel the hard planes of his chest. The need to cling to someone, even though it would be temporary. His hands worked under her shirt. It had been a long time since she'd given in to a one-night stand. Her hormones squashed any rational thoughts out of her brain, seeking the one thing her body wanted from Cash—to escape.

He stepped into her, urging her backward until her legs hit the edge of a couch. Then he eased her back, his hand cradling her gently, like something he treasured, lowering her onto a cushion. Her shirt stuck to her skin. She peeled it off, warmer without it, and leaned back. He fell against her. Boots hit the ground—his, then hers. His hands tangled in her hair, skimmed her rib cage. She broke away to steal a few breaths. His lips trailed kisses over her neck, her collarbone. She shifted under him, capturing one of his thighs between her legs. This was insane. But she'd never been known for being levelheaded.

She arched into him, urging him on, focused on riding out the streak of need he'd sparked inside her. The length of his thigh pressed against her, applying pressure exactly where she needed it. A moan rose from the back of her throat. He toyed with her, sliding his leg up and down against her, teasing her to the brink of a cliff she hadn't visited in way too long. As she hung at the edge, ready to catapult herself over, he paused, hovering above her.

She gripped his arms, lifted her hips, searching for the friction she needed.

Denied.

Her eyes adjusted to the dim light filtering in from the front windows. She expected a cocky grin, a smug, self-satisfied smirk. But instead, his eyes filled with heat. Deep, intense heat.

She worked his T-shirt up his abs until he whipped it over his head. This was happening. This horrible, awful, very bad thing was happening between them. And it felt so incredibly good.

⚜

Need took over. Edged out any rational thought from his brain. And thank goodness for that, because rational thought would tell him this was a monumental mistake. Then Jinx moved under him. The ripped-up, black leggings sailed over his shoulder. His hand traveled over soft skin that pebbled under his touch. He lifted his lips from her neck long enough to shed his jeans and boxer briefs. She stretched beneath him, rubbing every exposed inch against him. Skin on skin. Groaning, he felt for his jeans on the floor. Condom in the wallet. The just-in-case protection he'd carried around with him for longer than he cared to remember.

Her hair fanned out behind her onto the arm of the couch. So many reasons why this was a bad idea. As he struggled to remember just one of them, his radio crackled.

"Cash, you there?" Tippy asked over the radio.

Dammit, couldn't the man figure something out on his own for once? Cash tried to ignore him, to refocus his attention on the woman sprawled out naked underneath him.

"If you can hear me, we got a situation over here," Tippy continued, his voice filling the weighted silence.

"You need to go?" Jinx made a move to roll out from under him.

"No. He can handle whatever's going on." He brushed her hair back from her cheek. "I'm otherwise engaged, wouldn't you say?"

She nodded, then pulled his head down to hers, their lips connecting. Her body rubbed against his, urging him on.

The radio crackled again. "Last chance. I've got your brother here. Caused a bit of a fuss out at the Deere dealership. Figured you might want to get your hands on him before I take him in."

Cash scrambled for the radio. "What's he done?"

"Finally. I figured you were asleep, since you hadn't answered yet."

He ran his tongue over his lower lip; the taste of Jinx's lip balm lingered. "Nah, just wrapping something up. Who is it, Presley?"

Tippy chuckled. "Believe it or not, it's Statler."

Cash struggled to his feet, already feeling around on the floor for his underwear. "You sure? What the hell did he do?"

"I'd…uh…rather not say over the air. Can you come and get him?"

"I'll be there in ten." He tossed the radio onto a cushion, then leaned down to where Jinx sat on the edge of the couch. "I'm sorry. You okay?"

"Yeah, I'm fine. Is everything okay?"

"I don't know. It's one of my brothers. I've gotta go see what the hell he's gotten himself into. You sure you're all right?" He caught her hand as she stood from the couch.

"Yeah. Why wouldn't I be?"

"Well, we just—"

"We got caught up." She shrugged. "Can I use your bathroom?"

He pointed across the living room to a hall. "Second door on the left."

"Thanks." She let his hand fall. Her bare ass sashayed across the room.

Cash cradled his head in his hands. What the hell? Yeah, they'd almost defiled his sofa. But he didn't do casual sex. He didn't get "caught up" either. Always the epitome of calm and controlled, he maintained a tight rein on his actions and emotions. Things didn't catch him off guard.

Until now.

He made his way to the bedroom to grab a fresh set of clothes. If she wanted to play this off as a spur of the moment, casual hookup, he'd roll along with that. Seemed the most logical explanation anyway, since he still hadn't figured out how he'd gone from threatening to arrest her to almost burying himself inside her.

Stress.

Lack of sleep.

Worry over Kenzie.

All that must have had something to do with his momentary lapse of control. That and this woman threw him off guard. Something about her rang silent alarms. He hadn't been able to pinpoint it…yet.

The clock over the mantel chimed four o'clock. He straightened the couch cushions, flipped on the table-side lamp, and waited for her to exit the bathroom.

"Hey, Cash?" The door cracked open.

"Yeah?" He was on his feet, headed her way before she stuck her head out the doorway.

"You have a T-shirt or something I can sleep in? All of my things are wet."

He padded into the bedroom and grabbed a shirt from the top of his drawer along with a pair of shorts. "Here you go."

A few minutes later, she emerged from the bathroom. With his shirt hanging down to graze her knees, she looked so young, so vulnerable, so frightened. Where was the badass biker chick who'd been slinging comebacks at him from across the bar?

Jinx held the shorts out to him. "They don't fit. But thanks for trying. I'll just lay my stuff out to dry. They'll be fine by morning." She moved past him to retrieve her shirt and pants from the hardwood floor. Seemed to take her much longer than necessary to drape them over his kitchen chairs before she turned back toward him.

"Is the offer for the couch still good?" She'd scrubbed her face free of makeup and twisted her hair up on top of her head, making her look even younger than he'd originally suspected.

"Um, yeah. Or if you want, you can go ahead and take the bed. I don't know how long I'll be but—"

"Couch is good. Maybe just a blanket?"

So they were going to ignore it. Not even acknowledge it. Is that how casual hookups went nowadays? He was way too far out of practice to know for sure, but this was fine by him.

He pulled a fluffy fleece blanket from the linen closet and a pillow to go with it. "Here. You need anything else?"

"Nope. I'm good. Thanks for…um…everything. I'll get out of your way by morning." She glanced around the open-concept first floor. "What time will Kenzie be home?"

"Not until after breakfast. They usually move pretty slow in the mornings."

"That's good. I wouldn't want her to be confused if she found me here."

"Yeah." He hadn't been thinking with his head. His daughter didn't need to get caught up wishing and hoping that Jinx would stick around.

"So…um…good night?" She held the blanket against her chest, essentially giving him a major brush-off.

"Good night. You need anything before I get back, give me a call."

"I won't."

He nodded, sure she wouldn't. He edged toward the front door, wondering what the hell had just happened and what he was supposed to do about it.

Jinx stared at the ceiling for hours. When Cash returned just after six, she pretended to already be asleep. He must have left his bedroom door cracked. Probably wanted to make sure she didn't steal anything. Even so, his steady breathing soothed her numb nerves. Listening to him breathe in and out, a reminder she was in *his* house, on *his* couch, at *his* mercy, gave her a sense of security but also set her on the edge of a panic attack. She vacillated until the sun began to spread a pinkish, reddish glow through the early morning sky, and she finally closed her eyes.

Clanging pots and the smell of fresh-brewed coffee woke her. Paradise. Wade hated the smell of coffee, so it had been months since she'd treated herself to a hot cup of homemade brew. She cracked an eyelid to find herself nose to nose with Kenzie's freckled face.

"She's awake, Daddy!"

"Kenzie, I told you to let Jinx sleep. She was up late last night." Cash's bare feet slapped the floor as he crept close to Kenzie, slung an arm around her waist, and pulled her away from the couch.

"But her eyes are open, see?" Kenzie twisted in his arms, pointing a finger her direction.

"So they are." The two of them towered over her. The smell of bodywash drifted off Cash. That and the damp hair meant he'd probably just showered. That would be a luxury. Maybe she could beg a quick shower before she hoofed it into town to see if Dixie's offer was still good.

"Morning." She squinted up at them. Father and daughter. Fragments of the night before flitted through her head. She'd almost done a dad. And a freaking cop at that. So much for making better choices.

"It's not morning anymore." Kenzie beamed. "Daddy said you slept like you were dead."

"What time is it?"

Cash glanced to the clock. "Almost one."

"Oh my gosh." She threw the blanket aside. The cooler air hit her bare legs. No pants. That's right. Her leggings and her panties were still draped over one of his kitchen chairs. Kenzie had turned toward the kitchen. At least she hadn't just flashed Cash's daughter from the waist down.

The look on Cash's face showed he'd caught a glimpse though. Otherwise, why had the smile morphed into the same kind of dark intensity she'd seen last night?

"Kenzie, why don't you go get Hendrix? Jinx probably wants to say hi."

"Okay." She skipped to the hall, calling out behind her. "He spent the night at Nana and Papa's last night."

As soon as she disappeared around the corner, Cash gathered Jinx's clothes and tossed them to her. "Sorry about that. I forgot you didn't have pants on."

"Thanks. Everything turn out okay with your brother last night?"

"Yeah. Statler somehow got locked into the cab of a combine over at the Deere dealership."

"A combine?"

"A big tractor kind of thing. Presley had a hand in it. My brothers need to grow up and stop trying to outprank each other."

"Mmm." Jinx nodded, making the walk of shame from the couch toward the bathroom, the fuzzy blanket wrapped around her hips. Before she reached the sanctity of the bathroom, Cash cleared his throat, drawing her attention.

Her lacy, black boy shorts dangled from his finger. "Forgot something."

She snagged them from his outstretched hand. Could things get much worse?

The front door opened. Ann and Tom bustled in, arms full of bags. Jinx froze, her foot in midair. No way. Hello, much worse.

"There she is." Ann set her bags on the foyer floor and moved toward Jinx. "How are you feeling this morning? When Cash told us what happened, well, we brought you some necessities."

What could Cash have told them? Surely not that they'd almost had hot, wild, primal sex on the cowhide sectional? She felt like she was standing in the middle of a stage, spotlights trained on her, buck naked, so uncomfortable to be the center of their attention. Her gaze traveled across the room to meet his.

"Sorry." Cash stepped between his mom and Jinx. "Mom, she just woke up. I think she's feeling better but is still a little out of it. Maybe you could come back later?"

Ann reached around him and placed her palm on Jinx's

forehead. "You do feel a little warm. It's probably one of those twenty-four-hour bugs that's been going around. Let's move you into Cash's room. I'll just throw some clean sheets on the bed, and we'll get you settled, okay?" Without waiting for a response, she moved down the hall, toward Cash's room. "Kenzie, be a doll and come help Nana."

Kenzie held Hendrix out to Jinx. "Be right back."

Jinx scooped him up with one hand, the other still holding the blanket tight around her middle. Hendrix wiggled in her grip, trying to smother her face in kisses. Jinx glared at Cash, willing him to provide some sort of explanation. Before he could speak, Tom crossed to the kitchen table and set down his bags.

"Good thing Cash found you when he did. The creek rose last night. Flooded several acres. It's gonna be a mess out there for a while."

"I'm just going to go freshen up." Jinx focused on the open bathroom door. If she could reach the room, she could close the door and pinch herself out of this whacked dream she must have been having.

"Ann brought you something dry to wear." Tom rummaged through a bag, pulled out a silky nightgown, and held it out toward Jinx.

She just stared.

Cash took it from his dad's hands and shuffled toward her. "I'll explain later, okay?" he muttered.

Speechless, she took the nightie and continued to the bathroom. Finally, she clicked the door closed behind her and flipped the lock. How long could she hide? Long enough for her hookup's parents to leave the building? Maybe they'd take his daughter with them. She'd picked the wrong guy to engage in a night of bumping uglies.

She held the nightgown out in front of her. Tiny purple and pink flowers on a light blue background. Not nearly as sexy as what it looked like in Cash's huge paw. But still. There was no way she was going to slip into lingerie picked out by her...her...her what? Her boss's mom? She'd found herself in the middle of some crazy situations over the years. But never, ever had she woken up the morning after to find herself face-to-face with a guy's kid or parents. A knife-wielding ex? Hell yeah. She'd even been chased out of bed by a jealous Rottweiler once. But Mom and Dad and the rest of the family? This was a first.

And a last.

Engine be damned. She could catch a bus to New Orleans and come back after the holidays to get her bike. If she called Jamie and told her she'd changed her mind about waiting for her bike to get fixed, she could be on her way later this afternoon. As soon as she ditched Cash and the rest of the Walkers.

She cracked open the door and peeked out. Cash and his parents sat at the oversize wooden kitchen table. Her gaze darted around the room, at least as much as she could see from the skinny crack in the doorway. The house was a blend of rustic and modern. Exposed stone walls met with log-cabin siding. The couch she'd spent the night on took up half of the living room. A cowhide print, splotches of brown and white, the couch faced a floor-to-ceiling stone fireplace. The kitchen sparkled. Stainless-steel appliances, everything in its place.

Except her. She was definitely out of place.

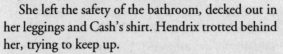

Cash lifted a mug to his mouth and glanced her way. His eyebrows rose. He'd seen her.

She left the safety of the bathroom, decked out in her leggings and Cash's shirt. Hendrix trotted behind her, trying to keep up.

"Did the nightgown not fit?" Ann pushed back from the table and stood. "We can get a different size if you want."

"No, it's not that." Jinx's stomach sank, thudding like a heavy rock into her boots. "I need to get going. Thanks for letting me crash here last night. I—"

"But Daddy made pancakes. He made me wait until you got up to have some. You can't leave before pancakes." Kenzie tugged on her hand, pulling her toward the table.

Cash stood and held out a chair. "No, you can't leave before pancakes."

"Nana and I made Hendrix a poncho last night." Kenzie let go of her hand and ran to the other room, returning with a red-and-green fleecy square of fabric. "Nana had it left over from when she made last year's pajamas."

"Wow, I'm sure he'll appreciate that. Thanks." Jinx smiled as Kenzie slipped the poncho over the dog's head. He held perfectly still while she secured it under his belly, then pranced around her in a circle. Traitor.

"Nana makes jammies for all of us every year. She said I'm big enough to help this time." Kenzie rocked back on her heels, a giant, proud smile plastered across her face.

"Do you want syrup?" Cash asked, dangling the bottle of syrup from his fingers.

"Syrup," Jinx mumbled.

"It's just syrup," Cash added.

Jinx buried her face in her hands. He didn't understand. She didn't do syrup. She didn't do dads. She didn't do breakfasts the morning after. She didn't do any of this.

"You know what? I'm not very hungry. I'll just grab my stuff and head out."

"Where are you going to go?" Cash cocked a hip.

"Mr. and Mrs. Walker, it's been nice…uh…seeing you again. Kenzie, thanks for taking care of Hendrix. I'm going to head into town and check on my bike."

"I can run you over to Dwight's later."

"That's okay. I can walk."

Cash's gaze drilled into her. "Why are you so damn stubborn?"

"You owe the curse jar!" Kenzie piped up, her mouth stuffed full of pancakes.

"Why are you such a bully?" Jinx demanded.

"I'm just offering you breakfast. Have a pancake, Jinx. Would it kill you to sit down and eat a fucking pancake?"

Kenzie's eyes widened at the f-bomb.

Ann pushed back from the table. "I think we'll head out. Cash, Jinx, Kenzie, you're all invited for dinner at the house tonight." She pressed a kiss to Kenzie's temple and scooted toward the front door. Tom followed.

Cash set the bottle of syrup on the table and held up a finger. "Can you wait here, please? I'll be back in just a minute."

He trailed his parents to the front door.

"Daddy owes the curse jar a whole bunch now." Kenzie struggled to separate a bite of pancake from the stack.

"Want some help with that?"

The little girl nodded. Jinx sat down next to her and picked up a knife and fork. She cut the stack of hotcakes into bite-size pieces, then popped one into her mouth.

Kenzie grinned up at her. "Daddy makes good pancakes, doesn't he?"

Jinx nodded. No denying the man had skills. She lifted a pancake off the platter in the center of the table and plopped it on the plate in front of her. Looked like he'd made enough to feed the whole county. May as well walk to town on a full stomach.

Cash returned to the table, a bashful grin pasted on his scruffy face. "I'm sorry. Sorry for being a bully and sorry about the intrusion with my folks. I told them you got caught out in the rain last night and all your stuff got soaked through. Mom wanted to fix up a batch of chicken soup and go shopping for a dry wardrobe for you. Nice to see she settled for a nightgown."

"Why?" Jinx asked, already stabbing another bite of pancake.

"Why what?"

"Your parents don't know me at all. Why would they care?"

Cash shook his head. "Mom's never met a stranger. Careful or she'll suck you right into the fold along with everyone else. It's what she does. Now, if you want to finish your pancakes, I can give you a ride over to Dwight's."

"Oh, I don't want to put you out, not after you've done so much already."

Cash chuckled. "I let you sleep on my couch. As

far as I'm concerned, that rates right up there with handing you a tissue or loaning you a cup of sugar on the *putting me out* scale."

"Still"—Jinx made a point to meet his gaze—"I do appreciate it."

The smile he gave her sent a wave of warmth crashing through her. "Don't mention it. Kenzie and I have to head into town this afternoon anyway. You're not putting us out at all."

"Okay then, I'd love a ride." The urge to buy that bus ticket to New Orleans subsided. "Can you take me to Dixie's instead?" Jinx speared the last bite of pancake. She could do this. She'd survived worse. Moving in with Dixie was the right thing to do. Putting some distance between herself and Cash and Kenzie would be good for her. She couldn't afford to make connections, not even with the darling little girl—and especially not with her disarming dad.

⟶

"Here we are." Cash eased the truck to a stop in front of Armadillo Antiques. He hadn't been inside in years. "I think you get to the apartment above by those steps over there."

Jinx looked out the window.

"You want us to help you get your stuff upstairs?"

"I want to see Jinx's new apartment." Kenzie unbuckled and leaned over the back of the seat.

Cash shrugged. "It's up to Jinx."

"Can we?" Kenzie bounced up and down, making the seat back shake.

"Um, sure. I bet Dixie won't mind." Jinx grabbed

her backpack and climbed out of the truck. Kenzie catapulted over the seat, then raced up the stairs ahead of them.

"Hold up a sec, Kenz." Cash snagged the rest of Jinx's things from the bed of the truck.

Jinx's hand closed over his. "I can get that."

Warmth traveled from where their hands touched, filtering through his limbs. For a split second, he was sorry Jinx would be staying at Dixie's. He banished the thought before he had time to mull it over. What had happened between them last night was a temporary lapse in judgment. He'd make sure he didn't let himself lapse again.

"Well, hi, y'all." Dixie swung the door wide open and stood at the top of the steps. "Come on in."

Kenzie raced past her. It wasn't worth his breath to try to reissue his warning to slow down.

Dixie gave Jinx a hug as she reached the landing. "I'm so excited you decided to take me up on my offer. It's not much, but consider half of it yours."

With her hands full, Jinx didn't return the embrace. Cash stood two steps lower and waited for Dixie to release her grip.

"Thanks, Dixie. I really appreciate you letting me stay here." Jinx passed into the apartment, and Dixie followed.

"It's you who's doing me a favor. It'll be nice to split the rent."

"You know it's only for a month—maybe six weeks tops." Jinx set her bag down on the edge of the couch.

Cash's gaze bounced from the frilly, pink-and-white

curtains to the lacy tablecloth. In her heavy black boots and motorcycle jacket, Jinx couldn't have looked more out of place if she'd tried. Everything in Dixie's apartment was pink, white, or pink-and-white checkered.

"I love it here." Kenzie spread her arms wide and turned in a circle. "Can we make my room look like this, Daddy?"

Jinx shot him a smile. His face heated a few degrees, and he wondered if she'd read his mind. "We'll see, Tadpole. I promised you we'd paint it this year."

"My room is too babyish." She turned to Jinx with a furry pink pillow in her arms. "Daddy says I can paint it whatever color I want, and I want pink."

"All right, pink it is." Cash set Jinx's stuff down on the floor.

"When can we paint it, Daddy? Today?"

"Not today, Kenz. We'll get it done though. Maybe over your Christmas break." He shook his head. "Always something to do with you around, kiddo."

"Where's Jinx's room?" Kenzie peeked through an open doorway into one of the bedrooms. "Is it this one?"

"No, that's mine." Dixie walked to the second doorway. "It's in here."

Kenzie entered the room first. "Oh my gosh, it's beautiful."

Cash let Dixie and Jinx go ahead of him and didn't follow the women in. He stopped in the doorway, trying to find something to focus on that wasn't pink. A white dresser stood against the back wall. Ah, relief. If Kenzie wanted this kind of a setup for her room makeover, he'd be screwed.

"I may have gone a little overboard on the monochromatic color scheme." Dixie smoothed down the pink paisley comforter. "You're welcome to change it."

"It's fine." Jinx took in a breath. "I won't be here long enough for it to matter."

"What do you think, Daddy? Do you love it? Can I have my room just like this?" Kenzie wrapped her arms around his legs.

Dixie and Jinx gave him their full attention, probably waiting for him to make some snide comment about the overabundance of feminine frill. "It's... um...definitely cheery in here."

The corners of Jinx's mouth tugged upward. Could they possibly be in agreement on something? That Dixie's place was complete overkill?

"We ought to let Jinx get settled. Let's hit the grocery store while we're in town. Nana wants us to pick up a few things for her for dinner. What do you say, Kenzie?"

"Do I have to say goodbye to Hendrix?" She turned the puppy dog eyes on him.

"He's got to stay with Jinx, hon. But maybe you can watch him if she has to work a double shift sometime." He looked to Jinx to gauge her reaction.

"That would be great." Jinx knelt down in front of Kenzie to give her a hug. "You can come say hi to him whenever you want, okay?"

Kenzie nodded. He recognized the brave face she tried to put on every once in a while. But her lower lip trembled as she handed Hendrix over to Jinx. Damn, he'd better start putting the word out that Santa might need to bring a puppy for Christmas.

Hendrix licked her across the face a few times, turning her pouty lip into a smile. "I love you, Hendrix." She kissed him on top of the head. Before she even stood up, she had already moved on to her next big request. "Can I pick out some ice cream at the store?"

"We'll see." Cash took his daughter's hand and turned to face Jinx. "So, I guess I'll see you around."

"Probably." She cocked a hip.

He looked to Dixie, who glanced at Jinx, who gazed at a spot on the floor. An awkward silence bounced between the three of them.

"Isn't Jinx coming to dinner at Nana's tonight?" Kenzie twisted her hand out of his grip. "Nana said she was invited."

"Oh, um…I'd probably better stay here and get settled. Next time, okay?"

Kenzie let out a dramatic sigh. "You promise?"

A crease appeared between Jinx's eyebrows. "Sure. If your Nana invites me again and I don't have to work."

Kenzie thrust her hand out. "Pinky promise."

"You drive a hard bargain, Kenzie Walker." Jinx curled her pinky finger around Kenzie's. "Okay, I promise."

"Let's go, Kenz. I'm sure Jinx wants to settle in. Take care. You too, Dixie." For half a heartbeat, he thought maybe he should ask for a private word with Jinx. But hell, no sense in making a mountain out of the molehill they'd gotten themselves into last night. Move on, that's what he'd do. He led Kenzie down the steps and out to the curb.

"What are you smiling so much about, Tadpole?"

"Jinx promised she'd come for dinner next time. I'm gonna ask Nana to invite her over for tomorrow night."

His heart sank. So much for getting Jinx out of his life. Looked like his daughter had already attached herself to the hardheaded bartender. Like a leech. Like a barnacle. Like a little girl who needed a friend.

He vowed to seriously consider his mom's suggestion from the other day. Maybe it was time to open
his mind and his heart to finding him and Kenzie
someone to take Lori Lynne's place. Not that she'd
given him any encouragement, but over his dead
body would it be the inked bartender who'd already
gotten under his skin.

JINX WOKE TO THE SOUND OF SOMEONE BANGING ON THE front door. She startled, trying to remember where she was for a moment. Right. Dixie's. She'd worked a double shift the night before and didn't get to bed until after three a.m.

Bang-bang-bang. It sounded like someone was hitting the front door with a hammer.

"Coming!" She tossed a Mariners sweatshirt on over her pajamas and made her way toward the door. Dixie was spending the day with her grandma, so Jinx had the apartment to herself. She'd planned on catching up on her sleep until whoever stood on the other side of the door decided to kill that idea.

Before she opened the door, she peered through the peephole. Their landlord, Mrs. Boswell, stood on the stoop. Shoot. Was Dixie late on the rent? Why else would the eccentric antique store owner be knocking on the door during business hours? She should be downstairs.

Jinx cracked the door open. She'd only met the woman once, the day after she'd moved in. Mrs. Boswell had gripped her hand, then flipped it over to trace some lines along her palm. She must have liked what she saw, because she told Dixie that Jinx was okay to move in.

"Good morning, Mrs. Boswell. Can I help you with something?" Jinx asked.

"Something is not right. My Armando is not happy." The older woman pushed her way into the apartment. "I need to see your palm again."

"I don't understand. Who's not happy?" Jinx shut the door and turned to see Mrs. Boswell wringing her hands together.

"Armando. My husband."

"Oh." Jinx could have sworn Dixie had told her Mrs. Boswell was a widow. Maybe Armando was her second husband. "Where is Armando? Did he say why he isn't happy?"

"No. Armando, God rest his soul"—she made the sign of the cross—"is dead."

Taken aback at that revelation, Jinx didn't know how to respond. "Um, okay. Then why don't you think he's happy?"

Mrs. Boswell flung her right arm out wide. "All day and all night, he bangs the armoire door. Something has upset him. That something must be you. Give me your palm."

Jinx squinted at the landlord, wondering if she'd lost her marbles. Dixie had said she was a little eccentric but harmless. Not wanting to rock the boat, she held her hand out to the woman.

Her forehead creased in concentration, Mrs. Boswell traced the lines of Jinx's palm. "Ah, hard times behind you. Good times ahead. A strong love line—you are a good girl. I do not see the problem for my Armando."

"I don't understand. How does your Armando know there's a problem?" She'd met some interesting people in her various stints behind the bar. But Mrs. Boswell seemed to be in a league of her own.

Mrs. Boswell slumped into a pink floral upholstered chair, mumbling to herself in some language Jinx couldn't comprehend. Jinx sat on the couch and rubbed her palms over her thighs, wondering how she could get rid of the loopy landlord so she could go back to bed.

Hendrix trotted out of the bedroom and sat in front of Jinx. At the sight of the dog, Mrs. Boswell leapt to her feet and jumped onto the chair. "Get it away!"

"The dog?" Jinx scooped Hendrix up in her arms. "This is Hendrix. He won't hurt you."

"Get it away!" Mrs. Boswell repeated. She waved her arms out in front of her.

Jinx took Hendrix to the bedroom and shut him inside, hoping that would calm the woman down. "It's okay. I put him in the bedroom."

In a move Jinx didn't think possible, Mrs. Boswell hopped from the chair and scurried to the door. "It's that creature. That is why my Armando cannot rest. He must go."

Jinx shook her head. "I don't understand. He's just a dog."

"No, no, no." Mrs. Boswell pointed a finger at Jinx's nose. "My room, my rules. No demons allowed."

"Are you saying I can't live here?" She crossed her arms. This was ridiculous. Dixie had said she'd cleared it with the landlord and it was fine for Jinx to move in, Hendrix too. What was the problem?

"No. You are okay. But the demon no." Mrs. Boswell peered past her toward the closed bedroom door. Jinx's gaze followed. "One more night. Then go."

"You've got to be kidding." She turned around to see Mrs. Boswell retreating down the steps. "Unbelievable." Just when she thought she could finally let down her guard and relax a little… She should have known better. Hadn't life taught her that as soon as things started to look up, they usually dropped into a downward spiral?

—Htt—

Cash entered the Rose, both eager and apprehensive to set sights on Jinx again. It had been almost a week since they'd had their botched hookup. He'd thought about her all week long, like how was she settling in at Dixie's? Had she been having a hard time getting him out of her head too?

He was early for the Saturday night crowd, but she was already there. Seeing her talking to Dixie behind the bar from across the room, his chest expanded. Something weird and bubbly percolated up inside. What the hell? He took in a deep breath and closed the distance between them. The least he could do was say hi. As he approached the bar, he couldn't help but overhear their conversation.

"I'm so sorry. I had no idea she'd bring up Armando." Dixie leaned on the bar, a deep line creasing her brow.

"It's okay, really. I'll just find somewhere to pitch my tent." Jinx unloaded glass after glass from the dish rack and slid them into the grooves over her head.

"Good evening, ladies." Cash tipped his hat their way.

Dixie wheeled to face him. "Cash, is it illegal for Mrs. Boswell to kick Jinx out?"

He looked from Dixie to Jinx and back again. "I can't say without knowing the situation. What happened?"

"It's not a big deal." Jinx put the empty rack on the bar next to her. "What are you doing working on Saturday? I thought you only worked Friday nights?"

"Did you miss me last night?" Cash winked at Jinx. A blush crept over her chest and up her neck.

"No. Just asking, that's all."

Dixie brought a fist down on the bar. "It *is* a big deal. Mrs. Boswell said Hendrix is a demon, and her dead husband who lives in the armoire said he can't live there anymore. It's not fair."

"Doesn't matter." Jinx covered Dixie's fist with her hand. "She's the boss. Life isn't always fair. In fact, I'd say life is never fair."

"Well, if you have to go, I'll go too." Dixie nodded to herself.

"Don't be silly. Like I said, I'll figure something out." Jinx grabbed the dish rack and headed toward the kitchen.

Dixie turned to Cash. "What are we going to do? She can't sleep out in that tent again. It's getting too cold outside."

"You're right." Cash bit his bottom lip. "Let me think something through. I may have an idea."

"Well, good." Dixie tucked her order pad into her apron. "That woman deserves a break." She whirled away from the bar, heading toward some newcomers who'd just sat down at a table.

Cash leaned on his elbows, waiting for Jinx to return. He did have an idea, but would Jinx go for it? He wouldn't know unless he tried.

She stalked from the kitchen to back behind the bar. "What's up, cowboy? Lose your way? I believe you work the door." Chin raised, she shot a glance at the front door. "Or did someone hire you to harass me tonight?"

"Sounds like you need a place to live." He'd ease into the conversation, feel her out, and then propose his plan.

"Yeah, thanks to an armoire-dwelling ghost."

His mouth quirked into a grin. "I've been thinking—"

"Don't hurt yourself." She shook her head.

"Come on now. I've been thinking what with you needing a place to live and me needing someone to help Kenzie with her reading, maybe we can work something out."

She looked up at him, surprise evident in the way her eyes rounded. "What? You want me to move in with *you*?"

He laughed. "Not exactly what I had in mind. I figure if you can help Kenzie with her reading, I'll let you stay in the bunkhouse until your bike's ready. Sound good?"

Her eyes narrowed. "That's it?"

"Yeah. What did you think I was going to propose?" Based on last Friday night, Cash could think of a few more bullet points to add to the list. But she clearly wasn't looking for a long-term solution, and he needed to find some stability for his daughter. For the umpteenth time, he reminded himself the inked-up bartender wasn't his type.

The short conversation with his mom the other day had gotten him thinking. Even when he thought he'd been putting Kenzie first, he hadn't. He'd done the best he could without Lori Lynne. But now his little girl was growing up. She needed more female influences in her life. With his mom and dad making plans to travel more and Charlie and Beck about to have a baby of their own, it was time he stopped relying on his family for everything.

Kenzie needed help with her reading, and there was no telling how long it would take for her to get a tutor through school. She and Jinx had obviously formed some sort of bond. If Kenzie was willing to work with Jinx, he wouldn't have to be the bad guy anymore. They could spend their free time doing the things they loved together, instead of him forcing her to work on flash cards and being held accountable to the damn reading timer so much.

Jinx fiddled with a coaster. "All I have to do is help Kenzie with her reading?"

So suspicious. For a split second, his ice-cold heart thawed toward Jinx. Who had hurt her so much that she couldn't take his words at face value?

"Yep. Don't get too excited. The bunkhouse is a mess. No one's stayed there for years. It's probably full of snakes and spiders. And helping Kenzie won't be much of a picnic either. She's stubborn as a mule and has the attention span of a gnat."

A soft laugh escaped her lips. "Sounds good to me. When do I start?" She tilted her chin up and met his gaze. He could see the doubt in her clear gray eyes.

"You have plans tomorrow morning?"

"Nothing except for getting kicked out of my apartment."

"Okay then." He slapped a palm against the bar. "Kenzie and I will pick you up at Dixie's at, say, ten?"

She nodded.

"Good. Then we can go check it out."

The truck bounced over the washed-out dirt road leading to the abandoned bunkhouse. It sat in a clearing about half a mile from Cash's place, but he hadn't been inside for a couple of years.

The screen on the long front porch had a few holes, possibly places where something had chewed through to get inside. Nothing that couldn't be fixed up quick. He held the door open for Jinx and Kenzie as they stomped up the steps and stood on the porch.

"What's that smell, Daddy?" Kenzie pinched her nose.

"We'll see." He held his breath as the old wooden door swung inward. The building was fairly basic. A room full of bunk beds sat to the left, a small kitchen area and living room to the right. They'd added running water and a bathroom to an addition off the back a few decades ago. It wasn't anything special and not somewhere he'd want to spend a lot of time, but it sure as hell had to be better than a tent, especially at this time of year.

Jinx didn't say a word, just took it all in, slowly spinning in a circle in the middle of the space.

"Think this will work?" he asked, searching for the source of the foul smell. It was like something died a while ago and had been decaying ever since.

She smiled, a genuine, no-holds-barred kind of smile. "This is great, but I can't accept it."

"What do you mean you can't accept it? I'm not giving it to you, just offering you a place to stay until your bike gets fixed."

The smile on her face contradicted her refusal. "It's too much. Maybe we could work something out where I pay you a little rent and you let me keep my tent set up—"

"The spot where you had your tent is under eighteen inches of water right now." He clenched a fist, then released it. Why was she so reluctant to take any help? "Besides, it's November. Your sleeping bag looks like it's only rated to about forty degrees. Give it another week or two, and you'll be freezing your ass off out there."

"Curse jar, Daddy!" Kenzie skipped around them in a circle.

"Kenzie, honey, can you stop running around?"

Her boots stopped clomping over the wooden floor. "Can I go play outside?" Her fingers still pinched her nose shut, so the nasal tone of her voice made him smile.

Jinx let out a chuckle and shuffled her feet while she appeared to mull over his valid argument.

Cash ruffled his daughter's hair. "Yeah. Just stay close, okay?"

Kenzie scampered off, Hendrix at her heels, leaving him and Jinx alone.

"All I need to do is help Kenzie with her reading?" Jinx glanced up at him, her eyes reflecting a mixture of wariness and hope.

Who was this woman, and what had happened to her to make her so skittish? "Yeah. That's what I said. What, did you think a repeat of last week would be part of the deal too?"

She looked away.

"Hey." Cash lowered his voice. "Sorry. I didn't mean to make you uncomfortable. What happened before… I'm sorry. It won't happen again."

"Good." She moved to the dustcover draped over the

long, wooden kitchen table. "I'll help Kenzie with her reading, but I still want to pay you rent. Otherwise, the deal's off."

"Fine." He held out a hand. "Should we shake on it?"

Her bracelets jangled together as she slid her hand in his. "Thanks for this." Her gaze met his, her eyes shiny like they were holding back tears.

The momentary glimpse behind her walls lasted only a second, maybe even less, before she pulled her hand away. But he'd seen it. There was something underneath her armor. Something soft behind the ink, the metal, the attitude.

"Yeah. You're welcome. I've got some stuff up at the house we can use to start cleaning this place up. Why don't Kenzie and I run back and get it?"

"That would be great." She shook her head, like she wanted to shake any kind of emotion away.

"Back in a bit." Before he said something stupid and scared her off, he called for Kenzie and made for the truck.

~HH~

Half an hour later, he pulled up in front of the bunkhouse again. Jinx had opened all the windows to air the place out. Music drifted out the open front door. He stood on the porch for a moment, enjoying the sound of a strumming guitar. But where in the hell had she found that? As he entered the front room, the music stopped. Jinx sat on the edge of the couch, holding a crappy old guitar in her lap.

Kenzie spun into the room behind him, clapping her hands together in time to the beat.

"Don't stop on account of me." Cash gestured to the guitar. "You know how to play?"

Jinx stood and set the guitar on the couch. "Just a little. My dad taught me when I was a kid. But I haven't played in years. I found this in the bunk room. Do you mind if I mess around on it?"

Cash moved closer to get a better look. The guitar must have been left by one of the ranch hands. The last time anyone stayed in the bunkhouse had been over a decade ago. "Have at it."

"Thanks." The smile she gave him was worth at least twenty old guitars. Finally, something breached that wall of bitter sarcasm she'd built. She should smile more often. It softened her hard edges, put a shine in her eyes. He thought about telling her that, but figured if he did, she'd make sure she never gave him another genuine smile as long as he lived.

So instead, he took a look around the bunkhouse. In the short time he'd been gone, it already looked better. The dustcovers had been removed from all the furniture and sat folded in a pile by the door. She'd found some cleaning supplies somewhere and had already wiped down the counters and table. The smell of lemon and thick dust hung in the air. A little elbow grease and effort were all it would take.

"Here's the stuff I picked up when I packed your tent." Cash set her small bundle of belongings on the table.

"Thanks."

"You sure travel light." He wasn't big on material things, but even he'd have to have more than a few days' worth of clothes to make the kind of trip Jinx had undertaken.

"I shipped the rest of my stuff to my girlfriend's place.

Thought I wouldn't need much just to make the drive."
She shrugged. "I don't suppose there's a washing
machine or dryer hiding in one of these closets?"

"You can use the laundry room at my place if you
have anything to wash."

"Thanks. By the way, I found the source of the
smell. Might have been a possum at one point. It's in
a bag out front."

"It does smell much better in here, doesn't it,
Kenz?"

"Much." Kenzie nodded her head. "Show her
what you got her, Daddy."

He set a laundry basket down on the table. "So I
brought you some stuff. A set of sheets, some towels.
Even found a couple of things in the back of the
closet that might fit until you have a chance to do
laundry or pick up some clothes."

"Oh, you don't have to do that. I'll be fine with
my sleeping bag and planned on going into town later
today to get some clothes."

"Just take it, okay? I don't need any of it and was
planning on getting rid of it anyway." Why couldn't
the woman just say thanks and accept a little help?

"I don't need your charity, you know."

"It's not charity. You're saving me a trip into town
to drop off the donation, all right?"

She rolled her eyes but wandered over to pick
through the basket. "Fine."

Good. At least that was settled. He'd feel better
knowing she at least had a set of sheets out here. "I've
got to fill out some paperwork. How about I pick you
up about five thirty?"

Her brow furrowed. "For what?"

"Dinner at the big house. Mom called and invited you. Kenzie will go nuts if you tell her you're not coming."

Kenzie tugged at his leg. "Daddy, can I stay with Jinx?"

Cash glanced toward Jinx, gauging her response.

Jinx shrugged. "She can keep an eye on Hendrix while I sweep the place out. If that's okay with you?"

He bit back the instinctive no on the tip of his tongue. If Jinx was going to be spending a lot of time with his daughter, he'd have to extend some degree of trust. He'd be home, just a few hundred yards away. And Jinx didn't have a vehicle, so it wasn't like she could take off with her or anything. "Sure. Kenzie, you be a good listener, okay?"

She nodded.

With a weird feeling settling in his chest, he turned toward the door. Right before he walked through to the porch, he spun around. Kenzie held both of Jinx's hands in hers, swinging them back and forth, beaming up at her. Kenzie deserved a friend, but hopefully she wouldn't get too attached.

She was only two when her mother had taken off. She didn't remember what it felt like to be left behind. But he did. Since then, he'd sworn not to be stupid enough to let himself be dragged through that kind of emotional hell again. He could protect himself, knew how to stifle any threat of feelings or attachment. But he feared for his daughter. Feared that if she got too close to Jinx, her little heart might shatter when the time came for Jinx to move on. Jinx wouldn't be around long enough for Kenzie to get too close. And if all she was doing was helping her with her reading, he'd have to make sure that didn't happen. For Kenzie's sake...and his.

chapter
TEN

By the time Cash was due to return, Jinx had scrubbed the top layer of dust off every surface inside the rustic log building, including the walls. She'd made up the lower bunk closest to the window so she could wake up every morning and look out on the woods. The creek she'd camped by ran close to the back of the bunkhouse, and the sound of gurgling water played as background music. The accommodations might have been sparse, but she'd be more than comfortable here—more comfortable than she could remember being anywhere else over the past several years.

"What do you think?" She turned to Kenzie, who had done a fine job of smearing window cleaner all over the lower panes of glass.

"I think it's better." The little girl's face conveyed the doubt she must have felt inside.

Jinx smiled. "Yep, much better than it was. We'd better get cleaned up. Your dad's going to be here soon."

Kenzie picked through the basket Cash had brought over. "Are you gonna wear one of these?"

"Oh. I'm not usually a big fan of dresses. How about you?"

"Sometimes. Aunt Charlie wears dresses now. So she has room for the baby."

"Yeah, well, I don't need room for a baby, so maybe I'll stick to my leggings."

Kenzie made a sour face like she'd sucked on a pickle. "You're all dirty."

Jinx evaluated the once-black leggings that had turned gray from cleaning. "Yeah, you're right. Okay, let's see how bad these dresses are."

Fifteen minutes later, she'd taken a quick, ice-cold shower in the unheated bathroom and towel-dried her hair. Standing over the two least offensive options, she asked Kenzie, "What do you think?"

"I like the pink one." Kenzie fingered the flowy, pink skirt of the dress on the left.

"Of course you do." Jinx remembered how enamored Kenzie had been with Dixie's apartment. "I think the blue one suits me better." Jinx held the hanger up in front of her. With a belt and a long-sleeve T-shirt underneath, it might be doable.

Heavy footsteps sounded on the porch, followed by a knock on the front door. "Kenzie? Jinx? Y'all ready?"

"Daddy's back!" Kenzie hopped off the bunk and ran to the front door, leaving the door to the bedroom open behind her.

Jinx crossed the room and pressed the door shut. "Be out in a sec."

"Take your time. Mom won't mind if we're late. She'll just put us in charge of dishes." Cash's boots clomped around the room, probably checking out the progress she'd made while he was gone.

She slipped the dress over her head and fiddled with it. Too bad she didn't have a full-length mirror. Swiping some lip gloss over her lips, she tried to check out her reflection in her tiny compact. How bad could it be? At least the blue in the dress matched a few shades in her hair.

"Okay, ready." She yanked the door open and stepped into the main room.

Cash turned. His gaze traveled over her, the warmth in his eyes chasing any lingering chill away. He let out a low wolf whistle. "Well, Ms. Jinx, I do say, you clean up real nice."

With an exaggerated eye roll, she slid her feet into her boots and donned her leather jacket. There, that felt better.

He looked pretty good himself. He'd swapped out his sweats for a pair of snug jeans. He had on a collared, long-sleeve shirt that looked like it had even been ironed and a cowboy hat with his untamed hair curling out under the edge.

His hand reached for hers. Her jumpy reflexes instinctively made her want to pull away, but he held fast.

"Your key." He pressed a shiny gold key into her palm and closed her fingers around it.

He was close enough for her to catch a whiff of aftershave or cologne or whatever he'd used in the shower. It made her want to plant her nose in his chest and inhale the fresh scent of strength and security. Why was he being so nice to her? In her experience, people didn't just do things for others out of kindness. They always had an ulterior motive. Helping Kenzie didn't seem big enough. How long would it take for him to reveal what he really wanted?

For now, she needed to let herself enjoy her newfound luck. "Thanks."

He squeezed her hand and gave her a quick wink. "Don't mention it. Now, you ready to meet the family?"

Kenzie clipped Hendrix's leash on, then grabbed Jinx's hand with one of hers and her dad's with the other. "Swing me!"

"Let's get off the porch first." Cash pulled the door closed behind them and waited for Jinx to turn the key in the lock.

They swung Kenzie between them all the way down the steps to the truck.

"Now hop on in, and let's try not to be the last ones to Nana's." Cash held the passenger door open for the two of them.

Kenzie scrambled into the back. Jinx climbed into the front. He waited for her to adjust the skirt around her legs and closed the door.

By the time they arrived at Tom and Ann's, Jinx had worked herself into a jangled bundle of nerves. Why had she agreed to a family dinner? She didn't do well in crowds. Based on what Cash and Kenzie joked about on the drive over, she was in for a hell of a big get-together.

Walking up the flagstone path to the front door, she made a fist and pressed it against her gut, trying to break up the horde of nerves that was misfiring in her stomach. Cash caught up to her and bumped her shoulder with his.

"Relax. They don't bite."

She took a step to the side, separating herself from the rugged deputy. Wouldn't do any good for his family to get the false impression there was something going on between them. Kenzie ran ahead, cradling Hendrix in her arms, and flung open the door.

A mixture of laughter and loud voices surrounded Jinx as she crossed the threshold into the house. The noise came from the left, most likely the direction of the kitchen. She stood in a warm foyer that led into a huge, open living room. The mix of country, comfort, and chic seemed to match Cash's parents. She could easily picture him growing up here, hanging his stocking from the massive mantel and learning how to read next to the floor-to-ceiling fireplace.

"Jinx, you made it." Ann gave her a hug and a quick kiss on the cheek. "It's so good to see you. Can I take your jacket?"

"Hey, Mom." Cash wrapped his mom in a big bear hug. "I'll hang up the coats." He helped Jinx shrug out of her jacket, then draped it over a coatrack that appeared to be made out of cow horns.

"One of Strait's creations. Don't ask." Cash set his hand at the small of her back, propelling her toward the kitchen.

"Is that one of your brothers?" Charlie had mentioned something about having a slew of brothers, although Jinx hadn't paid much attention to their names.

"Yeah. He's the next to youngest. Went off to Nashville to find fame and fortune."

She caught the edge in his voice. Cash struck her as someone who valued control, power, and the ability to make a quick decision. She had a lot more go-with-the-flow in her. Yet another good reason to steer clear.

They entered the kitchen to find a group of Walkers crowded around the large granite island. A variety of appetizers were spread out over the counter. Her stomach grumbled.

Ann clapped her hands together. "Thanks for your attention. This is Jinx. She works with Charlie at the Rose and is going to be staying at the old bunkhouse on Cash's property. Y'all make her feel welcome."

Jinx wanted to curl up inside herself and die as the sea of curious faces turned her way. Charlie smiled from across the island. Jinx tried to grin in return—at least one friendly face. And there was Charlie's husband, Beck. Make that two. The rest of the clan spoke all at once. A hand reached for hers, and a towheaded boy tapped her on the arm.

Cash stepped in. "Hey, one at a time. Let me do the introductions. Jinx, meet Waylon and Darby. They pretty much run the ranch now that Dad is semiretired. They've got four kids running around here. This one here is Ryder, then there's Luke, Allie, and June. Over there's my brother Statler, the nerd. He has his own CPA firm. You met my dad already." Tom smiled and waved from his spot in the doorway leading into another room. "Anyone know if Presley's coming?"

"Wouldn't count on it." Charlie dipped a chip into a bowl of salsa. "He closed down the Rose last night. Saw him leaving with a pair of—"

"Yeah, I figured." Cash leaned against the counter. "You know Angelo and Shep."

Jinx nodded at her coworkers.

"That's pretty much it. I'll point out which kid is which if you can catch 'em. Hell, I can barely keep track of them all."

"Curse jar!" Kenzie's voice floated out of the other room.

"If you'll excuse me for a minute." Cash made for the doorway, disappearing past his dad.

"So, Jinx, is it?" A smiley brunette sidled up next to her. Darby, that's right. Married to one of the Walker brothers, although she couldn't remember which one. "I love your hair."

"Thanks." Jinx fingered a strand of her air-dried hair. She'd run a brush through it, but with no hair dryer, it had probably frizzed out on her. No mirror meant she couldn't feel too bad about how frightful she might look.

"So what's your story? Charlie told me you were driving cross-country on a motorcycle and broke down by Cash's place?"

"That's right."

"And you're working at the Rose now. That's good, hon, real good. With the baby coming soon and Beck getting the brewery up and running, Charlie's going to need an extra set of hands around that place."

"Oh, I'm not staying very long. Just until my bike gets fixed," Jinx insisted.

Darby eyed her over a tortilla chip. "But the baby's due right around New Year's. You'll at least stay through the holidays, won't you? The whole town does the Jingle Bell Jamboree. It's so much fun, and the Rambling Rose is a big part of that."

Christmas was over six weeks away. Surely, she'd be well on her way before that. "Um, we'll see."

Charlie nudged Darby with her elbow. "Don't scare her off, Darbs. I'm working on her to stick around. Hoping maybe she'll find Holiday too irresistible to leave behind."

"I don't know about that." Jinx took a step back and bumped into Ann. "I'm so sorry."

"That's okay, sugar. I'm so glad you could join us tonight." Ann patted her shoulder. "Now, if you girls will stop gabbing and help me set the table, we can get this crowd fed."

Darby and Charlie dismissed Jinx's offer to help, so she wandered into the other room in search of Cash or Kenzie. A huge flat-screen TV had a football game going, the players almost life-size. Kenzie sat at a kid-size table in the corner, coloring, with Hendrix curled into a ball on her lap.

Jinx put her hand on Kenzie's chair and peered over her shoulder. "What are you making?"

"I'm trying to draw a reindeer, but it's not working." She held up her paper.

"Want to let me try?"

Kenzie handed her the pencil and watched while Jinx sketched the outline of a reindeer. "Can you give him sunglasses?"

"Sure." She added a pair of dark glasses.

"And a cowboy hat?" Kenzie pointed to the antlers. "And some candy canes."

"Is this a Texas reindeer?" Jinx laughed as she sketched to the girl's specifications. When she was done, she held it up. "You want to color it in now?"

"You draw real good." Kenzie picked out a brown crayon and began to fill in the face.

"Dinner!" Ann summoned them all to the dining room.

Kenzie grabbed her sheet and took Jinx's hand. "You can sit by me."

"That sounds great. But Hendrix better stay here,

don't you think?" Jinx lifted the chair and looped his leash underneath the leg. "Don't you get into any trouble." Then she followed Kenzie into the dining room and took a seat. Cash sat on her other side.

"How are you doing?" he asked.

"Surviving." She managed a nervous grin, then tucked her napkin into her lap.

Tom motioned for everyone to hold hands while he said the blessing. Sandwiched between Kenzie and Cash, Jinx closed her eyes, letting herself feel their hands in hers. Kenzie's little fingers squeezed hers, like a butterfly beating its wings against her palm. Cash's firm grip left no room for wiggling. Strength flowed through his hand to hers, bolstering her courage, filling her full of unwelcome tingles too.

As soon as they dropped hands, the Walkers started passing around platters full of food. Ann had made a roast with potatoes and homemade gravy. Jinx's mouth watered as Cash held the platter for her to help herself. Conversation flowed around her, and she began to settle in. So this is what a family dinner looked like. She sipped some red wine, took the buttered roll Kenzie offered, and enjoyed being in the presence of a group of people who clearly loved each other.

Maybe it was the wine, the warmth from the fireplace in the other room, or the nearness of so many Walkers, but she let herself imagine what it would be like to be a part of a family like this. Inside jokes flew around the table. The siblings spoke over each other like they were still kids. With no brothers or sisters of her own, she'd never felt so much a part of something and so very alone at the same time.

As they finished their meal, Kenzie held up the reindeer picture. "Look what Jinx made for me."

"That's really good. Did she help you color that?" Beck asked.

"No, she drew it."

"Really?" Darby swirled her wine. "You seem to have a talent for art."

Jinx tried to slide down in her chair. "I just mess around."

"Hey, Darby, weren't you saying you needed some help with the set design for the Christmas play at school?" Charlie asked.

Darby shot her a conspiratorial grin. "Why, yes, yes, I was. Jinx, how would you feel about helping a very untalented room mother make hundreds of elementary kids very, very happy?"

"Oh, I don't know." Jinx dabbed at her mouth with her napkin. "I don't think I'll be around that long."

"So you can help while you're here. It'll still be better than me trying to do it on my own." Darby took a sip of her wine.

"You'd have so much fun. Those kids have been working so hard on the Christmas play. It's a highlight of the Jingle Bell Jamboree." Ann nodded.

"I suppose I can pitch in a little," Jinx said.

"Don't let them talk you into anything you don't want to do," Cash warned.

"No, it's fine. I'd love to help." Whether her spirits lifted because of the sense of family camaraderie or the glass of wine, Jinx found herself agreeing and actually looking forward to it.

"Okay then." Cash pushed back from the table. "Do we have dessert tonight?"

Ann stood. "I was going to wait until Thanksgiving, but Dwight brought over a bag full of pecans from his tree."

Cash's eyes lit up like a kid in a candy store. "Pecan pie? Did you make a pecan pie today?"

Kenzie leaned close to Jinx. "Pecan pie is Daddy's favorite."

"I'll help serve it up." Cash got to his feet.

"You just want to help so you make sure you get the biggest piece," Charlie joked.

He grinned. "You've got me all figured out, Sis. Here"—he leaned over Jinx—"let me clear your place for you."

As he reached for her plate, a crash came from the kitchen. Jinx spun in her chair, catching a glimpse of Hendrix on top of the kitchen island.

"What in tarnation is that?" Statler pointed to the dog, who didn't appear startled. He stood on the counter, lapping up the remains of something spread over the granite.

"It's Hendrix!" Kenzie raced into the kitchen with Cash right behind her.

"Watch out for broken glass." He scooped up his daughter before she cut her feet on the shards of the broken pie plate on the floor. "My pie! Please tell me that wasn't my pecan pie."

Jinx grabbed the devil dog from the counter. Maybe Armando was right and he really was a little demon. "How did you get loose?" She fingered the frayed end of his now-much-shorter leash.

"Looks like he chewed right through." Waylon held a palm over his belly and clapped Cash on the back with the other. "You're SOL on that pie, Bro."

"What's all the fuss?" Ann broke into the circle surrounding the mess on the floor, a broom in her hand. "I'll make you another pie for Thanksgiving, Cash."

"What's SOL mean?" Kenzie asked.

"Don't you worry about that," Ann said. "Be a big helper and grab that bag of cookies from the pantry, will you?"

Kenzie scrambled away from her dad to do her nana's bidding. She returned a minute later with a half-full bag of store-bought vanilla wafers.

"I'm so sorry about the mess. I'm going to take him outside for a minute." Jinx whirled around, trying to remember which way was out in the huge monstrosity of a house.

Cash caught up to her as she struggled with the front door.

She swatted his hand away. "I got it."

"I'm just trying to help."

"I don't need help." A mixture of feelings swirled inside her. Wasn't she just thinking it would be nice to fit in, have a family who cared about her? But not Cash's family. It was too much. They were too much. They smiled too much and were way too willing to help—who did things like that? Especially for a total stranger?

"Hey, are you okay?" Cash followed her into the yard.

"Yeah, I'm so sorry about the pie. I needed some fresh air."

"My family can be a bit much." He leaned up against a tree while she squatted to hold on to Hendrix's shortened leash.

"They're great. It's just—"

"You don't have to help with the play, you know."

"I know. I want to. I just don't think I'll be here that long, and I don't want to disappoint anyone."

He pushed off the tree and squatted next to her. "Hey, look here."

She met his gaze, saw the sympathy in his eyes. "You too?"

"What?"

She picked up Hendrix and stood. "I don't like people feeling sorry for me. I'm not some charity case."

"Hey, no one said anything about you being a charity case." Cash stood, towering over her. "You had a stretch of bad luck. You'll get your bike fixed and be on your way. It's okay to let people help you every once in a while."

"I'm not used to that. I've been on my own for so long, it just feels weird, especially since…I mean, you're strangers."

He moved closer, invading her personal space. "Why have you been on your own?"

"Forget it. I don't want to talk about it. I'll help with the play. For as long as I'm in town. Okay?"

Arms crossed over his chest, his gaze drilled into her. "Okay."

"Good." She nodded.

Charlie, Darby, and a handful of kids came out the front door, breaking the awkward interaction between her and Cash.

"Ryder wants y'all to watch him shoot off his stomp rocket," Darby said.

Thankful for the interruption, Jinx handed what remained of Hendrix's leash to Cash. "Can you watch him? I'm going to go help clean up."

"Sure."

It had only been a couple of weeks. She had a job, a place to stay, and a volunteer gig in town. She'd never felt more unsettled in her life.

—*HH*—

Cash entered the kitchen through the garage, wiping his boots on the doormat before kicking them off. He almost called out to let Jinx and Kenzie know he was home, but the sound of Kenzie's giggles made him pause. Ever since Jinx had entered their lives and begun spending her afternoons with Kenzie, working on her reading, his daughter seemed to laugh a lot more. He set his keys on the counter and tiptoed to the doorway, not wanting to break up whatever fun was going on in the other room.

The two sat side by side on the sectional, shoulders hunched over the coffee table, their backs toward him. "Is Jinx your real name?" Kenzie asked.

One of these days, he'd have to reward his little interrogator.

"No. Just a nickname that stuck."

"So what is your real name?"

"Oh, it's… You sure you want to know?"

Kenzie's pigtails bounced up and down.

Jinx took in a deep breath. "It's Joy. Kinda crazy, huh?"

His daughter's shoulders lifted up in a shrug. "I like it. It's pretty."

"Thanks. Nobody calls me that anymore."

"Not even your mom?"

A sharp punch of laughter escaped Jinx's lips. "Especially not my mom. She's…let's just say not part of my life anymore."

Kenzie put a comforting hand on Jinx's arm, causing Cash's stomach to hitch into a knot.

"My mommy's not a part of my life anymore either." The way she said it didn't just tug at his heartstrings; it gutted him. Made him more resolved than ever to give his girl everything she deserved.

Jinx wrapped an arm around Kenzie's shoulders and pulled her against her side. "I'm sorry, kiddo."

Before the conversation derailed into a total train wreck, Cash cleared his throat. Both of them turned around, surprise evident on their faces at being caught deep in conversation.

"How's the reading going today?" He walked around the couch and gathered Kenzie into his arms.

"Hi, Daddy!" Her kisses landed on his cheeks, chasing away the stress of his day job, reminding him what was important.

"Hi, Tadpole. Did you have a good day?"

"Yep. I got a part in the play. I'm the star on the Christmas tree."

Cash tilted his head. "A star?"

"Not just *a* star. I'm the special, sparkly one on top. Jinx is going to make a big tree, and my face is going to stick out of it, and I get to stand on top of everyone else, and it's gonna be sick!"

He glanced over Kenzie's head to Jinx, who stifled a laugh. "Care to interpret here?"

She stood and gave Kenzie a teasing tap on the nose. "What she means is that we're going to build the front of a huge tree out of plywood with cutouts for all the kids' heads. We'll need scaffolding for the back so they have a tiered framework to stand on.

Some of the kids will be ornaments, but Kenzie is going to be the most special gold star on top."

"Hmm. Okay. That makes a little more sense. What's this about it being 'sick' though?"

"Oh, that means cool, Daddy." Kenzie rolled her eyes, smiling at Jinx.

"Why do I suddenly feel about a hundred years old here?" He tickled Kenzie until she couldn't catch her breath, then tossed her onto the couch cushion and picked up her book from the table. "Did you go up a level in reading, honey?"

"Yeah, I'm a prairie dog now. Ms. Pepper says if I keep this up, I'll be an armadillo before Christmas break." She bounced on the cushion, using it like a trampoline.

"Wow, a prairie dog. That's fantastic. Does that mean I need to start calling you my little prairie dog instead of my tadpole?"

She stopped bouncing and walked to the edge of the cushion. Putting a hand on either side of his face, she pulled him toward her and planted a smushy kiss on his lips. "No. I always wanna be your tadpole, Daddy."

His heart surged with love for this little miracle of his. "So what do you want for dinner tonight? Should we drive Jinx to work, then eat at the Rose to celebrate your big achievement?"

"I really don't mind the walk." Jinx gathered the books into a stack on the table. "It's good for me."

"You still want to argue with me about this?" He'd been driving her to work and making sure whoever pulled the overnight shift at the sheriff's office brought her home every night. Yet every day, they had the same conversation. "It's in my best interest to make sure you get to and from safely. If something happened to you, I'd have to listen to Kenzie read 'See Spot run' five hundred thousand times."

"Anyone ever accuse you of being a little overprotective?" She swatted him with one of the early reader books. "You really do sound like you're a hundred years old now. Spot went out of style in the '50s or '60s."

"I can't help it. I don't want anything to happen to the people I care about." Cash caught her hand in his.

Her gaze met his. For a brief second, her carefree attitude slipped, and he recognized the same desire he'd seen in her eyes before. It would be so easy to pull her against his chest, slip an arm around her back, and nestle his nose against the warm pulse of her neck. Images from the night they'd almost spent together on this same couch had played through his mind on a loop ever since it had happened. But she wasn't long-term material. She definitely wasn't his type. Then why did his body rev into hot-and-bothered mode every time he got close to her?

"Okay, you can drive me. But only because I know how much Kenzie likes to take Hendrix for a ride in the truck."

"Hey, I'll take it." Instead of kissing her like he'd been dreaming about, he let go of her hand. "You need to run by the bunkhouse before we head out?"

She slung her backpack over her shoulder. "Nope. I've got it all here. Kenzie, do you want to bring Hendrix? If your dad says it's okay, you can take care of him tonight, and I'll get him in the morning."

"Watch this, Daddy! Jinx taught me how to do a

trick with him." Kenzie told Hendrix to sit, then nodded to Jinx. The first bars of "Jingle Bells" started to play from Jinx's phone. Hendrix sat up on his hind legs and began to howl along with the song. Kenzie collapsed into a fit of giggles on the couch while the little dog sang along. The tune finally came to a finish, and Hendrix wrapped up his show with a particularly long "Ow-ow-ooowah!"

Kenzie tossed a treat to Hendrix, who caught it in the air.

"Wow, I didn't know Chihuahuas could howl. That was pretty cool." Cash held his hand out for a high five. How could something that small make so much freaking noise? He hadn't quite forgiven the dumb dog for eating his entire pie, but Kenzie sure seemed to love the little guy.

"We're gonna teach him more stuff too. Aren't we, Jinx?"

Jinx nodded. Kenzie took Hendrix into her bedroom to grab his leash.

Taking advantage of the moment alone, Cash cleared his throat. "Oh, hey, I need to ask you something."

"What's that?"

"You up for taking part in the Turkey Trotter tomorrow morning?" He crossed his arms across his chest and cocked a hip against the back of the couch.

Jinx raised an eyebrow. "I'm almost afraid to ask. What's a Turkey Trotter?"

"It's a kind of a race. Teams of four. You run a little, do stupid stunts at each station. It's a Thanksgiving tradition around here."

Her eyebrows furrowed. "Running? No thanks. I'm not much of a runner. I think I'll just watch."

"You don't want to miss out, do you?"

"On running? Yeah, I don't mind."

"It's not just running. They have stations along the

race where you have to do certain challenges. The team that ends the course with the most completed challenges wins five hundred bucks. Each."

"What?" Her head jerked up, obviously interested in the mention of the cash prize.

"Yeah. A little bit of fun on Thanksgiving morning, then we all head over to Mom and Dad's for dinner."

"And everyone in your family does this?"

"Not everyone. But between my brothers and me, a Walker has been part of the winning team the past seven out of ten years. Waylon, Darby, and I are signed up. My cousin Brittany was supposed to round out our team, but she decided to stay in Dallas for the holiday instead."

"Really?"

"Yep. I know you can use the money. You want to be part of the team?"

She thrust her hand at his chest. "Deal."

"Great. It'll be fun. Now, let's get you to work. I know it's apple-cinnamon pork chop night, and I'm starving."

He held the door open for Jinx and Kenzie as they walked through. Jinx had been avoiding him in close quarters. Running the course with her would put them in some interesting situations. Might be a chance to get close without her backing away. Would give him a chance to see if the sparks between them were anything more than remnants from their almost one-night stand.

ELEVEN

"On your mark, get set, go!"

A shot rang out, making Jinx almost jump right out of her borrowed running shoes. Cash grabbed her hand and pulled her along behind him. What in the hell had she agreed to? Twenty teams, each one dressed more ridiculous than the next, jostled for the lead. Darby and Waylon jogged beside her. They'd come up with a name and costumes long before Jinx had joined the team—the Tasseled Turkeys.

Cash swore it was his cousin's idea. Who knew where Darby had found the hundreds of tassels she'd sewn onto the matching golden-yellow sweatshirts they had on? Obviously, Brittany had a few inches on her, since Jinx had to roll up the sweatpants so she wouldn't keep tripping on them.

They reached the first station and stopped next to a five-gallon bucket filled with stuffing mix.

"What do we need to do?" Cash asked.

The race volunteer held out a wooden spoon. "Stuff the turkey. Take a spoon full of stuffing mix, and carry it in your teeth down to the other end. You dump it in the turkey, then race back for the next person to take their turn."

"How big is that turkey down there?" Darby pointed

across the field to where a row of turkeys were lined up, ready to be stuffed.

"Aw, I'd say they're about twenty pounders. Don't want to make it too easy on us, right?" Waylon grabbed the spoon. "I'll go first. Get ready!"

He took off toward the turkey, the spoon clenched between his teeth. Darby went next, then Cash, and finally, it was Jinx's turn. She scooped up a spoonful of stuffing and ran as fast as she could. By the time she got to the turkey at the other side, only a couple of cubes of bread remained on her spoon. At the rate she was going, this could take all night.

The crowd of spectators cheered as the teams finished the first station. Finally, after it seemed like she'd run a marathon back and forth between the bucket and the turkey, their turkey was stuffed enough to move on.

"Let's go. Half the teams are ahead of us, so we've got to pick up the pace." Cash grabbed Jinx's hand and urged her on to the next challenge. They stopped in front of a huge inflatable pool filled with some sort of grain.

The station leader gestured to the pool. "Welcome to the corn bin. Two team members have to jump in and find a wishbone. Once you grab it, make a wish, and break it, you can move on."

"Y'all want to take this one?" Darby asked. "We'll do the next."

Cash lifted an eyebrow. "Whaddaya say?"

Jinx nodded. "Sure, let's go." How bad could it be? She lifted a foot and stepped over the edge. She sank into three feet of dried corn kernels.

Cash belly flopped into the bin next to her and began digging through the kernels. A whitish dust covered his face and shirt. "Come on in, Jinx. Feels great!"

Another team jumped in with Cash. Jinx climbed in and ran her hands through the corn. Kernels went everywhere. They flowed into her shoes, infiltrated her sweatpants, and crept up her sleeves. Her fingers combed through, finding nothing but corn. A guy from the other team held a wishbone up in the air.

"Crap, they got theirs already. Keep digging." Cash dove under the corn, fully submerged. He came up a few seconds later, the dust coating his hair, his face, even his eyelashes. "Got it!"

They staggered to the edge of the tub and over the side. Jinx grabbed one side of the bone, and Cash held the other.

"You got a wish in mind?" he asked.

She nodded, even though no wish had fully formed in her head. Her bike still needed to be fixed. Wishing for a windfall of cash would help. Wishing to win the race would put her closer to her goal. But something else hovered at the edge of her mind. Could she wish for more of the feeling she got when she was around Cash and Kenzie? Not that she wanted to stay in Holiday. But being around the two of them made her feel needed, like a part of something. She'd never experienced that before and wasn't sure she wanted to let it go.

Before she settled on a wish, Cash pulled and the bone snapped. He held the bigger half. She didn't need to even make a wish, since his was the one that would come true. Assuming he even believed in the mysterious wish-granting powers of half a turkey wishbone. The station helper stamped their card, and the four of them jogged to the next challenge.

The volunteer manning the next station handed Darby something that looked like a pointy potato and explained the goal. "Y'all line up and pass the yam from one to the next without using your hands. Get it to the line over there, and you can move on. Drop it, and you have to start over."

Should be easy enough. Jinx had done relays like this back in school. Darby stuck the yam under her chin and turned to Waylon. "Get over here so I can pass it on to you."

Waylon leaned in but couldn't get close enough because of his beard. The yam dropped to the ground.

"Dammit, Waylon. Try again." Cash picked up the yam and thrust it at his brother.

There was no way that vegetable was going to fit under Waylon's chin.

"Here, let me try." Jinx held out her hand. Waylon passed her the yam, and she tucked it under her chin. "Who's next?"

"Give it here." Cash crowded into her space. His chin hit her at eye level. He'd have to crouch down a bit if he wanted to line up for the yam.

"Bend down a little," Jinx said. She raised up to her toes while he leaned over a bit. His whiskers scraped against her cheek as he tried to transfer the yam between them. He was close enough that she could see the flecks of gold in his eyes. Close enough that she could smell the lingering scent of soap on his skin. Close enough that she could feel her heart leap into an erratic rhythm of its own.

The yam was transferred, and Cash turned to pass it to Darby.

"You're next, Jinx." Darby pointed to her husband. "You sit this one out, honey. I love you, but you don't have the neck for it."

They got into a groove, passing the yam from Darby to Jinx to Cash. Every time Cash leaned in to tuck his chin against her neck, her breath hitched. By the time they got to the other side, she was surprised she hadn't hyperventilated. What had gotten into her?

At the next station, Waylon and Darby had to take on another team in a chicken fight in a tub of gelatin. Teams had to win two out of three to move on. Darby won her first two meets, taking down Angelo's girlfriend twice in a row. Jinx was glad to not have to do that one. Sandwiching Cash's head between her thighs would have been unbearable. Especially when her nerve endings still sizzled from the pass-the-sweet-potato challenge.

After four of the five challenges, Team Tasseled Turkeys was neck and neck with Team Gyrating Giblets. Waylon and Cash had a special interest in beating their brother Presley, who was competing with his girl of the month along with Shep from the bar and his girlfriend. With only one more stop before they made a dash to the finish, Jinx was afraid of what the final challenge might be. The four of them approached the last station. A herd of horses stomped around inside a makeshift enclosure.

She'd seen horses before. The Walkers even had some that grazed close to the bunkhouse. But she'd never been this close to one of the giant beasts.

She half listened while the station helper explained the challenge. Something about riding into the patch of trees and bringing back some sort of rings. She couldn't tear her eyes away from the large, stomping, snorting, tail-swooshing animals.

"Why don't you pick one?" Cash pointed to the corral. "A fast one, okay?"

Jinx squinted at the group. "How can I tell which one is fast?"

"It's just a feeling. Hurry though. Presley's right on our tail."

Jinx pointed to a shiny black horse with a jet-black mane. "That one."

The station helper opened the gate for them. "That one's Hell's Fury. Good luck to y'all."

Hell's Fury didn't appear to be furious at all. Jinx couldn't even tell if it was male or female, and she didn't want to ask Cash and seem even more stupid than she already felt. The horse stretched its neck to reach a particularly tall patch of grass just outside the fence line. Its lips twitched, revealing a row of huge teeth, making her wonder if horses bit their riders very often.

"Come on. Get on." Cash made a basket out of his hands. "Put your foot in my hands and I'll hoist you up."

She did, somehow managing to settle herself in the saddle. Cash slung himself into position behind her, aligning his front against her back. Before she had a chance to take in the feeling of being that close, he kicked his feet into the horse's side, and they took off. Her thighs squeezed against the horse's back as she grabbed on to the knob sticking up from the saddle for dear life. Cash wrapped an arm around her middle, securing her, holding her even tighter against him.

Hell's Fury raced across the field toward the stand of trees like someone had lit a fire under his ass. Or her ass. Did it even matter? Trapped against Cash's chest, her butt bumping up and down on the hard saddle, Jinx stopped caring if her vehicle of death was male or female.

"There's the first ring." Cash's arm left her waist so he could point at a bright-blue object in a tree up ahead.

Feeling like she was about to slide off, Jinx scrambled, reaching behind her to grab on to Cash to steady herself.

"Easy there, Annie Oakley." He pulled up on the reins, and the horse slowed, giving him the chance to snag the ring out of the tree. "Don't tell me you've never ridden before."

"Do I look like I've ever been on the back of a horse?" she ground out between clenched teeth.

"Well, now that you mention it, you do seem a bit uptight."

"Uptight?" Her heart pounded like it wanted to take off into flight, rising up from her chest, sticking in her throat. It made it hard to choke out a response. "I think you're trying to kill me."

"Now why would I want to do that?" He clucked his tongue, and they took off again.

In that moment, she could think of a few hundred good reasons for Cash to meet his demise. Not wanting to give him the satisfaction of besting her, she chanted to herself, trying to calm the fear flooding her bloodstream.

Cash pulled up on the reins next to another tree. "Grab that one, will you?"

She stretched for the ring, just out of her reach. "Can you get closer?"

Hell's Fury pranced around, circling the tree. Finally, Cash got the horse positioned directly under the ring, and Jinx was able to grab it.

"One more to go." They dashed off toward the last ring as Presley and his partner reached them. "Hang on. We've got this."

Jinx's teeth knocked against each other as he urged the horse to go faster and faster. The last ring hung on a low branch just up ahead. Tassels twirling, butt bouncing up and down in the saddle, Jinx would have prayed if she'd been the praying type. Instead, she closed her eyes, trying to keep the protein bar she'd scarfed down for breakfast from ending up all over the front of her shirt.

"Duck!" Cash yelled, jerking Jinx to the side.

"What?" She struggled against him, trying to stay in the saddle. Her eyes opened just in time to see the rough bark of the tree. Her brain tried to make sense of why the tree branch would be so close as her head jerked backward. Her body followed, flying through the air and landing with a jarring thud on the dry, hard ground. A part of her was aware of Cash wheeling the horse around, of him jumping to the ground while it was still moving, of him cradling her head in his hands.

"Wiggle your toes. Move your fingers. Is anything broken?" Cash's face hovered over hers. She wanted to tell him not to worry, that she was just fine—no thanks to him—but her tongue wouldn't get out of the way, so her lips couldn't form the words.

Presley stopped next to them and hopped off the horse. "Hell, what happened?"

"She fell off. She needs an ambulance. Go get the EMT or something." The concern in Cash's eyes would have been funny if she could remember how to laugh.

"You okay, Jinx?" Presley leaned over her, his head opposite Cash's.

She stared up at the two Walker brothers, her gaze darting back and forth between them. "I'm…"

"What? You're what? Are you okay?" Cash's eyebrows wrinkled, making her think of that kid's book about the furry caterpillar or something.

"Let her talk." Presley pushed his brother away. "You're what?"

"I'm okay. I think I'm okay." She struggled to sit up.

"Maybe you should wait for the doctor." Cash put a restraining hand on her shoulder.

She pushed it away. "I'm fine. I just have a hell of a headache."

Waylon, Darby, and a guy wearing a medical vest crowded around them.

"You okay, hon?" Darby huffed in and out, breathless from running out to meet them.

"Yeah. I think so."

The medic knelt down next to her, probing her head, asking her to move her fingers, her toes. After a quick check, he told them nothing appeared to be broken, but she might have a concussion and should go to the hospital to see if she needed treatment.

"I'll take her." Cash's statement didn't allow for questions. He insisted on scooping her up like a child and carrying her back to the parking lot.

Darby led the horse, Waylon at her side.

Jinx rested her head against Cash's chest. "I guess this is one way to get out of celebrating Thanksgiving with your family."

"I'm just glad you're okay."

"Me too. I'll be fine, really."

"By the way, takes more than a visit to the hospital to shake my mom's good intentions." He squeezed her tighter against him, leaving her to wonder what exactly he meant.

~#~

Cash had been fielding phone calls from his family for over an hour. All he wanted to do was sit in the hard plastic chair by Jinx's bedside, hold her hand, and see if he could make her smile. It was his damn fault she fell off the horse. If he hadn't been so worried about beating Presley this year, none of this would have happened.

He should have let Waylon and Darby do the final challenge. But Waylon had about forty pounds on him, so he knew they had a better chance of staying ahead of Presley if the horse didn't have to cart Waylon's fat ass around.

He ended a call with Statler and was about to reenter the hospital room when his phone buzzed again. Dammit. Charlie. She'd volunteered to keep an eye on Kenzie while he and Jinx were at the hospital. Better not ignore this one.

"Yeah?"

"Hey. Just wanted to give you a heads-up. Mom's on her way over." He could practically hear the smile in her voice.

"What do you mean she's on her way over? She's hosting Thanksgiving at her place this afternoon."

"Well, that was before your girlfriend ended up being admitted."

"Whoa. She's not my girlfriend."

"Okay. Then what would you call her? Your pet project? Your indentured servant?"

"Hey, that's not fair." His lungs squeezed together. He and Jinx were friends. That's all. "We're friends. She's like the sister I never had."

"Hmm. As your only sister, I'm going to have to take offense to that. Besides, the things you want to do with Jinx are not the kind of things you'd do with a family member."

How would she know what he wanted to do with Jinx? Unless...had Jinx confided in Charlie? "What in the hell has she told you?"

"Nothing, Einstein. But it doesn't take a super sleuth to see the way you look at her when you don't think anyone's watching. And when's the last time you went out of your way to give someone a ride anywhere? You've been driving her back and forth to work since she got into town."

"She doesn't have a vehicle."

"Yeah, well, you don't have a life—at least you didn't until she got stranded here."

That wasn't true at all. He had a life. He had Kenzie. He had a job he loved and a family who backed him up, at least most of the time. "I'm not discussing this with you right now."

"Good idea. Mom ought to be there in a few minutes. You'd better brace yourself for the impact. Don't worry about Kenzie. She's playing with that dog Jinx has. He's really cute. You should get her one."

"She's already got Chucky." Plus the pony his dad had bought her for her fifth birthday.

"Chucky isn't a cat. He's more like a Tasmanian devil in a cat suit. Anyway, I'll let you go. Good luck with Mom. I'll plan on keeping Kenzie overnight."

"Thanks, Sis."

"My pleasure. Give Jinx a hug from me."

"We'll see."

He ended the call and went to slide his phone into his back pocket out of habit. Damn. He still had on the stupid tasseled sweats. The Turkey Trotter event was well known in Holiday but not so much in the bigger city of San Marcos. He'd received his fair share of odd looks and smirks from the hospital staff.

Jinx opened her eyes as he entered the room. They'd hooked her up to an IV since she seemed slightly dehydrated. Other than that, they suspected a mild concussion. Once the doctor came in to confirm, they'd probably send her home. Between Cash and his brothers, the Walker family had seen their fair share of head injuries over the years. Presley was the worst. He'd tried to jump off the roof of the house onto the back of a horse, convinced he wanted to be a stuntman in the movies when he was twelve. Then he got himself sidelined playing high school football when he bet a guy he could make a hit so hard he could crack his helmet. Unfortunately, he won that one but also broke four bones in his hand.

"How are you feeling?" Cash set his hand on her arm.

"The same as I was when you asked me five minutes ago." Her blue-gray eyes sparkled at him, still full of fire and sass. "I'm sorry we lost."

"That's okay." By the time they'd gotten Jinx to the truck, three different teams had stopped to pitch in, meaning the unlikely pairing of Whitey and Dwight had secured the win. "There's always next year."

"Next year?" Her eyes rounded.

"Sure. We'll win back the title then. By the way, Charlie called. I guess Mom is driving over to check on you."

"What? Why?"

He almost laughed at the shock registered on her face. "Who knows? Be sure you ask her when she gets here."

"Ask her what?" His mom pushed open the door to Jinx's room, her arms full of foil-covered dishes. His dad followed, a huge tote bag in one hand, a thermal carafe in the other.

"What's all this?" Cash asked, moving toward his mom to take a few of the dishes.

"If you and Jinx can't come to Thanksgiving, we'll bring Thanksgiving to you." Ann unloaded everything to Cash and walked to Jinx's side. She ran her hand over Jinx's forehead. "How are you feeling, sweetie?"

"Oh, I'll be fine. Just a bump."

"She'll be ready for riding lessons in no time." Cash set the food on the rolling table. "You brought enough food to feed the whole hospital, Mom. Did you leave anything at home?"

Tom lifted his eyebrows. "Really? You know better than that, Son. This is maybe ten percent of what she's got back at the house."

"I'll fix plates for y'all, and then we'll take care of feeding those fine folks who have to work on the holiday." Ann started unwrapping dishes. "Tom, hand me those plates from the bag, please?"

"I got it, Dad." Cash reached into the tote bag for the plates and plasticware. "Anyone tell you you're crazy, Mom?"

"Only every single day of my life. Now, Jinx, do you like white or dark meat?"

"Oh, it doesn't matter. I can't believe you did this. You're missing out on dinner with the family. I—"

Cash noticed the shift in his mom's shoulders, the bristle in her spine.

"Now, honey, you listen to me. You're just like family. You're helping out with Kenzie, you're living with Cash…why, I couldn't let you go without a Thanksgiving dinner."

How Jinx's face could have paled any further was beyond him, but her skin took on the shade of the bleached, starchy pillowcase behind her head.

"She's not exactly living with me, Mom."

Him mom waved his comment away. "You know what I mean. Besides, I had to get you your turkey dinner."

"Yeah, speaking of dinner, please tell me you brought me a piece of pecan pie?" Cash poked around in the bag, hoping he'd come across a pie pan or at least a slice wrapped up in foil.

Ann continued to dish up a little bit of everything onto a plate for Jinx. "Sure did."

Cash dug through the bag for a pie-size box. "This one?"

"Yes. I know how much you enjoy your pecan pie. But dinner first, okay?"

Jinx laughed. "That sounds like what you say to Kenzie."

Cash winked and lifted the lid to peek in on the pie. His mouth watered. He could almost taste it. Until he saw a big, fat piece of pumpkin pie nestled into the box. "Mom, I thought you said you brought me pecan."

She peered into the box. "I did. I asked Statler to put it in a box just for you."

"Well, he got me good this time." Cash dropped the box back into the bag.

"When are you boys going to stop pranking each other?" Ann asked.

"After I get even with Statler." Cash leaned against the bed. Second year in a row he'd missed out on his mom's prize-winning pecan pie. Last year, he'd had to work, and by the time he had gotten home, his brothers had licked the pie plate clean. Dammit. Well, priorities and all. He would much rather be sitting by Jinx, even if it meant he would miss his mom's special dessert.

By the time Ann had fixed plates for all of them, including Jinx's nurse and the woman from registration, the doctor entered the room.

"So this is where the party is." He offered a hand to Jinx. "I'm Dr. Stafford. Looks like it's just what we expected. You're a lucky lady. Things could have been much worse...broken bones, a back injury. Looks like you're going to walk out of here tonight with just a mild concussion."

"That's great news." Ann set her plate down. "What can I fix you for dinner, Dr. Stafford?"

"Oh, nothing, thank you though. My shift ends soon, so I'll get to go home for dinner." He flipped open a chart. "I'm assuming you have somewhere to stay tonight?"

"She can stay with me." Cash's statement didn't

leave room for protests or arguing. But leave it to Jinx to try anyway.

"Oh, I'm sure that's not necessary. I'll—"

"Actually, Ms. Jacobs, it is. We'll want someone monitoring you in case things get worse." He turned to Cash. "You'll need to keep an eye on her for the next twenty-four hours, preferably forty-eight. I'll send you home with a sheet listing the things to watch for."

Cash shook the doctor's hand. "Thanks, Doc. I'll take good care of her."

Dr. Stafford nodded. "I'll send in the nurse to get her unhooked from the IV, then you're free to go. Oh, there is a note in the file about needing your insurance card."

"Yeah, about that." Jinx twisted her hands together. "I don't exactly have—"

"I'll take care of it on the way out. After all, I'm the idiot who crashed her into the tree." Cash held the door open for the doctor. Jinx glared at him, a silent fist to the gut. But he wasn't sorry for speaking up. It was his fault she was on the horse in the first place. He gave her one of his best grins; she looked away.

"Well, that's great news." Ann scurried around the room, putting lids back on containers. "Tom, help me move this stuff to the staff lounge? Let's get out of here so the kids can pack it up and head home."

His dad complied for a change, and within a few minutes, they'd left, taking all the food, chaos, and hungry members of the staff who'd heard there was a home-cooked turkey dinner in room 212 with them.

"What do you say, Jinx?" Eyebrows raised, Cash took a seat by the bed.

She'd started peeling the tape off her arm where they'd attached her IV. "I think you're pretty pleased with yourself for rescuing me again."

"What?"

"You've got to stop being so nice. What's wrong with you people?" She winced as she ripped the tape from her arm.

"Don't you want to wait for the nurse to do that?"

"Hand me a tissue?" She nodded toward the box of tissues secured to the wall.

He pulled a few and passed them to her just in time for her to slide the needle out of her hand. Holding the tissue over the insertion point, she let the tubing and IV drop to the floor.

"It's not right. I can't keep taking your charity. Your mom, your sister...hospital charges... For fuck's sake, I'll never be able to repay everyone."

"Hey—" He reached for her hand, covering it with his as she pressed down on the tissue to curb the bleeding. "It's not like that. We like you. My mom might have freaked you out a bit, but she's right. You are kind of part of the family now, at least while you're still in town. And that's what family does—they look out for each other, especially during the tough times."

She glanced up at him, her eyes shiny with unshed tears. "That's what I'm talking about. I'm not your family. I don't have any family. Do you know how lucky you are to have that kind of support? People aren't like that."

He wanted to wrap her in his arms, this tough, tatted, badass biker chick who could be reduced to tears by a paper plate full of turkey and trimmings. "What happened to your family, Jinx? Who hurt you so bad?"

She opened her mouth, about to speak. The door squeaked, and a nurse entered the room.

"I'm here to take out the… Oh." She rounded the bed where Jinx still held the tissue to her arm. "Looks like it's already been taken care of."

Jinx closed her eyes, breathed in and out a few times, her jaw clenched, her body as rigid as an unbending old oak.

The nurse moved next to the bed. "Can I take a look? Let me swab it with some alcohol and get a bandage on that, okay?"

By the time the nurse finished, any sign of weakness or willingness to share had disappeared— another missed opportunity to learn more about the mysterious woman who'd crashed into his life. He held the door open for her, and in their matching, tasseled, yellow sweats, they marched toward the parking lot.

SHE WOKE TO THE SOUND OF THE TELEVISION. SOME infomercial about the only pan a person would ever need. It could sauté, fry, poach, boil. A real one-stop shop. Kind of like the Walker family. In the dim light cast by the TV screen, she evaluated the sound-asleep caretaker next to her. He appeared to be hell-bent on following the instructions the doctor had given. Cash had insisted on sitting in the chair in the bedroom while she slept. He must have thought she was going to die in her sleep or something. She'd finally convinced him to sit on the bed so he could at least see the TV.

He'd leaned against the headboard on top of the covers while she snuggled underneath. She'd almost laughed at how careful and gentle he'd been. Every time he moved, he checked to make sure he hadn't jostled her too much. He'd been waking her up every two hours all night long to make sure she was still alive. The effort must have got to him, since he was obviously sound asleep.

Jinx took the opportunity to look him over. With his eyes closed, he couldn't shoot her that exasperated glare she'd grown so used to. Long, dark lashes fanned over his cheeks, making her curse the fact that guys always seemed to get the eyelashes to die for. So unfair.

A layer of scruff covered his chin and upper lip. He

looked so much more relaxed in his sleep than he did awake. Vulnerable. Soft. All the hard edges were erased when he closed his eyes. She lay there, watching the hypnotic rise and fall of his chest until she couldn't ignore her thirst or nature's inconvenient call.

Rising from the bed, she moved as cautiously as she could, not wanting to wake him. She'd almost reached the bathroom when her foot landed on a creaky board.

"Where you headed?" Cash squinted at her, one eye open, the other squeezed shut tight.

"Bathroom and to get a drink of water. I'd also like to get out of these sweats."

"You need some help with that?"

"That would be a hard no to that offer."

He sat up taller, swinging his legs over the side. "Hey, I'm here for you. Whatever it takes. Squeeze your cheeks, help you get undressed, kiss your boo-boos."

She couldn't help but smile. "My boo-boos definitely do *not* need to be kissed." *Especially by you*, she wanted to add. Kisses from Cash would lead her down a road she'd vowed to avoid. She didn't need to tangle with Deputy Do-Good any more than she needed another knock to the head.

"All right, but if you change your mind…" His words trailed off, his laughter following her into the bathroom.

"I won't." She reached the sanctity of the master bath and closed the door behind her.

She took care of business, then washed her hands

in the huge basin sink. The mirror above reflected an almost unrecognizable version of herself. Her hair hung in tangled strands, a few twigs and dry leaves caught up in knots. A line of mascara streaked down her cheek. She rubbed it away, then splashed her face with cold water.

What a mess. Her ass ached from riding in the saddle. Her head throbbed from the impact of the fall. Her hands shook as she pushed her hair behind her ears.

"You okay in there?" Cash's voice came through the door, like he was standing outside, talking directly into the wood.

"Yeah, be out in a sec, jailer."

"Glad to hear your sense of humor didn't get knocked out of you."

Nope. Just her pride, her air of independence, and her common sense. Why else would she have agreed to come back to Cash's place instead of going straight to the bunkhouse?

"I hung a T-shirt on the door handle. Oh, and I got you some water. Put it on the nightstand."

"Thanks," she said, cracking open the door. She reached a hand out and snagged the T-shirt. It felt good to slip into something clean. She hadn't bothered when Cash had first brought her back. As she left the bathroom, she flipped the light switch so he couldn't see what a mess she'd become. Although, if he'd been with her since the hospital, he probably had already seen her at her worst.

He put an arm around her back, leading her toward the bed. "You dizzy at all? Nauseous?"

"I'm fine. Other than a splitting headache, I think I'm going to survive. You can stop monitoring my every movement."

"I don't mind. It's my fault you were on the damn horse. I should have had Waylon and Darby do it."

"Really? I thought you liked scaring the shit out of me and squeezing me so tight my guts almost popped out."

He pulled back the covers so she could slide underneath. "I did enjoy sharing a saddle with you. But I didn't mean for you to get hurt."

"I know. Seriously, stop blaming yourself. I'll be fine."

He pulled the covers up to her chin, tucking her in like she imagined a parent might tuck in a child. Not that she would know. She'd put herself to bed for as long as she could remember.

"Can I get you anything?" He hovered over her.

"There is one thing."

"What? Just name it."

"Do you have a comb or brush? I'd love to get some of this crap out of my hair."

"Yeah, I'm sure Kenzie's got something. Let me go look."

She waited, listening to the salesman on the TV rave about the patented nonstick coating. That's what she needed—a nonstick coating of her own. That way, she wouldn't get attached. To Cash. To Kenzie. To the Rambling Rose. To Holiday.

By the time Cash returned, her eyes had closed. The mattress dipped as he sat down on the bed next to her. His fingers slid through her hair, gentle, caressing, careful. She tried to reach up and push his hand away, but her muscles wouldn't muster the energy to obey her brain.

She drifted off to sleep with the feel of Cash's hands in her hair, the solid weight of him beside her.

HH

"Hey, take it easy. You don't want another concussion, do you?" Cash peered up at Jinx, who straddled a ladder above him, reaching for the top of the plywood Christmas tree.

"I can take care of myself," she shouted down at him, waving a paintbrush dripping with bright-green paint.

He never doubted that for a second, especially since she'd hightailed it back to the bunkhouse after only spending one night at his place. But it hadn't even been a week since she'd been in the hospital, for crying out loud. She ought to be taking it easy. A splash of paint landed at his feet, splattering onto his boots.

She smiled down at him. "Sorry."

He grabbed the drill and moved to the other side of the stage. The scenery for the play was really coming together. Thanks to Jinx. Darby hadn't realized what a hidden talent Jinx possessed. None of them had. The entire PTA raved about how she'd come in, made a plan, and began putting the whole thing together. In an effort to keep up with the doctor's orders and make sure she didn't overdo it, he'd decided to sneak over on his lunch hour several times a week to help out. With the play only a couple of weeks away, they ought to have it done in plenty of time.

Jinx scrambled down the ladder faster than he would have liked. The woman was nothing short of frustrating. It made him want to tear his hair out just trying to put the brakes on her. Charlie had her coordinating a ton of stuff at the Rose for the upcoming Jingle Bell Jamboree. His mom had pressed her into service helping to decorate some of the storefront windows downtown for the holidays. Hell, even his dad had commented on what a great job she was doing helping Kenzie with her reading.

He hated to admit it, but his life had become a whole lot easier once she fell into it, making him even more aware of how hard it was to manage fatherhood, his family, and a career as a single dad.

"When do you think you'll have the scaffolding for the kids built?" She looked like a kid herself in a pair of Charlie's old overalls. A smudge of green paint covered her cheek.

He leaned close, swiping his thumb over the paint. Not such a great idea. He'd gotten it off her cheek, but now it covered his thumb. Jinx held out the edge of her shirt.

"Just wipe it on this. My shirt is pretty much shot anyway."

"If you insist." He wiped his thumb on the edge of her shirt, adding green to the color palette she'd collected. "How late are you planning on staying?"

"I was going to walk home in time to meet Kenzie's bus so we can work on her reading. Charlie needs me at the Rose by five. Will you be home by then?"

He nodded. To anyone else, this might have seemed like quite the domestic conversation. Trading work schedules and coordinating child care were the types of things parents did. He doubted Jinx realized how wedged into their daily lives she'd become. And in such a short time.

"I can give you a ride if you want. I've got to head that way anyway to serve some papers to someone."

"Uh-oh. Something bad?" She raised a brow.

"Nah. I can tell you all about it on the way. What do you say?"

She tilted her head to the side like she was trying to get a read on him. "You sure you have to go that way? I don't want to put you out."

"How many times do I have to tell you you're not putting me out? I do need to run into the mini-mart on the way though. You up for a stop?"

"Sure."

"All right, let's go." He led the way out of the school to where his truck sat in the parking lot. He waited until Jinx buckled up, then pulled out onto the main road. "So, I've been meaning to ask you something."

"Oh?" She raised an eyebrow, always skeptical.

"Nothing bad. I have to spend most of next week up in Dallas for some training. I was going to ask Mom and Dad if they'd look after Kenzie, but Mom mentioned wanting to squeeze in a quick visit with her sister before the holidays. Aunt Doris lives up by Tulsa, and I don't want Kenzie to miss that much school—"

"I'd be happy to." She let out a breath, nodding in apparent relief. "She's got an assessment next week anyway. You don't want her to miss that."

He reached for her hand, then thought better of it. "Thanks. I really appreciate it."

"My pleasure. With everything you and your family have done for me lately, I don't think hanging with Kenzie will even come close to evening the score."

He wasn't worried about keeping things even. There was still something about her that nagged at the back of his brain. But she'd done nothing in the past couple of weeks to earn his doubt.

She'd done exactly the opposite.

She showed up on time for her shifts at the Rose, went above and beyond helping out with the Christmas play scenery. Charlie had commissioned her to paint a mural on a wall of the Rose. And he and Jinx had even settled into some sort of warped, slightly flirtatious vibe. It would be fine with him if she decided to stick around for a while.

He already knew the answer to the question he wanted to ask but needed to hear her confirm it. "You talk to Dwight lately?"

"Yeah." Her eyes sparked with excitement. "He ought to have everything fixed before Christmas."

He'd been after Dwight for an update. That was pretty much what he'd been told too. Dwight said she came by a couple of times a week and paid him in cash. Probably her tip money from working the bar at the Rose. She still talked about trying to get to New Orleans in time for the holidays. Kenzie would be crushed. He hated to admit it to anyone, especially himself, but he was going to miss her too. More than he should.

He pulled into a spot in front of the convenience store. Jinx climbed out of the truck before he even had the keys out of the ignition. He took large strides toward the door so he could hold it open for her.

"Thanks, Deputy." She brushed past him into the store and headed for the candy aisle. "I promised Kenzie a treat if she made it through her library book today. Does she like gummy bears or jelly beans better?"

"Either one. As long as it's sugar." He grabbed a couple of light bulbs from the shelf and placed them on the checkout counter.

Jinx stepped next to him. "Lightbulbs? That's your emergency?"

"Yeah." Cash paid for his purchase. "I noticed the light on the bunkhouse front porch was out. I don't want you tripping and falling in the dark."

"Oooh, lookie there." Dwight came up behind them.

"What are you oohing over?" Cash turned to face him.

"Mistletoe." Dwight pointed over their heads. A sad sprig of mistletoe dangled over the checkout.

Jinx glanced up. "Oh crap."

"It's bad luck not to kiss under the mistletoe. I'm game if you are." Dwight puckered his lips.

"No. Absolutely not." Jinx tossed a couple of dollars down on the counter. "Keep the change. I'm out of here."

"Oh, come on. If you won't kiss me, I dare you to lay one on Cash here," Dwight teased.

"She's not going to do it." Cash tucked his change into his pocket. "Just drop it."

"I bet she will," Dwight said. "Hey, Jinx, give Cash a kiss, and I'll take ten bucks off your repair job."

She stopped at the door and slowly whirled around.

"I said drop it, Dwight." Cash tucked the brown bag under his arm. "Let's go, Jinx."

"A hundred," she countered.

"Wait, what are you doing?" Cash glanced back and forth between Jinx and Dwight. Both of them were crazy.

"Now if I was getting the kiss…" Dwight pointed to his lips.

"No way." She clamped her hand to her hip.

Dwight let out an exaggerated sigh. "Can't blame me for trying. Fifty bucks, final offer."

"Fine." Jinx held out a hand.

Dwight reached out and shook it. "You've got yourself a deal."

"What's going on here?" Cash couldn't tell for sure, but it seemed like he was about to lock lips with the woman he'd been trying to avoid thinking about locking lips with.

"You're about to get a fifty-dollar kiss. Are you game?" Jinx asked.

"With a proposition like that, how could I refuse?" Cash tried to make his voice light. He wasn't sure exactly how this had gone down, but he didn't want to look like a complete jackass in front of Dwight.

"It will only hurt for a sec, cowboy." Jinx reached up and pulled his head close to hers.

Their lips touched. Shock, warmth, and desire flooded his system. He dipped her low, deepening the kiss. Her body responded, pulling him closer. The fluorescent lights and the beep of the cash register faded into the background. He wasn't aware of anything else but this woman, this kiss.

Too soon, the moment ended. Jinx pressed against him, trying to break away. He set her upright as Dwight let out a low whistle.

"Whoo-ey! That was some kiss. Hopefully, they caught it on the Kissmas Cam."

"What are you talking about?" Jinx asked.

Dwight pointed above them. "The town does a Kissmas Cam every year. Captures shots of mistletoe kisses, then plays them on the big screen during the Jingle Bell Jamboree."

Jinx turned on Dwight. "So everyone's going

to stand around and watch Cash and me kiss on some huge TV?"

"Yeah. Social media too. What's the big deal?" Dwight shrugged. "It's all in good fun. Best kiss gets free tickets to the annual chili cook-off in the spring."

With a shake of her head, Jinx stomped away. So much for the spirit of the season.

Cash swatted Dwight on the shoulder. "Thanks, dumbass."

"Hey, you got a hell of a kiss out of it," Dwight called after him.

It had been a hell of a kiss. There was something between them. Even if neither of them wanted to acknowledge it, he couldn't pretend anymore.

She was a wonder with his daughter, but it was more than that. Hers was the smile he wanted to see when he got home from work in the afternoons. Not that they engaged in deep conversations beyond the typical check-in, but having a woman in the house had its perks. He didn't have to do everything with Kenzie on his own anymore. And there was still that crackle of tension and attraction that rubbed along his nerve endings when they brushed hands or ended up sitting next to each other on the couch. He wasn't ready to shut all that down yet, no matter how irritating it was to not be one hundred percent in control.

THIRTEEN

JINX TOSSED AND TURNED ALL NIGHT LONG. SHE COULDN'T help but replay that kiss in her head. Over and over and over again. She needed to establish some ground rules with Cash, and fast. Like no more touching. No more being nice. And definitely no more kissing.

The man did something to her insides. Made it impossible to think when he was around. She'd had the hots for guys before. But things always went down on her terms. This was different. Usually, the more time she spent around a guy, the less time she wanted to be with him.

Like Wade.

Hooking up with him had seemed like a good idea at the time. He'd needed a bartender, and she had needed a place to live. At first, he was generous, letting her move in and giving her an advance. But the more she'd gotten to know him, the more she'd realized she was in over her head, and not in a good way. The man had a mean streak and a violent side, and she'd gotten out before she'd had to deal too much with either.

With Cash, the more she got to know him, the more she wanted to stay. The more she wanted to stay, the more she thought she ought to put as much distance as she could between herself and Holiday, Texas. Guys like Cash didn't pick girls like her for more than a one-night stand or a few weeks of fun. He walked the line while she ran in circles. He kept the peace while she created chaos wherever she went.

The sooner she could get out of Holiday, the sooner she'd be able to rid herself of the uncomfortable feelings he stirred up inside.

As the dark of night gave way to the misty gray morning light, she finally stopped trying to force herself back to sleep. It was no use. She flung the covers off and decided to walk to Dwight's. It had been a few days since she'd checked her numbers against his. Knowing how much longer she had to spend in Holiday would definitely improve her mood. She left the bunkhouse and began the long trek into town.

Dwight wasn't in the office when she peeked in. A loud banging noise came from the garage. She rounded the corner and entered the bay as he wheeled himself out from underneath a gigantic old four-door sedan.

"You okay? I heard that noise."

"Just a muffler falling off." He got to his feet. "Damn tailpipe rusted out. I barely touched it."

She pulled her jacket tighter around her. "So…um… about my bike."

Dwight snagged a rag out of his coveralls pocket, wiping his permanently stained hands on the dirty piece of flannel. "Told you last week—I'm still waiting on that final part to come in from San Bernardino. Once I get it, I'll need a few days."

"And then?"

"Then you'll be free to ride off into the sunset."

As if. She didn't bother to remind him she'd be heading southeast. Catching a sunrise would be more likely.

"Did they give you a delivery estimate?"

"Yeah. Said it would be here about two weeks after they received payment in full." He leveled his gaze at her.

"How much do I still owe?"

He pulled a tiny notebook out of his pocket. His fingers twitched like he was counting in his head. Murmuring to himself, he looked skyward. Finally, after enough time passed that he should have been able to do whatever complicated calculation he needed to in his head at least five times, he scribbled something in the notebook.

"Five hundred after you won that fifty-buck bet."

She nodded. Unfortunately, that matched her estimate as well. If only she could pay the guy off in money-laundered gift cards. She drew the line there though. She wanted to tell Cash about them, and had started to on multiple occasions, but always stopped herself. Instead, she'd slipped a couple into the Salvation Army kettle in front of the mini-mart and dropped a few into a toy collection bin. But she refused to use them for herself.

She just needed to amp up her game at the bar and try to appeal to some big tippers.

"I'm working on it. Here's another hundred." She handed over what she had left of her last couple of nights' worth of tips.

Dwight pocketed it, made a note in the notebook, and flipped the cover shut. "Heard some folks around town sayin' you're doing some sign making?"

Her eyes cut to the dust-covered office windows. Probably hadn't seen the business side of a squeegee in years. "Yeah. I've done the windows down at the diner for the holidays and am making some decorations for the Jingle Bell Jamboree."

"Huh." He flipped the ever-present toothpick from side to side between his lips. "Think you might wanna paint me up some candy canes or something in the front window? I can knock some money off what you still owe on the bike."

"Sure. I'd be up for that. How about I stop by on Sunday? I don't have to work that day."

He thrust his hand toward her. "You got yourself a deal. Come around three. When you're done, I'll treat you to some barbecue across the street."

The scent of oil, gasoline, and desperation rose off him in waves. She'd decided a while ago that Dwight was relatively harmless. Rolling her eyes, she shook her head. "Nice try, Romeo. I'll stop by on Sunday. But I'll be doing dinner on my own."

"You eatin' Sunday dinner at the Walkers?"

"What do you know about that?"

He shrugged. "Folks talk."

"And what do folks say when they talk, huh?" She took a menacing half step toward him. Her five-foot-four frame shouldn't strike fear in the heart of a guy who probably outweighed her by at least double. But he stepped back.

"Just that they've been seein' you and Cash together. A lot. And that kiss yesterday… Ain't none of my business—"

"That's right. It ain't." Sheesh, she needed to get out of here if she was going to start talking like Dwight. "I mean, it isn't."

He must have realized she wasn't going to physically attack. His shoulders relaxed, and he looped his thumbs into his pockets. "I know you ain't from around here, so you probably don't know about Cash and Lori Lynne Evans. Damn shame about her. And Cash gettin' left to raise that little girl all on his own."

Jinx narrowed her eyes into slits. She didn't usually get sucked into gossip. But she did want to learn more about Cash. Didn't she? No, not like this. If Cash wanted to tell her something about his past, he would.

"I've got to go. See you on Sunday." Before Dwight could suck her in with another tantalizing tidbit, she made a beeline for the door.

She'd wondered what had happened between Cash and Kenzie's mom. Charlie had started talking about it once at the bar, but then Statler had shown up to go over some numbers. As someone who appreciated keeping her own skeletons in the closet, she didn't need to go looking for Cash's.

Glad that was settled. She tucked her chin against her chest and walked into the wind. Whoever this Lori Lynne was, something bad must have happened. Poor Kenzie. Jinx's heart squeezed. She knew what it was like to grow up without a parent. To lose someone she loved.

When her dad died, her life had fallen apart. She'd pieced it back together as best she could and moved on. That was the key, the moving-on part. She couldn't afford to stick around or put down any kind of roots. Not in a place as small as Holiday. Roots had a way of growing out of control, like a weed. Before she knew it, they'd sprawl and tumble, snake around her neck, and practically choke the life right out of her.

She'd keep her end of the bargain and watch Kenzie next week. No need to go back on her word. But once Cash got back in town, she'd either need to have the money to get her bike fixed or buy that bus ticket. Before those roots started to grow.

Because she could already feel them taking hold.

HH

Cash cursed himself for the umpteenth time since yesterday. Hell, every time he found himself in the same room with Jinx, he seemed to screw it up. What had possessed him to deep dip her and lay one on her in front of the Kissmas Cam? He could tell Kenzie had her heart set on him and Jinx getting together. At seven, she couldn't see past the mermaid hair and the fun she was having with Hendrix around. But Jinx wasn't the type of woman to settle in a place like Holiday, no matter how hard Kenzie wished for it. How could he protect his little girl's heart if he couldn't keep his own under control?

The training up in Dallas couldn't have come at a better time. The break would do him good. Put some distance between the two of them. Give him a chance to get his priorities straight again. He tapped his fingers on the steering wheel along with the beat of some song he didn't recognize. What the hell was that? Kenzie must have flipped the station this morning when she climbed into the truck. They usually listened to country, but this was some sort of psychedelic garbage. He pressed the preset button and let the steel guitar soothe his rattled nerves. He ought to have enough time to stop in at the station and wrap up some paperwork before getting Kenzie over to his folks' house and heading to the Rose for his off-duty shift tonight.

A few hours later, he stood on the front porch of the Rambling Rose, checking IDs. Classes wouldn't be out for the holidays for another couple of weeks, so the kids came in droves from San Marcos, Austin, and San Antonio. They thought some backwoods honky-tonk out in the sticks would be an easy place to sneak in with a fake ID. He'd already busted a handful of underage kids. It wasn't too hard when the ID stated their hometown as Albuquerque and the frat boys didn't have a clue how to spell it. One of the bouncers came out to give him a break, so Cash wandered inside to grab a water from the bar.

The band had the crowd on its feet. A combo of rockabilly, swing, and country blasted through the speakers. Bodies bounced and swayed along to the music. Cash estimated they were pushing their max occupancy based on the number of arms waving in the air and the sheen of sweat breaking out on his forehead. The temp inside had to be pushing ninety degrees.

He made his way toward the bar, fighting through a pulsing sea of limbs and torsos. When he got to the edge, a cold chill wrapped around his neck, squeezing his breath out, stalling his heart.

Jinx leaned over the bar, that damn micro tank top stretched tight over her chest. One of those kids who didn't look old enough to drive, much less be sitting on a stool at the Rose, swept his tongue across her neck then slammed a shot of what Cash could only assume must be tequila. Before Cash could grab him by the back of his neck, he snagged the lemon Jinx held between her lips with his teeth. What the actual fuck? Cash pushed people out of his way, reaching the bar just as the kid slapped a twenty on the bar and called for another shot.

"We're out of tequila." Cash wadded up the twenty and pushed it at the kid.

"I don't think so." The jerk gestured toward Jinx, who held a full bottle of Cuervo in her hand and had just poured another shot.

Cash grabbed it off the bar, tossed it back, and slammed the shot glass down. "I said we're out of tequila."

"Hey, asshole—" The kid pushed a palm into Cash's chest, but his buddies held him back.

"What in the hell do you think you're doing?" Jinx levered herself halfway over the bar to grab the collar of his shirt, jerking his attention from the kid being swallowed by the crowd to the cleavage spilling out of her tank top.

Air. He needed air. The sweat and stench of hundreds of bodies pressing close together made him struggle to take in a deep breath.

"Shep, cover me for a minute?" Jinx let go of his shirt and rounded the bar. She grabbed his arm and began to drag him down the hall. "We need to talk."

Something inside him snapped. "You're absolutely right." He thrust his arm around her waist as they forced their way through the crowd toward the back hall.

Finally, they made it into the utility room. He slammed the door behind them, leaned up against it, and tried to shut the blaring music and chatter of the crowd out. Jinx rounded on him as he let her go.

"What"—she swatted at his chest—"in the hell was that?"

He caught her wrists, pulling her closer. "I saw that kid using you like a…a… Damn, I couldn't handle it. I don't know what got into me. What were you thinking?"

The fire in her eyes blazed. "I was making tips. Good tips. Enough to pay for my bike and get the hell out of here. Away from—"

"From what?" He had to know. What was she so afraid of?

"From this." Her hands still caught up in his, she gestured around the room with her head.

"From this or from me?" He tilted his head down, trying to get her to meet his gaze.

She let out a sigh and, with it, the anger he sensed boiling underneath the surface. "What do you want from me?"

Well, shit. That was the million-dollar question now, wasn't it? He dropped her hands and doubled over, pressing his palms to his thighs. "I don't know. But I saw him sliding his tongue all over your neck and it…" He shook his head. How could he explain the white-hot rage that had flooded his system? It didn't make sense to him—how could he have lost all shred of control?

Her hands clamped to her hips. "You don't own me, you know. Yes, we have an arrangement, and I appreciate the place to stay, but what I choose to do on my own time is my business."

"Your business?" Anger burned through his belly. He studied the tips of her motorcycle boots as his stomach ignited from within.

"Yes. My business. You can't boss me around—"

He ran his hand down his cheek, rubbing the scruff on his chin. "Dammit. You're worth so much more than that. Don't you know how much…how special…hell, how important you are to…to Kenzie?"

"To Kenzie? This has nothing to do with Kenzie."

His heart clenched. What the hell was wrong with him? He was being an A-1 douchebag, and he didn't care. All he cared about was the feeling of utter helplessness when he'd seen that kid's tongue meet the sweet skin of Jinx's neck. He didn't like it—the loss of control. It made him feel like he was losing his fucking mind.

"You're an asshole." She covered her eyes with her hands and turned away.

He deserved it. Taking in a deep breath, he put a hand on her shoulder. "You're right."

"Hell yeah, I'm right." She dropped her hands as she whipped around to face him. "Wait, what?"

"I said you're right. I *am* an asshole." He tucked his thumbs in his front pockets and searched her face for the slightest sign of understanding.

Her head cocked to the side, the swoop of teal hair hanging down on the right side of her face. She lifted a hand and ran it over the shaved hair on the left side of her head, fiddled with an earring, and then pursed her lips. "Go on."

"I don't know what's going on with me lately. I'm not myself. I'm… There's something right here." He closed his hand into a fist and pounded his chest. "I'm sorry. I'll figure it out."

"You'd better. You can't just manhandle me. I'm not like one of those guys you can cuff and throw in the back of your truck."

Cash raised his hands in surrender. "I know. I'm sorry."

She straightened her shirt. "You better be. What I do on my time is up to me."

"Up to you," Cash agreed.

"That's right." She moved to stand in front of the sink, trying to put herself back together.

His gaze traveled over her, this stranger who'd infiltrated his life, dug her heels into his world, taken up space inside his heart.

"You've got no claim to me." She nodded to herself in the mirror.

No claim. She was right. They'd almost gotten carried away on his couch once. And he'd kissed her under the mistletoe. That didn't exactly constitute a relationship. His heart pounded, sending blood whooshing through his ears. He almost didn't even hear himself speak. "What if I want one?"

Jinx's hand hovered in midair. Her gaze met his in the mirror. "Want one what?"

He moved behind her so close he could smell the scent of her skin. "A claim."

FOURTEEN

A CLAIM? HER STOMACH TIGHTENED, TWISTING IN ON itself. Oh God, she didn't do claims. She couldn't.

"Stop it, Cash. You don't mean it." She studied their reflection in the mirror. His head bent toward her neck, and she could almost feel his lips on her skin.

"What if I do?" His breath tickled the spot where her neck curved into her shoulder. A shiver raced through her.

Her eyes met his. Desire and need simmered in their depths. Her heart surged in her chest. He couldn't mean it. A man like Cash needed stability. He had a kid, for crying out loud. She wasn't exactly stepmom material. How could she be with the kind of role model she'd had? No, her life would never mesh with his, not in a permanent or even semipermanent way.

"I can't. I can't give you what you need."

His finger traced the feather tattoo behind her ear, then slid lower, down her neck and across her collarbone. "What is it you think I need?"

She tried to tamp down the ache pooling between her thighs. "You need someone you can count on. For Kenzie. Not someone who's going to be out of here as soon as possible."

Cash shook his head, nestling the scruff of his chin

against the curve of her neck. Her hands grabbed the edges of the sink before her knees gave out.

"What about what I *want*?" His voice vibrated through her, his lips connecting, searing her skin at each point they touched.

She arched into him, her resolve scattering like ashes in a strong wind.

Want.

He wanted her. She could feel it through the front of his jeans, pressing against her backside. When was the last time a man wanted her? Really, truly wanted her? Would it be so wrong to give in? He was a grown man. Could make his own decisions. Live with the consequences of his actions. It wasn't her job to protect him. Every time she tried to help someone else, it backfired. Maybe it was time to be selfish for a change. She wouldn't be here long. Cash could pick up whatever pieces he needed to once she left.

She nudged into him, pressing her ass against his crotch. A low groan rumbled through his chest. He slid her tank up her back. Placing a hand on either side of her, he trailed kisses from her neck down between her shoulder blades. His lips continued down, over her bra strap, across her lower back, stopping at the edge of her miniskirt.

If he was waiting for encouragement, she'd give it to him. She lifted the edge of her skirt, shimmying it up over her hips. He stood behind her and met her gaze in the mirror. She nodded.

His hands left the edges of the sink long enough to unbuckle his jeans and slide on a condom. Then they were back, running over her thighs, slipping her boy shorts down her legs. Her breath caught as he reached a hand around her navel, his fingers tracing a line across her stomach, zeroing in on the apex of her thighs. As he entered her from behind, his fingers found their mark, and she bucked against him.

With her back at his front, he was in control, and she didn't like it. She tried to spin, but his arm clamped around her middle. "Let me make you feel good. I've got you."

She met his gaze in the mirror and stopped trying to take over. Gentle, tender kisses landed on her neck, her collarbone, behind her ear. He slowed the rhythm, barely moving, letting her feel each sensation as it hit her. When they'd almost hooked up before, it had been a relentless, erratic, heart-pounding frenzy. That was what she was used to. Not this slow, erotic dance. It was like he was taking pieces of her with him each time he pushed in and pulled back.

It felt like more. More than just sex. More than just a quick one-night stand.

She could do the fucking. But this, this pull on her heart, the tenderness, the connection…it was too much.

"Let go," Cash whispered into her neck before rimming her ear with his tongue. His fingers caressed her, igniting a slow burn that glowed deep down inside.

"I can't." Tears burned behind her eyelids. She fought through the surge of emotion welling up inside her chest. What the hell was happening? Her body had never betrayed her like this before. Sex was sex. That's all. She bucked against him, trying to increase the pace, trying to get him off so she could bury herself back inside her shell and avoid this terrifying feeling.

But instead of moving with her, he stopped.

"Jinx."

She ignored him.

"Jinx, look at me."

Reluctantly, she met his gaze. The kindness, the caring, the empathy shone bright in the dim light from the bare overhead bulb. That's one thing she couldn't stand. She didn't want his sympathy.

"I can't do this with you."

"Just let go. I've got you."

Eyes locked in the mirror, he moved against her. Gentle. So tender, it gutted her. She didn't deserve this kind of attention. She couldn't give him what he needed; he knew that. Why not walk away?

Her body hummed under his touch. The glow sparked, igniting a burn that coiled in her core, then began to spread. She stopped trying to reason with herself. Sensation took over. Cash's hand on her breast, his breath on her neck, his fingers coaxing her to a slow, intense climax.

Like a wave that started a mile offshore, her release built, slowly rolling into itself until she couldn't hold it back. It crashed over her, sending her reeling, so she couldn't tell which way was up. She didn't have a choice but to ride it out, letting each sensation dissipate until she felt herself floating back down.

Strong arms anchored her. "That's it. Let it go. Give in to me." Cash thrust, filling her, finally letting himself take his own pleasure.

She watched his reflection in the mirror. Muscles taut, his jaw slack, eyes closed as he came down from his own release.

This man, this good man, wanted her. When was the last time someone cared enough about her to fight for her attention? Never.

"You okay?" He nuzzled into her neck.

For once in her life, she didn't feel the urge to pull away first. "Yeah, actually, I am."

His gaze met hers in the mirror. "It's going to be okay, Jinx."

She nodded. Maybe she owed it to herself to explore this new feeling. To see if she could be the woman he wanted *and* needed. At least for a little while, until she left Holiday and everyone in it behind.

⟶

"You look pretty darn pleased with yourself." Jinx slung her bag over her shoulder while Cash held the door open for her.

Something had shifted between them tonight, like she'd decided to stop fighting the attraction and give in to it. Truth was, he *was* pretty darn pleased with himself. After the quick stint in the utility room, she'd burrowed into him. The hard shell she'd coated her heart with had cracked, and he felt like he'd been given special access to a buried part of her. Now he had to figure out how to avoid screwing it all up.

With his arm draped over her shoulder on their way out of the Rambling Rose, he figured they were off to a good start. She hadn't shrugged him off yet, not even when Charlie had raised an eyebrow at them while saying good night. Progress was progress.

He led her around to the passenger side of his truck and opened the door, another first. Not that he hadn't tried before, but she'd always scrambled ahead, opening the door for herself.

"I am pretty pleased with myself," he admitted. Her eyebrow lifted. "It's not every night I get to bust up a fight *and* take a tumble in the storeroom with a beautiful woman."

She swung her legs into the cab. "Hmm. You seemed pretty comfortable in that storeroom."

He stepped on the running board and planted a kiss on her cheek. "You're the first gal I've tumbled with in the storeroom. Cross my heart."

Her palm flattened against the front of his wrinkled undershirt. "Is that what I felt against my backside earlier? Your heartbeat? And here I thought cowboys were heartless savages."

"No, that was something else entirely. And lucky for you, I'm not a cowboy. That's Waylon's department." He shut the door and rounded the front of the truck to climb in beside her.

The air held a chill—as much as mid-December in the Hill Country could muster. But still, it reminded him that the holidays would soon be upon them. Could he convince Jinx to stick around through Christmas? He'd take the time he could get with her. Even though it went against everything he'd been telling himself he needed, he couldn't fight the feelings being around her brought up.

Logically, there was no reason he ought to be attracted to Jinx. She wasn't his type. A half-shaved head of blue hair. Enough metal to build a barbed-wire fence. Definitely not. But then again, Lori

Lynne had supposedly been his type, and look where that had gotten him.

"We headed to my place or yours?" he asked.

"You're being fairly presumptuous, aren't you?" The side-eye glance she gave him lacked the frostiness from earlier.

He turned the key in the ignition and fired up the truck. "Based on recent events, I thought you might want to invite me in when I drop you off tonight."

She buckled her seat belt, clicking it into place. "Isn't my place technically your place anyway?"

"Good point. My place it is."

Jinx twisted a piece of hair between her fingers. "You really want to do this?"

"What, drive you home?"

"You know what I mean. I'm not sticking around. I don't want you to get any ideas."

"The only ideas I'm getting are you and me on my memory foam mattress, not bending over some chipped porcelain sink. You with me on that?"

"Casual. No expectations."

Cash reached over and squeezed her exposed knee. "Well, I expect I'll have some expectations."

"That's what I'm talking about."

"Not what I meant. I expect we'll spend more time awake than asleep."

"I sure hope so. You snore."

He eased the truck out of the gravel lot and onto the pavement. "Well, I guess you'd better keep me up then."

"Oh, I'll keep you up all right. You'll just need to make sure you can stay up, old man." Her smile flashed white in the seat next to him.

"Old, huh? How old do you think I am?"

She rolled her eyes. "How old do I think you actually are, or how old do I think you act?"

His jaw just about dropped. "Wha—both. How old are you, pretty, young thing?"

"Twenty-three. My guess is you're about forty, but you act like you're going on seventy."

His jaw did drop at that. Seventy? Forty? Hell, he'd barely crossed the threshold of thirty-five. "Damn, you're harsh. I'm thirty-five, not forty."

"Seriously? Thirty-five? That's still old." She shook her head back and forth. Mocking. Teasing.

When was the last time he'd joked around with a woman? Typically, he didn't let his guard down enough to crack a smile unless he was talking to Kenzie. Every once in a while, his mom or Charlie could coax a grin out of him. It felt good to banter for a change.

They made the rest of the drive in comfortable silence. The edge of tension that usually hung between them had dissolved. Probably not for long. If he tended to keep things wrapped up tight inside, then Jinx was like a safety deposit box locked inside a vault in comparison. He still didn't know much about her: where exactly she'd come from, what kind of life she'd led growing up. She still didn't even know that he'd overheard her share her real name with Kenzie. Maybe she'd be more willing to share now.

The truck came to rest in front of his garage. "Need anything from the bunkhouse?"

"Nah. But promise me you'll make sure I'm out of here before Kenzie shows up in the morning."

"I think that can be arranged." He stepped out of the truck and walked around to open her door, but she beat him to it.

Hand in hand, they walked to the front door, and he swung it open. Before he could drop his keys on the entry table and hang up his jacket, she kicked off her boots and started making her way toward the bedroom.

He followed behind, picking up the trail of clothes she left in her wake. Her jacket. The tank top. The skirt came next, followed by a bra. Last but not least, the boy shorts sat on the floor in the doorway of the bedroom. He tossed the pile of clothing into the chair in the corner and stripped down himself. Then he joined Jinx under the covers in the hopes that she would indeed keep him up all night.

chapter

FIFTEEN

She woke to warm breath on her ear. Cash's arms wrapped around her, cradling her against him. Whiskers scraped against her cheek as she eased herself out from his embrace. He grunted and readjusted. She tucked her hands under her head and studied him in sleep. His hair, usually hidden under a cowboy hat, stuck out in all directions. Dark lashes rested on his cheeks, and a tiny smattering of freckles splayed across his nose, so faint she hadn't noticed them before. Sleep erased the barrier he'd constructed, and the man in front of her looked nothing like the hard-nosed brute she'd gone head-to-head with on previous occasions. In cop mode, he seemed invincible, like nothing could touch him. Here, next to her in bed, he looked like a man—a man who could be hurt.

She didn't want that kind of power.

The relationships—if she could even call them that—she'd been involved in in the past stemmed from her desire for one thing: survival. Emotions were never involved. She had no problem spending a couple of weeks warming some guy's bed for the chance to sleep indoors for a while or, in the case of Wade, a few months taking his shit in exchange for a place to stay and the good tips she managed at the bar.

But she'd kept her heart out of it. The last time she'd

loved someone with her whole heart and soul, he'd died.
Since then, she had made a habit out of keeping her
feelings buried—deep under thick layers of protection.
She'd do anything to avoid the pain and heartache she'd
felt when her dad died. Anything.

Her toes met the cold wood floor as she slid out of
bed, grabbed her clothes from the chair, and took refuge
in the bathroom for a few minutes. She had to pull herself
together. Cash made her want things she'd never thought
possible. Things she'd never thought she deserved.

A few minutes later, she sat on a barstool while she
waited for a pot of coffee to brew, tapping her feet against
the kitchen island. Her mom had spent her entire life
dependent on a man. When Jinx's dad died, she hadn't
known what to do with herself, so before the grass even
started to grow over his burial plot, she'd moved them in
with a guy she'd met at a bar. When that didn't work out,
they'd lived in the back of an SUV for a couple of weeks
until she met someone else. She had a thing for cops.
Thought those who were committed to protect and serve
would carry that responsibility through to their personal
lives. And so it went. Until the last guy had assumed that
Jinx was part of the deal too.

When she wouldn't give in to snuggling with her new
"stepfather," he had told her to get with the program or
get the hell out. She had chosen the latter option and had
been on her own ever since.

Watching her mom choose a man over her own
daughter had taught her a few things. First, she never
wanted to put that much faith and hope into another
human being ever again. It was a guaranteed path to
pain. Second, she must not be worth very much if her

own mother would stick with a relative stranger over her own flesh and blood.

The coffeepot let out a final burst of steam. Jinx poured half the carafe into a travel mug and left the pot on for Cash. She couldn't afford to get caught by Kenzie at her dad's place again. That kid was smart, much smarter than Jinx had been at her age.

She shrugged her jacket over her shoulders and slipped her feet into her boots. With a final look around Cash's living room, she pulled the heavy wood door closed behind her and made the trek to the bunkhouse. Kenzie had taken to pet-sitting Hendrix overnight on the nights her dad worked at the Rose, so Jinx entered the bunkhouse to a lonely stillness. She changed into her leggings and curled up on her lower bunk, letting the quiet swallow her.

The fuzzy edges of early morning transformed the inside of the cabin. A dark lump on the bunk next to her slowly morphed into the outline of her backpack. The thin mattress creaked as she flipped onto her back, staring at the bunk above. The stillness hadn't bothered her before. She'd welcomed it, like a break in a raging storm. But now, compared to the cozy warmth of Cash's cabin, the bunkhouse seemed barren.

She punched her pillow and twisted onto her side. This was enough for now. She had a place to stay, a good-paying job, and an apartment waiting for her in New Orleans. That was as much as she could hope for, as much as she deserved.

Jinx sat up straight, jerked from a dreamless sleep by a loud banging noise that came from the front door. She tossed the covers aside and stumbled to her feet. The sky outside the wavy paned window gave no hint to what time of day it might be. Gray clouds hung low, blotting out the sun and reminding her that winter in Texas looked a lot different than it did in LA.

With her sweatshirt pulled tight around her, she answered the door. Cash and Kenzie stood on the front porch. Hendrix nestled in Kenzie's arms, a tiny Santa hat secured to his head.

"Well, there you are." Cash held out a thermal mug of coffee.

"Of course she's here, Daddy. She lives here." Kenzie skipped into the open living area, her little pink boots clunking across the wide-planked floor. "Look what Nana made for Hendrix, Jinx. She said she'll sew him a coat too. Won't that be awesome?"

"Yeah, awesome." Jinx rubbed her eyes, not sure how Hendrix would feel about being a fashion model, since he barely tolerated a collar when she tried to put it on him.

Cash grinned, then leaned in and brushed a kiss along Jinx's cheek as he followed his daughter.

The contact made her reel backward, and she knocked her head on the door.

"You okay?" Cash's brow furrowed.

The poor man must be getting whiplash, trying to keep up with her mood swings. When she was with him, she wanted to believe there was a chance for her to find a happily ever after. But then reality would set in, and she'd come to her senses. Whatever was going on between them had her head and heart trapped in some sort of spin cycle.

"Yeah. I'm exhausted though. What time is it?" Jinx closed the door behind them.

"Nine o'clock." Cash shrugged his shoulders. "I'm taking Kenzie into town for breakfast with Santa, and she wouldn't go without you."

Jinx groaned. She'd come back to the bunkhouse around six. That meant she'd gotten a total of maybe four hours of sleep. No wonder the backs of her eyelids felt like steel wool every time she blinked.

"You've gotta come." Kenzie sidled up next to her. "They have cinnamon rolls and juice, and Daddy said they might even have a real live reindeer."

"Hmm. Cinnamon rolls and juice. That *is* tempting." Jinx scratched Hendrix under the collar. "I didn't know they had reindeer in Texas."

Kenzie leveled her with an eye roll that would have looked more appropriate coming from someone three times her age. "The reindeer is from the North Pole, Jinx. Duh."

Jinx bit her lip to keep from laughing and met Cash's gaze. "Of course."

It had been a very long time since she'd been around a kid during the holidays. Back before Wade, she'd worked at a diner. The waitress there had a grandson who'd visited over Easter. But when his grandma suggested they go to the community center for an Easter egg hunt, he'd shaken his head and said he'd rather go hunt for rabbits in the desert with his BB gun. That the Easter bunny was for babies and losers. He was five. Hopefully, Kenzie had a few more years of believing in the magic of Christmas before she became as cynical.

"So what do you say? Want to join us for

breakfast?" Cash leaned against the counter. "It's not every day you get to meet one of Santa's official reindeer."

"Do I have time to shower?" She still had a layer of salt and sweat covering her skin from her late night at the bar.

"If you make it quick." Cash crossed the room and snagged her jacket from the hook by the front door.

"Five minutes. And I need to brush my teeth too." Jinx grabbed some clothes and headed toward the bathroom.

Eight minutes later, she emerged to find Kenzie tapping her foot by the door.

"We're going to miss the reindeer." Kenzie thrust her arms into her coat.

"Okay, I'm sorry. Let's go." Jinx shrugged into the jacket Cash held out for her.

"For what it's worth, I'm tired this morning too," he whispered into her ear as he helped her into her coat.

"I was up too late. All that talking—"

"And sex," he mumbled. "Don't forget about the sex."

She batted his hand away. A low chuckle vibrated through his chest.

She'd never be able to forget about the sex. Cash took sex to a whole new level. That was a given.

ℋ

Cash threaded his fingers through Jinx's on the way into the community center. It felt natural, not like he hadn't held hands with a woman over the age of seven in more than five years. Entering the room hand in hand would be making a statement. Nothing went unnoticed in a town the size of Holiday. "This okay?"

She glanced down at their entwined fingers. "It's your funeral, buddy."

His brow crinkled. Why did he constantly feel like he was forcing things on her? Somehow, even though he still felt like there was something off with her, he'd chalked up his feelings of apprehension as fear of getting attached. He'd decided to budge from his adamant stance. Why was letting someone close such a battle for her? "What do you mean by that?"

Shrugging her shoulders, she looked around the crowded hall. "Nobody here knows me. You're the one they'll be talking about. I'll be out of here in a couple of weeks."

Kenzie ran ahead to get in line for Santa, so Cash stopped short and pulled Jinx to the side. "I don't give a crap about what anyone else thinks. Are *you* okay with this?"

She met his gaze. A flicker of vulnerability flashed through her bluish-gray eyes before that familiar hard glint slid back in place. "Just don't lay one on me like you did at the mini-mart, 'kay?"

"Hey, you started it." He grinned. "I'll do my best to keep my lips off you."

"I'd appreciate that, cowboy."

"At least until later," he muttered to himself.

"Should we go find Kenzie before she eats all the cinnamon rolls?" Jinx raised a brow.

Cash scanned the crowd, looking for the lopsided topknot in the sea of bows and festive hair bands. Poor kid. He should have thought to dress her up in her Christmas dress for her picture with Santa.

Instead of locating his daughter, his gaze landed on Dixie King, who sliced through the crowd like a knife through butter, heading their way.

"Hi there, Deputy Walker." Dixie stopped short in front of them. She looked down toward their joined hands, then bit her lip before a sly grin slid over her face. "Wasn't expecting to see you here this morning, Jinx."

Jinx rolled her eyes toward Cash. He couldn't tell if it was a secret gal pal signal or a cry for help, so he waited. "I wasn't exactly planning on being here."

"Kenzie really wanted her to come." Cash cleared his throat. His voice had come out somewhat squeaky. What the hell was up with that?

"Mmm." Dixie nodded in exaggerated agreement. "Kenzie. By the way, where is that adorable daughter of yours?"

"She's…um"—Cash scanned the heads of the crowd again—"maybe I'd better go look for her. Will you be okay?" For a moment, he shut out the chatter of the crowd, turning his full attention on Jinx.

Dixie's hand landed on his arm. "Of course she'll be okay. She'll be with me. I need to ask her some questions about some stuff she's helping me plan at the Rose."

"You know, I'm standing right here." Jinx slid her hand from his. The sudden lack of warmth made him realize how much he'd enjoyed holding hands with someone for a change. An adult someone. "I don't need a babysitter. I've managed to survive this long on my own."

"Get on outta here, Cash. Go rustle up your daughter, and find us some coffee, will you?" Dixie linked her arm through Jinx's, leading her toward an empty table.

As they moved away, Dixie chattering like an amped-up squirrel, Jinx laughed. The sound washed over him. She'd giggled and let out a couple of obnoxious laugh-type snorts when they'd been together. But nothing like the sound that poured out of her at something Dixie said. In that moment, he vowed to do whatever he could to get her to make that noise again.

He ducked under a makeshift candy-cane arch and found his daughter wedged between his mother's knees. She had a hairbrush in one hand and Kenzie's mass of untamed curls in the other.

"When's the last time you worked a brush through this child's hair?"

Cash winced under his mom's disapproving stare. "She likes to brush it herself."

"Hi, Daddy." Kenzie beamed up at him. "Where's Jinx? I want her to see me sit in Santa's lap."

"You brought Jinx with you?" The hairbrush paused in his mother's hand.

"Yeah. We woke her up to come with us." Kenzie twisted a candy cane around her finger.

Cash braced himself for the onslaught of questions and comments.

Instead, his mother focused her attention back on Kenzie's nest of hair. "Well, isn't that nice. I bet she'll have a real good time."

What? No interrogation? No loaded remarks?

"Do you want one braid or two, doll baby?" She bent her head toward Kenzie's ear. "I brought some Christmas ribbon I can weave through it if you want."

"Two, Nana. Can you do two, please?"

"You bet, sugar. Cash, why don't you go find your father? He's supposed to take over the raffle ticket table at ten, and I bet he's out bending poor Cooper's ear about growing grapes again. Did he tell you he wants to start making wine? I thought we were going to retire now that Waylon's taken over."

"Sure, Mom. Kenzie, you stay here with Nana while I go find Papa, okay? When I come back, we'll get in line for Santa."

"But first we find Jinx." Kenzie nodded, confident her grown-ups would bend to her will.

Cash gave her a wink, not missing the knowing smile his mom cast his way. Women. They spoke a language all their own. He'd been happily oblivious to it for so long. Looked like his time for blessed ignorance had run out.

He ducked outside in search of his dad.

"Yo, Cash." Dwight ambled across the parking lot, headed his way.

"What are you doing here? Going to sit in Santa's lap?"

"Hell no. But I wouldn't miss the bake sale. I've gotta get my hands on one of your mom's pumpkin pies. She make any pecan this time?"

Cash's stomach rumbled at the mention of his mom's pecan pie. "No. But she promised for Christmas. Hey, can I ask you something?"

"Sure. Just make it quick."

"About Jinx's bike. She said it's almost ready. You think you'll have it done before Christmas?"

"At the rate I'm going, I don't know why not."

"Would there be anything that might delay your work?"

"What are you gettin' at? You want me to break something else?"

"No, nothing like that. I just know Kenzie will be crushed if she leaves before the holidays, that's all."

"Then why don't you ask her to stay?" Dwight squinted at him from under the brim of his baseball cap.

How could he tell the man that's the one thing he could never do? "It's not that easy."

Dwight shrugged. "All right. You want me to take a hammer to it, you just let me know."

"Um, no. Definitely do not damage the bike. We clear on that?" Cash shook the hand Dwight thrust at him.

"Fine. But if you want to make a move, you're running out of time." Dwight dropped his hand.

How could Dwight somehow sound like the voice of reason? "Thanks. I'll keep that in mind."

Cash managed to find his father, exactly where his mom thought he would be. Tom had cornered Cooper Justice by the juice table. Cooper had some fancy degree from Texas A&M and had taken over a failing tract of land on the outskirts of town and turned it into a working vineyard. Tom had been keeping an eye on his progress and got a wild hair to try his hand at wine making as well. As he approached, Cash caught tidbits of the conversation. Something about the acidity of soil. His mom was wasting her time hoping his dad would fully retire and leave the ranching to Waylon. He'd go to the grave with a handful of Texas dirt in his grip. It was in his blood.

By the time he'd rustled up his dad, snagged three cups of coffee, and made his way back to the table where he'd left Jinx, the line for Santa stretched around the perimeter of the room.

"Here you go, ladies. Coffee, as requested." Cash set the three cups down and collapsed into a chair. "It's going to take us an hour to get through that line now."

Dixie checked her watch. "Better get to it then. Santa's only here until eleven."

"Who'd you sweet-talk into taking on the role this year?" Cash scooted his chair closer to Jinx.

"Kermit volunteered again. He only comes into town once a year. Poor guy, out there all alone. I wish he'd socialize more." Dixie stood. "Thanks, Jinx, for saying you'll help. See you tomorrow night."

"What's tomorrow night?" Cash gave Dixie a small wave, then turned his attention toward Jinx.

"I don't know. Something about a fund-raiser auction she wants me to help with."

He nodded. "That's right. The elf thing. Good. Now should we go find Kenzie and get in line?" The more Jinx got involved in the town, the more she might want to stay.

Jinx grabbed her coffee and scooted her chair back. "There she is. Why don't you go get in line, and I'll grab her?"

Cash held the back of her chair as she stood. "Sounds good."

He took up a spot at the back of the line while he watched Jinx fetch Kenzie. The way his daughter smiled up at Jinx filled his heart with warmth. For a moment, he could see the possibilities—making pancakes on Saturday mornings together, swinging Kenzie between them on a walk to the park—possibilities he'd never allowed himself to imagine. Maybe it was time to open up his heart again. Maybe it was time to take a chance.

chapter

SIXTEEN

Jinx and Kenzie joined Cash in the long line for Santa. "You want more coffee?" Cash offered. "I'm going to go grab a refill."

"Sure." She handed him her cup, then leaned against the wall. Kenzie moved in closer, resting her shoulder against Jinx's side. Jinx wrapped an arm loosely around her. This kid reminded her so much of herself as a child. At least before her dad died. Up until that point, she had been curious, had laughed a lot, and was always ready for a hug. Just like Kenzie. But then it all went to hell.

Not willing to let herself go there, she ran a hand over Kenzie's hair. "You've got Christmas break coming up soon. What do you want to do over vacation?" All kids loved Christmas break, right?

"I want to ride my pony."

Jinx nodded. "That sounds like fun."

"And play with all my new toys." Kenzie tapped her index finger to her lips, no doubt giving the question the level of seriousness it deserved in the mind of a seven-year-old. "Can we have a sleepover?"

"You want to invite some friends over to stay the night?" Jinx had never invited friends over to her place as a kid. She'd never really had good enough friends, plus the idea of exposing anyone else to her mom and the current deadbeat boyfriend almost gave her hives.

"Yeah. You." Kenzie giggled and poked Jinx in the belly.

Cash returned, two fresh cups of coffee in hand. "Y'all haven't moved much."

"Jinx is going to spend the night, okay, Daddy?" Kenzie peered up at them, her gaze bouncing between them.

He'd been about to swallow a sip of coffee. Instead, he spurted brown liquid from his mouth and let it dribble down his chin. "Say what?" He lifted a thin paper napkin to wipe his chin clean.

"We can watch a movie and eat popcorn. It'll be fun. Just like Aunt Darby and Uncle Waylon do when I go over there."

"And when is this supposed to be happening?" Cash asked.

"Can we do it tonight? Oh, please!"

"Jinx has to work tonight, Tadpole. Some other time, okay?" He nudged her forward in line.

A sleepover… Jinx mulled the idea over, expecting to feel the telltale signs of an oncoming freak-out at the mere thought of spending an official night with Kenzie and Cash. Instead of the walls of her chest squeezing together, she took in a deep breath. Her lungs expanded. Her heart warmed at the thought of snuggling next to Cash on the sectional with Kenzie tucked between them. The fact that she wasn't having a panic attack almost sent her reeling headfirst into a panic attack. As she listened to Cash tell a particularly bad holiday joke, she tried to figure out what that meant.

By the time they reached Santa, Cash had exhausted all his cheesy jokes and even a few he looked up on his phone. The man would stop at nothing to amuse his little girl. Jinx used to take up major real estate in someone's heart like that. She hadn't let herself remember how it felt to be the center of someone's world in a long, long time. It hurt too much. Being around the two of them made her miss it. Even though the pain still cut like a hacksaw through her chest when she let herself recall the happy days before her dad died, she'd found herself reliving them more in the past couple of weeks than she had in years.

Kenzie was lucky to have a dad like Cash. He might come across as callous, stubborn, and bullheaded in his interactions with grown-ups, but he melted like a pat of butter on a stack of his homemade buttermilk pancakes when it came to Kenzie.

"Ho, ho, ho! Happy holidays, Kenzie. Hop on up here and tell Santa what you want for Christmas this year." Santa patted his thigh with a gloved hand.

Kenzie clambered onto his lap, leaving Jinx and Cash behind.

Cash leaned into her, whispering against her ear, "Are you next?"

"For what?" Jinx asked.

"Sitting on Santa's lap and telling him what you want for Christmas."

"I'm not going to give some pervy old man a thrill. Besides, Santa never came through for me as a kid, so why would that change now?" She regretted the words as soon as she said them. "Sorry, it's just that Christmas was never a big deal when I was growing up."

"Well then, you're in for a treat, Ms. Jacobs." Cash's mouth split into a grin. "Christmastime is the best time to be in Holiday." He whipped his phone out of his pocket.

"What are you doing?"

"Texting Charlie. Telling her I want to steal her star employee for the evening and make you late for work tonight."

Jinx wrapped her hand around his arm. "No, I can't."

"Did she tell you how slow it would be? Nobody's going to be there anyway. It's the annual tree-lighting ceremony."

"She did say we probably wouldn't have anyone come in until later because of that."

"What do you say? I think it's high time you see how much fun embracing the holiday spirit can be. I can run you over after."

"But—"

He held his phone out to her, showing her Charlie's reply. "Charlie said it's okay."

Jinx flip-flopped back and forth. He couldn't just take control of her schedule like that. But on the other hand, the thought of spending the evening with Cash and Kenzie did sound pretty appealing.

"Okay. But we have to leave early so I can get to the Rose before the crowd."

"You're going to love it, I promise. It's the kickoff for the Jingle Bell Jamboree. Kenzie and I always go." He leaned in close to nibble on her earlobe. "And if you're really good, I'll let you sit on my lap later and tell me what you want for Christmas."

Smiling, she nudged an elbow into his ribs. "I told you I wasn't up for giving a pervy old man a thrill."

"Oh, sweetheart, I plan on being the one delivering the thrills."

chapter
SEVENTEEN

THE SMALL DOWNTOWN SPARKLED LIKE SOMEONE HAD
doused it in spray-on glitter. Twinkle lights outlined
the buildings, and iridescent snowflakes dangled from
the streetlights. Two of the Belgian draft horses from
Waylon's stock pulled a flatbed wagon that had been
decked out to look like Santa's sled and was full of kids.
Bells hung from the horses' necks, jingling and jangling
as they passed through the main street of town. The diner
had gone so far as to rent several snow cone machines
and were making "snow" for the Make It Before It Melts
snowman contest.

"What do you want to do first?" Cash asked. He held
Kenzie's hand in her pink-and-purple-striped glove in one
hand and Jinx's ring-clad fingers in the other.

"Can we make a snowman?" Kenzie pulled them
toward the snowman contest. "They ran out of snow last
year before we got a chance to do it. Remember, Daddy?"

He and Jinx followed behind her, linked together like
a three-person chain.

"Be careful with that critter, Kenz." Cash nodded
toward where Hendrix nestled against her chest. His
mother had made Kenzie a carrier for him like that infant
sling thing he'd seen on Charlie's baby shower registry.

Kenzie dropped his hand to pat Hendrix on the head

and adjust his little Santa hat. "Don't worry, Daddy. He's fine."

"Until he pees on you," Cash muttered under his breath.

"It's like fifty-some degrees out. How's she going to make a snowman?" Jinx stepped next to him as they stopped in front of a long table.

Ruth, one of the regular waitresses from the diner, set a tub of freshly shaved ice in front of Kenzie. "Here you go, sweets. Build your creation, then make sure we get a picture of it before it starts to melt so we can enter you in the contest."

Kenzie gripped the sides of the tub, trying to lift it up off the table. Cash stood behind her to put his hands over hers. "Where should we do our building?" he asked.

"Over there." Kenzie nodded toward an empty spot in front of Whitey's Western Wear. Together, they hefted the tub of snow.

"What are we trying to do here?" Jinx didn't appear to be all in on this one.

"We've got to make a snowman or something before the snow melts. Kenzie, what do you want to make?" Cash dumped the bucket onto the plastic tablecloth. The ice had already started melting. Water ran off the edge of the table to drip onto the sidewalk.

"We could just make a snowman." Kenzie shrugged.

"You want to win?" Cash couldn't keep his competitive side from coming out. Didn't matter if it was a friendly family football game or a snowman-building contest geared toward kids.

"What do you win?" Jinx stood a little more than a foot back from the table.

"Bragging rights. Oh, and your picture on the wall of the diner. Big stakes here, huh?"

Jinx shook her head. "If you say so."

Kenzie took off a glove to dip a finger into the snow. "How about a snow family? A daddy, a mommy, and a little girl."

Cash glanced to Jinx to gauge her reaction. Her eyes widened. "How about we do Pork Chop out of snow?" he suggested. Steering Kenzie away from creating the perfect snow family seemed like a better option.

"Can we do Pork Chop with her mom and dad?" Kenzie didn't seem ready to give up on the idea of a happy family holiday, even if it had to be pig-friendly.

The corner of Jinx's mouth tugged up. She took a step toward Kenzie to swipe at the end of her braid. "Now that I have to see."

Yeah, he wanted to see how they were going to pull that off too. "Okay, let's get moving." Cash dug his hands into the ice, smashing it together to form a denser ball. "Kenzie, why don't you get started on Pork Chop, okay?"

She tossed her other glove onto the table and grabbed two handfuls of snow.

"What are you waiting for, a special invitation?" Cash flung a glob of snow at Jinx.

"Careful, cowboy. Paybacks are hell." She rolled her eyes at Kenzie. "I know, I know. The curse jar."

Cash couldn't keep his grin to himself. As they molded the frozen bits of ice into something resembling a trio of pigs, he let himself wonder what it would be like to actually be a family of three. He'd been so focused on his baby girl for so long, trying to give her everything she needed. But there were certain things he couldn't do for her. His mom was right. Kenzie needed a positive female role model in her life. Until now, he'd assumed his mom or his sister could fill that role. They'd done a fantastic job of being there for her. But they couldn't be everywhere forever.

Now, with Charlie starting her own family and his mom and dad talking about retiring and spending half the year traipsing around the country in an RV, he had to give serious thought to who would fill that void. Watching Kenzie with Jinx made him more aware than ever of how much she'd been missing out on without a mom in her life—how much he'd been missing out on without someone to share his life with too.

Aside from making the parenting stuff easier, there'd been a hole in his heart since Lori Lynne had left. They hadn't been right for each other. Odds were it never would have lasted, even if she hadn't walked out on them. But he'd opened himself up to the idea of sharing his life, his love, and his heart with someone when she'd told him she was pregnant. He'd been excited about the possibility of a future, of building the kind of life his mom and dad shared.

Looking at Jinx, the polar opposite of the type of woman he'd expected to share a future with, the possibility of forever didn't seem so unimaginable.

"There. What do you think?" Jinx lifted her hands off the pile of snow she'd been molding to reveal a pretty good-looking pig.

"That's perfect!" Kenzie hopped up and down in front of her puddle of melted ice. "Will you do mine too? Please?"

"I'll help you with it. Hurry, before it all turns to water." Jinx and Kenzie set to constructing another pig.

By the time they had finished, Cash had perfected his version of papa pig. He set his snow creation in between the two they'd made. "There we go. They're perfect."

"Don't you mean… Oh, forget it." Jinx shook her head.

"What?" Cash pressed.

"Nothing. It's too cheesy, even for the two of you."

"Come on, Jinx. Tell us." Kenzie grabbed on to her arm with both hands.

"I was just going to say"—Jinx snorted, channeling her inner sow—"don't you mean they're pork-fect?"

"Aw, you're right. Way too cheesy." Cash grabbed a handful of leftover ice and lunged at her, trying to slide it down her back before she wriggled away.

Kenzie erupted into a fit of giggles and joined in the chase. Hendrix yipped and yapped from his perch while Cash caught Jinx in one arm and wrapped the other around Kenzie, pulling them all together for a group hug. He couldn't remember the last time his heart had felt so light or that everything had seemed so right in his world.

"Y'all done? I'd better get a picture of that before it melts." Ruth held her phone out to snap a picture of the trio of snow pigs. "Now let me get one of the three of you. Smile and say cheese."

"Cheese!" Kenzie smiled so hard, Cash could barely see her eyes.

Ruth checked her screen. "I'll text that one to you, Deputy. It's perfect."

"You mean pork-fect?" Kenzie clapped her hands together.

Jinx burst out laughing. Cash could barely catch his breath. He'd never again be able to think of anything as *perfect* without remembering the magic of this night.

"Okay, enough hog humor. Let's go see what other trouble we can cause." He lifted Kenzie onto his shoulders and took hold of Jinx's hand. "The tree lighting ought to be happening soon. Should we go check?"

"Giddyup, Daddy." Kenzie pummeled his chest with her heels, urging him forward.

They joined what appeared to be the entire town of Holiday plus a good portion of the surrounding communities near the giant pine tree at the end of the downtown area. As promised, a big flat screen sat next to the tree, pictures from the Kissmas Cams captured all over town playing while the church choir sang Christmas carols. Someone had even set up a petting zoo for the kids.

"What's on the tree?" Jinx rose to her tiptoes, trying to see over the heads of the small crowd in front of them.

"They pick a theme every year. I think this time it's a down-home country Christmas." He squinted at the tree. "Looks like they have it decked out in a chili pepper garland."

Kenzie let go of his ears to tap on his head. "Can we get a tree this big?"

"Aw, Tadpole, this wouldn't fit in the house." The tree had to be at least thirty feet tall. "But I promise we'll get a tree this year."

"A real one?"

"Yep."

"Don't you usually have a tree?" Jinx squeezed his hand.

"Well, we normally spend Christmas Eve at the big

house with my mom and dad. They love seeing Kenzie wake up on Christmas morning to find out what Santa brought her. Seems silly to decorate when it's just the two of us, y'know?" When he said it out loud, it sounded like a pathetic excuse. "You ever put up a tree for the holidays?"

"Me?" Jinx screwed her mouth into a frown. "I'm usually the one working the holiday shifts, since I don't have kids or family. Everyone else wants those days off. I'll take the overtime and the extra holiday pay every time."

"But not this year." He stated it like it was a foregone conclusion. A fact.

"Not this year?"

"Nope."

"But by Christmas, my bike should be fixed."

Cash lifted their linked hands and pressed a kiss against her palm. "Don't say it, okay?"

"But—"

He shook his head. "Let's not talk about it tonight." He knew she couldn't wait to get out of town, put hundreds of miles between them. But he didn't want to hear it tonight. It had been such a perfect day, he couldn't stand for her to spoil it with talk about leaving.

"Kenzie, let's go get your picture taken with Pork Chop." Cash began to make his way toward the tree. Every year, Charlie brought the Rambling Rose's pig mascot to the Jingle Bell Jamboree to pose for pictures. For a donation to their charity of choice, festivalgoers could snap a photo next to the pig.

"Is she wearing a costume?" Jinx asked.

"She always dresses up like an oinking elf," Kenzie said. "Oh, look, there's you and Daddy kissing!"

Cash looked toward the screen, where he and Jinx stood lip to lip under the mistletoe at the mini-mart.

"Great, just great." Jinx tucked her chin against her chest.

"Don't be embarrassed. They manage to get everyone eventually." Cash kept his eyes on the screen where the next picture showed Presley with a blond on one side and a brunette on the other. They both had their lips pressed to his cheeks while he smiled directly into the camera. One of these days, his brother would get what was coming to him. The sooner the better.

When they reached the line to pose with Pork Chop, Cash lifted Kenzie off his shoulders and set her on her feet.

"Here." Jinx reached for the dog. "Why don't you let me take him to go potty while you get your picture taken?" Kenzie passed her the leash, and Jinx turned toward a patch of grass on the other side of the street. "Back in a sec."

While Cash waited for the family in front of them to arrange themselves around Pork Chop, Charlie walked over.

"How's it going?" he asked.

"Okay. Pork Chop is a hit. Blows my mind what a great marketing stunt the pig mascot has been."

"And how are you feeling?" She must have been wearing Beck's coat. The sleeves were rolled up, and it reached down to her knees.

Charlie sighed. "I'm tired of being fat. I'm tired of being hangry all the time. But most of all, I'm tired of being tired."

"Wish I could tell you it gets easier, but that would be a lie."

"I know." She put her hand on Cash's shoulder. "Oh no."

"What?" He turned to see what had gotten her attention. Pork Chop stood, shaking off the jingle bells and elf hat they'd secured around her head. The family who'd just had their picture snapped with her backed away. The pig squealed, then took off like a missile toward the other side of the street—where Jinx stood with Hendrix.

Cash raced after her, trying to nab the red-and-white leash trailing behind her. The crowd in front of the tree parted. Hendrix leapt out of Jinx's arms, and Pork Chop banked left, running around the back side of the tree. Jinx met Cash in front of the risers where the choir had just started on the chorus of "Rocking Around the Christmas Tree."

"Where did they go?" Jinx asked.

"Around back. You go that way, and I'll go this way. Hopefully, we'll catch them." Cash started around his side.

Hendrix ran past with Pork Chop hot on his heels. Her hoof caught in the extension cord that was hooked to the speakers. One of them went down. Cash dove for it, trying to prevent it from crashing to the pavement. He missed.

Hendrix passed him again, then Pork Chop came around the tree, the speaker and a string of lighted snowflakes dragging behind her. As he scrambled to his feet, Jinx stopped next to him.

"We've got to catch them." She huffed and puffed, trying to catch her breath. "They're going to take out all the A/V equipment."

Cash put his arms out, forcing the crowd to move back from the tree. The lights strung over the choir popped off the backdrop. Some of the choir members continued to sing about everyone dancing merrily while the rest rapidly vacated the risers.

Pork Chop made another lap, this time crashing through the banner advertising the tree lighting. Her vision blocked by the sign, she paused to shake her head. Hendrix jumped up, trying to pull the banner from her eyes.

"Now!" Cash made a grab for the pig.

Right before his hand closed around her collar, she turned on him, knocking him into the base of the tree. As the automatic timer started the countdown, the tree listed left, then right.

10...9...8...7... Cash tried to wrap his arms around the trunk to straighten it.

6...5...4... Jinx joined him in the mess of branches, but the tree continued to sway.

3...2...1... The tree lit up for a brief moment. The crowd oohed and aahed.

Then it fell. Cash watched as the tree tilted backward in slow motion. Ornaments crashed to the ground, while the prerecorded message from the mayor played on fast-forward, making him sound like one of the Chipmunks.

The power went out. Then silence.

No lights.

No music.

No tree.

EIGHTEEN

JINX SET HER BACKPACK DOWN ON THE FLOOR BEHIND the stage at the Rambling Rose. She hadn't been too crazy about the idea of helping Dixie with the fund-raising auction tonight, especially after the fiasco with the tree yesterday. It had taken them all evening to clean up the mess from the broken ornaments and restring the tree with lights. Her picture had even made the front page of the paper, and video some of the people in the crowd had captured on their cell phones had gone viral. If she saw one more clip of her and Cash tumbling into the tree as it fell, she'd swear off the internet forever.

Tonight was her only night off this week, and she'd hoped to spend some time with Cash and Kenzie. But she'd promised Dixie she'd help with the charity auction, and she didn't want to piss off one of the few people who was still willing to speak to her.

Dixie swished by in a ridiculous holiday ensemble. "Right on time. But where's your costume?"

"Where's my what?" Jinx glanced down at her standard black leggings.

"Your costume. Where's your elf costume?" Dixie crossed her arms over her chest. The jingle bells rimming her red-and-green skirt jangled.

Jinx copied her stance. Two could play at this game. "Hey, nobody said anything about a costume. You just asked if I could help out with the fund-raiser." She'd already spent two hours at Dwight's that afternoon painting a whole winter wonderland scene on the windows of the gas station—after she'd spent an hour cleaning decades of grime away. She'd assumed Dixie just needed some help with artwork or something.

"Yes. The Naughty or Nice Elf Auction. As an elf. That means you need to dress the part, just like everyone else." Dixie gestured to a dozen or so people dressed in similar garb behind the stage. "Do you have anything with you that will work?"

The entire town was living in some sort of holiday-crazed twilight zone.

Dixie held out a red-and-green costume. "Lucky for you I have an extra. It'll look so cute on you. Come on. It's for a good cause."

Jinx eyed what appeared to be a scrap piece of material rimmed in some fake fur. "I am not parading around a stage in *that*."

"You said you'd help." Dixie's perfectly painted pink lips pursed into a pout. "Please? You'll only be out there for a couple of minutes."

Jinx clamped her hands to her hips. "Hard no. Absolutely not." The piece of material Dixie held by the fingertips looked more like a fuzzy negligee than an elf costume. "I don't want to be *that* kind of Santa's helper."

Dixie rolled her eyes. "No one's going to think you're that kind of helper. Trust me."

"You're the one who called it a Naughty or Nice Elf Auction. What kind of help are you trying to sell here?"

"I told you. You're on the hook for four hours. Whoever makes the highest bid will have you do some holiday shopping or wrap presents or something. Nothing naughty. We just call it that because it sounds more exciting than calling it the Nice Elf Auction." Dixie waved the strip of fabric. "Come on. The money goes to a women's shelter in Austin. It's a really good cause. Please?"

"I can't believe I let you talk me into this." Why did they have to support a women's shelter? Jinx could have refused if it had been any other kind of event. But doing something for women caught in abusive relationships was a no-brainer. She snagged the costume out of Dixie's hand and stepped into the makeshift backstage dressing room.

"Yay!" Dixie clapped her hands together. "Thanks so much!"

"I'm just trying it on. No promises." Jinx stripped down to her boy shorts to pull the costume up and over her hips. The faux fur–trimmed skirt hit her midthigh. She shimmied the strapless top up over her bra and attempted to zip up the backside. "I can't get the zipper. Can you help me out?"

Dixie flung the curtain back and squealed. "Oh my gosh, you look so adorable."

"Just zip me up." Jinx held the top against her chest while Dixie slid the zipper closed. "Why can't I wear your outfit?"

"Are you kidding me? My daddy would tan my hide if he saw me out in public in something like that."

Jinx let her gaze roam up and down Dixie's much

more modest ensemble: curly-toed slippers, red-and-white-striped tights, a skirt ending at the knees.

"So I have to be the slutty elf because you're afraid of your dad?" She'd love to recall exactly how she'd let Dixie talk her into this. Sure, she'd offered to help at the fund-raiser, but no one had bothered to tell her she'd be selling her services to the highest bidder.

Usually closed on Sunday nights, the Rambling Rose had opened especially for the big event. Dixie bragged that folks came from places as far away as Austin and San Antonio for the annual fund-raiser. Yeehaw. Somehow knowing she was doing her part in providing help to vulnerable women didn't quite make up for the fact that she was about to make her debut as Ho-Ho Holly on the Rambling Rose's stage in front of hundreds of strangers.

"There you go." Dixie stepped back, satisfied with her handiwork. "Hmm. Your bra straps are showing. You've got to lose the straps, or the bra's got to go."

"Hey, I showed up. I put on the costume. But there is no way in hell I'm going out there without a bra on."

Dixie sighed and clucked her tongue. "Charlie! Can you come give us an opinion?"

Charlie wobbled over to where Dixie and Jinx stood, eyes locked in a stare down. "What's up?"

"The bra straps. They don't really gel with the holiday vibe, wouldn't you agree?" Dixie asked.

"Yeah, it's too late for Halloween." Charlie tilted her head. "What does the rest of your bra look like?"

"What?" Jinx covered her shoulders with her hands. "They're supposed to look like spider webs. I picked it up on clearance."

Dixie held out a hand. "The bra."

"Whatever." Jinx jerked the straps down and managed to twist herself out of the bra without losing the top half of the costume. "Better?"

"Much," Charlie and Dixie answered in unison.

"Let's get this over with." Jinx stepped to the edge of the stage as Presley took the mic.

"Ladies and gentlemen, welcome to the tenth annual Naughty or Nice Elf Auction. We've got a great lineup for a great cause tonight. Just a few house rules before we get started. Our elves are volunteers. You're bidding on a four-hour block of their time to help with your holiday preparations. But you can't have them do anything you wouldn't do yourself." Presley shielded his eyes from the spotlight and scanned the audience. "I'm talking to you, Dwight."

The crowd let out a low rumble of laughter.

"All right. Bids are binding, and all volunteer hours need to be used before December thirty-first. Let's get started. First up, our own Dixie King."

Dixie twirled onto the stage, her curly-toed slippers jingling as she skipped over to Presley's side.

"Can we get the bidding started at fifty bucks?"

Several hands rose into the air. Jinx waited, the anxiousness in her stomach clawing its way up her throat. Dixie worked the crowd, blowing kisses to the bidders, while Presley pushed for a higher amount.

Finally, after two of the Rose's regulars battled it out with their bidding cards, Presley announced the final winning bid. "Sold for two hundred bucks to Charity King."

Dixie skipped across the stage to where Jinx stood

clutching the edge of the curtain. "At least that was more than last year."

"Is that your mom?"

"Yep. My folks would never let me go to someone else. Daddy hates this auction, but he knows it's for a good cause." She adjusted the row of giant bells lining the front of Jinx's costume. "Statler's up next. We'll save you for a little later."

Jinx took in a deep breath through her nose and blew it out of her mouth while Charlie's brother strode onto the stage in a red-and-green-striped onesie.

"Ladies, eat your hearts out. Here comes Holiday's second-most-eligible bachelor." Presley lowered his voice a notch. "We all know who's first on that list, don't we?"

Statler threw a fake punch at his brother, then crossed his arms over his chest. "Can we get this over with?"

Jinx could relate—she felt the same way. Presley made a few jokes and even managed to coax a smile from Statler as the bids stacked up. Finally, it was down to two people.

"Going once, going twice..." Presley waited, drawing out the moment. "Sold to Mrs. Holbein for two hundred and thirty bucks!"

"Oh no." Dixie gripped Jinx's arm.

"What's wrong?"

"That's my gram. My daddy's going to blow a gasket when he realizes she just bought a bachelor elf." The bells on Dixie's costume jingled as she sprinted away.

Jinx stood in the wings, her anxiety rising as other volunteer elves took their turns onstage. All too soon, it was her turn.

"Next up, we have the Rose's newest little elf. Come

on out here, Jinx." Presley raised his hand, beckoning her onto the stage.

Dixie reappeared from nowhere, shoved a holiday headband onto Jinx's head, and gave her a gentle nudge from behind. With a lump the size of an ostrich egg lodged in her throat, Jinx stepped onto the stage.

The bright light blinded her. She couldn't see beyond the first two or three feet into the audience. It was probably better that way. Presley moved closer, talking about how she'd just recently joined the staff. Then he leaned in and held the microphone out to her.

"Can you tell us about any special talents you have?"

"What?"

Presley smiled at the crowd. "You know, are you an expert baker? Have a special recipe for eggnog? Know how to knit a scarf? We need to let the bidders know your area of expertise."

Area of expertise? Running away. That was one thing she excelled at. Probably not the kind of skill he was looking for.

"Um, I can draw. Other than that, I've got nothing."

"Okay, drawing. Ladies and gentlemen, we've got Jinx, the drawing elf. Who will start the bidding at fifty bucks?"

She stood, squinting into the light while voices called out to each other across the room. Presley repeated bids, upping the amounts, pushing the crowd for more.

"Two hundred and fifty dollars. Going once, going twice."

"Five hundred."

Jinx's heart revved into freak-out mode. She'd recognize Cash's voice anywhere.

"Five hundred?" Presley repeated.

Cash stepped closer to the front edge of the stage. "That's what I said."

"Sold for five hundred big ones. Thanks, Big Brother."

She tried to force her feet to move, to carry her off to the side of the stage where she could get out of the spotlight. But instead, she froze. Her feet wouldn't budge, like they'd been cemented in place. Cash levered himself onto the stage, wrapped an arm around her shoulders, and led her to the side.

Dixie jumped up and down, her bells jingling like crazy. "That was awesome! Congratulations, Jinx. You too, Cash. That was super generous of you."

"Hell, I couldn't let Cooper get his hands on her. He'd have her out stomping on grapes or something." He whipped around to face Jinx. "You're welcome, by the way."

"You're welcome? Don't I already spend enough time helping you?" Her reaction didn't make sense to him. She could see it in the confusion clouding his eyes. It didn't make sense to her either—except for the feeling that it was too much. He was getting too close. Helping him out with Kenzie and sharing some mutually beneficial time between the sheets was one thing. But going public, making a huge statement by doubling the highest bid, that was commitment. And the one thing she'd never done was commit. Not to anyone or anything.

Suddenly, the lights, the costume, the stifling heat backstage behind the curtain became too much. Jinx whirled around, desperate for a way out. The red light from an EXIT sign caught her eye. She brushed past Cash, swept by Dixie, and pushed through the back door to the sanctity of the parking lot. She had to get out of here. Out of the Rose. Out of Holiday. Before it was too late.

⁓⁂⁓

"Jinx!" Cash let the back door to the Rose slam behind him. The gravel parking lot overflowed with cars, but she was nowhere in sight. She couldn't have gone far. While he walked through the lot, he peered between the rows of trucks and cars. Damn, he hoped she hadn't taken off down the highway in that ensemble. She'd freeze to death before he could find her. He'd just make a loop around the building. If he didn't see her by then, he'd head toward home and hope he came across her on the way.

As he neared the pigpen, he picked up the faint sound of someone crying. Or it could have been Pork Chop pigging out over the evening bucket of scraps. Either way, he needed to investigate.

There she was. Huddled against a wooden beam under the tin roof of the pigpen, Jinx had her arms wrapped around her waist. Pork Chop nudged her through the fence, and she looked up just in time to notice Cash approaching.

"Go away. I don't want you to see me like this." Her voice hitched, raw with emotion.

"Hell, Jinx, I've seen you in a lot worse shape. Remember the tassels?" He hooked his thumbs into his belt loops and kept walking, slow and steady like he was approaching a spooked mare.

She let out what he'd consider a little bit of a laugh. "Those were pretty awful."

"What's wrong? What did I do this time?" He stopped in front of her and resisted the urge to reach out and pull her into him. She had to be freezing in that getup. "I figured you could paint unicorns and rainbows all over Kenzie's walls. That's worth at least five hundred bucks."

She covered her face with her hands. "It's not you. It's me."

"Now come on. You don't expect me to believe that, do you?" He wanted to lift her chin, get a good look at her eyes. See if he could see beyond the lies. Instead, he held his ground. He didn't want to scare her off by pushing too hard too fast.

"I don't belong here. This is too…too…" Her hands flailed, gesturing at everything all at once.

"Too what?"

Finally, she met his gaze. "Too much. It's all too much."

Cash slipped his jacket off and draped it over her shoulders. "I don't know what to say to that. Are you talking about the town or me specifically?"

She let out a huge sigh and pulled the jacket tight. "It's everything. People are too nice."

"Well, that is the one thing I've never been accused of before."

Unshed tears pooled in her eyes. "Especially you."

Cash glanced down at the pig bumping against his leg. His hand slipped through the wide gap in the fence to scratch behind Pork Chop's ears. "What's so wrong with being nice? The way I see it, you've hit a rough patch and could use a hand. You're helping me out with Kenzie. I just happened to have somewhere for you to stay—"

"People don't help me. Don't you get it?"

Cash took a step closer. "People don't help? Or is it more like you don't let them?"

She backed up against the wall. "I can't."

"No, baby"—he pulled her into his chest—"you won't. Let me in, Jinx. I'm scared too."

She didn't yield, just stood stiff in his arms, her palms against his chest. "Do you know how I got the nickname Jinx?"

Cash whispered along her hairline. "Do you want to tell me?"

"From my mom. She said I was deadweight. That I jinxed her from being able to keep a man." Her laugh came out half-bark, half-cry. "I was ten."

"I'm so sorry."

"You tell a kid something like that and they believe it. Sticks with them, you know?" She sniffled, then rubbed her hand under her nose.

He slipped his hand under the jacket to rub circles on her back and tried to think of something to say to erase the years of hurt. Her shoulders heaved up and down. Tears soaked the front of his favorite button-down plaid shirt. Didn't matter. What mattered was right here in front of him. How could he convince her she wasn't a jinx? Especially to him.

Minutes passed. The waterworks ceased. Her breathing slowed.

"You okay?" His hand stopped circling her back.

She tried to bury her head in his neck. "I'm sorry."

"For what?" The only person who needed to apologize was over a thousand miles away. If he ever happened to run into Jinx's mom, he'd make sure she spent the rest of her life trying to make things up to her daughter.

"For ruining your night. For being a hot mess. For destroying your shirt." Dark black streaks crossed her cheeks. "I'll replace it."

He didn't even look down. "I don't care about the shirt."

"No?"

"No. And you didn't ruin my night. I came here for you. Charlie sent me a text and told me Dixie suckered you into going up on the auction block. I couldn't let anyone else win the nicest elf in the auction, now, could I?"

She blew out a laugh. "I'm the worst elf. I'm sure they'll refund your money if you ask for it."

"I don't want my money back." He pulled away.

"What *do* you want?" Her breath came out in puffs in the chilly night air.

"Honestly?"

She nodded.

"I don't know. But I want to figure it out. And whatever it is, I know I want you to be a part of it."

"Why? I ruin everything. I'm bad luck. Like a rotten penny that keeps turning up. Or a black cat. Or a—"

He cut off the rest of her words with a kiss. The salty taste of her misery on his lips made him want to prove to her that her mom was wrong. She yielded slightly, her lips responding to his kiss. It wasn't all in his head. There *was* something between them.

He pulled back to meet her gaze. "That's not true. Kenzie adores you. You've been a huge help at the school, and Charlie would be lost without you right now. You're a good person. Your mom was wrong."

She met his gaze, her eyes brimming with tears again. "I don't know who I am anymore."

"Then we'll find out together. Let me be part of your journey. That's all I'm asking."

Her head tilted toward his chest in an almost imperceptible nod. The blood pounded through his ears. She was game. He'd done a great job of convincing her. Now he needed to convince himself he was worth the effort.

chapter
NINETEEN

"KENZIE, COME ON. YOU'RE GOING TO BE LATE FOR school!" Jinx shoved the crustless peanut butter and jelly sandwich into a plastic bag with one hand while she licked the sticky strawberry jam off her finger.

Kenzie skipped into the kitchen, still in her favorite Disney princess pj's. "I can't have peanut butter for lunch."

"What do you mean?"

"Zander Lewis is allergic. If he even breathes it, he can die." Her eyes rounded. "His mom said so to our class."

"What does your dad fix you for lunch then?" Jinx snagged the offensive, allergy-ridden sandwich from the pink-and-purple lunchbox and tossed it on the counter. Looked like she'd be eating PB&J for lunch today.

"Daddy makes me eat school lunch, but it's always so disgusting." Kenzie stuck out her tongue and faked gagging.

"I'll figure something out. Go get dressed. If you miss the bus—"

"Will you drive me to school today, Jinx? Pleeeeeeeease?" Kenzie grabbed her hand and pulled on her arm. "Puhleeeeeeease?"

Where did she get her flair for the dramatic? Not from her dad—he was as cut-and-dried as they came. "You're making me crazy, kiddo. Get your clothes on and then we'll talk about it, okay?"

"Okay." Kenzie stuck out her lower lip. "But Tanner farts on the bus. He thinks it's so funny. Why are boys so gross?"

Jinx rolled her eyes. "Second-grade boys are gross. Sometimes they get better as they get older. Get dressed!"

"Daddy still farts though." Kenzie's nose wrinkled. "I don't think I ever want to kiss a boy."

"Good plan. Now no more talking until you come back fully dressed." Jinx pointed in the general direction of the bedroom.

Kenzie dragged her feet in a sullen march to find her clothes. They were on day three of Cash being up in Dallas for training with two more to go. How would she ever survive? Just getting the kid up and out the door used up all her energy for the day.

The bus honked on the main road out front. Jinx thrust her feet into a pair of boots by the door and scrambled halfway down the long gravel driveway to wave the driver on. No sense holding up a whole bus route for an uncooperative drama queen. The kids on the bus pressed their noses against the glass as they pulled back onto the road. Shoot. She had on one of Cash's long T-shirts and a pair of his cowboy boots. Nothing like a little show before school for the elementary kids.

She trudged back to the house to find Kenzie dolled up in the outfit they'd picked out the night before. Thank God for small favors. At least that battle had ended. She rummaged through the pantry, then tossed a nut-free protein bar and an apple into the lunch box along with a tube of yogurt and a juice box. That would have to do.

"Sit right here for five minutes, okay? I need to run a brush through my hair and throw on some clothes." Cash had borrowed his dad's truck so she could have his to cart Kenzie around this week. But she'd have to put on something besides her pajamas if she was going to run Kenzie to school. "Hey, make sure your bag is all packed up—your math worksheet, that reading page, oh, and the permission slip for your field trip next week."

Kenzie yelled back to her. "I need to bring in some frosting for the gingerbread houses."

Jinx had barely pulled on a pair of leggings. "What?" She stuck her head out of the doorway to Cash's bedroom. The space that should have been a guest room had been filled with workout machines, and he'd insisted she couldn't sleep on his couch for a week. Sleeping in his bed, taking over his space, felt more natural than she'd imagined.

Cabinet doors slammed, then something thudded onto the kitchen floor. "Uh-oh!"

"What in the hell is going on out here?" Jinx rounded the corner to the kitchen.

Kenzie was sprawled in the middle of a powdered sugar explosion. Fine, white dust covered her hair, the countertops, and the floor. She didn't move except to point at a jar full of dollar bills on the counter. "You owe the curse-word jar."

"First, you tell me what happened."

"I need to bring frosting. We're making gingerbread houses, and Daddy said I could do the frosting."

"Then why did you throw powdered sugar all over the kitchen?"

"That's how Nana does it." Her lower lip quivered.

Hendrix hopped through the sugar explosion, licking piles of powdered sugar from the floor.

Jinx needed to come up with something quick or she'd have a crying, sugarcoated second grader on her hands as well as a hopped-up dog. "Tell you what. Let's get you cleaned up, and I'll swing by the store and get some frosting after I drop you off at school."

"But it won't be like Nana's." The lip wobbled. Tears filled Kenzie's eyes.

Before she had a chance to think about it, Jinx said, "I'll make frosting then, okay?"

Kenzie wiped a powdery hand across her cheek. "Do you have Nana's recipe?"

"Not quite. But I've got something almost as good."

"What?"

"Google." Jinx tapped her phone. "Now come on. It looks like it snowed in the kitchen. Let's get you desugared and off to school." She reached down to pick up Hendrix, brushing the white dust off his back.

Kenzie took her hand and let Jinx pull her to her feet. "I'm sorry."

"I know, kiddo." She brushed the sugar off Kenzie's hair, her shirt, her leggings. How did Cash do it? This parenting thing was tough.

An hour later, she stood in the kitchen, willing the slop in the silver mixing bowl to miraculously turn into something resembling some form of icing. She'd dropped Kenzie off, then picked up the ingredients to make what promised to be melt-in-your-mouth buttercream frosting. It looked more like the consistency of milk. She dumped more sugar in the bowl and kept the mixer going. A huge cloud of white poofed into the air.

Jinx traced the fallout with her eyes as particles of powdered sugar drifted down to cover every available surface in the kitchen.

"Oh, screw it." She didn't wait for the dust to settle. Cash's keys felt heavy in her hand as she stomped toward the truck.

The tiny market in town had two cans of Betty Crocker French vanilla frosting. Jinx bought both. Plus a plastic-ware container to transfer it to so she could hide any evidence of it being store-bought. By the time she pulled into the elementary school parking lot, she never wanted to think about buttercream again.

She followed the instructions and slid her ID through the security system.

A grizzled voice came through the speaker. "Come on in. The security system isn't working today."

Jinx set the container of frosting down on the admin's desk with a little more force than it required.

"What's this?"

"Frosting. For Kenzie Walker. She said they were making gingerbread houses or something."

"Just add it to the stack over there." The woman pointed to a teetering tower of Betty Crocker French vanilla containers on the table by the door. "Most kids just bring in the store-bought kind."

Jinx took in a few deep breaths. *Don't lose your shit. Not at Kenzie's school.* She pulled together a sugar-sweet smile and added her container to the table. Doing everything Kenzie's way wasn't working. It was time she tried figuring things out on her own.

Cash parked his dad's old farm truck in the lot of the Dallas hotel. Hopefully, the ancient beast would make it home. He'd left his own truck behind so Jinx would have a way to shuttle Kenzie around. The training had been going well, but it had brought up some major concerns. Drug traffic across south Texas was on the rise, especially around the little neck of the woods he called home. The suppliers from Mexico were getting more and more sophisticated. He'd have to keep his eyes and ears open.

He contemplated which delivery joint to call for dinner while he passed through the dingy hotel lobby. They'd tried to encompass the holiday spirit but failed. A few sprigs of fake pine needles curved around the reception desk. Christmas carols played in the background, and a lopsided tree occupied a corner. Holiday preparations would be in full swing at home. He and Kenzie hadn't had a chance to go get their tree yet. He couldn't wait to let her wake up in her own bed on Christmas morning instead of sleeping over at the big house. Sure would be nice if Jinx was around to celebrate the holiday as well.

Maybe he was getting ahead of himself. He wasn't the kind of guy who dove into the unknown headfirst. But that seemed to be what he was doing with Jinx. Just thinking about her made him hyperaware of the emptiness of his hotel room. He pulled out his phone and pressed the button to video chat. He'd been calling to check in every night, but tonight, he wanted to see her.

The phone buzzed, waiting for someone on the other end to pick up. Finally, right before he gave up, Kenzie's face appeared on his screen.

"Hi, Daddy!"

"Kenzie, is that you?"

She giggled. "Yep."

"What are you doing, Tadpole? It looks like you went swimming in sawdust." White powder covered her face and clung to her hair.

"Jinx made it snow!"

"Did she? Is…uh…Jinx there, sweetheart?" He could tell they were in the kitchen. But what the hell was all that white stuff? It didn't snow in Holiday. At least not for real. Not unless she'd borrowed the snow cone machine from the diner.

"Hey." Jinx's face filled his screen. White powder was dusted across her nose.

"What's going on? Kenzie said you made it snow."

"I had an altercation with your mixer."

"I'm not sure I get what you—"

Jinx's face disappeared. Her phone skittered across the floor. It looked like it had landed screen side up. He could make out the ceiling of his kitchen and the edge of a countertop. A tongue lapped the screen.

"Sorry about that. Kenzie dumped a handful of snow over my head. Hendrix sends kisses."

"We're making snow angels, Daddy!"

Jinx tilted the phone to show his baby girl moving her arms and legs up and down while she lay in the middle of the kitchen floor.

"It's just powdered sugar." Jinx's voice came from off-screen. "We tried to make frosting this morning, and, well, let's just say it didn't work out."

"How many inches of snow fell in my kitchen today?" His mom would drop dead on the spot if she saw the state of his floors right now. But the smile on Kenzie's face made it worthwhile.

"There wasn't significant accumulation." Her face appeared again. "Don't worry. I'll clean it up before you get back."

"Hell, I'm not worried."

"Daddy owes the curse jar!" Kenzie's face smooshed next to Jinx's. "When do you come home, Daddy?"

"Friday, Tadpole. I'll be home in time for dinner. How about I take you two girls out to eat when I get back?"

"I've got a shift at the Rose that night. I figured you'd be back in time."

"Of course. Kenzie and I can drop you off for work and stay for dinner." He'd told Charlie he wouldn't be in this weekend. After spending most of a week away from Kenzie, he wanted them to have the whole weekend together.

"Okay, Daddy. I love you." Her lips puckered and made contact with the camera. Where would he be without his little girl? She'd been his light, his purpose, his whole heart for the past seven years.

"Love you too. You be good for Jinx, you hear?"

She disappeared from the screen. "Can we have a snowball fight, Jinx?"

The dog yipped. Sounded like they had quite the party going on at home.

"Hold up a minute. Let me say goodbye to your dad, okay?" Jinx faced him head-on.

"Things going okay?" With his folks up in Tulsa and Charlie ready to pop any day, he hadn't wanted to ask Darby and Waylon to watch Kenzie. His brother

Presley was never an option, and Statler wasn't around enough. Hopefully, he hadn't tossed Jinx in over her head.

"Yeah, she's a handful, but we're having fun."

Her smile made his heart twinge. Hell, he wanted to be covered in powdered sugar, having a snow day with his girls, not five hours away. "I miss you." His admission surprised him. Not because it wasn't true, but because he hadn't planned on blurting it out.

She raised an eyebrow. "You do?"

"Yeah." He swallowed. His throat had gone dry, as he thought about the various ways he could get that powdered sugar off her cheek if he were there.

"What part of me do you miss the most, huh, cowboy?" Teasing, she licked her lips.

"Why don't you call me back later and I'll let you know?" He gripped the phone tighter. Phone sex had never been one of his hot buttons, but he could see himself going there with Jinx.

"Why don't you just show me when I see you on Friday?" She winked.

A burn started low in his gut. Friday wouldn't come soon enough.

"Let's go, Jinx. You said you'd help me make cookies." Kenzie wrapped her arms around Jinx's shoulders. Her face appeared on-screen again.

"No more mixing in my kitchen," Cash warned.

"Don't worry. They're slice and bake. I know my limits and won't commit to homemade."

"Bye, Daddy!"

"Bye, sweetie. Talk to you later on tonight, Jinx?"

"I think I'll be vacuuming the kitchen all night. We'll talk to you tomorrow, okay?"

She blew him a discreet kiss, then disconnected.

He took in a deep breath, letting visions of him and a sugarcoated Jinx play across his mind. How sweet it would be if he could live in his head for the rest of the night. Before he could pull up the number for the pizza place across the street, his phone pinged with an incoming text. He scrolled through the message, his mind already moving on from Kenzie and Jinx.

One of the guys from the DEA wanted to grab a bite and talk about a case he was working. Might as well. It would do him good to get out of this hotel room for a bit. He responded that he'd be down in the lobby in fifteen minutes. That would give him enough time to grab a quick shower. Hopefully, whatever the guy needed help with wouldn't be coming too close to home.

✻

Cash nursed his beer while Dan, the agent from Hidalgo, a tiny town on the Texas-Mexico border, signaled the waitress for another round. They'd been sitting at a table in the crowded bar area for fifteen minutes, making small talk. Cash was ready for the guy to get to the point.

"Thanks for coming out tonight. I know it's been a long day." The agent traded his empty glass for a full one.

The waitress signaled to Cash's beer. "Did you want another one?"

"No. I'm good. But I will take a burger with fries."

"Make that two." Dan held up two fingers as if the

poor waitress couldn't count. He waited for her to turn back toward the kitchen before he spoke. "I wanted to talk to you about a case I've been working on."

"You're talking about something down in Hidalgo, right?" Cash couldn't see what that had to do with his sleepy, little county in the Hill Country. Over three hundred miles separated them. And Conroe County wasn't known for being a hot spot for drug smuggling. Most of that action took place along the border.

"Yes and no. We've got information that connects one of the cartels we've been watching with some contacts from your area."

"Who?" Beyond some small players in neighboring towns, Cash wasn't aware of anyone who might warrant watching.

"Does the name Wade Boyd ring a bell?" Dan asked.

Cash shook his head.

Dan pulled up a mug shot on his phone and tilted it toward Cash. "Guy is from Louisiana and lives out in LA now but has a brother in your area. One of our informants said there's word that a large shipment might be moving through soon. Straight up 281 then over to Conroe County, where they're going to sit on it for a few weeks before moving it west."

"Why?"

Dan leaned back on his stool. "Who knows why these motherfuckers do half the crap they do, right? My guess is that his little brother finally wants a piece of the action. Wade's got active warrants out on him in Texas and Louisiana. Maybe he convinced someone else to do the dirty work so he didn't have to come so close to home."

Cash drummed his fingers on the table. "You have any more details?"

"I'll send over a copy of my files. Best I can tell, it'll go down sometime between now and the end of the year. Just keep an eye out for us, will you?"

"Of course."

"Oh, and he likes to use gift cards to pay off his runners. If you hear of anyone flashing some high-dollar cash cards around town, I'd appreciate a heads-up."

Cash's mouth went dry. He didn't trust himself to speak, so he nodded at Dan as two burger platters clattered to the table. His thoughts immediately went to Jinx. She'd had a handful of gift cards on her the night they'd met. He'd always thought it was a little strange. But he'd reasoned with himself that it wasn't exactly illegal to carry around a gift card. And she'd done nothing else in the time she'd been with him to warrant any suspicions. Yeah, he'd keep his eyes out but Jinx couldn't be involved in anything. He'd know it if she was.

He decided to order that second beer after all. He'd need something to help him sleep. Between missing Jinx and Kenzie and trying to make sense of why a shipment wouldn't take the typical route up the California coast, he'd probably be awake for hours.

chapter
TWENTY

JINX ROLLED OVER. HER ARM BUMPED INTO SOMETHING hard. She cracked an eye open to see a dark shape under the sheets next to her. Her heart pounded into her throat, and she reached for the first thing she could grab from Cash's nightstand. She scrambled from the bed, clutched whatever she'd snagged in her hand, and flipped on the lamp.

Cash winced at the onslaught of bright light. Jinx lowered the haunted house made out of Popsicle sticks she'd been clutching like a weapon.

"Hell of a welcome home." Cash covered his arm with his eyes. "Can you turn off the light, please?"

"I almost killed you. You can't just crawl into bed with someone without any warning."

He peered up at her, a doubtful slant to his brow. "You were going to attack me with Kenzie's Halloween craft?"

Jinx set the house back on the nightstand. "No. I don't know. Whatever. But you can't surprise me like that."

She turned off the lamp, her heart still thumping erratically in her chest.

"Come here." His hand patted the sheets where she'd been nestled in beside him just moments before.

Jinx slid back under the covers and took his hand in hers. "I'm not joking. You scared the crap out of me."

He scooted closer to put his hand on her chest. "Wow. Your heart's really racing."

"Tell me about it." She let him snuggle around her. Usually, she needed her own space in bed, couldn't stand to be smothered by another body in her personal bubble. But with Cash, the comforting feel of him curled around her calmed her. He surrounded her like a protective shell. "What are you doing home anyway? We weren't expecting you until tomorrow night."

"Mmm." He snuggled his cheek against the back of her neck. "Got done early. I ran by Statler's house to get even with him for my Thanksgiving pie prank. Then I came home. Missed my girls."

His girls. It wasn't the first time he'd said it, but it was the first time she truly felt like it fit. She'd been fighting the connection, fighting the long-buried desire to belong somewhere, to someone. The more time she spent with Cash and Kenzie, the more she felt like it would be possible for her to fit in. She'd spent so much time feeling like she must be the embodiment of her mother's nickname. There had to be something wrong with her. That was the only explanation for why she jinxed everyone and everything she touched. Cash made her realize she wasn't to blame for everything that had ever gone bad in her mom's life. He gave her hope.

"What prank did you play in the middle of the night?" Charlie had told her all about the back-and-forth pranks the brothers liked to pull on each other. Some of them sounded downright dangerous.

"Dumped pink glitter into the defrost vent in his

truck. When he turns it on tomorrow morning, he'll get a face full of sparkles."

"You're vicious." Jinx snuggled closer. "Are you sure you're responsible for upholding the law?"

"He deserves it. It's his fault we were interrupted that first night I brought you home."

She smiled into his chest. "That's right. I never did find out what happened."

"Presley locked him in the cab of a combine over at the Deere dealership with a lady friend, then tossed the keys into a runoff pond. Took us over an hour before we dredged them out of the muck."

"Boys will be boys, I guess."

"Some boys will be boys. Others grow up to be men." He twined his fingers with hers.

"Whatever." She squeezed his hand. "You know I can't be here when Kenzie wakes up. She can't see us in bed together." Kenzie needed stability. Jinx knew what it was like to see her mom waking up next to someone new every couple of months. She wouldn't do that to Cash's daughter.

His breath tickled her ear, sent goose bumps down her side. "I know. I set my alarm for five. I'll move out to the couch then."

"Okay, good." Sleep tugged at her eyelids. "I'm glad you're back."

He nestled closer. "Me too."

She was exhausted. Hanging out with a seven-year-old for four days would do that to a gal. But she couldn't turn off her brain long enough to fall asleep. By the end of the weekend, she'd have enough money to pay off Dwight. That meant, within two weeks, she could be on her way east. Jamie had been texting to check in. The job was still hers if she wanted it, but they needed to know before the end of the year. For some reason, she'd hesitated sending back an immediate confirmation. What was that all about?

Did she want to stay in Holiday? She tried to picture working at a bar in the heart of the French Quarter—the tourists, Mardi Gras partygoers, and people on vacation. Instead, all she could see was a vision of Cash and Kenzie, holding hands, playing with Hendrix, making snow-sugar angels on the kitchen floor.

She'd almost fallen asleep when the soft pitter-patter of tiny footsteps came from down the hall.

"Jinx?" Kenzie's whisper startled her to a seated position. Already sound asleep again, Cash didn't move.

"I'm right here, honey. What's wrong?" She moved toward the direction of the whisper before Kenzie crawled into bed and found out her daddy had come home early.

"I had a bad dream."

Jinx's arm closed around Kenzie's shoulder. "Hey, let's get you back up in bed. I'll sit with you until you fall asleep again, okay?"

"Okay." Kenzie let her lead the way back upstairs to her bedroom. Why couldn't she be so compliant when fully awake?

After she got her snuggled under the covers, Jinx lay down next to her. "Want to tell me about your dream?"

"I dreamed Santa couldn't find my house. He had my presents, but he got lost."

Jinx smoothed the hair back from her forehead. "You don't have to worry about that. Santa has supersmart

GPS on his sleigh. He doesn't get lost." Oh, to have the troubles of a kid again. Jinx wanted to smile at the simplicity of Kenzie's concerns. "Plus, he has Rudolph, right?"

"I guess so."

"What's wrong?"

"Can Santa bring whatever you ask for?"

How would Cash answer a question like that? Santa had stopped visiting her house when her dad passed away. She'd known better than to believe in the magic of Christmas long before other kids in her class stopped believing. "Sure. As long as his elves can make it in their workshop."

"What if it's something they can't make?" Kenzie battled a yawn but lost.

"Then he'll order it online, I guess." That was a plausible explanation, right? Even Santa had access to the internet.

"Okay." Kenzie curled her little body into Jinx. "Will you sing me a song, Jinx?"

"Sure." She'd left the guitar in Kenzie's room last night, so she reached for it. As her fingers strummed the strings, her memory took over, and she managed a halfway decent version of "Silent Night." Kenzie's eyes hadn't closed yet, so she half assed it through "Jingle Bells" and "Rudolph the Red-Nosed Reindeer." "Close your eyes, Kenz."

"One more?"

"Okay." She tried a few chords in an effort to remember how to start the fingering for the song her dad had always played for the holidays. He'd been an over-the-road truck driver before he'd had the accident that took his life. With tears welling in the corners of her eyes, Jinx sang along to the one song she knew by heart. "I'll be home for Christmas…"

Kenzie's eyelids drifted shut. "Good night, Jinx."

Jinx finished the song, letting the last note fade before

she leaned over and pressed a kiss to her forehead. "Good night, sweetie." An unfamiliar feeling bloomed in her chest. She wanted to protect Kenzie from the sad truth of the world. The poor girl already had to make it without a mom. Life was so unfair. But at least she had Cash. There was no doubt he was a devoted dad. Kenzie deserved his full attention. Jinx wouldn't get in the way of that.

She waited until Kenzie's breathing evened out, then tiptoed out of her room. She'd never been involved with someone with a kid before. It threw a whole new complication into the mix. But the more time she spent around Cash and his precocious little girl, the more she wanted that kind of complication. She'd never pictured herself with kids. Hell, she'd never pictured herself sticking around the same place for longer than six months at a time. For some reason, her typical urge to flee was slowly being replaced by a sense of belonging.

A calm, peaceful quiet had settled over the house, the kind she'd never experienced anywhere else but here, at Cash's place. Finally, sure of what she wanted to do about the job in New Orleans, Jinx shot off a text to Jamie. She'd have to find someone else to take the bartending job. Jinx was staying put.

"Let's play hooky today." Cash wrapped his arms around Jinx while she stood at the kitchen counter.

"Don't you have to go to work?" She held a butter knife in one hand and a jar of jelly in the other. Somehow, seeing her making lunch for his daughter made him all warm and tingly inside.

He nudged into her backside. "My calendar is clear. I thought I'd still be up in Dallas today. Whaddaya say?"

"What's hooky?" Kenzie dropped her cereal bowl in the sink.

"Hooky is when you skip out on work or school and do something fun instead." Cash moved away from Jinx to pull his daughter into his side.

"Can I come?" Kenzie wrapped her arms around his thigh. "Please, Daddy? I wanna play hooky too."

Jinx pursed her lips and leveled him with a scathing eye roll. "Hooky, really? Next you'll be teaching her to do keg stands and roll her own fatties."

"*Fatty* isn't a nice word." Kenzie waggled a finger at Jinx.

Cash almost laughed out loud. "You're absolutely right, Tadpole. I think Jinx ought to add a dollar to the curse jar for that."

Kenzie's nod brushed his hip.

"Fine." Jinx dug in her backpack for a dollar bill, then stuffed it into the overflowing jar. "What do you do when it's all filled up like this?"

Kenzie beamed up at him. In unison, they both shouted, "Diner Day!"

"What in the he—I mean, what in the world does that mean?" Jinx popped a hand onto her hip.

"You tell her, Tadpole."

"It means we get to go out to breakfast at the place with the giant sprinkle pancakes." Kenzie let go of his leg to hop up and down.

"You mean at the Rose?" Jinx asked.

Cash shook his head, in sync with his daughter. "The diner downtown. They only serve the sprinkle pancakes for breakfast."

"Well, that explains why I've never seen them on the menu." Jinx turned her attention back to the half-made sandwich on the counter. "I'm never out the door early enough to make it anywhere for breakfast."

Kenzie tugged on his jeans. "Jinx isn't a morning person."

"Really?" He played along. "Seems to me she gets up very early in the morning."

"Nah, I just stay up late, old man."

"Hey, I can stay up pretty late too."

Jinx raised an eyebrow at him while a sly grin spread over her face. Oh, it was on. He'd take a great deal of pleasure in reminding her just how late and how early he'd be willing to get up for her.

"Kenzie, honey, your bus is going to be here in a few minutes," Jinx reminded them.

"But we're hooking today, right?" Her lip stuck out in that pout he loved and hated.

Before he could respond, Jinx put her hands on Kenzie's shoulders and twirled her around. With a gentle nudge, she sent Kenzie in the direction of the mudroom. "Get your boots on and grab your backpack. Lunch is almost ready. And no one is hooking or playing hooky today."

Good God. First Kenzie wanted to be pregnant, and now she wanted to spend a Friday hooking. He'd have to have a serious talk with his little girl. But first, to convince Jinx to drop whatever plans she had for the day and play with him instead.

"Come on." He put a hand on the top of Kenzie's head. "Which boots do you want to wear today?"

"The ones like Jinx has." Kenzie skipped ahead to pull two heavy-soled black boots from the shoe bin.

"Where did you get those?" He cast a glance toward Jinx, who shrugged.

"Jinx got 'em for me. They're just like hers." The big black boots swallowed her little feet, a stark contrast to the hot-pink ropers she usually wore.

"Hmm." Eyes narrowed, he tried to determine how he felt about his little girl channeling her inner Goth.

"Do you like them, Daddy?" Kenzie twisted first one foot, then the other, showing off her new footwear.

"I'm sure they'll grow on me." He swooped her up, cradled her in his arms, and blew a raspberry on her neck. Her squeal of laughter cemented this moment in his brain. This is what life could be like if he let it. He and Kenzie didn't have to be on their own anymore. Instead of shutting everyone out and doing things on his own like he had been for the past seven years, maybe it was time to take a chance and put himself out there. He'd thought about it while he was up in Dallas. It was time to officially ask Jinx to stay.

Jinx walked over, Kenzie's pink Disney princess lunch box in hand, and dropped a kiss on his squirming daughter's forehead. "Lunch is ready."

Kenzie reached for her insulated lunch box, but Jinx didn't release her grip.

"Promise me you'll eat your growing food before you have the cookie?" A smile lingered under the mock stern look.

Kenzie nodded. "I promise."

"Good." Jinx let go. "Now you and your daddy better get down the driveway before the bus leaves you again."

"Again?" Cash set Kenzie on the ground. "What's this about *again*?"

"Come on, Daddy!" Kenzie wrapped her hand around his, pulling him toward the hooks holding their coats.

He twisted back to make eye contact with Jinx over Kenzie's head. "I'll be back."

She swatted at him with a dish towel. "I'm counting on it, cowboy."

Warmth radiated from his chest, an unfamiliar but not unwelcome sensation. When did he get so lucky?

TWENTY-ONE

By the time Cash returned, she'd finished cleaning up the kitchen and managed to sneak in a quick shower. He shut the door behind him, not even bothering to take off his boots.

"Okay, what do you want to do today? I can take you into Austin to do a little Christmas shopping. I need to pick up some stuff for Kenzie, and I could treat you to lunch." He put a hand on the counter on either side of her, trapping her backside against him. "Or we can just hang out here all day."

"I can't play hooky with you today. You might not have to go to work, but I do." Jinx squirmed under Cash's touch. God, when he did that thing with his mouth on her neck, she could feel her resolve wash away as easy as water down a drain.

"But you work nights. Why do you have to go in this morning?" He brushed her hair out of his way, clearing the path for more kisses.

"You keep that up, and I'll get fired." She twisted around to face him. Her arms encircled his neck, and she leaned into him. Solid. Like a rock. He could be her rock if she'd let him. It would be so nice to be able to count on someone for a change. Cash could be that someone for her, she knew it.

"I'm related to your boss." He thrust his hands into the back pockets of her jeans, kneading her ass. "I'm sure she'd let it slide if you were a little late."

This man, dammit, he drove her crazy. "I have ten minutes before I have to leave. The director of the women's foundation is coming by to pick up the check from the auction today, along with the bags of donations, and then I wanted to get some work done on Kenzie's walls." She wasn't going to mention the stack of gift cards she'd hidden within the bags of clothes Charlie had pulled together. They weren't doing anyone any good stashed under the kitchen cabinet in the bunkhouse. Plus, she was anxious to get rid of more of them and break ties with her past.

She laced her fingers together behind his neck. "Unless you want me toodling around in your truck all day, you'll have to drive me."

He nuzzled the sensitive spot on her neck, his whiskers scratching her skin. "Ten minutes is a long time."

"Is it?"

"Oh yeah. I can do a lot in ten minutes."

"Really?"

He urged her backward, toward the kitchen table. "Sure. In ten minutes, I can mount a horse, rope a calf, and have enough time left over to down a beer."

"I'm not impressed." Her butt hit the edge of the table. "What else can you do in ten minutes?"

"I can take down a bad guy, cuff him up, and deliver him to the county jail. Better?" He edged a thigh in between her legs, his mouth continuing to make contact with her collarbone, her jaw, her cheek.

"Still not impressed." Her eyes drifted closed as he palmed her breast through the thin fabric of her T-shirt.

"Damn, woman. What's it going to take?" He smiled against her neck. "In ten minutes, I bet I can make you come at least twice on this kitchen table."

She arched into him. "Now you're talking."

His hands went under her shirt, edging it up, over her head. Desire darkened his brown eyes to almost black. He traced the outline of the hourglass tattoo that wrapped around her rib cage. "You're so fucking beautiful."

She unbuttoned her jeans and slid them down her legs. "You better get busy, cowboy. You've already wasted two minutes yapping."

He licked his lips, whipped his shirt over his head, and forced her backward until her bare back met the rigid wood of the table. Within seconds, he'd removed any remaining barrier between them. Leaning over her, wearing nothing but a smile and a condom, he set a hand on either side of her and thrust. She pulled her knees up to wrap her legs around his waist. Her hands gripped the edge of the table to keep from sliding across the top as he drove into her again.

She opened for him, taking everything he gave her. This man, this incredible man, was offering her things she'd never thought she'd deserve. She'd take it. Take every last bit of what he wanted to give her, for however long it lasted. She was done running, done fighting. She wanted to be a part of his life, to try to build a future. To look forward for a change, instead of always looking behind her. Emotion swelled inside her, and she let the last barrier fall away.

As she exploded around him, her hands gripped his

arms, and she levered herself up, clinging to his chest like they were the last two people on the face of the earth. Like he was the only one who could save her.

His hands cupped her ass as he carried her to the bedroom. They fell to the bed, still entwined. She pushed him onto his back, taking control, slowing things down. Up and down, she slid over him, drawing him in, relishing the low groan rumbling through his chest. His hands gripped her hips, urging her to move faster. She toyed with him, speeding up for a few moments, then coming to a grinding halt.

He wouldn't stand for that. Flipping her over, he rained kisses down on her neck. She met him thrust for thrust, building toward the inevitable release. The release she craved.

Finally, she crested again. Her body paused, her hips suspended in midair. She let the feeling wash over her, not wanting to disturb the swell of intense pleasure sweeping over every inch of her.

Cash cradled her, held her tight against him, waiting for her to finish. When she let her hips drift back toward the bed, he increased his rhythm, finding his own release. A groan ripped through him, and she clenched around him, wanting to give him the same pleasure he'd given her. He stilled, his breath coming in short bursts against her ear.

She opened her eyes. A smug grin was plastered on his face.

"What are you so proud of?" she asked.

He twisted his wrist her way, showing off his watch. "Seven minutes."

Jinx shook her head. "Doesn't count, cowboy."

He dropped down next to her and flung his arm over his head. "What in the hell do you mean it doesn't count? From what I could tell, you came twice, just like I said you would."

Propping herself up on an elbow, she nudged a finger into his chest. "You said you'd make me come twice on the kitchen table."

Comprehension swept over him, lighting up another kind of grin. He grabbed her finger. "That's a technicality."

She kissed the scruff of his jawline before she climbed off the bed. "More like a technical foul. Sorry, doesn't count."

"Wait a minute." Cash sat up. "You can't be serious."

She cast a smile over her shoulder as she walked toward the kitchen to retrieve her clothes. "If you're nice to me, maybe I'll let you have another shot at it later."

His deep rumble of laughter sent tingles racing through her, from the tips of her toes upward. "Oh, it's on, babe. It's on."

She laughed, relishing the lightness that filled her. She'd made the right decision. As crazy as the idea of staying put for a change was, her place was here with Cash. For as long as he and Kenzie would have her. Now she just needed to figure out how to tell him she'd decided to stay.

⎯⎯⟋⟍⎯⎯

Cash threaded his fingers with Jinx's while Kenzie gripped his other hand. He liked the feel of being sandwiched between the two of them. Based on the sideways glances and nods he'd caught as they walked through the crowd at the second weekend of the Jingle Bell Jamboree, most of the town felt the same way.

"Y'all want some hot cocoa?" Cash nodded toward a tent where members of the Holiday Chamber of

Commerce handed out steaming paper cups to people passing by.

"With marshmallows?" Kenzie asked.

"Of course." He led them over to a table lined with cups.

Twinkle lights wrapped around the edges and legs of the tent. Glittery ornaments hung down. He bonked his head on one when he leaned in to grab a cup of cocoa for Kenzie.

"Watch yourself there." Maybelle, the resident hairdresser and senior square dance champion, smiled and pointed up. "Looks like you owe someone a kiss."

Cash glanced up. A sprig of mistletoe hung directly overhead. He glanced toward Jinx, who gave a slight shake of her head. "Aw, come here, Tadpole."

Kenzie took a step back. "Don't kiss me, Daddy. Kiss Jinx."

He cocked his head, raising an eyebrow at Jinx. "Whaddaya say?"

She bit her lower lip, probably debating whether or not she wanted to go all in with him. After all, the Kissmas Cam was watching.

Her voice came out barely more than a whisper. "Okay."

His heart thumped against his chest. He set the cup of cocoa down on the table. Pulling her close, he wrapped one arm behind her back, then dipped her low. Kenzie jumped up and down, clapping her hands. Cash met Jinx's lips with his. She molded against him, surrendering herself to the kiss.

A chorus of claps sounded around them. He

reached up and took his cowboy hat off, then used it to shield their kiss from the audience that had gathered.

Jinx pulled away first. He set her upright but kept hold of her hand. She squeezed, giving him a smile that conveyed the new intimacy they shared.

"My turn!" Kenzie crashed into their legs, wrapping an arm around each of them. "Kiss me now!"

Jinx laughed, a peal of laughter that brightened his already cheery mood.

"On three?" Cash leaned down. Jinx nodded and did the same, both of them lining up to catch Kenzie on a cheek. "One, two, three." They planted smacking smooches on the soft cheeks of his baby girl.

Kenzie thrust an arm around each of their shoulders and lifted her feet off the ground. She dangled in midair while she giggled in delight.

"Well, ain't this the picture-perfect scene?" Dwight stopped in front of them, passing the ever-present toothpick from one side of his mouth to the other.

"Hey, Dwight." Cash stood, Kenzie hanging from her grip around his neck.

Dwight nodded. "Deputy. Hey, Jinx."

"Hi. Are you having fun at the festival?"

"Yeah. You haven't been around lately. Wanted to let you know that part came in."

Jinx shifted her weight from one foot to the other. "Oh. Thanks."

"Bike should be ready next week." He lifted a brow. "Figured you're still in a big ole hurry to get it finished."

"Right. Next week." Cash felt the shift in her vibe, like she'd just stepped ten feet away, although she hadn't moved. The virtual distance between them widened.

"Well, y'all have a good night." Dwight tipped his ball cap before he wandered away.

Kenzie snagged the cocoa off the table and gripped it with both hands, oblivious to what had just happened. "Where are the marshmallows, Daddy?"

"Over here, sweetheart." Maybelle rounded the table to lead Kenzie to a big bowl of star-shaped marshmallows.

Cash jammed his hands into his front pockets. "So, next week. That's...uh...soon."

"Yeah, it is." Jinx wheeled away. "I wasn't exactly planning on having this conversation right now."

"Hey." Cash caught up to her. "You've been nothing but up-front about where you stand on this from the get-go."

"You're right. I have."

He reached for her hands, drawing them together between them. The thought of her leaving now, when things had just started to heat up between them, made him cringe inside. But that was his problem, not hers. He'd known all along she didn't have plans to stick around. Sure, he'd hoped, but it was time to man up and face the facts.

"You've got to go. I know that." He kissed her hands. Every part of him wanted to ask her to stay. But he'd done that once, a lifetime ago, and he realized he couldn't do it again.

"I do?"

The questioning tone caught him off guard. He met her gaze, searching for meaning in the depths of her eyes. "Don't you?"

"Do I?"

He sucked at head games. Was she being a smart-ass, or was there a chance she might have changed her mind? Only one way to find out. "Are you fucking with me?"

She grinned. "Not yet. I figured we ought to keep that to the privacy of your home. Or the bunkhouse, assuming you'll let me stay there until I can find a place of my own."

Silence stretched between them while her words sank in. "Don't jerk me around here. I don't think my heart could take it. You're really thinking about sticking around?"

Her shoulders rose as she took a deep inhale. He held his breath while he waited for an answer. With her head tilted to the side, she gave a slight shrug. "Would that be okay?"

"Would that be okay? Hell, that would be fantastic. I've been dying to ask you, but it has to be your call. You sure about this?" He hadn't thought she'd ever come to that decision. He'd hoped, even offered a half-assed prayer to whomever might be looking down on him from above, that she'd come to her senses. But he didn't really think it would happen.

"I don't want to be in the way. Kenzie's got to be your priority. I know what it's like to have someone come in and tear a family apart."

"Oh, baby." He brushed her hair away from the side of her face. "Kenzie loves you."

Her head jerked up at the mention of the l-word. He wanted her to know though. He'd been so scared of spooking her, he hadn't wanted to push things too far.

She squeezed his hands in hers. "She's a special kid. I really lo—care about her too." Her eyes offered an apology, like she was sorry she couldn't bring herself to say the actual word.

Cash nodded. "She is. And so are you. You don't have

to say it, Jinx. I can't imagine how hard it must be for you to trust your feelings. We've got time. Lots of it, okay?"

A tear rolled down one cheek. She nodded, then wiped it away. "Can I ask you a question?"

"Of course."

"What ever happened with Kenzie's mom?"

He snugged her against him. "You sure you want to know? It's not a happy ending."

"I figured. But hey, I specialize in unhappy endings, so lay it on me."

Cash let out a long breath. "All right. We dated in college. But she didn't want to move to the sticks, so we broke up after graduation. Over the years, we hooked up on occasion, and she got pregnant." He stopped, glancing at her for some sign to continue.

She nodded. "Go on."

"I wanted to do the right thing, so I convinced her to move back here with me. We were going to wait until after the baby came to get married. But after Kenzie arrived, she decided she couldn't hack it. She missed her friends, missed her family." He hung his head. "We had an awful fight. I told her she had to stay, that she didn't have a choice. She took Kenzie up to Dallas. I kept thinking she'd come back. Finally, I went up to get her, but I couldn't find them anywhere. Turns out Lori Lynne had left Kenzie with some people she'd just met so she could go out with some guy she'd been dating online. The people turned Kenzie over to child protective services."

Jinx bit her lip. "I had no idea."

Cash shrugged. "How could you? I don't talk

about it. I went for full custody, and she let me have it. A few months after that, I got a call she overdosed. Her folks were interested in keeping in touch for the first year or so, but I haven't heard from them since. Kenzie deserves more, you know?"

"She's lucky she has you for a dad." Her arms went around his waist, and she held tight.

Before she could say anything else, Kenzie reappeared. "I got marshmallows. Can we go ride the Ferris wheel?"

"Sure. Just give us a minute, okay?" He ruffled Kenzie's hair with one hand while holding Jinx against him with the other.

"What's wrong with Jinx?" Kenzie tugged on her jacket. "Daddy, did you make her cry?"

Jinx lifted her head, wiped her cheeks, and leaned down toward Kenzie. "It's okay. Your daddy didn't make me sad. He said something that made me happy."

"He did?"

Jinx nodded.

"Then why are you crying?" Confusion furrowed Kenzie's brow.

"It's complicated. Should we grab a gingerbread funnel cake before we ride the Ferris wheel?"

"With powdered sugar?"

Thank goodness his daughter could be easily distracted with the promise of sugar.

"Extra powdered sugar," Jinx promised. Eyes bright, she faced Cash. "I know I'm kind of messed up, and I don't have a real good sense of what it takes to be a family. But I want to get there. Will you help me?"

Now he was the one held hostage by raw emotion. "Absolutely. We'll get there together."

Kenzie thrust a hand to her hip. "No more grown-up stuff. Are we getting a funnel cake or not?"

"Let's go, Tadpole." Cash wrapped an arm around Jinx's shoulder and scooped Kenzie up in the other. "Whatever my girls want tonight, it's all yours."

TWENTY-TWO

THE NEXT SEVERAL DAYS PASSED IN A BLUR. JINX SPENT almost every waking moment either with Kenzie and Cash or at work. Charlie was due any moment, and with each passing day, she piled more and more responsibility for running the Rambling Rose on Jinx. The newfound sense of purpose agreed with her. It's not like she hadn't done a good job before, but she'd always had one foot out the door. Now that she'd decided to stay, she had a vested interest in the town, the Rose, and especially anything that had to do with the Walker family.

Surprisingly, it didn't scare the hell out of her. With Cash at her side, she could do almost anything. She spent her days working on the scenery for the upcoming Christmas play and her nights either at the Rose or on Cash's couch, snuggled up with him and Kenzie, watching Christmas specials. She'd never had that experience with her parents, so it was like getting a second chance to enjoy the holiday season. Seeing the magic of Christmas through Kenzie's eyes was something she especially enjoyed. And this morning, if she could get her butt in gear, they had plans to go cut down a tree.

Cash and Kenzie had never had their own Christmas tree, and neither had Jinx. This would be the start of a holiday tradition for all of them, something they could truly call their own. Jinx couldn't wait to see the look on Kenzie's face when she stepped back to see a fully decorated tree. It had been a long time since Jinx had hung an ornament or draped tinsel on a pine bough. It had to have been before her dad died.

She gathered the shoebox full of ornaments she and Kenzie had made on her way out of the bunkhouse. They'd strung popcorn kernels, wrapped yarn around Popsicle sticks to make snowflakes, and created angels out of paper doilies. At least they'd have something to get them started.

Cash met her at his front door. "We still on for tree shopping? Kenzie's been up for an hour already, talking my ear off about whether we should get a Leyland cypress or a Virginia pine. How the hell does she know so much about trees?"

Jinx laughed. "We looked them up online. She wanted to see what kind of trees you have in Texas."

"You eat anything yet?" He helped her take off her coat and tossed it on a hook by the door. "Kenzie's finishing up some pancakes in the kitchen. We've got plenty if you want some."

She'd just left his place a few hours before. Putting Kenzie to bed together, then bunking down in Cash's room had become routine. She always made sure to be gone before Kenzie woke up though. Cash assured her his daughter would be able to handle it if Jinx moved in permanently, but she still needed her own space—even if it meant sneaking out in the middle of the night and trying to fall back asleep on the thin bunkhouse mattress instead of nestled against Cash.

"Pancakes sound good."

"Jinx!" Kenzie scrambled out of her chair to wrap Jinx in a pint-size hug.

"Hey, kiddo." Jinx leaned over, folding her arms around her. She might not be able to admit her feelings for Cash yet, but Kenzie had infiltrated her heart, and Jinx was powerless against her. "I just saw you last night."

"I know. But I missed you." Kenzie smiled up at her, then snuggled her head into Jinx's stomach again.

Truth was, Jinx had missed her too. More than she'd ever expected. Cash had been trying to get her to move more stuff over to his place. Maybe after the holidays, they could talk about it.

"I taught Hendrix a new trick. Wanna see?" Kenzie jerked away, heading back to the table, where Hendrix sat on a place mat.

"Hey, he shouldn't be on the table while you're eating," Jinx warned.

Kenzie rolled her eyes. "That's what Daddy says. But he's keeping me company."

Cash set a giant plate of pancakes down on the table. "Come eat."

Jinx swept Hendrix up in her arms. Since she'd been spending so much time at Cash's, she'd been leaving him in Kenzie's care. It didn't make sense to have him living in the bunkhouse by himself all the time. "Where's his crate?"

"It's up in Kenzie's room." Cash reached for Hendrix. "Let me get him. I'll go put him back while you eat. Kenzie, you can show us your trick after breakfast, okay?"

"Okay," she grumbled.

Jinx took a seat next to her and dug into Cash's pancakes. It was nice to know that Hendrix had carved out a special place in Kenzie's heart. A few minutes later, they'd started making plans for a morning out at Kermit's Christmas Tree Farm.

"So who's Kermit, exactly?" Jinx asked between bites.

"Kermit the Hermit." Kenzie nodded, then stuffed another huge bite of pancake into her mouth.

"Kenzie, that's not nice." Cash tapped her on top of her head.

Sufficiently shamed, her shoulders slumped. "That's what everybody calls him."

"Doesn't make it right." Cash turned his body toward Jinx. "He owns a slice of land out past the Rose. Doesn't come to town but maybe once or twice a year."

Jinx took another bite of pancake. Cash didn't do much in the kitchen, but holy buttermilk, the man had serious pancake-making skills. "So does this Kermit guy live out there all by himself?"

"Yep. He just opens up the back gate to his property and lets people cut down the trees he's marked. It's all honor system. He doesn't come out much, so I doubt we'll actually see him there."

"Sounds cool." Jinx shoved another bite into her mouth. "Let's go."

"Can Hendrix come with us?" Kenzie asked. "Nana made him a new coat, and it's perfect for cutting down a Christmas tree."

"When does your nana have time to sew clothes for Hendrix?" Jinx asked.

Kenzie shrugged. "She likes it. Nana said she's going to make him pajamas for Christmas that match mine."

Jinx shook her head. She could barely get a collar around his neck, but Kenzie appeared to be able to dress him up like a Barbie doll, and he still loved her. If even the dog was settling in and feeling at home, Jinx was more convinced than ever that she'd made the right decision.

⸻ ⊞ ⸻

The truck bumped over the deep ruts carved into the dirt road leading toward the Walker's horse barn. Jinx, Kenzie, and a well-dressed Hendrix bounced up and down and side to side while Cash eased the truck to a stop next to a rusty old tractor. "Ready to find the perfect Christmas tree?"

"I thought we were going to a Christmas tree farm." Jinx eyed the barn with suspicion. "Are you hiding trees in the barn?"

Cash grinned. Oh, this was going to be fun. "Not exactly. I thought it would be fun to do it the old-fashioned way."

Kenzie hopped over the seat to land between them. "It's a surprise. Daddy told me not to tell you we're riding horses, so I didn't."

Cash shook his head while he patted his daughter on the head. "You kinda just did, kiddo."

Realization washed over her. She clapped a hand to her mouth. "Oops."

"It's okay. We're already here. Jinx is going to find out soon enough what we have planned."

Jinx hadn't moved, just sat frozen in place, one hand on the door handle, the other flat on the dash in front of her.

"Come on, Jinx. Daddy says you get to ride Lou today." Kenzie shook her shoulder, jostling Jinx out of whatever trance she'd fallen into.

"We're cutting down a Christmas tree," Jinx said. Cash nodded.

"On a horse." She twisted to face him.

"Not exactly. I think we'll have to dismount to actually cut the tree down," Cash said.

Kenzie's head pivoted back and forth, tracking the conversation.

"You remember the last time I was on a horse it didn't end so well, right?" Jinx crossed her arms across her chest.

"Right." Cash bit back a grin. "But you've got to admit, those were extenuating circumstances."

Her mouth gaped open. "I almost died."

Cash stepped down onto the running board and offered Kenzie a hand. "That's stretching it a bit. Besides, you told me you wanted to learn how to ride. Kenzie and I thought this would help. If you don't want to do it, you don't have to, right, Kenz?"

Kenzie nodded. "That's right."

"Someday. I said I might want to learn how to ride *someday*." Her jaw clenched, Jinx climbed out of the truck and fell into step beside him. "I don't think I can get back on a horse."

"I figured you might feel that way." Cash ducked into the stall where they kept the saddles. "Kenzie, come get your helmet, and grab one for Jinx too."

He was under no illusion that strapping a helmet to her head would alleviate her anxiety of getting back up on a horse. But he didn't want to offer her the easy out yet. Better to see if she'd push past her fear first.

"Cash, I can't—"

"I don't buy that for a minute. You can do

anything you set your mind to. I've seen you do it. Now, if you decide to ride today, you've got three choices. You can ride Star—she's Charlie's horse. Wouldn't hurt a fly." He stepped in front of Star's stall and offered the mare an apple he'd picked out of the barrel in the saddle room.

"She looks gentle." Jinx reached a tentative hand out to rub it along Star's nose. The horse sniffed, then nuzzled her palm, looking for another treat.

"Gentle but greedy." Cash took a few steps to stand in front of the next stall. "Option two is I can saddle up Melvin for you."

Jinx moved next to him. "What is that?"

The donkey hung his head over the stall door, nudging Cash's shirt pocket.

"I want to give it to him." Kenzie climbed onto the bottom rail and thrust a carrot at Melvin. "Here you go."

"Melvin might not look like much, but he was a blue-ribbon winner in the Conroe County Fair two years ago." Cash scratched Melvin behind the ear. The donkey pawed at the dirt and let out a bit of a whinny. "I think he likes you."

"Yeah, but what is he?" Jinx brushed a hand over Melvin's cheek.

"He's a donkey," Kenzie chimed in.

"A donkey. You want me to ride a donkey?"

Cash shrugged. "Not just a donkey. A blue-ribbon-winning donkey. Not every jackass can add that to his résumé."

Jinx cast a glance upward, muttering something under her breath.

"Ready for option three?" he asked.

"Sure. I can't wait." Sarcasm dripped from her voice like molasses from an overfull spoon.

Cash moved to the stall at the end. "Meet Lou."

"No. Give me the donkey."

"What's wrong with Lou?" He pulled on a mask of mock innocence. "Lou's an icon around here."

"Hi, Lou." Kenzie opened the stall door and stepped in with the giant Texas longhorn.

"Oh my gosh, don't let her do that. She's going to get stabbed or impaled or…oh hell, what's that word?" Jinx made a move to grab for Kenzie's arm.

"Don't spook him." Cash flung an arm around her waist, jerking her backward as Lou turned his head to find out what all the commotion was about. His left horn missed Jinx's face by a mere inch.

"Gored. She's going to get gored." Jinx struggled to get to Kenzie, who held a handful of hay out to the giant horned beast.

Lou sniffed the hay, then gently took a nibble. "He's not going to hurt her. We raised that one by hand after his mama died during birth. It's fine. He'd rather be around people. We keep the door to the pasture open for him, but he likes to hang out in the barn and keep an eye on things."

"You're crazy, Cash Walker. There's no way I'm getting on the back of that cow."

"Oh, honey. Your roots are showing." Cash hung a hand over the rail of the stall.

Jinx's hand went to her hair. "I was wondering if I should dye it back to brown."

Cash gave her a blank look until it dawned on him they were talking in circles. "Not those roots.

I was talking about your West Coast roots. You really are something, you know. Besides, I like your hair blue. Kenzie would be devastated if you changed it."

"I'm so glad I provide the fodder for your amusement." She turned to go.

He caught her hand and twirled her around. "Lou isn't a cow. He's a Texas longhorn. And yes, we've ridden him before. He's slow and reliable. He won't bolt on you, and trust me, he'd be more eager to get back to the barn than you would."

"I doubt that."

"You wanna feed him some, Jinx?" Kenzie held a handful of hay out to Jinx.

"That's okay. I'm good. Tell you what. Why don't you and Kenzie go get the tree, and I'll just wait right over here in the truck?"

"Jiiiiiiiinx." Kenzie coupled her whine with a pout. "You have to come with us, or it don't count."

"Doesn't," both Jinx and Cash corrected at the same time.

"Are you sure I can do this?" she asked Cash.

Before he could respond, Kenzie reached through the fence and tugged on Jinx's jacket. "You told me it was okay to be scared but it's not okay not to try. Remember?"

Jinx closed her eyes and took in a slow breath. "That was about reading, not flirting with death."

Cash let out a low laugh. "It's okay. We can drive the truck to the tree farm. Kenzie, say goodbye to Lou."

Jinx shook her head. "Give me the damn horse."

Kenzie's mouth opened, but before she could say anything, Jinx put up a hand, palm out.

"Yes, I know I owe the curse jar. Now get me on the horse before I change my ever-lovin' mind."

Cash and Kenzie raced around the barn, running a quick brush over the horses before getting them saddled up.

"You ready for this?" Cash led Star out to the front of the barn where Jinx stood, probably cursing him with every four-letter word she knew.

"If I crack my head open again, it's on you." She pushed off the split-rail fence and approached the horse.

He handed her a helmet. "This ought to help with the head cracking."

She plopped it on top of her head. "I feel so much better now."

"You don't have to do this, you know." He held Star's reins with one hand while he secured the helmet under Jinx's chin.

"I'm not going to say you're right, but I want to. I've got to get past what happened."

"Atta girl." He lifted his hat to lean down and kiss her. Star wouldn't stand for being ignored. She tried to nibble on the brim of his Stetson. "Oh hell no, you don't."

Jinx laughed. "Wouldn't hurt a fly, huh?"

"She's eager to go. Charlie hasn't been over to ride for a while, so she hasn't been getting the exercise she needs. If the two of you hit it off, maybe you can take her out from time to time."

"Let's not get ahead of ourselves. Are you going to help me mount this thing?"

"Just put your foot in the stirrup, and I'll boost you up." He draped the reins over the saddle horn.

Jinx lifted her foot into the stirrup and pulled

herself up and into the saddle. He barely got to palm her ass before she'd slung her leg over and straddled the large mare.

He squinted against the early morning sun as he peered up at her. "You're a natural."

"We'll see about that."

Within a few minutes, he'd helped Kenzie into the saddle of the pony his dad had bought her and had taken a seat on his own mount.

"Ladies, shall we?" He pointed his horse east. They could get to what remained of Kermit's Christmas Tree Farm by cutting through a couple of neighbors' acreages.

"Let's go, Daddy." Kenzie urged her pony into a trot. "We're going to get the best Christmas tree ever."

Cash glanced back to Jinx, who held on to the saddle horn with both hands. "You okay back there?"

"So far. But no running. Nice and slow."

Nice and slow. That seemed to be her MO in so many areas of her life. He nodded and waited for her to draw up even with him. He'd go nice and slow—on the horse and in their relationship. If that's what it took to keep her moving forward, he was all in. No matter how many hours it would take them to find the perfect tree.

chapter

TWENTY-THREE

Jinx settled into the easy sway of Star's slow gait. It was almost nice. She'd spent so much time inside over the past couple of weeks, she hadn't realized how much she missed the fresh air and the wide-open spaces. Cash pointed out property lines and told her stories about the neighbors whose lands they crossed. As they neared Kermit's property, he filled her in on the history of the farm.

"Why do they call him Kermit the Hermit?" she asked.

"Like I said before, he doesn't get out much. Once upon a time, this place was huge—the only cut-your-own tree farm for miles around. We used to come out here every year. We'd all climb into the back of Dad's pickup. Mom would pack thermoses of cocoa, and we'd sing made-up Christmas carols at the top of our lungs."

"What happened?"

"When Kermit's wife died, he kind of fell out of touch with the town. The lady's circle from one of the churches made him meals for a solid year. The mayor even came to visit him." Cash's parents had taken a turn trying to coax the old man back to civilization.

"But he didn't care?"

"Nope. He grieved alone, only reaching out when he

needed something he couldn't take care of himself. Which wasn't too often."

"How does he get by?"

"He still lets folks cut down trees on a part of his land. It's all on an honor system. There's a cash box near the road."

They'd reached an old rusty gate on the trail. Cash climbed off his horse and swung it wide open. "We're here."

"So what do we do, just ride into the field and tag the one we want?" Jinx looked suspicious.

Cash swung himself back onto his horse. "Nope. This is a do-it-yourself kinda place."

"Let's go." Kenzie raced ahead.

"Don't go too far, Tadpole. Stay where I can see you."

She disappeared in between two rows of trees, obviously oblivious to his warning.

"Kenzie!" His voice boomed through the countryside.

"I'm right here, Daddy." She reappeared between two different rows of trees.

"Stay close."

"Okay, okay." Kenzie turned her horse around and stayed close by.

Jinx breathed in the scent of pine trees. She'd expected Texas to be full of tumbleweeds and cactus, not beautiful rows and rows of pines. She raised her gaze to enjoy the view of Cash riding a few feet in front of her. Unlike her, he was an absolute natural on a horse. He swayed back and forth in the saddle, instinctively matching the horse's gait with the movements of his body. He must have felt her gaze on his back; he twisted in the saddle to shoot a smile her way.

Her breath hitched. She'd never been this happy

before. Never thought she deserved it. He brought
out feelings in her that she didn't know she was even
capable of.

"Kenzie thinks she found a tree." He pulled up,
stopping his horse until she caught up. "Do we have
enough ornaments for that?"

Jinx followed the line of his arm, her gaze resting
on a giant pine that towered over its neighbors.
"You've got to be kidding. That's got to be at least,
what, twelve feet tall?"

He shrugged and climbed out of the saddle. "Let's
measure. If we put it in the front room, we've got the
height."

"Yeah, but how in the world are you going to get
that home?" She swung her leg over the saddle, trying
to find the ground. Cash slung an arm around her
waist, catching her before she tumbled into a heap.

"Need a hand there?" He slid her foot out of the
stirrup and set her upright, both feet finally firmly
planted on the ground.

"Thanks." The tree appeared even taller now that
she wasn't sitting six feet off the ground.

"It's perfect!" Kenzie trotted in circles around it
on the back of her pony. "It's the most perfectest
Christmas tree ever."

"You sure you don't want to look at one of these?"
Cash gestured around them to the sea of five- to
six-foot trees.

"Nope."

He smiled an apology at Jinx, a dad clearly
wrapped around his little girl's finger. "Let me get
the saw." He passed both sets of reins to Jinx. "Can

you tie them up to a tree or something? They shouldn't run, but they might not like the sound of the saw when I get it going."

Jinx took the leather leads and loosely draped them around a branch of a tree. "Yeah, we're going to need more ornaments."

By the time Cash had sawed through the thick trunk of the tree, the sun sat directly overhead. "Y'all want to take a break for lunch before we head back?"

"Lunch?" Jinx wondered where they'd be able to grab a sandwich with nothing but trees and fields around them.

"Daddy and I packed a picnic." Kenzie pulled something out of a pocket on the side of her saddle.

"When did you have time to do that?" She helped Kenzie spread out the blanket.

Kenzie beamed. "Are you surprised?"

"I sure am. You're definitely making this a day to remember."

Cash joined them on the blanket, spreading out the picnic feast. "PB&J, grapes, and Rice Krispies squares."

"Perfect." She meant it. The sun overhead, the man she'd been waiting for all her life next to her, and the promise of many tomorrows between them filled her heart with a joy she didn't know she had the capacity for. "I think this is going to be my new very favorite best day."

Kenzie giggled. "What's a very favorite best day?"

It was a game she had played with her dad. She hadn't thought about it in years. Hadn't had a reason to. "Every time you have a really good day, you have to think to yourself…is this the very best day? Better than all the others? If so, then you can declare it as your new very favorite best day."

"How many new very favorite best days can you have?" Kenzie picked a few grapes off of the bunch.

"As many as you want. But you can only have one at a time. That's why it has to be the most very favorite best day ever."

"And today is yours?" Cash asked.

"Yep."

"Well then, it's mine too." He leaned across the blanket and kissed her on the lips.

"I want it to be my new very favorite best day too," Kenzie whined.

Jinx laughed. "I already called it. You two have to find your own days. This one's mine."

"That's not fair." Cash nudged Kenzie. "What do we do when someone's not being fair?"

Kenzie didn't say anything, just sat there like she was thinking too hard. "We tell a grown-up?"

Jinx laughed again while Cash shook his head. "Not that kind of not fair. Jinx isn't being fair because she won't share her day. What do you say we tickle her?"

Kenzie's eyes lit up, and she attacked, her fingers ready to deliver some serious tickles. Jinx tumbled over to the blanket, laughing so hard she snorted. This was the first. The first of her new very favorite best days. Her decision to stay with Cash and Kenzie meant she had an unlimited number ahead of her.

<hr>

"There we go." Cash crawled out from under the tree to admire his handiwork. The massive tree Kenzie had selected stretched toward the dark wooden beams lining the two-story ceiling of his living room.

"I think it's still crooked." Jinx stood on the steps, her head tilted at a slight angle.

Kenzie's mouth puckered.

"Which way do I need to move it?" He'd been trying to get the damn tree to stand up for the past hour. The trunk was too big to fit into the stand he'd pulled out of the barn, so Presley had run by with a giant galvanized metal tub earlier. And thank goodness for that. It had taken him, Cash, *and* Jinx to wrestle the tree inside the house. Hopefully, the tub would hold it upright.

"A little to the right." Jinx tapped her finger to her lip. "Just a couple of degrees."

He stuck his hand in between the branches to grasp the rough bark of the trunk. "Better?"

"Now a little to the left."

"You sure?"

"Um, yeah." She didn't sound so sure.

He nudged the tree an inch to the left.

"Perfect." Kenzie clapped her hands together. "Now can we put ornaments on?"

He brushed his hands off on his jeans. "Don't you want lights first?"

"Oh. Yes. Lots of lights."

As he ripped open a box of the lights she and Jinx had picked out, his phone buzzed in his pocket. Tempted to let it go to voicemail, he read over the package. Programmable to dance to music? What happened to regular old twinkle lights? His phone buzzed again. Charlie.

"Hey, Sis. That baby here yet?" The smile on his lips faded as her sobs hit him square in the gut. "What's wrong?"

Jinx caught his gaze from across the room.

"Charlie? Slow down. What happened?"

Her cries faded, and Beck's voice came on the line. "Hey, Cash. Your mom just called."

"They're still up in Tulsa? Supposed to be coming home tomorrow." Something wasn't right.

"Your dad fell off a ladder and broke his hip. He's okay. Your mom said they're going to take him into surgery first thing in the morning to try to repair some of the damage. Charlie's ready to jump in the truck and head up there, but I don't think she should travel, not with the baby coming any day."

"No. Of course not. What do we need to do?" he asked.

Jinx crossed the room and pressed her hand to his back. It wasn't much, but that small gesture gave him more comfort in that moment than he could have hoped for.

"I'm not sure yet. Sit tight, I suppose. We'll call Waylon and Statler to let them know. You want to try to track down Presley and Strait?"

"Yeah, sure. Presley just left here about a half hour ago. You keep me posted. How's Mom doing?" Jinx rubbed small circles on his back. He leaned into her, drawing on her strength.

"As well as can be expected. He's in good hands, and her sister's with her." Aunt Doris would make sure the doctors were doing everything they could. She pretty much defined the term *ballbuster*, or at least she had when she lived down the road. They never got away with a thing while she was in charge.

"All right. Give Charlie a hug for me. Tell her everything is going to be okay."

"Will do." Beck disconnected, and Cash stood with the phone pressed against his ear.

"What's going on?" Jinx's voice pulled him back.

He ran a hand over his chin. "My dad fell off a ladder and broke his hip."

She gasped, then clapped her hand to her mouth. "Oh my gosh. Is he okay?"

"Yeah. Beck said he'll be fine. But my mom's got to be worried half to death. They're going to take him into surgery in the morning." Cash staggered to the edge of the couch. "What am I supposed to do?"

"He's still up in Tulsa, right?"

Cash nodded as he dropped down onto a cushion.

Kenzie rushed to his side and curled up against him. "Is Papa going to be okay?" Fat tears slid down her cheeks.

Hell, he had to hold it together for his kid. He shook off the shock. Pulling Kenzie tight, he assured her, "Papa's going to be fine, Tadpole. Nana's with him. He's probably just going to need to stay off his feet for a while, okay?"

Jinx made eye contact over Kenzie's head. She wasn't buying his little white lies. He didn't blame her. The truth was, this reality check had him a little bit scared.

"Hey, Kenzie. Why don't we go get some dinner started while your dad makes some phone calls?"

Cash nodded, grateful she was there to distract his daughter. Even though Presley had just left a little bit ago, there was no telling where he was headed. Might take him hours to get a hold of him. And he hadn't talked to Strait in months. No one had.

"I think we've got a box of mac and cheese in the pantry." Jinx held out her hand.

Kenzie took it. "You promise Papa's going to be okay?"

His heart wrenched in two. How could he promise a thing like that? What if the surgery somehow went wrong?

Jinx saved him again. "Nobody can make a promise like that. But your daddy can promise that the doctors up in Tulsa are supersmart and doing everything they can for your papa, okay?"

"Okay." His daughter suddenly seemed so much smaller than her seven years. She let Jinx lead her into the kitchen. He listened to them chatter back and forth about little things, things that didn't matter a hill of beans when his mom and dad sat in a hospital hundreds of miles away.

He took the phone into the bedroom for some privacy and pulled up Presley's number. His brother was probably out chasing skirts or running the table at the pool hall in the next town over. When it went to voicemail, he disconnected. Strait didn't answer either. With Charlie banned from traveling and two of his four brothers not willing to pick up their phones, his course of action became crystal clear.

He had to go to Tulsa.

The sooner the better.

Now he just had to ask Jinx to take care of Kenzie for him again. Decision made, he strolled into the kitchen. Jinx and Kenzie were bent over Jinx's phone, giggling and whispering back and forth. He tried to make his voice light. Kenzie didn't need to worry about her papa being in the hospital. She needed to be thinking about Santa and Christmas and decorating that monstrosity that still listed a little to the left in his family room. She'd be okay with Jinx.

Thankful he had someone to lean on, he wrapped his arms around both of them. "Group hug."

He'd draw on their love and support and carry it with him to share with his mom and dad. Everything was going to be fine—as long as he had Jinx and Kenzie waiting for him when he got back.

chapter

TWENTY-FOUR

Of course he had to go to Tulsa. Jinx would never deny him the chance to be at his father's side, not if she was able to offer some assistance in making that happen. So here she was, wrist deep in soapy water, cleaning up the breakfast dishes while Kenzie got dressed to start another week of school. Cash said he'd call her when he got there and give her an update on Tom's condition. Charlie had promised to come over tonight to put Kenzie to bed so Jinx and Beck could handle things at the Rose. Charlie's doctor didn't want her standing so much at the honky-tonk anymore. Too stubborn to go on complete bed rest, she'd agreed to hang out with Kenzie so that Jinx could still help out at the Rose.

Jinx was amazed at the way the Walker clan rallied when one of their own needed help. Darby had volunteered to make dinner for everyone tonight, and Jinx found herself looking forward to the sense of camaraderie—something that would have scared the crap out her just a few months ago.

"You about ready, Kenzie?" She wiped her hands on the dish towel hanging from the stove. "We've only got ten minutes until the bus gets here."

Kenzie padded into the kitchen, still in her footed kitty cat pajamas. "Do I have to go to school today?"

The puppy dog eyes didn't jibe with the cat print but managed to be effective just the same. Jinx gathered her into a hug and rested her chin on top of Kenzie's untamed tangle of curls.

"I think it would keep your mind off things if you were surrounded by your friends. Aren't you making those gingerbread houses today?" She warred back and forth with herself. The poor girl could use an extra helping of love today. But it would probably be better if she stuck to her routine.

"They're not real gingerbread houses. The teacher makes us use graham crackers. Not like the ones I always make with Nana and Papa." The mention of her grandpa's name brought on a fresh round of tears.

"It's okay, honey. Your papa is a strong man. He's doing everything he can to get better." Jinx had dealt with the unexpected passing of her dad when she was about Kenzie's age. She'd never forget the deep ache she'd felt when her mom had said her dad was gone and never coming back. At eight years old, she didn't fully comprehend what that meant, but she knew enough to know she'd never see him again. Her heart shattered for Kenzie. Even though Tom had only broken a hip, it was still scary to be a kid and not fully understand what was going on.

Kenzie snugged her little arms tight as far as she could reach around Jinx's middle. "I miss my daddy."

"I miss your daddy too." It felt natural to admit it. "Now, why don't you go get dressed, and I'll drive you to school today?"

"Do I have to? I don't feel good. My tummy hurts, and I have a sore throat, and I think I might be getting the measles." Kenzie grabbed her stomach and flung a hand to her forehead. "Can you take my temperature?"

Kenzie was just worried about her papa and missing her dad. Jinx couldn't do anything about that, but she could try to distract both of them. "You know what?"

"What?" Kenzie's head nestled into Jinx's stomach, muffling her words.

"I think we need to play hooky today." Hopefully, Cash would understand. She didn't think he'd be too upset if she kept Kenzie out of school for the day. What would she miss out on? Making fake gingerbread houses out of graham crackers?

"Really?" A giant wet spot lingered where Kenzie's tears had soaked into Jinx's shirt.

"Really. A girls' day. Just you and me. What do you say?"

"What do we do on girls' day?" Kenzie wiped at her nose.

"Whatever you want. As long as it's girl stuff. We can paint our nails, go Christmas shopping, maybe even make some more of those cookies." Jinx hadn't the slightest idea what real girlfriends did on a girls' day, since she'd never had any. But based on the chick flicks and sitcoms she'd seen, she figured her ideas weren't too off base.

"Real cookies?" The pout came, forcing Kenzie's lower lip to jut out.

That meant no slice and bake. Was she up for it? Kenzie's eyes held a glimmer of hope. "Yeah, sure. Real cookies. Why not?"

"Yay! Oh, can we make gingerbread houses instead?" Her whole body lit up.

Jinx froze. She didn't even know what went

into gingerbread houses. But she couldn't deny Kenzie, especially when she didn't know if her nana would be able to keep the tradition going with her this year.

"Um, sure. Yes, definitely. I bet we can find a recipe or something online." Or a shop where they could buy the pieces and assemble it themselves. Or a bakery where they could get a gingerbread cupcake.

"Can I have a Coke while we make gingerbread houses?" Kenzie bit her bottom lip, anticipating the denial.

Jinx knew Kenzie was playing her now, trying to see how far she could push it. "We'll see, okay?"

"Okay." Kenzie dropped her gaze to the ground.

"Let's get started. We're going to need a grocery list if we're going to make a real gingerbread house. Can you find me a notebook or piece of paper or something from your daddy's desk?"

Kenzie took off on her errand while Jinx pulled up the internet on her phone. So many choices. Settling for the one titled "Easy Gingerbread Houses for Kids," she scanned the recipe while she waited for the notebook.

"Here you go." Kenzie handed her a small spiral pad, the kind Jinx had seen Cash carry with him while out on patrol.

She went to flip the page filled with his chicken scratch when a name caught her attention. *Wade Boyd.* Why the hell would Wade's name be on a page in Cash's notebook? Her stomach churned, the scrambled eggs she'd scarfed down for breakfast threatening to reappear. The blood drained from her face, leaving her feeling numb. Her vision tunneled. She couldn't see past that name. *Wade Boyd.*

"Jinx?" Kenzie grabbed her hand, pulling Jinx's attention away from the notebook. "Did you find a recipe?"

She didn't want to think about Wade yet. Actually, she didn't want to think about him at all, ever again. But it looked like Cash already knew something about Wade. The question was...*what*?

"Jinx?" Kenzie shook her arm. "Are you okay?"

"Yeah, I'm just trying to remember what we need." She flipped the page over but could still see the name in her mind. She needed to tell Cash about her history with Wade and find out why he'd written down his name. But first, she needed to give Kenzie a good day. Committed to making the biggest and best gingerbread house the girl had ever seen, Jinx picked up a pen and began to make a list.

Cash nudged the heavy hospital door open enough to peek around the corner. "Anybody home?"

His mom startled. "Cash. What are you doing here?" She rose out of her chair to meet him by the door.

"I thought you might need some moral support." He wrapped his mom in a hug. Her usually rigid shoulders slumped against him.

"You didn't need to come, Son. Where's Kenzie?" His mom's arms clung to him, her desperate need for support at complete odds with her words.

"Jinx is taking care of her. I needed to be here. How's he doing?"

Ann nodded and wiped at her eyes with a wadded-up tissue she held in her hand. "Come see for yourself. He's been in and out because of the painkillers, but he's doing great." She led him toward the side of the bed. "He's going to be fine. Just fine."

Cash stepped next to his dad. "What the hell were you doing on a ladder?"

Tom had the decency to plaster on a sheepish grin. "Hanging holiday lights over your aunt Doris's stoop. Damn ladder wasn't steady. She's got one of those cheap aluminum ones. I should have known better."

"Hell yeah, you should have known better." The poor man looked like shit. Like he'd spent the past couple of days on the wrong end of a pissed-off bucking bronc. "Kenzie sends her love."

His dad tried to sit up higher in bed. Cash reached behind him to fluff his pillow. "You tell Kenzie I'm going to be good as new. Won't be but a couple of weeks until we're out riding ponies together again."

His mom cleared her throat. "You mean after you finish your rehab, right, honey?"

"Oh, I'm not going to need all that nonsense." He gestured for Cash to lean closer. "They want me to spend a couple of weeks at some nursing home for old folks."

"It's not a nursing home. It's a rehab facility." Ann rolled her eyes. "Your father thinks I'm going to abandon him at an old folks' home and leave him in Tulsa."

"I told her she deserves a younger model. Someone with two good hips, you know?" His dad beamed up at his mom, making Cash feel like he'd intruded on their intimate moment.

The door opened, and a nurse swept into the room.

"Let's let her do what she needs to do." Ann squeezed his shoulder. "They come in every so often to check vitals, and it's easier if we're not in the way."

Cash lingered, giving his dad one last grin before following his mom into the hall. He was glad he came.

Seeing his dad in good spirits eased his fear, and he couldn't wait to call Jinx and fill her in.

"Can I get you anything, Mom? Have you eaten yet today?" He'd left the house before breakfast and hadn't had a meal yet himself.

"Your Aunt Doris left right before you got here. She ran back to the house to grab some lunch for us. She ought to be back soon. He's going to be fine. The doctor wants him to go straight to a rehab facility from here, but if all goes well, he should be home before Christmas."

"That's great." Relief flooded his system. He was tempted to twirl his mom around in a hug, but the delivery of her good news didn't match the worried look she still wore. "What's wrong? Isn't that good news?"

She stared through the blinds on the window of his dad's door. "Yes, it's great news. But he's got no guarantee of a complete recovery. He's got to participate in home therapy and stick to a PT routine. Do you want to be the one to tell your dad he can't just hop on the back of a horse if he feels like it?"

"Oh shit."

"Cash Warren Walker, watch your language." Ann clenched her jaw and turned a narrow gaze his way.

"Sorry, Mom. I see what you mean about it not all being good news." His dad had learned how to ride before he'd learned how to walk.

"And he's got to start taking regular medications like calcium supplements. Just getting him to take a daily vitamin has been a huge accomplishment." She turned a worried gaze to her son.

He covered her hand with his. "He'll do what he needs to do. You, the ranch, his family…they're everything to him. He won't like it, but he'll play along."

"I hope you're right."

"Well, if he gives you any grief, he's got five grown sons who will kick his ass until he does what you tell him to. Does that make you feel better?"

She looked like she might scold him for a moment, then broke into a grin. "Oh, honey. I'm glad you came."

Cash pulled his mom into another hug. He knew his dad would do what it took, because that's what dads did. If roles were reversed and he had to make massive lifestyle changes to gain more time with Kenzie, he'd do whatever the hell the docs told him. Family was everything, especially for the Walkers. And now he was on the verge of building his own. His dad would be okay.

The door opened, and the nurse swept past. "You can go back in now. Everything looks great."

His mom nodded. Cash released her, and she took a step toward the door.

"Hey, you mind if I go make a couple of phone calls? I know Charlie's beside herself wondering what's going on up here. And I want to let Jinx know everything is okay."

"You go ahead. I should have called earlier, but I didn't want to take any time away from your dad." She touched his cheek. "Thanks for coming all this way. It means a lot."

"I'll be back in just a few minutes." He gave her hand a squeeze.

She entered the room and took a spot by his dad's bedside. Cash couldn't begin to imagine what might be running through her mind. His dad was her rock. They'd been together since junior high. Built a family, a home, and a life together. Neither one was whole without the other.

That's what he wanted in his life. He'd never had that sense with Lori Lynne. They'd been young and stupid and horny. But he saw hints of being able to build that kind of a future with Jinx. She was the one he wanted to call first. She was the one who infiltrated his thoughts. She was the one who made him feel like he could be the man he wanted to be. For Kenzie. For her. For himself.

chapter

TWENTY-FIVE

JINX PROPPED THE EXTENSION LADDER SHE'D FOUND hanging on the side of the bunkhouse against Cash's living room wall. She'd managed to get Kenzie off to school by promising she'd string the lights today. Whose idea was it to pick the tallest tree in Texas for a Christmas tree? She leaned back, letting her gaze drift from the huge metal pail at the base to the crooked point at the top. Getting a star to sit straight would be Cash's job. Jinx would be doing well just to get a few strands of lights looped around.

Kenzie couldn't wait to hang garland and drape tinsel over the giant pine. Cash had said he'd be home in time for dinner, and Jinx didn't have to go in to the Rose tonight, so she was hoping they'd be able to make an evening out of it. They'd hang ornaments, sing Christmas tunes, and maybe watch that vintage Rudolph special she'd recorded on the DVR. And after they put Kenzie to bed, she could ask him what he knew about Wade Boyd. She didn't want any secrets between them. The sooner she came clean about how she knew Wade, the better off she'd be.

As she climbed the ladder, a strand of lights coiled in her hand, she let her thoughts drift over memories of holidays past. Last year, she'd been in Vegas. She hadn't lasted long tending bar at that seedy joint off the Strip. The year before that, she'd been working at a ski resort in Colorado. She couldn't remember the last time she'd actually set up a tree with all the trimmings. Somehow, this seemed right. Usually, the holidays filled her with a sense of loss, made her ache for what might have been had her dad never passed.

But this year, she was looking forward to it. She'd even done some shopping for Kenzie and the rest of the Walkers. Nothing big. But she wanted to show them how much they'd come to mean to her. She still hadn't found the perfect gift for Cash.

Jinx tucked the end of the strand into the top boughs of the tree. The ladder wobbled a bit when she leaned in to pass the cord around the tree. Round and round she went, moving her feet down rung by rung as the top of the tree sparkled in pink, blue, green, and purple. Kenzie had picked the jewel-tone lights as opposed to the traditional colors. As long as the kid was happy—that's what mattered.

Having reached the end of the strand, Jinx clambered down the ladder to rip open another box. On her way back up the ladder, something within the tree caught her eye. She paused, searching through the greenery for whatever she'd seen—probably just a couple of loose branches or something.

About halfway down, she tucked the strand in to wrap it around a branch. Something brushed her hand. She screamed and fled. Right back up the ladder, giving her a perfect view of what had to be a thirty-foot snake wrapped around the branches of the tree. Okay, so maybe it was more like six feet long. But still, it seemed much, much larger from where she stood, perched at the top of the tall extension ladder.

If she could just climb past it, she could grab her phone from the end table and call someone to come take care of it. She'd lived with mice, been infested with cockroaches, and even had an overpopulation of kangaroo rats take over when she lived in a mobile home in the high desert. But she didn't do snakes.

She stepped down to a lower rung, trying to find the creature within the branches. No luck. Down one more rung. Still nothing. She moved her foot to the next rung. There, nestled among the dark-green needles. Oh hell no. She scrambled the three rungs back up to stand near the top again. It was only one o'clock. If nothing else, Kenzie would be home in another two hours. Surely, the snake would slither down by then.

Ht

"Jinx? Are you home?" Kenzie bounded through the front door, dropped her backpack on the floor, and turned an accusing gaze to where Jinx still clung to the top of the ladder. "You didn't meet my bus."

"I'm so sorry. Guess what?" Jinx didn't want to scare the crap out of the kid. *Stay calm.*

"What?"

"It's kind of a funny story." Well, maybe not yet. But it had potential. Assuming she and Kenzie didn't get eaten by the rogue rattler. She could see the headlines now… *Christmas Comes Early for Giant Rattler in the Form of Stupid Woman and Tasty Little Girl.*

"Why are you on a ladder? Are the lights done?" Kenzie moved toward the boxes of twinkle lights at the base of the tree.

"Stop!" Jinx wasn't a yeller, so her shout made Kenzie

stop in her tracks. "I don't want you to freak out, but there's a snake in this tree, and we need to call someone to help us get it out. See my phone over there on the table?"

Kenzie nodded, then turned her head to peer into the tree. "Is it a copperhead? Daddy says they're posiness."

"Poisonous," Jinx corrected. "I don't know what kind of snake it is, but I need you to stay away from the tree, okay?"

"Okay."

"Can you go get my phone? Do you know your Uncle Waylon's number?"

Kenzie shook her head.

"How about Uncle Statler?"

Another no.

A swell of panic squeezed her lungs, making it hard to take in a full breath. There was only one other thing she could think to do. "Kenzie, I want you to dial 911."

"Daddy says that's only for emergencies."

Jinx wanted to laugh, cry, and scream all at the same time. If this didn't qualify as an emergency, then she didn't know what did. She had to get off this ladder soon, or her legs were going to give out. "Honey, this *is* an emergency. Do you know how to dial that?"

Kenzie crossed the room to the table and picked up the phone. Her little fingers punched in the numbers before she lifted the phone to her ear.

Jinx gritted her teeth while she listened to the one-sided conversation.

"There's a snake in our tree."

Pause.

"It's in our house."

Pause.

"My daddy is with my papa. He's in the hospital. I don't have a mama, but Jinx is here."

Pause.

"She can't. She's on a ladder."

Pause.

"Oh, hi, Brandi. Okay." She pressed the "end" button. "Can I get a snack?"

Jinx took in a deep breath through her nose, warding off a claustrophobic sense of panic. "Is someone coming?"

"Yeah. Brandi's nice. She gives me suckers when I go to work with Daddy sometimes."

"So Brandi's sending someone over?"

"She said it will be a little while. Can I make hot cocoa?"

"Can you wait, sweetheart? I'll make you cocoa with marshmallows when I get down, okay?"

"I'm gonna go play in my room."

"Okay." Good idea. That would keep her away from the snake. "Will you make sure Hendrix is okay? But don't let him out." That's all she needed—a Chihuahua on the loose with a snake chasing him around the house.

Jinx rolled her neck, trying to dislodge the tension that had settled in. Standing on a ladder all afternoon would do that.

Finally, after what seemed like hours, the faint wail of sirens reached her. Sirens? All she needed was one cop. Or a husky ranch hand. As long as he or she came with gloves and hopefully a huge hoe. Or two hoes. Or at this point, even a shotgun. But seriously, what was with the sirens?

Blue and red lights flashed across the walls of the house through the front window. The sirens stopped, but the sound of voices took their place. Voices, as in more than one person. How many guys did this Brandi send over? A sharp knock sounded at the door.

"Come in!" Jinx yelled.

The door opened, and a handful of people trickled in. Jinx recognized Tippy, Cash's coworker, but the rest of them were strangers.

Tippy took off his hat. "So we received a call from Kenzie about a snake?"

Jinx's legs shook, the effort of clinging to the ladder finally taking its toll. "It's in the tree. When I tried to climb down the ladder, I saw it."

A woman with bright-red hair stepped out from behind Tippy. "What color was it?"

"What color? I don't know. I didn't get a good look at it. I was trying not to get eaten."

The woman didn't flinch, just pulled on a pair of long gloves, then took a stick out of her pocket. "Where did you last see it?"

"Um, are you just going to grab it?"

Tippy spoke up. "Jinx, this is Sage. She lives down the road a ways and knows how to handle just about any kind of wild animal."

"Even snakes?" Jinx eyed the woman.

"'Specially snakes. I've got a rattlesnake farm. Tastes like chicken." She moved toward the ladder and put a well-worn steel-toed boot on the first rung. The ladder shook. "Come here, you little bastard." Sage extended the stick to poke it into the branches.

"Are you getting the snake?" Kenzie piped up from the second-floor landing. "Is it a big one?"

"Don't know yet. Stay upstairs, okay?" Jinx closed her eyes, shuddering with every shake of the ladder.

Sage crept from rung to rung, finally stopping a few feet below Jinx. "This about where you saw it?"

"I don't know. I think so."

More strangers walked through the front door. How many people did it take to catch a snake? Jinx trembled on the ladder while the guys below stood around giving each other fist bumps and watching Sage poke around in the tree. Hendrix ran between their legs in a new outfit Kenzie had put on him. He had on suspenders and holiday-printed shorts over his bottom half.

"Kenzie, can you get Hendrix and take him upstairs?" All she needed was for her dog to become a snack for a hungry rattler.

"This what had you shakin' in your boots?" Sage reached a hand into the depths of the tree. Jinx cringed, trying to climb even farther up the ladder, anticipating the worst. Instead, Sage pulled out a snake.

It dangled from her hand, about five feet down. Jinx hadn't really seen a snake that big in person, but she expected it to slither or strike. Or at least do something besides just hang there.

"Is it dead?" she asked.

Sage dropped it to the ground. The tough guys who'd been watching each took a quick step back. The snake lay on the hardwood floor, not moving.

"Wasn't ever alive," Sage said. "That's a bummer too. That size would have made for a few good meals."

Jinx shuddered at the idea. "What do you mean it wasn't ever alive?"

"It's rubber. Fake." Sage climbed down the ladder and

kicked it with her boot. Hendrix grabbed hold of it, growling and snarling as he dragged it around the room.

Jinx's stomach rolled over. "Are you sure there's no real snake?"

"I been up and down this tree twice now," Sage said. "The only snake you've got was made in China. Besides, it's too cool out. Pretty unlikely to find a snake in a tree to begin with, but especially this time of year."

"It's just a fake snake?" Kenzie walked down the steps, her disappointment evident. "Who would put a fake snake in our Christmas tree?"

Jinx held tight to the ladder. Hendrix continued to drag the snake around the room, ripping chunks out of it. Only one person had had access to their tree besides the three of them. It had to have been Presley. The Walker brothers had taken their holiday pranking one step too far.

Tippy and the other spectators shook their heads, clearly amused at her mistake. If she could disappear inside herself, Jinx would have chosen that moment in time to vanish. Maybe transport herself somewhere where snakes didn't exist. Like Antarctica.

HH

Cash pulled off the blacktop onto the long gravel drive. It would be good to be home. He'd have enough time to cuddle with Kenzie before she went to bed, then lose himself in Jinx's arms. Hospitals creeped him out. Something about the smell of death and illness mingling with antiseptic and alcohol. Made him feel like he was coming down with something every time he passed through the automatic sliding glass doors.

As he approached the house, he eased his foot onto the brake. What in the hell was going on? Tippy's truck sat out front, lights flashing like at a crime scene. Two other vehicles he didn't recognize sat in the driveway. If something had happened to Kenzie... He wouldn't let himself think about it.

He raced from the cab, not even thinking to turn off the engine. The front door of the house sat cracked open. Cash burst through, running smack-dab into a woman on her way out.

"Damnation!" the woman cursed.

"Somebody want to tell me what the hell is going on in here?"

Kenzie stood at the bottom of the stairs. "Curse jar."

He'd stuff the damn curse jar with hundred-dollar bills as long as his baby was okay. He raced through the door to pull her into his arms. Had to make sure she was safe. "You okay, Tadpole?"

"Hi, Daddy. Jinx is having a—what did you call it, Tippy?"

"Hey, Cash." Tippy clapped a hand on his shoulder. "Welcome home."

"What the damn hell is going on?" He thrust a palm toward Kenzie before she could call him out again. "I know, I know. I'm overriding the curse jar for a few minutes."

"Ain't it obvious?" Tippy's head shook from side to side. "Your girlfriend got treed by a snake. Or I guess she got laddered by a rubber snake."

Cash screwed up his brow. "Say what?"

"There was a snake." Jinx stood at the top of the extension ladder. "Before you tell me I'm crazy, I know what I saw." She could have killed Tippy with the sour look she gave him. Full of piss and vinegar. May as well have been fire shooting from her eyes.

Cash felt the heat from her stare burn right through him as she turned her gaze on him.

"It was a rubber one, Deputy." The woman—he recognized her as Sage, the snake farmer from a few ranches over—held a long rubber snake up with Hendrix dangling from the end.

Tippy held his hand to his mouth and winked at Kenzie. "Nervous breakdown. That's what I called it."

"I am not having a nervous breakdown!" Jinx yelled from the ladder.

Cash took a step toward the ladder, but Tippy caught his arm. "Careful. You don't want to get bit."

"Thought you said it was just a rubber snake," Cash said.

"I didn't mean by the snake. I meant by her." Tippy pointed to the top of the ladder, where Jinx clutched the sides in a death grip.

"Very funny, Tippy. Remind me to put coal in your stocking this year." Jinx glared. She was like a treed cat—nervous and frozen with fear.

"Can everyone go on and get out of here, please? I'll handle things from here on out." Cash ushered the spectators from his family room. "Except you." He put a hand out to stop Tippy from leaving.

"Need me to take a hoe to that snake for you?" Tippy joked.

Cash ignored him, figuring he better step in and

take control of the situation before Jinx lost it even more than she already had. "Why don't you come on down from there?"

Her grip tightened. "Your brother's taken it too far this time. What else do you think he did to the tree? Rigged it with explosives?"

"Jinx, you can't stay on the ladder all night." But the set of her jaw and the determined glint in her eye said different. This wasn't how he'd pictured his homecoming. "You really think Presley did something else to this tree?"

She shrugged. "I don't know. But either that tree goes, or I go. You choose."

Cash shook his head. "Fine. Tippy, help me haul the tree out of here, will you?"

Tippy looked like he'd been enjoying the entertainment until Cash pressed him into service. "Hey, there could really be a snake in that tree."

"Not likely." Cash bent down to unhook the trunk from the complicated rigging system he'd installed.

"But what if there is?" Tippy shifted from foot to foot.

Cash almost felt sorry for the guy. Back when they were kids, they used to try to trap the snakes that slithered out to sun themselves on the hot asphalt. Tippy gave that up when he got bit by a nasty copperhead. Ever since then, he'd steered clear of anything that slithered.

"Snakes are more scared of you than you are of them, right, Daddy?" Kenzie called from the steps.

Tippy muttered under his breath, just low enough that Cash had to strain to hear him, "Not really."

"But what about our tree?" Kenzie stomped her foot.

"I'm so sorry," Jinx called down. "We'll get a new tree, one that doesn't have anything slithering inside it, okay?"

"Okay." Kenzie crossed her arms over her stomach and sat halfway up the steps.

With a lot of heaving and hefting and more than a few four-letter words, Cash and Tippy managed to get the tree through the front door. By the time Cash returned to the living room, Jinx had climbed down from the ladder. She and Kenzie stood at the top of the steps.

"I've got to sit down." Jinx lowered herself to sit on the top step.

Cash took the stairs two at a time. "How are my girls?"

"Hi, Daddy." Kenzie wrapped her arms around his legs. He hefted her onto his lap as he took a seat next to Jinx.

"You okay?"

She rested her head on his shoulder. "No."

"I'm sorry about the fake snake." His arm went around her shoulders. Kenzie snuggled between them.

"Three hours. I was on that ladder for three hours. This prank thing needs to end. Your brother is going to pay."

"So you think it was Presley?" Cash asked.

"Who else could it have been? He's the only one who's been over here since we got the tree."

"That's true. All right, we'll retaliate, then call it quits on the whole thing."

"Good. Hey, how's your dad doing?" Jinx asked.

Cash bounced Kenzie on his knee. "There's good news on that front. Should be home by Christmas."

"That's great."

"Yeah, Mom's freaking out about everything that

needs to be done. I told her we'll figure it out. She needs to worry about Dad right now."

"So Papa's going to be okay?" Kenzie asked.

"Better than okay. He'll be just fine." He kissed his daughter's soft cheek. She smelled like Jinx's lotion. "What did you girls do while I was gone?"

"Look, Daddy. Jinx painted my fingernails." Kenzie held her hand out, twisting it back and forth so the sparkles on her fingernails caught the light.

"Wow. That looks great."

Kenzie nodded. "And I did hers."

Jinx held her hands out for him to see. Red and green fingernail polish covered most of her nails and a good portion of her fingertips too. He tried not to laugh. Seeing Kenzie bloom under Jinx's care was just the kind of holiday cheer he needed. It had become obvious his daughter benefitted from having the soft touch of a woman around. Not that Jinx looked like she had very many soft edges. But he'd figured out something pretty important about the woman he was falling for. She was kind of like that fire-roasted mango salsa his mama made. The first bite made his eyes water, packed a punch, and made his tongue feel like it was on fire. But if he made it past that initial burn, he was rewarded with a sweet, lingering aftertaste that always made him go back for more.

Tippy interrupted their little reunion. "Need anything else, Deputy?"

"Nah, I think I can handle things from here." Cash stood and met his coworker at the bottom of the stairs.

"Hey. How do you want me to code this one? Domestic disturbance?" The smug smirk gave away Tippy's twisted sense of humor.

Cash scoffed. That's all he needed. "Can't you tag it with something like a wildlife intervention?"

"Whatever you say. See you at the office tomorrow." He clapped Cash on the back, then headed toward the door.

Cash watched him step around the tree they'd abandoned halfway down the walk.

"Want me to turn off your truck?" Tippy asked.

Cash had been in such a hurry to get inside, he'd left the driver's side door open and the engine running.

"Yeah, thanks."

Tippy climbed inside, cut the engine, and tossed the keys to Cash. "Have a good night now."

"Thanks, you too."

Cash had promised Kenzie a Christmas tree this year. With his mom still in Tulsa and their fresh-cut pine sprawled across the front lawn, he'd let Presley know it was now his responsibility. His brother would have to come through so Cash could keep his word.

But first, he needed to surround himself in the warmth and love of his two favorite females—even if one of them hadn't been able to acknowledge the newfound feelings between them yet.

chapter
TWENTY-SIX

JINX HAD BEEN ON EDGE ALL NIGHT. IT DIDN'T HELP that she'd been rendered motionless for an entire afternoon thanks to Cash and his brothers and their stupid pranking tradition. It was hard to stay mad at Cash. He seemed so happy to be home, so relieved about his dad's progress.

And now she needed to figure out an alternative tree, something without serpent-appealing branches, so that Kenzie could have a Christmas tree. Cash's idea to heft the responsibility to Presley wouldn't pan out. That meant it was up to her.

As she mulled over where to get a tree in a town the size of Holiday, her phone rang. Why would Geri be calling? Jinx hadn't heard from her since she had left LA. She'd sent a text to let Geri know she had settled in Texas for a bit, but that was the only communication they'd had. Dread bloomed in her gut. This couldn't be good.

"Hello?" Jinx tucked her phone between her ear and her shoulder while she attacked a cup crusted in cocoa and marshmallows with a sponge.

"Jinx, is that you?" The panic in Geri's voice kicked Jinx's heart into high gear.

"What's wrong?"

"Oh, honey. It's so good to hear your voice. Are you okay? Things are good down there?"

"Geri, what's going on?"

"I didn't want to tell him, I promise." Geri's voice wavered like she was trying to hold back tears.

"Tell who what?" Jinx immediately fast-forwarded to the worst. She pulled her hands out of the sink and wiped them on her pants. Wade must have figured out where she was. By now, he'd know the gift cards were missing and assume she'd taken them. It didn't take much to get him all riled up.

"Wade. He knows where you are. He was going to turn me in to the Humane Society, honey. I couldn't lose my cats."

"Oh, Geri." Jinx knew how much she cared about her rescue kitties. But why now? "What happened?"

"He made me tell him you were in Texas. Then he left town a few days ago but didn't say where he was going. I should have called you then, but my calico had her kittens, and her milk didn't come in, so I've been feeding them all with a dropper for the past couple of days."

"It's okay. What makes you think he's coming here?"

Geri blew her nose, then continued. "Last night, he called in to talk to the new girl he hired, Shelby. She works the taps but also does a lot of stuff back in the office."

Jinx could picture the kind of work Wade probably had her engaged in, and it didn't have anything to do with ten-key skills. "Go on."

"I picked up the extension and heard him say he's going to find you and take care of the problem right away, before it gets out of hand. Why else would he head that way unless he's coming after you?"

Jinx staggered to the table and dropped into a chair. *Why else would he head that way unless he's coming after you?* looped through her mind. Just when she thought she'd found a safe place to settle down. She couldn't—no, make that *wouldn't* let Wade kill what she had with Cash before it even had a chance to grow.

"Okay, I'll figure something out. Thanks for telling me."

"I'm so sorry, hon," Geri keened into the phone.

"It's okay. Everything will be fine." Jinx disconnected. It was time to tell Cash about Wade. He'd know what to do.

While she waited for him to put Kenzie to bed, she paced the kitchen. How should she start the conversation? *Hey, remember how I told you I worked at a bar in California before this? Well, my ex-boss, who also happens to be my ex-lover, is a major drug dealer and is probably tracking me down because I accidentally stole several thousand dollars' worth of the gift cards he's using to pay off his drug runners…*

No, that wouldn't do. While she ran through her options in her head, her phone pinged, so she took a quick peek at her incoming text. A picture of Kenzie with a stocky Santa in a crappy red suit had been sent from a number she didn't recognize. Something about the eyes underneath the gray-tinged eyebrows and the cocky smile looked off.

The picture had to have been taken at Kenzie's school. She could see the brick wall in the background and the flower beds out front that always looked like they needed weeding. It couldn't be from Kenzie's teacher—she wouldn't have Jinx's number. A cold knot formed in her gut. Wade. Under the beard, mustache, and thick, fake eyebrows, Wade mocked her. But how had he gotten to Kenzie?

She called the number. Voicemail picked up.

"Thanks for calling, Jinx. Do I have your attention? Cute kid you've got here. Funny how I was able to just walk right into her school. No security system, nobody checking IDs. Makes me wonder about what kind of job your new boyfriend is doing protecting the good citizens of Holiday, Texas. Now before you get any ideas about calling him for help, listen up. You meet me at ten o'clock Thursday night at that old dairy on the outskirts of town. Bring my cards. Fail to show up or get the cops involved, and somebody's going to get hurt. I just hope it isn't sweet Kenzie."

The message ended with a loud beep. Jinx stepped out the back door and stood on the concrete stoop. "Now you listen, you sorry sack of shit. You touch one precious hair on that kid's head, and I'll kill you. This is between you and me. Keep everyone else out of it."

Cash opened the door, spilling a wedge of light out onto the stoop. "Everything okay?"

She clicked her phone off. "Yeah."

"Who were you talking to?"

"Just somebody who had a question about my last job." She hated lying to him. But Wade didn't make idle threats. He might have been a huge asshole, but when he issued a warning, she knew he'd always follow through.

"Come back inside. It's cold out here."

She followed him into the house and leaned against the back of a chair at the kitchen table.

Cash came up behind her. "Kenzie's asleep." He nuzzled his lips against her neck.

Shivers raced up and down her spine at his touch. "I'm sure she's happy to have her daddy back."

"Mm-hmm." His lips trailed kisses down to her shoulder and back up again.

She wanted to moan, twist around in his arms, and lean into him. But that would only make things harder. So instead, she stiffened. "You know, it's been a really long day."

His hands circled her waist, coming to rest under her chest. She wouldn't have to do much to encourage him—a gentle nudge against his crotch, a tilt of the head to give him better access. Either of those movements or her choice of many others would ensure she'd be on her back and on the receiving end of his talented hands in mere moments. As tempting as that was, she needed time to think, to plan, to figure out how to get Wade away from Holiday.

"I think I'm going to head back to the bunkhouse and hit the sack early tonight." She ducked out of his arms to pick up the backpack she'd stuffed while he put Kenzie to bed.

His eyes narrowed slightly, like he was trying to get a read on her. "You sure?"

"Yeah. I'll be by in the morning before she leaves for school."

"You still upset about the snake fiasco? For what it's worth, I texted Presley that he has to find us a new tree."

"I know. I'm fine. Just tired." She stood on her tiptoes to give him a peck on the cheek. He could tell something was up. But she needed to be alone to figure out a plan. Being around Cash was too distracting. "I'll see you in the

morning." She shoved her feet into the boots she'd
left by the back door.

He held the door for her. "If you change your
mind…"

"I know where to find you," she finished. Her gaze
settled on him for a long moment. His jeans clung to
his hips, a form-fitting T-shirt stretched over those
broad shoulders, and three days' worth of stubble
covered his usually smooth cheeks. This was his home.
He belonged here—with his daughter, his family, his
life. Maybe she'd been wrong about fitting in.

He acted like he wanted to stop her, like he knew
something was up. But he didn't. Maybe if he had, he
would have changed her mind. But she didn't want
to dump her problems on him, not when he had so
much going on with his family. They needed to be
his priority, not digging her out of a mess she'd found
her way into all on her own. No, Wade was her fault.
She needed to deal with him by herself.

Things were so much easier when she only had
herself to worry about. Her heart skipped a beat at
the thought of being on her own again. She and
Hendrix had done okay by themselves. They'd had
nothing but open road between them and whatever
new adventure awaited.

Part of her missed that freedom. No one counted
on her. No one needed her. No one would be disappointed when she couldn't come through for them. But
spending time with Cash and Kenzie and the Walker
family had shown her another option. They'd woken
up a part of her that she didn't even know existed.

And she liked it.

Which meant she'd do anything to protect them.

Even if it meant leaving.

She could beat Wade to the punch. Draw him away from Holiday, away from the people she loved.

Loved.

The realization slammed into her like a two-by-four to the head. She actually felt physical pain at the thought. She loved them. All of them. Ann, Tom, Charlie, Beck, Waylon, Darby, their posse of kids. Kids...like Kenzie. Like the unborn baby Charlie was ready to pop out any day. And Cash. Yes, him most of all. He'd shown her the path to a place inside herself she thought she'd lost.

Life was a shit shack. How could she protect them if she didn't go? The truth pressed down on her, making her feel like Lou the longhorn was standing on her chest.

She couldn't.

With a last look back at Cash, she carved the image of him into her mind, silhouetted by the warm light of the kitchen, the smell of gingerbread still hanging in the air. His arms were wrapped around his middle, warding off the chill, and his feet were covered in those silly striped socks she and Kenzie had bought him last time they went into town. Then she turned forward, ready to face the future she deserved.

Cash knocked on the door to the bunkhouse. Jinx had been avoiding him for the past two days. He couldn't believe she was still that upset about the snake in the tree. They'd both been busy, him with trying to get caught up at work and her with finishing the scenery for the Christmas play. After tonight's performance, things ought to slow down a bit. Kenzie's break started tomorrow, and they'd have plenty of time to spend together.

He knocked again. Her footsteps came closer to the door, then it swung open. She stood in front of him, a sight for seriously sore eyes.

"Hey, Kenzie and I are going to head into town in a bit. Do you want to catch a ride with us?" He peered past her into the main room of the bunkhouse. Her backpack sat on the table, and everything else had been picked up and put away. It looked cleaner now than it had since she'd moved in.

"Dwight finished my bike and dropped it off this afternoon. I figured I'd take it out for a drive to test the new engine and meet you at the play." She toed at the edge of the door.

He reached for her shoulder, but she backed away. "What's wrong, Jinx? Are you still mad about that prank? I told you I'd get even with Presley."

She gave a slight shake of the head. "No, it's not that."

"Then what is it? You've been giving me an ice-cold shoulder ever since I got back from Tulsa."

"I'm sorry. I guess I'm nervous about tonight. Can we just get through the play?" She glanced up at him. Something passed across her face. Fear? Regret? For someone who spent most of his day getting a read on people, he couldn't figure out what had happened.

"Did I do something? Whatever it is, I'm sorry."

"You didn't do a thing. It's me. This is a hard time of year for me. The past keeps coming back. But I'm working on it. I'm going to put it behind me once and for all."

"Good." He leaned in to kiss her cheek. She bristled but didn't pull away. "Can we talk later? Maybe over a glass of wine after Kenzie gets to bed tonight?"

"That would be nice." She nodded. "I've got to get going. I promised I'd pick up a couple of things at the mini-mart on the way. I'll see you there."

"I'll be in the front row."

She gave him a half-hearted smile and shut the door.

Cash stood on the porch for a moment, wondering what he'd done and what he needed to do to fix it. Maybe it was the holidays, like she said. He knew she missed her dad. It had to be hard to not have family this time of year.

He hopped off the porch and made his way back home, vowing to give Jinx the best holiday she'd ever had. Between him and Kenzie, they'd make her stop looking back and give her a reason to start looking forward.

A half hour later, he gave Kenzie a kiss on the cheek in the wings of the makeshift stage. He had to get back out to where he'd saved seats in the front row of the elementary school cafeteria. No way could he miss his baby's theatrical debut.

"You got glitter on your lips." Kenzie ran her finger over his mouth.

Gold face paint covered her cheeks. Gold glitter specks covered her sparkly star costume. His mom would probably keel over if she saw how the finished costume had turned out without her help. Jinx had somehow managed to figure out how to run the fabric through his mom's old Singer. So what if the five points on the star weren't exactly the same length? It was art, for crying out loud.

"Break a leg, baby." He stood, ready to head back to the audience.

Her mouth opened in horror. "What?"

"It's just something people say to professional actors and such. It means good luck." He patted the top point of the star. A shower of gold sprinkles rained into her hair. She'd probably sparkle until Easter.

"Just say 'good luck' then." The look she gave him was part disgust, part wonderment at his fatherly stupidity.

"Got it. Good luck, Tadpole."

"Yeah, break a leg, Kenzie!" Jinx gave her a thumbs-up as she passed by. She'd been helping backstage, so he hadn't seen much of her since they'd arrived.

"What is it with you people?" Kenzie turned her scowl toward Jinx.

Cash let out a laugh. "See you on the flip side. I'm recording your show for Nana and Papa, so make sure you speak up, okay?"

Kenzie nodded, sending another rainfall of glitter to the ground around her.

Cash pushed through the door into the auditorium and located his sister, just about to take her seat. She was impossible to miss. Poor Charlie seemed to have doubled in size since he had seen her last week. She and Beck hadn't found out the gender of the baby; they wanted it to be a surprise. Based on the size of her stomach, he had to assume she had a future Aggie linebacker in there.

"Hey." He lifted what appeared to be a horse blanket off his sister's shoulders.

"My coat doesn't fit anymore. I've been reduced to wearing a blanket around my shoulders. Can you believe it?" She groaned as Cash helped her lower onto the uncomfortable folding chair.

"Where's Beck?" Cash scanned the overfilled lunch-room for a glimpse of his brother-in-law. He usually didn't stray more than a few feet from his wife's side these days.

"He ran back to the truck for my cushion. Nobody tells you about the hemorrhoids. I had no idea being pregnant was so glamorous." She looked miserable. He didn't remember Lori Lynne being so cranky at the end.

"Hang in there, Sis. Only a few more days, right?" The doctor said he'd induce on Monday if she hadn't delivered by then. Plenty of time for his mom and dad to get back to town.

"I don't know if I'm going to make it. Feels like this kid is going to shoot out at any moment." She leaned against the back of the chair. "Can you help me get my shoes off? Everything's too tight. I had to throw on Beck's boots in order to leave the house."

Cash leaned down and worked on releasing her swollen feet from Beck's well-worn work boots. Thank God women were the ones who got pregnant. He'd been through every kind of natural disaster and traumatic situation he could think of, but this forty-week misery would have done him in a long time ago. With Charlie settled, at least for the time being, he made his way down the line of relatives and friends who'd come out to watch the show. Even Presley had managed to get there on time. He'd be pissed as hell when he realized Cash had arranged for someone to cover his precious Jeep in red and green tinsel while he watched the show. But he'd get over it.

Cash's heart swelled with a newfound love and appreci-ation for the bonds of family. He'd closed off his emotions for so long after Lori Lynne had left. He'd been so bitter about what he'd lost, he couldn't appreciate what he still had. Now, all that had changed.

Darby passed out snacks to her brood, negotiating with them for forty-five minutes of good behavior. Statler pushed buttons on his phone, probably answering work emails or something. Presley took a swig from a flask he tucked back into his jacket pocket. When would someone come along and tame his youngest brother of his wild ways? At least he'd shown up. The only ones missing were his parents and Strait. He'd hoped his long-lost brother would make it home for the holidays this year, but something he wasn't willing to talk about yet kept him away.

As the lights dimmed, Beck slid into the seat next to Charlie. Cash pulled out his phone, ready to capture the show so his parents and Kenzie could watch it for years to come.

The play started with a group of kids and their dog, played by a very bedazzled Hendrix, bemoaning the fact that they didn't have money to buy Christmas presents or decorations for the holidays. Then the Christmas fairy descended from a cloud and told them if they could find the spirit of Christmas, they'd be rewarded. Cash laughed along with the rest of the crowd as the kids and Hendrix went on a scavenger hunt, looking for the mysterious spirit. They traipsed through a cookie-making contest, searched through a crowded mall, and stumbled over people watching the annual tree-lighting ceremony in downtown Holiday, complete with a reenactment of the tree topple in which Hendrix played himself as a kid in a pig costume chased him around the stage. Along the way, they helped some elderly people carry their packages to the car, located the lost parents of a kid at the tree festival, and helped a group of younger kids finish their cookies before the timer went off.

At the end of the play, the kids returned home to find the Christmas fairy had decorated their house with larger-than-life decorations. Kenzie delivered the last line of the play as the glowing star on top of the tree. When the spotlight hit her, the reflection from the pounds of gold glitter sent dazzling sparkles throughout the audience like a holiday disco ball.

Cash jumped to his feet along with the rest of the crowd, hooting and whistling their appreciation. Everyone but Charlie. She sat bent over with her giant belly drooping between widespread legs, huffing and puffing. Beck clenched her hand, coaching her through what appeared to be a strong contraction.

"Now? This is happening now?" Cash put a hand on Charlie's back as she practiced her breathing techniques.

"Sorry I don't have better timing."

Cash shifted into emergency responder mode. "Darby, can you tell Jinx I had to go? Will you see if she can grab Kenzie and maybe give them a ride back to the house?"

Darby nodded.

"Beck, I'm going to go get the truck. Meet you out front in two minutes, okay?"

"I'll have her there. Thanks."

Satisfied they had a plan, Cash stood to assess the best exit point from the school. Throngs of proud parents surged toward the stage. No sense in trying to sneak out that way. He turned his attention toward the doors. His odds of a quick departure didn't look good that way either. Forced to choose quickly, he opted for the back of the building. He nudged through the crowd, catching a glimpse of Jinx helping Kenzie down from her perch on the top of the plywood tree.

He tried to get her attention, but there were too many people between them. She'd never be able to hear him with all the chatter. His breath caught as she drew Kenzie in for a huge hug. He'd been so lucky to have her fall into their lives. It was time to start thinking about settling down. For real this time.

But first, he had to find a way to get to the front of the school to pick up his sister. He burst through the delivery door onto the receiving dock at the back of the school. This was worse than trying to get out of the parking lot on the last night of the Conroe County Fair. Why had the church next door decided to have their live nativity on the same night as the school play? Lines of cars snaked through the shared lot. Drivers honked. People flooded the parking lot, stepping between cars, totally disregarding any kind of traffic rules. Or common sense.

Cash barreled through the lot toward the truck with one thought on his mind—no niece or nephew of his was going to be born in the elementary school cafeteria where he'd grown up shooting spitballs at the ceiling.

TWENTY-SEVEN

JINX SCANNED THE TEXTS THAT HAD BEEN LIGHTING UP her phone throughout the performance. Wade was close. His messages taunted her, detailing the things he'd do to the people she loved if she didn't show.

Now to get Kenzie to her dad without losing the shred of control she'd managed to hang on to. She wouldn't say goodbye. She couldn't without suffering a complete emotional breakdown. And she didn't have time for that.

"Should we see if we can find your dad?" Jinx took Kenzie's smaller hand in hers. She'd miss this. To say she'd grown fond of Kenzie would be a lie. The little girl had taken hold of her heart like no one ever had before. She had a knack for worming her way in, past all Jinx's protective barriers. It wouldn't happen again; Jinx would make sure of that. Losing her dad had been one thing— she hadn't had a choice but to love him. Losing Kenzie and Cash would be a thousand times more devastating. She'd known the risks of opening up her heart to them and had done it anyway. She wouldn't make that kind of mistake again.

She should have known better. She *was* jinxed, doomed to destroy anyone and everyone who dared to get close to her.

Kenzie gave her hand a squeeze and held Hendrix's leash in her other. "Do you think Daddy saw me say my line?"

"Of course he did." Everyone in the room had been watching Kenzie. But Jinx had been watching Cash. The look of love and pride on his face had made her struggle to draw in a breath. That's what love between a daddy and his little girl should look like. That's the kind of love she'd felt from her own dad before he was taken away from her. She'd do absolutely everything within and even push the boundaries of things out of her control to make sure nothing she said or did would risk that sacred bond.

"Hendrix did real good too." Kenzie lifted the dog up to her face, laughing as he spread kisses over her cheeks.

Darby flagged them down over the heads of the kindergarteners standing between them. "Cash had to go. Charlie's in labor. Y'all need a ride home or to the hospital?"

"Can we go see the baby be born? Can we?" Kenzie bounced up and down. She'd been obsessed with worry about missing the baby's delivery. She and Jinx had had many conversations in which Kenzie had grilled her on where babies came from and how they got in and out of their mommy's tummies. Jinx had tried to talk around the topic so many times that now Kenzie had some confused notion that there would be a window that would open up in her aunt's stomach and the baby would just pop out like the drive-thru at Whataburger.

"Your dad would probably want you to go home

with Aunt Darby. Babies can take a while to arrive." Jinx actually didn't have a clue as to how long a baby might take to make an appearance, but she needed Kenzie to go with Darby. She couldn't make a meeting with Wade with a seven-year-old on the back of her bike.

"That's right, kiddo." Darby shifted the toddler on her hip. "Although Charlie does seem to do things her own way, doesn't she? I wouldn't be surprised if she had the baby arrive within a prescheduled thirty-minute window."

"See, Jinx? It is a window." Kenzie nodded, sure she'd figured out everything she needed to know about how babies found their way into the world.

Jinx wasn't about to start an argument with a seven-year-old. "I rode my bike, so can you take Kenzie home with you?"

"Sure. Want us to meet you at Cash's, or should we keep her overnight?" Darby asked.

"I've got something I need to take care of, so if you could have her stay over, that would be great."

"No problem. Let me get the rest of the brood gathered up, and we'll head out." She turned to start wrangling her kids.

Jinx dropped down so she was eye to eye with Kenzie. "So I've got some things I need to take care of. Will you look after Hendrix for me?"

"But we're still making Daddy's pie tomorrow, right?" Kenzie's big brown eyes widened.

Why was this so hard? She should have just walked away, not even bothered trying to hint at goodbye. Cash would understand. But Kenzie wouldn't. She'd look back on tonight and wonder what she'd done or said that had driven Jinx away. She had to know it wasn't her fault. Jinx tried again. "I think you might have to wait for your nana to get back to help you with the pie."

"But you promised. Nana won't have time to make it, and we were going to surprise Daddy with his favorite." Kenzie's brow furrowed. She looked just like her dad when she got upset—with the clenched jaw and hard glint in her eyes, it was like looking at a miniature Cash.

"Pie is too…"

"Too what?"

How could she explain to a kid that pie was too hard? Pie was a commitment. She didn't have the skill, the bandwidth, or the emotional capacity to make Cash a pie. Slice-and-bake cookies she could handle. But pie…a pie was something else entirely.

"Too complicated. Your nana is good with pie. All I'm good for is…"

"Nothin'." Kenzie twirled around and stomped off to join her Aunt Darby. Hendrix shot her a disappointed look before turning to follow.

Jinx hung her head and repeated Kenzie's last word: "Nothin'." That about summed it up. Even a kid could see her true colors. She stood to the side of the cafeteria as the rest of the Walkers shuffled through the side door and out into the parking lot.

She'd left a note in the bunkhouse for Cash, trying to explain herself. He'd be mad, but she hoped he'd understand. She had also told him she left something for Kenzie—Hendrix. It wasn't fair for him to live in the soft-side carrier on the back of her bike anymore. Kenzie loved the little guy and would take excellent care of him. Maybe someday, a long time from now,

Jinx would settle down and be able to handle the commitment to a pet again. Maybe.

Jinx slung her backpack over her shoulder and waded through the crowd out to the parking lot. She climbed onto her bike, enjoying the rumble as the engine came to life and hummed underneath her. It felt good to be on the move again. At least that's what she'd keep telling herself. As many times as it would take until she started to believe it.

HH

Cash tried calling Jinx again. It went straight to voicemail. *Dammit.* His truck sat in the middle of a gridlocked mess of vehicles. The school lot had been full when he arrived, so he'd taken a free spot in front of the church. How was he to know someone had booked both events for the same night? Folks came from miles around to see the live nativity with farm animals, people dressed up as Mary, Joseph, and the three wise men. Funny how neither he nor any of his brothers had ever been tapped for a role in that performance.

Before he could maneuver through the traffic to get to the curb, he caught sight of Beck's head bobbing above the crowd. He and Charlie must have seen him in the parking lot. Cash kept sight of them as they weaved their way through the line of cars and trucks. Then Charlie's head went down. Beck followed. Cash shoved the truck into park and hopped out.

The guy behind him laid on the horn and shouted out his window, "Hey, you can't just stop there."

Cash flashed his badge. Sometimes the hunk of metal came in handy.

He'd last seen Beck and Charlie between an oversize SUV and a conversion van. His heart skittered into an erratic beat as he searched for any trace of his sister. Beck emerged from between two cars, Charlie in his arms. Cash glanced back to his truck. They still had to get through the crowd gathered in front of the church and across the lawn to reach his truck on the other side. Beck might need help. Cash broke into a jog, heading toward his sister.

"Put me down." Charlie's voice came from somewhere under a pile of blankets snugged against Beck's chest. "I can walk, you know."

Beck set her down on the pavement. She immediately keeled over, moaning and reaching for something.

"What do you need?" Beck grasped her hand.

"I need to get to the hospital." She glanced up. Pain masked her face.

Cash had never felt so helpless in his life. "Here, let's help her walk together." Cash wrapped an arm around Charlie, and Beck did the same. Together, they hobbled, inch by inch, toward the truck.

Over the curb and onto the church lawn, the crowd parted for them as they made their way. Fifty yards, then forty-five sat between them and their goal. Charlie gripped his arm tighter than the blood pressure cuff he'd been subjected to at his last physical. Then something shifted.

"I need to stop." Charlie's feet stopped inching forward.

"We're almost there. Just a little bit farther." Cash willed her to keep moving.

"No. I can't." Charlie let go of his arm. "My water just broke. I think I'm having the baby right here."

"No, no, no." Beck tried to scoop her up in his arms. "I'll carry you the rest of the way."

"I can't." Charlie sank to her knees. "I'm not having my baby in the back seat of Cash's truck."

"So you're going to have it on the lawn of the First Baptist Church?" Beck argued.

Cash knew better than to pick a fight with his sister. Especially when it was clear she'd lost all access to the rational part of her brain. Or at least the most rational section. "What do you need?" His emergency responder training kicked in, and an eerie calm took over.

"I need to lie down."

"Can we get you inside?" He dropped to his knees next to Charlie. Keeping her calm was the most important thing he could do right now.

"No. I think the baby's coming. It's not supposed to go this fast, right? They said I'd have time." She grimaced as another contraction ripped through her.

"How long has she been having contractions?" Cash asked Beck.

Beck didn't answer. Poor guy appeared to be in shock.

"Beck!" Cash swatted him across the shin.

"What?" Beck shook off whatever thought had temporarily paralyzed him and dropped down next to Charlie.

"How long has she been having contractions? I need to know if we have time to get her somewhere else."

"They started this morning. But they were really far apart." Charlie winced. "I had some stuff I needed to get done around the house, and I didn't want to—Oh no. Here comes another one!"

Blankets. He needed blankets and preferably a pair of gloves. "Be right back." He clamped a hand to Beck's shoulder in an attempt at offering some reassurance, then sprinted toward his truck. Between his emergency first aid kit and the stuff he used for calving, he should be able to come up with something.

In the three minutes he'd been gone, Beck had managed to get Charlie closer to the makeshift manger and out of the wind. Cash spread a thick blanket out over the straw-covered plywood floor. Darby and Waylon must have seen the commotion from the school parking lot and were shooing people away as they got closer, their brood of kids in tow.

Waylon's booming voice could probably be heard all the way back at the ranch. "Nativity's closed for the night. Go on home."

Cash adjusted one of the floodlights to point toward Charlie. He'd helped birth calves and foals before. This couldn't be much different—except it was his sister, and she was about to give birth in a manger, surrounded by a menagerie of animals: a trio of cows, a handful of goats, and Pork Chop, the pig mascot from the Rambling Rose. Oh, and a couple hundred strangers who, despite Waylon's best threats, still milled around the lawn.

One of the goats nibbled on the brim of his hat. "Waylon, can you get these animals out of here?"

His big brother leaned down. "And where exactly would you like me to put them?"

"Isn't there a trailer somewhere?"

"They usually bring it back later, so it doesn't take up so much room in the parking lot. What's

Pork Chop doing here anyway? There wasn't a pig in the manger, was there?"

"How am I supposed to know?" Cash spread another blanket over the straw. "It's not like I was there." What did it matter whether there was a pig in the original nativity? If they were trying to re-create the scene, they were already out of luck. For sure his sister wasn't there that night, about to give birth.

"Would you please go make yourself useful?" Darby knelt down next to Charlie. "Call 911. Tell them we have a woman giving birth in a manger." She focused all her attention on Charlie. "You've got this, girl."

Charlie nodded as she hoo-hoo-hoo'd through another contraction.

"Who's in charge here?" Darby asked.

Cash glanced from Waylon, who had a kid in each arm, to Beck, whose face was as pale as the full moon that peeked out between the clouds from time to time.

"Can you do it, Darby?" Cash asked. She'd given birth before. She should be the one to issue orders.

"I've only ever been on the pushing end, not the receiving end of this process. But I can help."

"Cash." Charlie grabbed his hand. He hadn't decided if he should use the smaller latex gloves or ensure his protection by using the fingertip-to-shoulder ones he'd used for calving. Probably not the most sanitary choice. Then again, what was sanitary when he'd just put a knee into a pile of pig shit?

"What?"

"Tell me everything's going to be okay." Charlie never seemed to need anything from anyone. But in that moment, she needed his reassurance.

"Everything's going to be just fine. I promise. Beck, get down here. I need you to help me deliver your son."

"Is it a boy, Daddy?" Kenzie appeared next to him with Hendrix at her side.

"What are you doing here?" The last thing he needed was his daughter to distract him right now. She wasn't ready to witness a real live human birth. Where was Jinx? "We don't know yet, Tadpole. But it's about to get really messy in here. Can you go find Jinx?"

"She had to go take care of something."

"Had to take care of something? Did she say what?" It was hard to concentrate on Charlie while his mind raced with possibilities of where Jinx might be. He checked his phone. No text from Jinx, but Dan had called twice.

"Nope. But she's not helping me make your surprise tomorrow. I'm mad at her." Kenzie stuck her lower lip out in a pout and tapped her foot on the grass. Hendrix strained at the end of the leash, trying to get to Pork Chop. The lazy pig had zonked out between a bale of hay and a goat that kept trying to nibble on the edge of the blanket.

"Kenzie, honey, I need you to go help Uncle Waylon, okay?"

Charlie let out a howl, sending Kenzie scampering to the safety beyond the floodlight. Dammit, wasn't there a doctor in the crowd? Or at least a vet?

"It's coming." Charlie's head rolled back against the edge of a bale of hay.

"Don't push yet. The ambulance is on its way."

Or at least it better be. He tossed a glove to Beck. "Put this on, and don't let anything come out."

Beck glanced at the small latex glove. "How is this supposed to stop her?"

Charlie groaned. "This is an exit only. There's no pushing back in."

"Um, Cash?" Beck's ungloved hand held the blanket up high enough so he could peer underneath it.

"Waylon, how long until that ambulance gets here?" Cash willed his older brother to come through, but Waylon shook his head.

"Cash!" Beck nodded toward the mystery under the blanket.

He didn't want to look. Charlie was his sister. If he peeked under the blanket, he'd never be able to unsee whatever lurked beneath.

The damn dog had woken up the pig and they raced around the manger, crashing through bales of hay and taking out the croft where a plastic baby doll rested.

Cash sensed things were on the verge of crumbling down around him. He needed to do something. And fast.

Charlie groaned, clearly ignoring his directions not to push. Hell. Here goes nothing. He peered under the blanket. It took him a moment to make sense of what his eyes took in. Hair. Lots of hair. His niece or nephew had a full head of sandy-blond hair and was coming out, whether he was ready or not.

chapter
TWENTY-EIGHT

Jinx edged her bike up over the curb and sped past the crowd gathered on the grass for the live nativity. She fought the threat of tears as she made the turn to head out of town. It wouldn't do any good for Wade to catch her having feelings. He'd only figure out some way to use them against her. How could she have been so stupid as to hand out gift cards like they were Halloween candy? She didn't know what he'd do when he realized she was short. There wasn't anyone else to blame for this one. It was all on her.

She forced thoughts of Cash and Kenzie out of her head. That was the only way to move on. She'd just close the door on the last few months and not look back. It had always worked in the past. No reason why it wouldn't be the same now.

She pulled into the parking lot of the abandoned dairy. A light mist had started to fall. Jinx didn't mind. It matched her mood. A black SUV sat in the far corner. As she brought her bike to a stop, the door opened. The overhead dome light revealed Wade and a passenger. Jinx hadn't been expecting anyone else. In one of his many texts today, Wade had promised to come alone. It wouldn't be the first time he'd broken his word.

He stood next to the door, making no move to come

closer. Why did she have to always do everything? She took her time climbing off the bike, then slowly made her way toward him. Her attempt at getting a read on the situation wasn't working. She wasn't on her game. With her emotions racing all over the place like some train that had hopped the rails, she couldn't concentrate.

Wade took a few steps in her direction as she approached. "Long time no see, eh?"

"What do you want, Wade?" She thrust her hands in her pockets. Let him do the talking. She'd pressed the record button on her phone, just in case.

"I want what's mine. Nobody steals from me."

Her teeth ground together. Even the sound of his voice annoyed the hell out of her. "I didn't steal anything. All I did was take the cash you owed me out of the till."

"I don't give a fuck about the cash. You took off with over twenty thousand dollars in gift cards. Now be a good girl and hand 'em over so things don't get ugly."

"How did you find me?"

His lips curled into a sneer. "Your fucking face is plastered all over the internet. You always were a complete klutz. I've got that footage of you knocking down that tree playing on a loop at the bar. And who's the cowboy you've been locking lips with? I didn't think cops were your type."

Her stomach rolled. It was all her fault. Why couldn't she have kept to herself instead of tearing around town? "Who's that?" Jinx nodded toward the truck.

"None of your damn business, that's who." He took a step to the right, blocking her view of the guy in the front seat.

"Is that your drug-running buddy? The one you pay in gift cards?"

"I don't have all night. Give me the cards, Jinx."

"What would you say if I told you I don't have them anymore?"

"I'd say you'd better be lying, or I'm going to make you wish you were." His shoulders bunched toward his ears. He looked like a bull about to charge.

"I didn't take any gift cards. They were at the bottom of my bag. I didn't have anything to do with your side business. And you know I wouldn't take something that didn't belong to me."

"Yeah, that's right. You're destined for the sainthood." The thick sarcasm rolled off his tongue. "And I wouldn't have trusted you with anything more than running the bar. You did a piss-poor enough job of that."

She didn't care about the bar, but still, the slam stung. She'd left that place in much better shape than when he'd hired her. It didn't matter now. "Want to tell me how they got in my bag in the first place?" If she could keep him talking, maybe he'd admit she wasn't involved. That's all she wanted—an out from this situation.

"How the hell do I know? Fuckin' Geri. She was supposed to put them in the safe. How do you think Josh felt when he showed up to collect and I didn't have anything to give him?"

"So that's Josh in the truck?" Jinx tried to peer around his linebacker shoulders. "Is he the one who's been bringing you drugs?"

"Why so many questions? You wearing a wire?" Wade closed the distance between them, grabbed her wrist, and wrenched it back.

Pain shot through her arm. "Ow. No, I'm not wearing a wire. Let go. You're hurting me." She struggled against him. The man outweighed her by a good 125 pounds. It was like a mouse taking on an elephant—or a Chihuahua taking on a giant pig.

Josh got out of the truck. Jinx caught a glimpse of the gun in his hand as she brought her boot down on Wade's foot.

"You bitch!" Wade backhanded her across the cheek.

Jinx went down, breaking her fall with her injured hand. She'd pushed too far too fast. Wade veered toward fight mode—she should have known better than to bait him. She needed to figure out an exit strategy stat. "Fine. Take what's left." She flung the brown paper bag toward him. The shiny plastic gift cards scattered in a wide circle around his feet.

Josh immediately fell to his knees, trying to retrieve the cards.

Wade advanced on her, clawing at her jacket, trying to get to her chest. "Where is it?"

"Get off me." She scrambled backward, but he straddled her, squeezing her ribs together between his massive thighs. She struggled to take in a breath.

His hands groped at her chest. "Where's the fucking wire?"

She'd taken one of Cash's button-down plaid flannel shirts as a keepsake. Wade popped the buttons, ripping it apart. With her navel exposed, he must have realized she didn't have a mic taped to her chest. He paused, probably trying to figure out his next move. He'd never been a quick thinker, something she should be able to use to her advantage.

"I told you I wasn't wearing a wire, you sad sack of shit. Get off me." Jinx levered herself up as far as she could and spat in his face. She wouldn't go down without a fight.

At first, he didn't react. Then he calmly reached up to wipe the spittle off his cheek. A cold glint shone in his eyes: dangerous, venomous, lethal. "You're going to regret that."

"I doubt it." She pushed up and did it again.

Wade wrapped his meaty paws around her throat. She clawed at him, trying to get him to let go. "I knew you were trouble when I first met you, Jinx. Hell, who wouldn't with a name like that."

"Let me go," she rasped. "You got what you came for."

"Not yet. Where's your phone?"

She forced the words through her constricting throat. "I lost it."

He squeezed. She coughed, trying to grasp a breath. Her legs kicked out, and her hips bucked, anything she could do to give herself a chance to catch her breath.

Josh nudged Wade on the shoulder. "Yo, come on. Let's roll."

Wade gave a final squeeze. Jinx tried to blink away the gray fuzziness that threatened the edges of her vision. He let go, rising to his feet. Then he fumbled through her jacket pockets until he found her phone.

"You won't be needing this anymore." He stood over her, dropped her phone to the gravel, and stomped on it, crushing it to pieces under what she now recognized as fake cowboy boots.

Jinx rolled to her side, the fight drained from her. Her hands rubbed at her neck, attempting to ease the pain. She tried to yell, but her voice came out as a croak. "I hope you rot in hell."

"Oh yeah?" Wade turned and took two giant steps toward her. "I'll be sure to save you a seat."

She curled in on herself, letting the tears come.

Cash watched the paramedic close the doors of the ambulance. The lights came on, the sirens blared, and the driver pulled away from the manger with Charlie, Beck, and baby Sully safe inside. Darby and Waylon had taken their kids and Kenzie back to their place. As Cash trudged across the grass to get to his truck, he turned his attention to his phone.

Dan had called five times while he'd been playing delivery nurse to his little sister. He cued up the first message to find out what was going on.

As the messages played, Cash broke into a run. Dammit. How could the drug drop be going on now? Evidently, Dan had traced Wade to the dairy outside of town. He didn't need backup but thought Cash might want to know that they'd identified the local connection—Jinx. There had to be some mistake.

With his heart battering the walls of his chest, he threw his truck into gear and floored it out of the parking lot, hopping the curb and fishtailing through the grass to reach the road. Could she really be involved? He tried to banish the thought from taking root in his brain. This was Jinx they were talking about—the woman who'd cared for his daughter, helped his sister, brought his heart back to life.

A vision of Jinx scrambling to recover those gift cards flashed across his mind. He'd been suspicious of her at the start, but she'd proven herself to him and everyone else. What if he should have listened to his gut? He'd gotten so caught up in the idea of having her around that he'd silenced his intuition. Hell, he'd probably put Kenzie at risk, maybe even his entire family.

Guilt wrapped around him like one of those plastic tarps they used out at the ranch, suffocating him, making it hard to take in a breath. What if something had happened to one of them? What if something had happened to Kenzie? He'd never be able to forgive himself if a break in his guard had resulted in his little girl getting hurt.

He'd let Jinx get under his skin, let her infiltrate his heart. He should have known better.

Jinx struggled to get up. Wade and Josh scurried around the lot, scrambling to pick up the scattered gift cards. She had to stop them. Her throat burned.

She rolled onto her side and closed her eyes. The truck engine started. Two doors slammed. She'd been so stupid. Why hadn't she left when she'd had the chance? She'd led Wade straight to Holiday. Right to Kenzie and Cash. The screech of tires made her open her eyes. Cash's truck sat at an odd angle, blocking the exit from the parking lot.

No! She tried to warn him, call out that Wade and his buddy were armed. Her voice wouldn't work. From her vantage point on the ground, she saw everything in slow motion. Wade revved the truck. Cash pulled his gun from its holster. Josh leaned out the passenger window, took aim, and fired.

Cash went down.

Jinx got to her hands and knees, trying to reach Cash. Gravel bit into her palms. Her leggings ripped on the sharp rocks. The pain didn't matter. She had to get to him. He had to be okay. She should have known something like this would happen. It always did. Everything she ever touched turned to shit.

⚯

Cash dropped to the ground as the gun went off, rolling out of the way of the black SUV. A quick pat down reassured him he was still alive. He popped up on his elbows and fired off a few rounds, tagging the SUV in the back two tires. It swerved out of control and crashed into the edge of the old brick building.

He let out a ragged breath as he collapsed. Dammit. He had to find her. Maybe they could still sort this mess out. She couldn't have been playing him all along, scoping out the whole town for the best place to do the drop. He hoped beyond all hope that she wasn't responsible for what had just happened. His heart thundered, sending blood whooshing through his veins, pounding in his ears. He'd seen her bike when he drove by the lot. She had to be here somewhere.

Flashing lights bounced against the building as the lot filled with squad cars. Cash staggered to his feet.

"Walker, you okay?" Dan clapped him on the shoulder.

"Yeah. It was touch and go there for a few, but I'm fine."

"Nice work. Do you mind if we take it from here?"

"Be my guest. But can I have a word with Jinx first?"

"I think that can be arranged." Dan pointed to the far side of the parking lot, where Jinx was leaning against the back of a squad car.

She must have stolen his shirt. It hung open, exposing the hourglass tattoo on her rib cage. The one he'd traced with his tongue on more than one occasion. She'd told him it meant something along the lines of *this too shall pass*—that time kept slipping away whether she wanted it to or not.

One of the DEA agents had cuffed her, but she didn't appear to be cooperating. Yep, that was Jinx. She kept gesturing toward something on the ground. The woman might possibly have played him for a fool, but he had enough decency to not let her stand in the rain with her shirt falling off around her. He shrugged out of his jacket as he approached.

"Cash, thank God you're safe. I thought…I thought you were dead." Her voice cracked. He couldn't tell if she'd been crying or just standing in the rain too long. At that point he wasn't sure it even mattered.

"Nope." He shrugged. "Looks like I'll live another day."

She tried to reach for him, but her hands were cuffed. "It's not what you think. I swear, I——"

"Then what is it?" His stomach twisted. He wanted to reach out, smooth the wet strands of hair away from her face and have her deny everything. He needed to know the truth. "Do you know Wade Boyd?"

Jinx's gaze dropped to her boots. "Yes, but I——"

"Was it all a setup to you?" Her admission sawed through him like a steak knife. His vision fuzzed at the edges. "All of it? Your bike breaking down? Kenzie? Me?"

Her head jerked up. Tears flowed down her

cheeks. "No, of course not. What I felt, I mean feel, for you and Kenzie is real. You've got to believe me."

"I want to, I really do. But you put my kid in danger… my family."

"I'm so sorry. I didn't mean for any of this to happen. Please, Cash. I should have come clean with you earlier, before things got so out of control."

He ran his hands down his cheeks. "Were you even going to say goodbye?"

The look she gave him pierced through his heart. He almost staggered from the sheer physical pain.

"I want to explain."

The agent behind Jinx gestured toward a squad car. "You can explain it to the judge." He nudged his chin toward Cash. "Time to take her in."

Cash nodded, then draped his jacket over her shoulders and pulled her shirt closed, snugging it around her midsection.

Jinx tried to lean into him, but he moved away. "I'm so sorry. I just wanted to—"

"I can't. I just can't." He'd wrapped all his hopes and dreams up in that hundred-pound package. Her admission that she knew Wade shattered him. Filleted him like a fish she'd yanked out of the lake and left gasping on the dock. And Kenzie—how was his daughter going to react when she found out Jinx wouldn't be coming back?

She didn't respond, just stood there, letting the rain soak his jacket, plaster her mermaid hair against her head.

He took a final long look, turned his back on her, and crossed the parking lot to his truck.

Happy fucking holidays. Because of Jinx, he had no tree, no heart, and no hope for providing Kenzie with a merry Christmas. He pulled out onto the highway, leaving the flashing lights and his heart behind. He deserved a hot shower and a tall drink. The shower would wash away the tension of being target practice, and the tall drink would make him forget all about the woman who'd stolen his heart.

Htt

A half hour later, he sat at his kitchen table, chilled to the bone. The scalding shower and healthy pour of Jack had done nothing to warm him. He'd sent Kenzie home with Waylon and Darby, Charlie and Beck had made it to the hospital, and Jinx was spending the night in a cell at the sheriff's office. He should have been glad her true colors had shone through—he'd almost made her a permanent part of their lives.

Who was he trying to kid? Evidence of her remained everywhere he looked. He eyed the bottle. Not even that seemed appealing.

He moved into the living room, figuring he'd turn on the TV to try to distract himself, when a knock sounded at the front door. Waylon didn't wait for him to answer, just pushed the door open and let himself in.

"What the hell are you doing here? Is Kenzie okay?"

"Yeah, she's zonked out with the rest of them." Waylon wiped his boots on the mat—the Christmas welcome mat Jinx had bought. "Sounds like you've had a crazy night."

Cash scoffed. "Yeah, you could say that."

"You weren't answering texts. Even tried to call. You okay?"

Ignoring Waylon's concern, Cash headed back to the kitchen. "Pour you a drink?"

Waylon followed him. "No thanks. What happened? You want to talk about it?"

"Nope." Cash set his glass in the sink. "I'm fine. You can go on home. No need to babysit me tonight."

"That's not why I'm here." Waylon pulled a chair out from the table. "Mind if I hang out for a while?"

Cash crossed his arms over his chest and leaned against the counter. "Suit yourself. Darby send you over?"

"Nah." Waylon wiped his hand across his thick beard. "Just wanted to talk, that's all." The Walker brothers spent a lot of time together—playing pool, working the ranch, and drinking beer. Talking wasn't their thing.

"Something bothering you, Big Bro?" Cash asked.

Waylon shifted in the chair, resetting his bulky frame. "What's going on?"

"I heard about what happened tonight." His fingertips tapped on the table, and his eyes roamed over the perimeter of the room.

"Of course you did."

"You really think Jinx is involved in some drug ring?" Waylon raised a brow.

Cash chewed on his lip, trying to figure out how to answer. He let out a long sigh. "If you had asked me yesterday, I would have threatened to sue you for slander. But now…" He stepped away from the counter and took a seat across from Waylon. "She was there. Why else would she be meeting her ex at the confirmed drop location if she wasn't involved? What other proof do you need?"

"She sure doesn't seem like the type."

"Yeah. I don't know how I missed it. I checked her

COWBOY CHRISTMAS JUBILEE   339

record right after Charlie hired her. She didn't have any priors." He funneled his hands through his hair. "That's what confuses me the most."

"What?"

"It seemed like I could trust her. I should have been able to tell. That's what I do for a living...I read people. If I can't trust my gut anymore, then I—"

"Then what?" Waylon held his gaze. "What if your gut wasn't wrong? What if she's innocent?"

Cash pushed back from the table. As much as he wanted to believe that, the facts didn't stack up. "And what if Santa really did cram his fat ass down the chimney? Jinx being innocent is about as likely as good ole Saint Nick showing up with a pecan pie for me and a bag full of presents for Kenzie."

"You could find out pretty easy, couldn't you?" Waylon pressed.

"What, how deep she's involved in this?" Cash pondered that thought for a moment. Yeah, he could call Dan for an update. The DEA agent didn't owe him anything, but he might feel like being generous with some information. But why bother? The sooner he worked Jinx out of his heart, the sooner he could get back to normal. And normal meant no lingering feelings for a woman who was all wrong for him.

"You know, I never thought Darby was the right woman for me." Waylon pulled on his beard.

"Look, I don't need some heart-to-heart from—"

"Would you let me finish?" Pissed-off blue eyes dared him to speak.

Hell, if his big brother wanted to try to impart

some wisdom before he took off, Cash wouldn't be able to stop him. He shook his head. "I'm all ears."

"Yeah, I can tell." Waylon cleared his throat. "As I was saying, I never thought Darby was the right woman for me. When we got married, she was barely nineteen. But we—"

"And she was three months pregnant. I don't see how this line of conversation relates to me."

Waylon pushed back from the table, knocking the chair over backward. "Would you shut the hell up for once?"

He'd poked the bear. His brother usually kept his cool, kind of like Cash. Better to hear him out. "Go on."

"Yes, she was pregnant. And come hell or high water, I was going to do the right thing. But I'd planned on asking her to marry me anyway. Folks never would have put us together. We're like oil and vinegar. She's sunshine, and I'm a cloudy day."

Waylon spoke the truth. None of them could understand what drew Darby and Waylon together in the first place.

"Once that woman got under my skin, I was a goner." Waylon set his chair upright and took a seat. "She wasn't what I was looking for, but I thank God every day she found me. Can you imagine what I'd be like if we'd never gotten together?"

Cash let out a laugh. "Yeah, you'd be an even bigger asshole than you already are."

Waylon matched his grin. "You're right about that."

Neither spoke for a long moment. Cash pondered what his brother had shared. He couldn't imagine Waylon without Darby. They'd seemed an odd couple from the start, but they were made for each other—no one would argue that fact.

Waylon pushed back from the table. "I'd better head back."

"Yeah, thanks for stopping over." Cash trailed him to the door.

"Think about what I said." He pulled his coat over his shoulders. "Or don't, and be a miserable jerk for the rest of your life."

"Thanks for the pep talk."

His brother pulled him in for a half hug. "Make the call."

Cash clapped him on the back. "See you tomorrow."

He stood in the doorway while Waylon trudged down the walk to his truck. Wouldn't take much effort to make one call. He'd find out he was right, that Jinx was up to her earrings in drug money, and he'd be able to sleep like a baby knowing he'd done the right thing.

Or, a little voice in his head taunted, he'd find out he was wrong, and he'd be up all night trying to figure out what the hell to do about it. With his fate in the hands of a stranger, he dialed the number.

"You're free to go, Miss Jacobs." The bailiff handed her a her backpack along with a small envelope containing the key to her motorcycle.

Jinx blinked against the bright morning light as she exited the station. She hadn't slept in over twenty-four hours, thanks to the all-night interrogation. Thankfully, when Wade had smashed her phone, the micro SD card had been unharmed. After the agent in charge finally listened to her recording, they realized she'd been telling the truth. Plus, Wade had copped some sort of bargain to shorten his jail time, probably selling out his buddy Josh, and confirmed she didn't have anything to do with the drugs.

For all intents and purposes, she was free. Then why couldn't she breathe? She checked the preprinted instructions on how to get her bike out of the impound lot. With any luck, she'd be in New Orleans before nightfall. Her heart squeezed. Holiday had become the closest thing to home she'd experienced since she'd left her old neighborhood in Seattle. But she couldn't stay. Not when Cash had looked at her with that deep hurt in his eyes. He blamed her for putting his town, his job, and his family at risk. And the kicker was he was right.

Everything she touched turned to crap. Everything she ever cared about fell apart. Why would Cash operate outside the parameters of her clearly defined, screwed-up life?

She hooked a left, figuring she'd walk the couple of miles down the road to the impound lot. A flash of yellow caught her eye. Her bike sat in the front space of the parking lot. Cash straddled the seat, a tentative smile etched into the scruff of a few days' growth of beard. She swallowed hard. No, no, no. She couldn't face him. Not like this. Her throat constricted, and her eyes watered. She tried to swallow again, but it was like a cactus blocked her throat.

When she didn't move forward, he climbed off the bike and took a few steps in her direction. "I figured you could use this."

She looked at the pavement, at the sparkly pine garland someone had woven throughout the scrubby hedge—anywhere but at Cash. "I was about to go pick it up."

"Saved you a trip then." His feet moved closer until the tips of his cowboy boots appeared at the edge of her vision.

Her breath stalled in her lungs. She could smell him—that intoxicating combination of sunshine and leather. Her gaze roamed up his denim-clad legs to the snug T-shirt, the hands that had held her not more than twenty-four hours before, and finally, his jaw. She wouldn't meet his eyes; she couldn't. His pulse ticked along the soft spot at the hollow of his neck. She wanted to nestle in, bury herself against him, feel his arms wrap around her.

Instead, she croaked out, "Thanks." She cleared her throat. "I see you got your jacket back."

"Yeah, Tippy ran it over last night." He shifted his weight from one foot to the other. "Jinx, I'm sorry."

Her stare drilled into his chest. Fire danced across her cheeks. "You don't need to apologize. I'm the one who should be saying I'm sorry."

"When you took off last night without telling anyone, I assumed you were part of it." He shrugged.

"I was only trying to keep Wade from getting to you and Kenzie. He was after his gift cards. They accidentally ended up in my bag when I left LA." She peeked at his face. His forehead creased.

"I know. The agent I met up in Dallas who was working the case filled me in. I thought you'd used me. Especially when he mentioned the gift cards. That time a handful fell out of your bag? He made me question everything. But I was wrong."

She wanted to smooth out the worry, kiss his heartache away.

"It was crazy last night. Between the play and the nativity set…so many people. When I saw you at the dairy, I assumed you were involved like the DEA said." His voice wavered.

She placed a palm over his heart. The rhythmic *thud-thud-thud* pulsed against her hand. "I'm sorry. I should have told you. I wanted to, but Wade threatened to hurt you or Kenzie if I brought you in. I heard Charlie had her baby last night. Were you at the hospital with her?"

His hand covered hers, sending warning chills racing up her arm. "She didn't make it to the hospital. My nephew was born the old-fashioned way—in a manger."

Jinx dared to meet his eyes. "Oh my gosh. Is everyone okay?"

"Yeah, Charlie and the baby are doing great. I'm scarred for life after having to deliver my sister's baby, but I'll survive." His mouth quirked into a half grin.

This man had been dragged through hell already. He didn't need her around—she was deadweight, always holding people back. He needed stability in his life. For himself and for Kenzie.

"I'm so sorry. I wanted to tell you everything, but I couldn't find the right words. Here, with you, I thought I'd finally found a place away from all the trouble that always seems to follow me. But instead, I brought it to you. To Kenzie." She wiped at the tears threatening to spill over onto her cheeks. "I can't—no, I won't—cause you any more trouble."

Cash's hands curled around her arms. "I should have listened to you last night. I know you were trying to tell me the truth, but I couldn't hear it. All I could think about was how I'd failed. I jumped to conclusions, and I was wrong."

"You almost died because of me. I heard the gun go off, and you fell, and I—" Her chest heaved, letting a sob escape.

He gathered her into his arms. "It's okay." His hand smoothed down her mess of hair. "It's not the first time I've been shot at, and it won't be the last."

"No." It took every ounce of willpower to wiggle her palms between them and push back against his chest. "My mom was right. I ruin everything and everyone I get close to. I won't do that to you and Kenzie."

"Kenzie loves you." He made a move to tuck her

hair behind her ear, but Jinx ducked out of the way. "I love you."

The dam broke. Tears flooded her cheeks. She didn't bother to wipe them away. "That's why I can't stay. I'm sorry. You both deserve better than me."

She brushed past him, stepping to the side when he tried to grab her arm.

"Jinx, wait!"

Turning, she let her gaze roam over the only man she'd ever thought about settling down with. It would probably be the last time she'd ever see him. Her breath caught in her throat, and she gasped. Ragged sobs ripped through her chest.

He didn't move, like he was afraid if he took a step toward her, she'd bolt. "I'll admit you and I don't seem like a natural fit. But we belong together. You're the June Carter to my Johnny Cash. Things didn't always go easy for them, but they knew they were meant to be together. Through thick and thin." He dropped his head, shaking it side to side, then leveled her with a penetrating gaze. "You, Jinx Jacobs, are everything I never knew I always wanted." He reached a hand out. A hand she wanted to grab, to hold on to, to cling to for the rest of her life. "I'm only going to ask once. Not because I don't care, but because I know this has got to be your decision. I want to wake up next to you every morning. I want you to be a permanent part of my and Kenzie's lives. We don't have to get married if that's not your thing. But let's give us a shot. For good. Please…come home?"

For a moment, their future hung between them. The possibility of wrapping the Walker family around her, of building a home with Cash and Kenzie seemed like a realistic option.

But she couldn't.

"I can't. I wish I could, but I just can't." She turned toward her bike, her boots carrying her farther and farther away from that unattainable dream. Her heart shattered into a billion pieces, but she didn't look back. She flung a leg over the seat of her bike, pulled her helmet on, and turned the engine over.

It was better this way.

If she stayed, she'd only mess up bigger next time.

꙳

Cash drifted through the next couple of days, trying to fake some holiday cheer so he wouldn't ruin Kenzie's Christmas. He had so much to be thankful for this year. His dad had been discharged from the physical therapy facility in Tulsa and had made it home in time for the holiday. Charlie and baby Sully were home from the hospital and doing just fine. Even Kenzie seemed to be handling the news of Jinx's departure pretty well. It helped that she'd been preoccupied with Hendrix. Her nana had humored her and made a whole wardrobe of costumes for the little guy. Cash couldn't wait to see what getup he would be forced to wear to Christmas Eve dinner.

Presley had even come through with a real tree. Coincidentally, he had shown up on the porch with it the same night the liquor store two counties over had reported a guy in a Santa costume coming in and stealing their Christmas tree from the front window. Of course, Presley denied having anything to do with the crime. The tiny bottles of booze on the new tree should have been a dead giveaway, but Cash couldn't summon the energy to take his brother in, not when he'd been tossing back one or two shot-size ornaments each night.

He wasn't in the mood for a big family get-together, but skipping out wasn't an option. He'd agreed to bring Kenzie to dinner, but then they were heading back to their place. He wanted Kenzie to wake up in her own house with her own tree on Christmas morning. They needed to start building new traditions for the two of them. He'd relied on his mom and dad to carry them along for so long. If he and Kenzie were going to be a family of two, they needed to find their own way and have some of their own celebrations.

Kenzie had spent the day with his mom, baking up a storm, so he headed straight from work to the big house. As he passed through town, the roar of a motorcycle engine made him rubberneck, looking for the source. Just the Oakley twins on those damn dirt bikes. He'd ticketed them a couple of times already for not having tags. Hell, it was Christmas Eve. He'd let it slide.

Every time he caught a glimpse of teal, he expected to see Jinx. A few days ago, some canary-yellow Volkswagen had been parked in front of Whitey's. Cash had almost hopped the curb and crashed through the front of the diner when it caught his eye.

He missed her. He hadn't heard from her since she blew out of town. As he turned into the drive of his parents' place, he wondered if she'd found what she was looking for in New Orleans. Pickup trucks in various sizes, shapes, and colors lined the drive and covered the front lawn. *Here goes nothing*, he thought. He practiced his everything's-just-fine grin in the rearview mirror. No doubt he'd spend the whole night with it plastered across his face.

Before he reached the front porch, Kenzie launched herself off the steps and into his arms. "Hi, Daddy."

He kissed the top of her head. "Hey, Tadpole. Your hair looks nice. Did you and Nana have fun today?" His mom must have gotten tired of trying to tame Kenzie's nest. She'd twisted it up into some sort of braid on top of her head, secured by a huge red-and-green sparkly bow.

"Yep."

"Did you make me a pecan pie?" That was about the only thing he had left to look forward to. That and the look on Kenzie's face when Santa brought her that new bicycle she'd been hinting at.

"We tried."

"What do you mean 'we tried'?"

"I don't think Nana will let me help with pies again." Kenzie puckered her lips. "But I made the cookies with the kisses on top, the ones Papa loves. And Aunt Charlie's here with baby Sully, and she let me help change his diaper, and Hendrix and I got to jump on the trampoline."

"Wait a minute. What happened to my pie?"

Kenzie shrugged her shoulders, then ran off with her cousins. He crossed the threshold into the house. The smells of gingerbread, mulled apple cider, and Angelo's smoked ribs wrapped around him like a security blanket.

"Cash is here. We can eat." Statler clapped him on the back. "How ya doin', Bro?"

The practiced smile slid into place. "Fine, just fine. Where's Mom?"

Statler pointed to the kitchen. Cash threaded

through his brothers, sister, aunts, uncles, cousins, and the extended family like Charlie's employees from the Rose and anyone else who didn't have a place to go for Christmas Eve dinner.

He stopped to drop a kiss on his sister's head. "How ya feeling?"

Charlie grinned up at him. "Like I got run over by a truck."

Cash held his finger out to little Sully, who wrapped his hand around it. "He's got a good grip. I'm sorry I didn't get you to the hospital."

"We're fine." She nestled into her husband's side. "It was a good thing you were there. I don't think Beck could have delivered a baby."

"Nope," Beck agreed.

"We'll get you out calving this spring. You'll be a pro in no time," Cash teased. He kissed his new nephew on the forehead and slid his finger out from the baby's grasp. Heading into the kitchen, the savory smells assaulted his nose. There was nothing like a Walker family Christmas Eve.

Presley handed him a cold Lone Star as he passed. "I have a feeling you're going to need a few of these to get through the night."

Cash clinked his bottle against his brother's. "Thanks."

"Hey, Cash, merry Christmas." Darby leaned against the kitchen island, putting the finishing touches on a platter of something deep-fried that smelled delicious. Waylon stood behind her, his arms wrapped around her midsection.

Damn, if his whole family didn't seem to be made up of happily-ever-after couples. Had he never noticed before, or had it just never bothered him?

"There you are." His mom wiped her hands on her apron. "Did you see Kenzie's hair?"

"Yeah, looks real pretty."

She took a huge dish of homemade baked beans out of the oven. "It does now."

"Yeah, sorry. I'm not so good with her hair. Thanks for putting it up. Hey, did you happen to make a pecan pie?"

Ann squinted up at him through her glasses. "No."

"Really? I've been looking forward to it."

She lifted onto her tiptoes to kiss him on the cheek. "Go ask your daughter why we didn't have a chance to make your pie today. Then see if Angelo needs help bringing in the ribs, will you?"

"What's Kenzie got to do with it?"

She bustled around the kitchen, grabbing serving platters from the cabinets, utensils from the drawer. "Just ask her. I'll make you one for your birthday next month though, okay? I promise."

"Sure. No big deal." His mom had been through enough over the past month. She didn't need him to make her feel guilty about a stupid pecan pie. Now to locate Kenzie to figure out what kind of trouble she'd caused.

"Have you heard from her?" Ann's voice dipped, low enough so that only he could hear her.

The reference to Jinx pierced through the protective shield he'd built around his heart. "No. I don't expect to." Sympathy flooded his mom's eyes. He didn't need or want anyone to feel sorry for him. "Angelo's out back, right?"

She placed her hand over his on the granite

countertop. Her wedding ring glinted under the overhead lights. "She might still come around."

"I'm going to go find Kenzie and see about those ribs." He slid his hand out from under his mom's. She meant well. But nothing would bring Jinx back. That was the only thing he was one hundred percent sure of.

He found Kenzie on the trampoline his dad had just purchased as a Christmas gift for all the grandkids. Her braid had come loose, and her hair flew around her face as she executed a super-sloppy flip. Holy crap. No wonder his mom was so pissed. The top of Kenzie's head was still the light brownish-blond it had always been—a nice mix of his dark-brown hair and Lori Lynne's almost white-blond. But the bottom three to four inches appeared to be a bright shade of blue. Only one place she could have gotten an idea like that.

"Kenzie Ann Walker!" His voice thundered from his chest.

His nieces and nephews stopped bouncing. Kenzie froze. He didn't usually yell, but this wasn't a usual situation.

"Come here, Tadpole." He spread the outer net circling the trampoline so she could climb out. "What did you do to your hair?"

Her lip trembled. "I took some of Jinx's stuff. I wanted to surprise her. For when she comes back."

He gathered her up in his arms. "Honey, I told you, Jinx isn't coming back."

Kenzie sandwiched his cheeks between her tiny palms. "Of course she is, Daddy. I asked Santa to bring her."

His heart stalled. "I thought you asked Santa for a bike for Christmas."

She smiled, like the idea of having to explain something

so simple to a grown-up was beneath her. "I did. But when Jinx left, I wrote him a letter and told him I changed my mind. Am I in trouble about my hair?"

How could he be mad about something like that when her heart was about to get smashed to smithereens? "No. We'll see if we can wash it out later. Go tell your cousins it's time to eat." He set her down and gave her a nudge toward the trampoline. He thought she'd been handling Jinx's departure a little too well. How was he to know she thought it was a temporary setback?

As much as he wanted to go after Jinx, he couldn't. That's what he'd done with Lori Lynne—tried to convince her to stay in Holiday when all she wanted to do was leave. He wouldn't do that again. If Jinx didn't want to stay, he couldn't force her. He'd gone all in, put his heart on the line, and she'd left anyway. He'd go on. He'd damn sure never lose control of his heart again, but he'd survive.

Only one thing had him worried now—what was he going to do when Santa didn't come through?

JINX WIPED DOWN THE BAR AND TOSSED THE RAG INTO the sink of soapy water. She'd already refilled all the ketchup bottles, rolled an entire bin full of silverware, and restocked the refrigerator in the bar area. She hadn't served a customer in over an hour. Jamie had warned her things would be slow on Christmas Eve, but this was ridiculous. The place was probably losing money by having to pay the electric bill.

She'd only worked two shifts since she had arrived, but she could already tell it wasn't going to be a good fit. Giant big-screen TVs and glaring neon signs filled every square inch of wall space. Management played a headache-inducing mix of techno crap. All the songs sounded the same. And the staff—everyone seemed super nice on the surface, but it was obvious there was major tension going on underneath. Even the customers had attitude. A kid had pinched her ass yesterday, and Jamie had to restrain her from beating the crap out of him. He couldn't have been more than seventeen.

She missed the laid-back family feel of the Rambling Rose. She missed the comforting camaraderie between the regular customers. But most of all, she missed Kenzie and Cash.

She'd finally felt like she belonged somewhere when she

was with them. Her mood had been in the garbage since she had driven out of Holiday. No sense crying over things that weren't meant to be. As long as she was wallowing in a pity party for one, she figured she may as well get her annual phone call to her mom over with. She dialed the number by heart.

"Hello?" Her mom's voice rasped through the line.

"Merry Christmas, Mom." Jinx took in a slow breath, bracing herself for the onslaught of accusations—she didn't call often enough, the least she could do was send a few bucks home. Which angle would her mother work tonight?

"What's so merry about it?" her mother growled through the phone line.

"I just wanted to see how you're doing."

"How the hell do you think I'm doing? Randy left last month. Cleaned out my checking account on his way out of town. You making good money where you are?"

Jinx braced herself for the inevitable guilt trip. "I'm doing okay."

A hacking cough racked through her mother. "I'm not going to be able to make rent next month. I couldn't make it through a shift without breaking down, so I got fired."

"I'm sorry you're having a tough time." Why did she think it would ever be any different? Her mother's worth had always been so wrapped up in whichever man she'd hitched herself to.

"Randy left me. You left me," her mother keened. "That's not what family does. Family sticks around. Supports each other through the tough times."

Jinx's pulse throbbed in her temple. "You're right."

"I need money, Jinxy girl. Wasn't I always good to you? I don't even have your phone number. That's no way to treat family."

Her mother was absolutely right. That was no way to treat family. But that was the kicker. The revelation began to crystallize in her mind. Her mother was no more family to her than the guy at the Texaco station where she'd filled up with gas this morning. And at least he'd wished her a merry Christmas.

"You're right, Mom."

"So what do you say? I'm the only family you've got left. Can you be a good girl and help your mama out?"

Jinx swallowed hard. There would be no turning back after this. "The thing is, Mom, you're not my family. You never have been. I've learned a little bit about families in the past couple of months."

"Why, I—"

"Let me finish. You're right. Family does stick around. Families do support each other through the tough times. Families love each other unconditionally." Like the way everyone had rallied around Ann and Tom when he'd broken his hip. Like the way the Walker family had welcomed her into its fold with open arms. Like the way Cash and Kenzie had gifted her their hearts without expecting anything in return.

"I'm your mother, Jinx."

No. She'd never been much of a mother. Mothers didn't berate their kids for being kids. Mothers didn't choose to believe strangers over the word of their own flesh and blood. Mothers didn't turn their backs on their daughters. Her mom had never been the kind of mom Jinx needed. Or any kind of mom at all.

"You had a chance at being my mom, but you blew it. I hope things turn around for you. I really do. But I can't be your daughter anymore. I've got to go. Bye."

Jinx disconnected to the sound of her mother's protests.

That hadn't been as hard as she'd thought it would be. Her mother had never given her much, but tonight, she'd given her the best gift possible—clarity.

Jinx had done the same kinds of unforgivable things to Cash and Kenzie her own mother had done to her. She'd turned her back on them. She'd left them high and dry when they needed her. She hadn't even told them how much she loved them.

With a crystal-clear sense of purpose, she headed to the break room to grab her things.

"Hey, some of us are heading down to see the bonfires across the levees after work. Want to come?" Jamie asked.

Jinx shook her head. "Nope. I've got to go."

"Oh, okay. So see you at home later?"

"No. I've got to go back. Will you let them know I quit?"

"What?" Jamie grabbed her arm. "You sure about this?"

"Yeah. It's the only thing I've ever been one hundred percent sure of in my entire life."

Jamie didn't say anything for a long moment. "Okay then. I hope you find what you're looking for."

Jinx nodded. She didn't have to go looking for anything. She already knew where to find exactly what she needed. Hopefully, it wasn't too late.

*Cash woke to the vibration of his phone alarm in his pocket. He must have fallen asleep right after Kenzie last night. He'd tucked her in and started reading *The Night Before Christmas*. They both must have crashed hard. Her head rested in the crook of his arm. Before he slipped out from under the covers, he took a moment to watch the rise and fall of her breath. She'd be devastated this morning when Santa didn't deliver. How was he going to piece her little heart back together? Especially since his own had cracked in two?

As he padded across her bedroom floor on bare feet, Hendrix hopped off the bed to follow.

"Ssh." Cash picked up the dog and snuggled him against his chest. He hadn't had a chance to set Kenzie's bike out by the tree yet, and he couldn't let Hendrix wake her up before Santa showed. Maybe the excitement of the new bike would make her forget about Jinx. He dismissed the ridiculous thought as soon as it entered his mind. His daughter had too much of him in her. The dogged persistence, sizable stubborn streak, and tenacity were some of his greatest strengths. They'd also proven to be huge weaknesses, seeing as how he hadn't had the sense to give up on forcing Jinx into a future she didn't want any part of before it was too late.

The lights on the tree glowed in the otherwise dark living room. He'd have to return it after Christmas. He and Kenzie would buy their own fake one when they went on sale, so they'd be set for next year. Cash set Hendrix on the couch. He'd assembled the bike last week and hid it in the storage shed out back. He slipped his feet into his boots and shrugged his coat on over his shoulders. As he crossed the porch, he could have sworn he smelled something baking. Wishful thinking. His stomach growled.

His mom had sent him home with a pan of homemade cinnamon rolls for breakfast. She'd been disappointed that he and Kenzie wouldn't be waking up in the big house on Christmas morning but seemed to understand. With the bike under one arm and the new saddle he'd bought her from Whitey's under the other, he reentered the living room. Two trips later, he'd arranged all the gifts under the tree. Jinx had wrapped everything for him while Kenzie was at school. Everywhere he turned, he saw signs she was no longer there. He wouldn't be able to fall back asleep, not with the combination of excitement over Kenzie's first home Christmas and the looming dread of her guaranteed disappointment hovering over him. He settled on the couch to wait for her to wake up.

By the time Kenzie's feet shuffled to the top of the stairs, the sun had risen, and Cash had downed a full pot of coffee.

"Good morning, Tadpole."

She rubbed the sleep out of her eyes while she clutched the stuffed reindeer Jinx had won for her at the Jingle Bell Jamboree.

"Merry Christmas." Cash met her at the top of the stairs.

"Did Santa come?" She put her arms up, letting Cash pick her up and carry her down the steps.

"He sure did."

Her eyes lit on the packages arranged under the tree. "It's a bike. Is that for me?"

Cash set her down, committing the look of sheer joy on her face into his memory. "Doesn't look like it will fit me, does it?"

Kenzie beamed up at him. "Can I try it?"

"Sure." He picked up the bike by the handles and set it on the hardwood floor in front of her. This would be her first bike without training wheels. No doubt she was ready for it, but was he?

She straddled the sparkly pink banana seat while he held the bike upright. "Can we take it outside and try it on the driveway?"

"How about you open your other presents first?"

Kenzie nodded, immediately drawn to the brand-new saddle with turquoise trim. "This is for me too?"

"Yeah. I guess Santa knew you needed a new saddle."

"Oh, Daddy, it's the best Christmas ever."

It only took about fifteen minutes to exchange gifts. Kenzie opened the new set of Junie B. Jones books Jinx had suggested. He opened the paper tie she'd colored for him at school. Jinx had left gifts for both of them. Kenzie loved the art set. And Cash appreciated the brand-new twelve-cup coffeepot. Although now that he was back to making coffee for one, he'd probably return it. The living room looked like a paper factory had exploded with all the wrapping paper strewn about. Finally, only a few presents remained—the ones he and Kenzie had wrapped for Jinx. Why hadn't he thought to put the gifts for Jinx in a closet or something?

"Can we go try my bike now, Daddy? I don't want to get dressed yet. Can I just wear my pajamas?"

"Sure." He snagged the new pink helmet he'd bought her along with the bike and lifted Hendrix off the couch to go with them. "Get your shoes and jacket on."

She raced around him, shoving her footed pajama-covered feet into her boots. "Let's go."

Kenzie flung the door open.

There on the red-and-white candy-cane-striped welcome mat, Jinx stood, her hand frozen in a fist, like she'd been just about to knock on the door.

"Jinx!" Kenzie flung her arms around her. "I knew Santa would bring you back!"

Jinx met his gaze over the top of his daughter's two-toned head of hair. She looked good. Great, actually. It could have been the fact that she was a sight for extremely sore eyes, but most likely, it was the tremulous smile she gave him. His heart stuttered, hopeful she hadn't just come back for Hendrix.

"Hi." One arm cradled Kenzie against her. The other held out a foil-wrapped package. "I just wanted to stop by and wish you a merry Christmas."

"You want to come in?"

"Looks like you're about to head out." She nodded toward the bike.

"We were. I mean, we are. But just to the driveway. Kenzie wanted to try out her new bike."

"Oh, good. I'm not sure how people would respond to your holiday look."

Cash glanced down. "What's wrong with this?" He gestured to the pajama pants that matched Kenzie's footed pj's. "I'm rocking this look." They were tiptoeing around the real question. He wanted to toss the bike to the ground, crush her in his arms, and make her swear she'd stay.

"Hendrix too?" She reached out to pet the squirming dog. His mom had made him a special pair of pj's to match everyone else's. "And the hat." Her gaze landed on the Santa hat he'd put on to get a laugh out of Kenzie.

He reached up to take it off.

"No, don't. I like it. Here. I made you something." She handed him the package.

"What are you doing here?" He glanced back and forth between the package and her face, looking for an answer, not wanting to get his hopes up.

"Just open it."

Kenzie spun around in front of Jinx to watch him undo the foil. As he turned it back, it hit him. The smell of fresh-baked pie crust made his mouth water.

"It's pie!" Kenzie hopped up and down, clapping her hands together.

"It's pecan pie." Cash held the pan with both hands. "You made me pecan pie?"

Kenzie looked up to Jinx. "I thought you said you didn't know how to make pie. When we made cookies, you said pie was too complicated."

Cash's brow furrowed.

Jinx took a few steps forward. "Pie is complicated. I used to think it was too big of a commitment."

"Pie is a commitment?" What did pie have to do with making a commitment?

"Yeah, all that measuring and rolling and rising and baking and mixing…" She tucked her hair behind her ear, casting a quick glance to her feet. "I couldn't commit to pie before."

His heart surged. "But now you can make pie?"

"I think I'm going to need some practice. I've never wanted to try."

"Can we make cherry pie? And apple pie?" Kenzie

bounced around the porch, unable to contain her excitement at all the kinds of pie she and Jinx would be able to make.

He cleared his throat, not trusting his voice not to crack. "Does this mean what I think it means?"

Jinx nodded. "I want to make pie with you, Cash Walker. I can't promise I won't burn the crust or that you won't get mad at me once in a while when I want to give up because it's too hard."

"It won't be too hard. Daddy and I will help you, right, Daddy?" Kenzie gripped his hand.

"Will you hold this for me a sec, Tadpole?" He handed the pie to Kenzie and set Hendrix down on the porch.

She took it, freeing up his hands to do what he'd wanted to do with them since he'd first laid eyes on Jinx. He tangled one hand in her hair and wrapped the other one around her waist, drawing her close. Her eyes held all the hope he hadn't wanted to let himself feel.

"We're going to make some great pie together," he muttered against her ear.

She nodded.

"Kiss her, Daddy! You're under the mistletoe."

Cash and Jinx looked up. Sure enough, a little sprig of mistletoe hung from the doorway.

"I think this is my new very favorite best day." He brought his lips close to hers, his senses flooded with her scent, the warmth of her breath on his cheek, the feel of her in his arms, back where she belonged.

"I love you, Cash." Truth shone in her eyes.

"I love you too, Joy."

"You know, I kind of like the name Jinx now."

"Really? I thought you hated it?"

"I hated it because I believed it. But you and Kenzie, you've shown me that being Jinx isn't always the curse my mom told me it was."

"All right then. I love you, Jinx."

Then he covered her mouth with his while his daughter stuck her finger into his pie and danced around them. They definitely needed to come up with some new family traditions. Maybe he'd start with making out under the mistletoe with the woman of his dreams.

EPILOGUE

Jinx held tight to Pork Chop's leash as Kenzie ran ahead to knock on the door of her nana and papa's house.

"Trick or treat!" Kenzie held out her bag, waiting for her nana to fill it with candy.

"Oh my goodness, you look adorable." Ann scooped handfuls of candy and dropped them into the bag. "The three little pigs, right?"

Kenzie beamed under the layer of pink stage makeup she and Jinx had worked on all afternoon. "And the big bad wolf too." She pointed to Hendrix, who sat on top of Pork Chop's back, looking anything but wolfish.

"Good job, girls." Ann stepped out onto the porch. "You headed over to the party at the Rambling Rose now?"

"Yes. Cash said he'd meet us there. He's supposed to be the third pig, but since he was running late, Kenzie insisted we bring Pork Chop along for now." Jinx gave Ann a half hug. "He had to finish some paperwork at the office but wouldn't miss the party."

"And how did you get Pork Chop over here?"

"In the Jeep." Jinx pointed to the sunshine-yellow Jeep she'd bought with her own money last summer. She still had the bike, but the Jeep made it easier to get Kenzie—and the menagerie of animals she'd collected—to and from everywhere.

"Don't worry, Nana. We buckle her in. She sits up front with Jinx, and me and Hendrix sit in back." Kenzie reached into the candy bowl for another handful of treats.

"Y'all better get going. Don't want to miss out. I'll see you there."

Fifteen minutes later, Jinx returned Pork Chop to her pen. Hendrix refused to leave her, so Jinx left the lovestruck pup with his soul mate.

"We can't go in without Pork Chop and Hendrix," Kenzie insisted. "Then we'd only be the two little pigs."

Jinx took her hand. "We can tell people the big bad wolf is out chasing the other little pig around the countryside. That's what he gets for building his house out of peanut shells, right?"

Kenzie giggled. "Straw. The first pig's house is out of straw."

"Oh yeah."

They entered the Rose, and Kenzie forgot all about the need for another pig. Black lights hung from the ceiling, making everything glow. The event had expanded from last year to include games, crafts, and activities. Costumed kids of all sizes and ages milled about.

Jinx searched for Cash in the purple light. He hadn't had time to get his face done but had strung a piece of pink paper around his head and drawn a pig snout on the front.

"Nice try, Deputy." She angled her lips to hit his under his makeshift snout.

"Hey, last-minute effort. Where's Kenzie?"

"I don't know. She was just here a second ago." Jinx looked around the room, settling on a group of kids clustered around something in the back corner. "What's that?"

Cash put an arm around her, and they made their way to the back. Someone had dragged Santa's chair over from the community center, and Kermit sat square in the middle of it—in full Santa gear.

"What's Santa doing at a Halloween party?" Jinx asked.

Cash shrugged his shoulders and nodded toward Santa. Kenzie had clambered up onto his lap, and they giggled over something she'd whispered in his ear.

"Seems like you're getting all your holidays in Holiday mixed up this year." Jinx pressed a palm flat against her belly, trying to suppress the slight nausea she felt.

"Hey, Kenz." Cash caught his daughter in a hug before she could race by. "What's Santa doing here tonight?"

"Hi, Daddy." She kissed him on the cheek. "Your costume is lame with a capital *L*." Forming her fingers into the shape of an *L*, she held them to her forehead.

"Where does she get this stuff?" He shot an accusing look at Jinx.

She shook her head. "Not me this time, I promise."

"So what were you giggling about with Santa?" He rubbed his scruffy chin against Kenzie's neck.

She kicked her feet at him and erupted into a fit of giggles. "It's a secret."

"Can I guess?"

"You'll never be able to guess," she promised.

"I'm going to try. Let's see. You asked for a new horse?"

Kenzie shook her head.

Cash tapped a finger to his mouth. "You asked for Papa to build you a tree house?"

"Nope."

"Well, I give up." Cash released Kenzie. "I guess I don't want to know what you asked Santa for anyway," he called out after her just as Kermit passed.

The older man stopped between Cash and Jinx. "You've got your hands full with that one."

"Tell me something I don't already know." Cash lifted his eyes to the ceiling and shook his head. "The gray hairs that one's going to cause me…"

Kermit's smile showed under his beard. "She asked for a baby brother."

"No shit?" Cash's eyebrows knit together.

"Curse jar!" Kenzie called from the drink table.

"You hear that, Jinx? A baby brother? How's Santa going to pull that one off?" He shook his head, a lopsided smile on his lips.

Jinx didn't respond, just pressed her palm over her still-flat belly. Flat for now.

"Jinx?" Cash's hands curled around her arms. "Why aren't you saying anything?"

She shrugged her shoulders. "Kenzie might have to settle for a sister instead. We ought to be able to find out in another couple of weeks if you decide you want to know the gender."

"Good luck, you two. And congratulations." Kermit continued toward the door.

"Cash? You okay?" Jinx asked. His face had gone a weird shade of green under the pink pig snout and with the help of the black lights.

"I'm going to be a dad again?"

She nodded.

"I'm going to be a dad again," he said a little louder than she would have liked.

"Hey, quiet. We don't need to tell everyone—"

He pulled a chair out from the table next to them and climbed onto it. "Hey, everyone. Listen up!" The crowd quieted, and "Monster Mash" playing through the speakers came to a screeching halt.

Cash tossed his hat into the air and yelled at the top of his lungs, "I'm going to be a dad again!"

All eyes landed on Jinx. She took in a deep breath and bit her lip. The silence lasted for suspended eternity—or, more likely, a few seconds. Then everyone started talking at once. She was passed around from Charlie to Dwight to Beck to Dixie to Ann to Waylon to Darby to people she hadn't even met yet. They all wrapped her in hugs, offered congratulations, and patted her tummy. Finally, she made her way back to Cash.

Kenzie burrowed in between them. "Family hug!"

Jinx wrapped her arms around the little girl while Cash captured them both in a giant bear hug. She'd never thought she could be so happy. This town, these people, they'd accepted her unconditionally and showered her with love—especially the two people in front of her.

Finally, for the first time in her life, Jinx welcomed the sense of community. Let it wash over her and fill her with a strange but very welcome sensation.

For the first time in her life, she was home.

Acknowledgments

Writing a manuscript is a solitary task. Turning it into a story worthy of being a real book is a Herculean undertaking requiring input and effort from dozens of people. I'd like to thank a few of them.

First, my publisher, Sourcebooks, especially my editor, Mary Altman, who saw something in my writing that made her willing to take a chance on an unknown author with a wild and crazy idea. You took my rough draft and pushed me to make it bigger, better, and more badass than I ever imagined. You're a rock star! And to the cover design department, a huge Thank You! You've given me gorgeous covers that will hang on my wall for eternity.

To Jessica Watterson, my agent, who responded to every email, provided reassurance and encouragement, and didn't block my number even though I'm sure she was tempted (many, many times). I will always sing your praises... You're a superhero!

To my fellow Romance Chicks: Christina, Jody, and Renee. Thanks for always being there with an inspiring word, the perfect GIF, and solutions to my burning plot issues no matter the time of day or night. I'm so fortunate to have found you.

To Jody, Paula, Joyce, Christine, Diane, Miguella, and LeAnne. Thanks for being critique partners, beta readers, cheerleaders, and soul sisters. Your feedback has made me a better writer and your friendship has kept me sane (mostly).

To my Romance Writers of America chapter mates

at From the Heart and Midwest Fiction Writers. Thanks for the support, the encouragement, and the reassurance that having fictional people talking in my head all the time is perfectly normal.

To Liz, Cheryl, Marissa, Lynne, and Laura, the word warriors in my original writing group. You were the first ones to read my early words, including the four-letter ones, and the first ones to tell me you thought I'd write a really good sex scene. I hope you're not disappointed, ladies!

To my family and friends, especially my sister, Carrie, who's read everything I've sent her. Your unwavering faith in me means more than you know.

Finally, most importantly, to my husband and my kiddos: Honey Bee, Glitter Bee, and Buzzle Bee. You believed in me before I ever believed in myself. Your support and encouragement have made all the difference. The four of you are my *why*.

About the Author

Dylann Crush writes contemporary romance with sizzle and sass. A romantic at heart, she loves her heroines spunky and her heroes super sexy. When she's not dreaming up steamy story lines, she can be found sipping a margarita and searching for the best Tex-Mex food in Minnesota. Although she grew up in Texas, she currently lives in a suburb of Minneapolis/St. Paul with her unflappable husband, three energetic kids, two chaotic canines, and a very chill cat. She loves to connect with readers, other authors, and fans of tequila. You can sign up for her newsletter at dylanncrush.com or connect with her on social media:

Facebook: facebook.com/dylanncrush
Twitter: twitter.com/DylannCrush
Pinterest: pinterest.com/dylanncrush
Instagram: instagram.com/dylanncrush
Amazon: amazon.com/author/dylanncrush
Goodreads: goodreads.com/dylanncrush
BookBub: bookbub.com/authors/dylann-crush
Book + Main: bookandmainbites.com/DylannCrush

ALL-AMERICAN COWBOY

First in an irresistibly charming contemporary cowboy series from debut author Dylann Crush. Welcome to your new favorite holiday!

Holiday, Texas, is the most celebratory town in the South—and no shindig is complete without one of its founding members. It's a real shame the last remaining Holiday is a city slicker, but what's that old saying about putting lipstick on a pig…?

Beck Holiday has no intention of being charmed by some crazy Texas town, but the minute he lays eyes on his grandfather's old honky-tonk—and Charlie Walker, the beautiful cowgirl who runs it—he wishes things could be different. And when he looks into Charlie's eyes, Beck may finally discover what it's like to truly belong.

MISTLETOE IN TEXAS

Bestselling author Kari Lynn Dell invites us to a
Texas Rodeo Christmas like no other!

Hank Brookman had all the makings of a top rodeo bullfighter
until one accident left him badly injured. Now, after years of
self-imposed exile, Hank's back and ready to make amends...
starting with the girl his heart can't live without.

Grace McKenna fell for Hank the day they met, but
they never saw eye to eye. That's part of why she never
told him that their night together resulted in one heck of
a surprise. Now that Hank's back, it's time for them to
face what's ahead and celebrate the Christmas season rodeo
style—together despite the odds.

"This talented writer knows rodeo and sexy cowboys!"

—B.J. Daniels, *New York Times* bestselling author

ROCKY MOUNTAIN COWBOY CHRISTMAS

Beloved author Katie Ruggle's new series brings pulse-pounding romantic suspense to a cowboy's Colorado Christmas

When single dad Steve Springfield moved his family to a Colorado Christmas tree ranch, he meant it to be a safe haven. He quickly finds himself fascinated by local folk artist Camille Brandt—it's too bad trouble is on her trail.

It's not long before Camille is falling for the enigmatic cowboy and his rambunctious children—he always seems to be coming to her rescue. As attraction blooms and danger intensifies, this Christmas romance may just prove itself to be worth fighting for.

For more info about Sourcebooks's books and authors, visit:

sourcebooks.com

NAVY SEAL COWBOYS

Three former Navy SEALs, injured in the line of duty, desperate for a new beginning...searching for a place to call their own.

By Nicole Helm

Cowboy SEAL Homecoming

Something in Becca Denton's big green eyes makes Alex Maguire want to set aside the mantle of the perfect soldier and discover the man he could have been...

Cowboy SEAL Redemption

When Jack Armstrong and local bad girl Rose Rogers pretend to be in love to throw his meddling family off his trail, he discovers hope in the most unlikely of places...

Cowboy SEAL Christmas

When the ranch's therapist, Monica Finley, tempts Gabe Cortez with all the holiday charm she can muster, it's hard to resist cozying up to her for Christmas.

YOU HAD ME AT COWBOY

These hockey-playing cowboys will melt your heart,
from USA Today bestselling author Jennie Marts

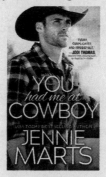

Mason James is the responsible one who stayed behind
to run the ranch when his brother Rock took off to play
hockey for the NHL. Women have used Mason to get to
his famous brother before, but he never expects to fall—
and fall hard—for one of them…

Tessa Kane is about to lose a job she desperately needs—
unless she's clever enough to snag a story on star player
Rockford James. But when her subject's brother starts to
win her heart, it's only a matter of time before he finds out
who she really is… Can the two take a chance on their love
story after all?

"Funny, complicated, and irresistible."

**—Jodi Thomas, *New York Times* bestselling
author, for *Caught Up in a Cowboy***

For more info about Sourcebooks's books and
authors, visit:

sourcebooks.com

Also by Dylann Crush

HOLIDAY, TEXAS

All-American Cowboy

Cowboy Christmas Jubilee